PENGUIN BOOKS

THE HAPPY PRISONER

The great-granddaughter of Charles Dickens, Miss Monica Dickens was educated at St Paul's School for Girls. She has been writing novels and autobiographical books since she was twenty-two, when she wrote *One Pair of Hands* about her experiences as a cook-general, the only job that her upbringing as a debutante had fitted her for.

During the war, Miss Dickens worked as a nurse in a hospital and subsequently she took a job in a munitions factory, turning out Spitfires. During the latter part of the war she was again working in a hospital. 'I would like to make it clear,' she says, 'that I did not take these jobs in order to write books. The books just came out of the experiences.'

After the war Miss Dickens gave up nursing to concentrate on her writing, and has published several novels, of which the latest is *Horses of Folly Foot* (1975). She has written a weekly column in a well-known woman's magazine. She is married to Commander Roy Stratton of the U.S. Navy, and has two daughters.

D0911577

THE HAPPY PRISONER

Monica Dickens

PENGUIN BOOKS
IN ASSOCIATION WITH
MICHAEL JOSEPH

Penguin Books Ltd, Harmondsworth, Middlesex, England
Penguin Books, 625 Madison Avenue, New York, New York 10022, U.S.A.
Penguin Books Australia Ltd, Ringwood, Victoria, Australia
Penguin Books Canada Ltd, 41 Steelcase Road West, Markham, Ontario, Canada
Penguin Books (N.Z.) Ltd, 182-190 Wairau Road, Auckland 10, New Zealand

—

First published 1946
Published in Penguin Books 1958
Reprinted 1960, 1961, 1965, 1967, 1969, 1973, 1976

—

Copyright © Monica Dickens, 1946

—

Made and printed in Great Britain
by Cox and Wyman Ltd,
London, Reading and Fakenham
Set in Monotype Times

TO
CHRISTOPHER
DICKENS

CHAPTER 1

THE moth, which had been clattering frantically inside his lamp-shade for the last ten minutes, suddenly dropped on to the open page of his book and lay there stunned, only a slight questing of the antennae showing that it was still alive. Because he was enjoying the book, Oliver went on reading until he came to the words which the moth obscured. He was just going to lift the book to shake it out of the window, when his eye was caught by the pattern on its wings and the needless perfection of its unimportant little body.

It was lying with wings half spread, the corners of the lower ones just showing inside the upper. They appeared to be made up of thousands of tiny fibres, weaving a pattern in browns and fawns that was like a priceless shawl or a piece of tapestry. At the edges, which were shaped like shells, with a tuft of down between each scallop, the fibres blended into a frieze of darker brown, which was continued at exactly the same point on the lower wings, so that when the two were spread the pattern would be continuous. This moth, which had seemed such a nuisance when it was trying to batter itself to death round his light, was really a show-piece, a miracle of skilled craftsmanship prodigally squandered on a single night's existence. (Was it only a single night? He must get someone to bring him a book on moths from the library. It would be a fascinating study on these September nights under the open window.)

If this pattern had been on a shawl or tapestry, it would have taken months or years of painful, eye-straining toil. It might have been someone's life-work, someone who would go blind over it and die without ever knowing that it was destined to endure and be treasured for hundreds of years. But Nature, who could mass-produce this kind of thing millions of times a day, could afford to squander it on an ephemeral thing like a moth, which, far from being treasured, was discouraged with camphor and closed windows. This moth, in fact, Oliver thought, was very lucky to be getting so much attention.

It had a velvet head and a dusty body. Its tail was a sandy tuft of finest hairs. Incredible that anything so soft could make such a metallic clatter against the ceiling and the parchment lampshade. It seemed to be rested now and was starting to weave its head about as if it meant to take off. Oliver lifted his book and shook it out of the window. Perversely, the moth clung. He slapped the book underneath, and then it was gone, although it would probably come in again to join the rest of the suicidal company whirring and slapping about his bedside light. Something horrid fell on to his sheet and crouched there, looking at him. It was a greenish-black flying beetle, with patent-leather scales, and claws, and a malevolent, hooded head. Moths were all right, but things like this were the drawback of having one's bed under the open window. He shook the sheet and it bounced into the air and fell on its back on the polished bedside table, where it squirmed, helpless as a sheep, with all its legs going in a frenzy of useless effort. He watched it until its agitations took it to the edge of the table and it fell off.

Glancing at the clock, he saw that he had frittered away nearly half an hour on moths and beetles. Before this new phase of his life, he had never had much time for idle musing. Thoughts which occurred to him he voiced in the first words that came into his head. Aspects of nature or the human character were noted by his mind only *en passant*. Their impact might be provocative enough at the moment and give rise to lively emotions or the embryo of an idea, but there was always something else clamouring for attention, and he passed on, dropping the thought undeveloped, like a new-born chick fallen from its nest. He realized now how much his superficial eye had missed and was surprised to find that his mind had nevertheless recorded and stored away many things behind his back. Now that retrospection was one of his favourite ways of passing the time, he often found himself remembering things of which at the time he had been only half aware.

If anyone had told him in the old days that it was possible to spend half an hour quite happily in contemplation of the veining on a rose petal or the pattern of a moth's wing, he would have dismissed it as not for him. Yogis and poets and philosophers did it no doubt, but not active young men who found it difficult

8

to sit still long enough to see a play through to its end. It was different now. He had got past the time of fret and exasperation, of refusal to relax and resign himself. He had gone through all that in hospital: nights and nights of lying fiddling with the sheet, with his mind going round like a caged squirrel, lighting one cigarette after another, following the night nurse with wide-open eyes, until at last, as much in exasperation for herself as in pity for him, she would give him the tablets from which he was supposed to have been weaned. He did not want them anyway. What use were they, he would argue in a cross mutter, which would make her glance apprehensively at the other sleeping patients. Oh, certainly, they made you sleep, but everything was twice as bad in the morning when realization, absent at the first moment of waking, came rushing back with the increased momentum of distance. On top of which, you had a headache and a taste in the mouth.

His transition to this comparatively contented, contemplative state had been so gradual that it was hard to say just how it had come about. It had crept on him with the lessening in intensity and frequency of his attacks of pain. When it was possible to be comfortable in one position for more than five minutes, it also became possible to read more than one chapter of a book at a time. As his preoccupation with himself diminished, he began to take a sympathetic interest in the working of someone else's mind, instead of becoming so irritated that he wanted only to have the author standing on the other side of the ward so that he might sling the book at his head. He went back, distrustfully at first and then with growing enthusiasm, to authors to whom he had thought himself permanently antagonized at school. He discovered that Shakespeare, Dickens, Thackeray, and Stevenson could transfigure the dreary waste between lunch and tea in which everyone but he seemed able to sleep. He had held out for a long time against Jane Austen, whom he had mistrusted ever since he had seen a performance of *Pride and Prejudice* at his sisters' school. He was reading *Emma* now, and the moth had fallen on to a piece of Woodhouse hypochondria.

He was just going to pursue this, when the door in the shadows on the other side of the room opened and his mother came in with his hot milk on a tray. She was a specialist in things like laying tables and arranging trays and dishing up delicate little helpings in separate dishes. It took time, but she did it quite beautifully: a spotless tray-cloth, glass, china, and silver polished to the last degree of sparkle, nothing forgotten, hot things sizzling and cold things iced, not too much of anything but more in the kitchen, butter not in a lump but in dewy curls, the morning paper crisp and unfolded instead of inside out with a smear of marmalade on it from someone else's breakfast. Often there were flowers – a few pansies, or a sprig of stock, or one perfect rose in the little cut-glass vase she kept especially for Oliver's tray.

Whenever possible, she liked to bring him his meals herself. She did not trust anyone, even the nurse, to do it properly, and if she went out to lunch, her enjoyment of it was quite spoiled by the thought of Oliver's. If Mrs Cowlin was ever left in charge, the poor woman was so frightened by all the instructions and warnings she had received that it seemed she would never get from the door to the bed without dropping the tray. She always forgot something, and went scurrying out for it in terror, to come creeping back with the knife, or mustard, or whatever it was, held placatingly out before her. Oliver's sisters forgot things, too, but would suggest hopefully how he could manage without. 'You can stir your coffee with the handle of the jam spoon, can't you, Ollie? And have you got a hankie? I've forgotten your napkin.'

His mother came heavily and carefully across the room carrying the glass of milk on a little round tray with a lace cloth. She never came blunderingly, like Violet, with a cracked cup slopping into an old saucer, or hastily, like Heather, as if she grudged the time, with a glass only half full of milk only half warm.

'Nearly time to settle, darling,' Mrs North said, using a word from his childhood. 'Is there anything you want?' She put down the milk, picked up his empty coffee-cup, and stood over him, watching him, stouter than ever in the dress into which she liked to change for dinner: sea-green silk, with bands of large white flowers running round all the ellipses of her body. She wore rimless pince-nez on a thin gold chain hooked behind one ear, and her grey hair, which was very mauve when she first came back from the hairdressers, but faded to a pleasing tint as the week went by, was swept smartly across the back of her head into a wig-like arrangement of waves and curls. Although she had lived

10

twenty years in England, she still would have passed unnoticed among a crowd of matrons in her native Philadelphia.

'Is there anything you want?' she repeated. 'Did Sandy leave you quite comfortable before she went?'

'Yes, thanks. I think I'll read a bit longer.'

'Well, don't settle late, dear. Oh, these awful moths! Don't they drive you crazy? Let me shut the window.'

'No, please, Ma.' He lifted a hand nervously as she bent forward. The thought of anyone leaning over his bed made him shrink with the fear of being hurt. 'I can shut it myself if I want to. I'm not *quite* paralysed, you know.'

'You must remember what Hugo said about the least possible movement. I don't trust you entirely. Goodness knows what you get up to when you're alone in here.'

'Oh, of course, I get up and dance round the room. You ought to look through the keyhole some time.'

'I'm sure you do too much. You hardly ever ring your bell for anything. I don't know what you think I gave it you for.'

'I hate that bell,' he said shortly.

'Well, for Heaven's sake, darling, why? It's a very charming bell.' She picked it up and rang it. 'It's a cow-bell; one of the girls brought it back that time we went to Davos.'

'I don't know – it's silly, I suppose. I just hate it.'

'There's that dinner-bell we used to use when we had a parlour-maid. You could have that if you like. Or maybe we could have someone come out and fix you an electric buzzer.'

'No, Ma, thanks, it isn't that. It isn't *the* bell, it's any bell. I just hate the idea of lying here and summoning people like a sultan clapping his hands.'

'But that's ridiculous, dear. How are we to know when you want anything? Of course, we know you're very sweet and considerate, but we all understand, and you must too, that you mustn't do one thing for yourself, not one thing. You're the most important person in this house. I want you to have everything. I only wish there were more I could do. ....' Her round, powdered chin quivered in its bed of soft flesh, her busy, decisive mouth weakened.

Oliver put out a hand. 'You do too much already,' he said. 'Forget about the bell; I was only drivelling.'

The door opened just far enough to admit the craven face of Mrs Cowlin, her cobweb of hair tied round with a baby blue ribbon. 'Oh, pardon,' she breathed. 'I thought I heard the Major's bell.'

'You took long enough to answer it,' said Mrs North, her self-control immediately restored by the necessity for militant action against inefficiency. 'I'm sorry, but I rang the bell by mistake. It's all right; he doesn't want anything.' Mrs Cowlin blinked and withdrew her head, shutting the door so that it opened again in a moment.

Mrs North gave a little click of impatience. 'If it wasn't for her husband being such a fine man, I don't believe I could put up with that haff-wit much longer.' She still said things like haff-wit sometimes. 'Still, we wouldn't get anyone else, and she never minds what you ask her to do. She seems quite to enjoy unstopping the scullery sink. Which reminds me, I must go back and see what she's broken. I heard an almighty crash a short while back.' She bent to kiss him, smelling of face-creams and Turkish cigarettes. 'Don't settle too late,' she repeated. 'Remember you've got an exciting day tomorrow.'

An exciting day? Oh yes, of course, his new nurse was coming tomorrow. 'I wonder what she's like. I bet she's even uglier than old Sandy.'

'If she knows her job half as well I shan't mind,' said his mother. 'Anyway, Hugo seemed to think her all right when he saw her in town.'

'If she's gummy and arch, and says: "Bottoms up" when she wants to rub my back, I shall sling her out,' Oliver said.

'Yes, dear, of course,' said his mother soothingly. It didn't do for him to get too lively at bedtime. She moved towards the door. 'Good night again, and – you'll ring the bell if you can't sleep, won't you?'

'You bet.' Oliver grinned. 'And listen!' he called after her, as she opened the door. 'Don't forget this new nurse is going to be as much yours as mine. I'm not going to have her here if she doesn't help you in the house. I hardly need a nurse now, anyway; it's ridiculous having one at all.'

'Now, Oliver.' His mother paused in the doorway, silhouetted in the light from the hall. 'Don't be that way. Of course she's

12

going to help in the house, she knows that; but not until she's done everything possible for you. Just you don't forget what I told you: you're the most important person in this house. And she'd better not either,' she added grimly, as she went out.

There had been a time when Oliver's mood of self-pity and invalid absorption would have fed on remarks like that. They simply irked him now. It was the same with the bell. He hated it because it emphasized his dependence. If he wanted anything, he put off ringing it as long as possible; but if nobody happened to come in and he had to ring it, he always imagined people looking up irritated from whatever they were doing, and someone getting up with a what-does-he-want-*now* expression, which they would try to fight down on the way to his room.

When he turned out the light, the scents of the country night outside the window seemed to grow stronger. Funny how you always got this extra wave of tree and flower smells with the first breath taken in the dark. It even happened in London. He could remember when he was a boy, in that house they had had when they first came back from America, how when he turned out the light and stood at the window of his little room that was like a passage, he could suddenly smell the sooty plane-tree bark and the bitter leaves, turning and glistening under the gas lamp.

His bed was level with the window-sill, so that even after he had thrown out two of his pillows, in defiance of orders to sleep propped up, he could see out of the open casement. There was no moon tonight, and the hump of the hill in the meadow opposite, with its mushroom of oaks and beeches on top, was darker than the sky. His room was on the ground floor, so that he could smell the grass of the lawn only a few feet below him. His bed was built into the window recess, occupying the whole bay like a wide window-seat, so that one of the small side windows formed its head. Through the window at the foot, half obscured by the hump of the cradle that kept the bedclothes off his leg, he could see the line of elms on the western boundary of their land, their rounded tops shaped like cloud masses. In the gap between them and the sentinel poplar in Fred's cottage garden a pale-green streak showed where the sunset had been.

The position of his bed, as Nurse Sanderson had frequently remarked, was inconvenient for nursing, but Oliver had decided

13

when they brought him home that he wanted it like that, so his mother had had it done and told Sandy that she must put up with it, just as she would tell this new nurse. She would probably tell her before she had a chance to complain. Mrs North was a great believer in getting her word in first.

Oliver hoped the nurse would not come too late tomorrow. He would not let his mother or his sisters do much for him. They usually hurt him, because they were as afraid to touch him as he was of their touch.

An owl screeched suddenly and Oliver's toes twitched. Would they never stop itching and twitching and feeling heat and cold? It would spoil his attraction for young David if they did, and he might not come to visit him so often. There was a distinct fascination about an uncle who could wiggle toes that were not there.

CHAPTER 2

ELIZABETH GRAY arrived before lunch. Oliver saw her from his bedroom window. Mrs North had taken her out through the drawing-room on to the stone steps which joined the two levels of lawn at the back of the house, and was pointing things out to her. Soon she would bring her in and show her Oliver, as she was now showing her the rose garden, and the neglected tennis court, and the fruit cage, and the herd of Herefords in the dip below the ha-ha wall, and the clump of trees on the hill-top where the Roman camp had been.

Thank goodness this girl was not going to crackle round him in hospital armour. Sandy had worn a mauve dress stiff as cardboard, a straining apron encircled by a belt with a vast buckle like a portcullis, and an outsize Army square which caught on beams and was whipped off her head if she ventured outside on a windy day.

Elizabeth wore a white overall with a half-belt nipping in her neat waist at the back, light stockings, and a little perky American cap on the back of her fair hair. His mother was wearing her second-best corsets, Oliver noticed. She really should have worn her best under that grey jersey suit, but she kept them for social

14

occasions. She wore a purple and green scarf tied in a big bow under her chins and her thick legs in grey silk stockings ran straight as tree trunks into high-heeled crocodile shoes, which made dents in the damp lawn. After fifteen years, she was still no more congruous in the country than a week-end visitor. He thought of calling out for her to bring the girl over to the window to be introduced, but decided not to spoil her pleasure in doing things in their right order. She would make quite a little ceremony of bringing Elizabeth into his room, leading her forward by the hand and saying: 'This is your new nurse. This is my son – Oliver, whom you're going to look after for me.' She had probably planned it out last night while she was doing her hair. This was the time when she laid most of her plans and did what she called her Figuring. Often, after she had kissed him good night, she would come in again in her quilted satin dressing-gown with a comb in her hand and some of her hair pinned flat to her head, to tell him something she had just thought of. Looking up from his book, he would agree, and ten minutes later she would be back again with a bit more of her hair in curls and an alternative idea.

'Don't read too long,' she would say going out, and he would say: 'Just going to finish this chapter,' and probably go on reading for another hour. Sometimes, when she drew back the curtains in her bedroom, she would see his light shining on to the lawn and would come down again to see whether he had gone to sleep with the lamp on.

He hoped they would come in soon. He was very uncomfortable. There were crumbs in his bed and his dressing wanted changing and the pillow in the small of his back had knotted itself into a hard lump. Heather had washed him after breakfast with a too dry sponge which did not rinse off all the soap, and Violet, coming in later, had set up his shaving things for him on the bed-table and had spilt some water which had now soaked right through the blankets and sheet to his pyjamas. He would also like to know what was for lunch before he started on the chocolate Bob had sent him from America.

When his mother turned to come indoors, she waved and smiled in his direction, although she could not see him behind the mullions of the open casement. When she was working in the garden or sitting in a deck-chair under the cedar, she would look up from time to time and wave to show him he was not forgotten.

She said something to Elizabeth, who also looked towards him. He was too far away to see her features, but the general effect was not unpleasing. Good.

When she came into his room, he saw that she had china-blue eyes in a smooth, well-mannered face, neither pretty nor plain, but strangely unanimated. Yet it was not a lethargic face; it was alert and intelligent and healthy, but controlled beyond its youth.

'This is your new nurse, darling,' said Mrs North. 'Elizabeth Gray. This is my son – Oliver. You're going to look after him for us, aren't you?' Elizabeth stepped forward, avoiding, either by accident or deliberately, the hand with which Mrs North was going to lead her up to the bed.

'How do you do?' she said politely, with a professional glance at the untidily made bed, the arrangement of the pillows, and the plaster on Oliver's chest where it showed under the open neck of his pyjamas. Being in bed gave you an advantage over people, Oliver always thought. Simply by turning your head, you could follow them as they moved about the room, conscious of your eyes. It was rather like being royalty. You waited at your ease for them to come to you, so much less at their ease because you were in bed and there was that hump under the quilt, which they were not sure whether they ought to notice or not. Even people whom he knew quite well were embarrassed when they first came to see him.

This girl seemed completely self-possessed, but of course she was used to seeing people in bed and to humps under quilts. They smiled at each other gravely, summing one another up, wondering how they were going to like seeing so much of each other.

'You'll find me an awful fraud,' said Oliver. 'Nothing wrong with me. I'm afraid I'm a dead loss as a case, but I don't suppose a bit of a rest will do you any harm.'

'Now, Oliver,' said Mrs North hastily, terrified that he might give the girl the wrong ideas, 'don't talk like that. It's no use your pretending you can do things for yourself, because you know quite well you can't. Miss Gray isn't going to think you lazy or spoiled. She's a nurse and she knows what a man with a heart may and mayn't do. We've had a long talk about you already and I've explained your condition exactly, so you needn't

16

start trying to muddle her.' She turned to Elizabeth. 'I told you, didn't I? A shell splinter just grazed the outer muscle of the heart. They say it's healing all right at last, but of course the least exertion . . .'

Elizabeth, who had formed her own opinion of the case long ago from her interview with Oliver's doctor, listened politely to what they both had to say, and when Mrs North at last decided to go and finish off the lunch, set about making Oliver comfortable as surely and successfully as if she had been nursing him for weeks.

*

It was a lovely afternoon. The sun, which had been in and out of clouds all morning, was standing in a clear blue sky by the time it reached the spot above the hill from where it shone on to his bed. The autumn and spring suns were better than the high suns of midsummer, which were only at the right angle for his low old window in the early morning and in the evening. This sun could shine into his room from two o'clock until it set behind the elms.

'Going out this afternoon?' he asked Elizabeth, when she came to fetch his coffee-cup. 'Wish I could show you round. It's rather a nice old place. We rent out most of the land and the farm buildings now, but Fred won't mind where you go. Fred Williams – he's our tenant. He lives in that cottage you can see by the poplar over there. My eldest sister works for him. D'you like farms? There's a couple of cart foals in the paddock by the front drive, they tell me, that might appeal to you. Don't worry about me if you want to go out. I shan't want a thing. Never do.'

'I might go out perhaps,' said Elizabeth, 'when I've done the washing up.'

'Don't let them work you too hard. I warn you, my mother is one of these people who would die at the sink sooner than leave the plates till tomorrow.'

He spoke lightly, but Elizabeth answered quite seriously, 'It's specified as part of my job that I should help in the house. Mrs North has drawn me up a time-table so that I can fit that in with my nursing.' She pulled a typed sheet of paper out of her pocket and showed it to Oliver.

He laughed. 'Isn't that typical? Every minute of the day accounted for, my poor Nurse Gray. "Off Duty: 2.30–4.30." You'll

17

find yourself going down to the village then to do some shopping and catch the London post. You wait. What's this? "Household chores!"' He laughed again. 'How the woman harks back to Ardmore, Pa. "9 a.m.: Major North's breakfast. 9.15: Make beds with me upstairs. 10 a.m.: Major North's dressing." How the devil does she know when I want my dressing done? "11.1: Help Mrs Cowlin prepare lunch, when I'm not doing it. Listen for Major North's bell – –" Look here, I *never* ring my bell. You can cut that out.' He rummaged on his bedside table for a pencil and Elizabeth stepped forward quickly and handed it to him. He scored heavily through a line.

'Thanks. I say,' he said, reading on, 'I hope you don't think we're expecting too much. It looks an awful lot set down like this, but half the things aren't necessary, and when you shake down and sort of get into the hang of things here, it'll boil down a bit.'

'It seems quite all right, thank you,' said Elizabeth, taking back the paper, folding it neatly, and putting it back into her pocket. It would help a lot, Oliver thought, if she would give some indication of what she thought of the household.

'What about your back?' she asked. 'You ought to have that rubbed at two, oughtn't you?'

'Good God, no. I'm not in hospital now, thank Heaven. You go away and do your "Household chores" and then get out into this sun. Get one of the girls to show you round. You've met them, have you – my sisters?'

'Oh yes. Mrs Sandys was at lunch with her little boy, and Miss North met me at Shrewsbury station. She didn't come to lunch. She came in after we'd started and cut herself a cheese sandwich to take out. She said she hadn't time for any more.'

'That sounds like old Vi,' said Oliver. 'She works like a black. She's a great soul; you'll like her.' He fixed Elizabeth with his eye, daring her to judge by appearances.

'She seems very nice. Well, if you're sure there's nothing you want . . .' She started towards the door. He liked the pert little point of her cap at the back.

'Nothing, thanks. I say – Nurse!' She turned, brightly prepared to hand him something or fetch a glass of water or shake up his pillows.

'Look, I don't think I'll call you Nurse, if you don't mind.

It seems silly when you're going to be more or less one of the family. I think I'd better call you Elizabeth, don't you?'

'Yes, whatever you like, Major North.'

'Sandy – that was the last nurse I had – used to call me Oliver, except when she called me Boysie. That was hell.' Elizabeth waited to see if he had anything more to say, and then went out, shutting the door carefully and quietly behind her.

*

Since Oliver had come home from the hospital, it had become the family custom to forgather in his room for a drink before dinner. At six o'clock, before she padded home to her cottage in the valley, Mrs Cowlin, looking ill-suited to anything so modern, would push open the door with her knee and bring in a tray of glasses, ice cubes, and gin, whisky, beer, or whatever Mrs North had managed to get in Shrewsbury from the grocer, who had known Oliver for years and was sorry about him. Then would come Oliver's younger sister Heather, with her small son David in pyjamas and a Jaeger dressing-gown, and a nursery tray containing his hot milk and one *petit beurre*, and a mug of cold milk and sandwiches, cake, or whatever wanted eating up, for Evelyn to have when she could be dragged indoors from the farm. Evelyn was the daughter of Mrs North's widowed brother, and had been staying at Hinkley during the war.

Heather would pour Oliver a drink and usually have one herself while David had his supper, but she did not stay long unless there were someone amusing to talk to. After five years of living at home during the war, it did not amuse her to talk to her family, and Oliver had now been home long enough for the novelty to have worn off. Mrs North would come in, have one sip of a drink, go out to do something to the dinner, come back for a nip, go out again, come back, like a bird making sallies at its drinking basin, or, rather, like a hippopotamus constantly being interrupted at its water-hole.

Violet usually managed to come in, unless they were working late in the fields. Sometimes Fred Williams came in with her to see Oliver. Mrs North did not like him very much and pretended that the room smelled of manure after he had gone. Sandy had always been there, with little finger crooked over a glass of sherry,

19

making gay conversation to anyone who would listen, the fur-belowed and trinketed silk into which she changed for dinner more unalluring even than her uniform.

Oliver liked to be washed and have his bed made before six so that he could be presentable for his At Home. He could enjoy his dinner more, too, if he was rid of the stickiness and creases and aches that had accumulated during the day. Elizabeth worked in silence, answering his remarks politely, but volunteering none of her own. He enjoyed her deft, assured touch. She never knocked him by mistake where it hurt, and although he was heavy for her, she had a knack of lifting and managed to make him very comfortable. She was slightly built, but her arms were firmly rounded and strong, with a bloom of youth and health. They looked nice coming out of the short sleeves of her white overall.

'You'll come back and have a drink, won't you, when you've changed?' Oliver asked when she had finished.

'I ought to be helping Mrs North with the dinner as soon as I've taken off my overall.' She was folding towels and gathering up his dirty pyjamas.

'Well, you don't have to brood over it like a witch, do you? You can come in and out. Ma always manages to. Come in!' he bellowed to a scrabbling at the door. The latch jumped madly and there was a thud and a precarious tinkle as Mrs Cowlin entered bowed over the tray of drinks. She put it down on a table, glanced furtively at Elizabeth from under her arras of hair, and crept out as if the floor of this room were made of thin ice.

'There you are,' said Oliver. 'Have one before you go.'

'I don't drink, thank you, Major North.'

'Why not? Taste or principle?'

'I won't have one, thank you. I don't drink,' she repeated, not answering his question. She took the washing-bowl out to the downstairs cloakroom to empty it. Oliver hoped she was not going to turn out to be like the nurse in hospital who was always smiling because she was pleased to find herself so holy. She used to tell him he must be born again, and he had caught her praying over him once when she thought he was asleep.

*

A miniature oak armchair, relic of some Elizabethan nursery, was kept in Oliver's room for David. At supper-time, he would carry it over to the bed and drag up the stool which he used for a table. As the window recess into which Oliver's bed was built was a step higher than the floor of the room, he had a bird's eye view of the little boy on his low chair. He could see the cow-lick on top of his head, where the black hair gave a swirl before it shot the rapids of his forehead. When David's head was bent over his biscuit or the knot hole in the stool, Oliver could see the arc of his lashes lying on the bulging, boneless cheeks; when it was tilted back to obey his mother's interjections of 'Drink up,' most of him was hidden by the big white china mug, except for two wet black eyes, which stared and stared and went on staring after he had lowered the mug and let out the breath he had been holding while he drank.

'Wipe your moustache,' said Oliver, throwing down his handkerchief.

'Yes,' said David, thinking of something else. 'Uncle Oliver, I want to tell you something. How do you cut your toenails, if you haven't any toes?'

'I don't. I file them usually. It's safer, when you can't see them.'

'I want to tell you another thing – –'

'You mean ask,' said Heather, from the table where she was mixing Oliver a drink.

'How do you know if you've got a hole in your sock if you can't see your big toe sticking out?'

'I can feel it. The edges of the hole cut into my toe when I wiggle it.'

'You shouldn't stuff him up, Ollie,' Heather said, bringing his drink over. 'It's going to be awfully awkward when you get up and he sees you really have only got one leg.'

'Perhaps I shall have my cork one by then. That'll be a great thrill. He'll be able to kick it as much as he wants.'

'Yes, till he kicks the good one by mistake.'

David had got up and gone to stare at the tent of bedclothes between the cradle and the foot of the bed. 'Are you wiggling them now? Are you? May I look under the sheet?'

'You may not,' said his mother, and bent to pick him up. 'Come on, you can go to bed if you've finished your milk. I've got heaps to do before dinner.'

David's face went scarlet and began to disintegrate. He beat his mother off with both hands. 'David – stop it!' She jerked her head away, her face as red as his from the same quickly-roused temper. 'Look what you're doing to my hair, you little fiend. You are *not* to kick me! Oh, Ollie – what does one do? I'm always having these struggles – stop it, David!' She managed to catch hold of both of his wrists in one hand and they stood breathing heavily at one another, furious. Heather's right hand looked as if it wanted to smack the child.

'Couldn't he stay a bit?' suggested Oliver mildly. 'It's early yet, and he hasn't had any reading.' David looked from one to the other judicially, wondering who would win, and saw Heather make a face at Oliver.

'Oh, Ollie, *really*,' she said. 'Why suggest it? I did want to get him settled early. I've got Susan to feed, and I must change and do my face. Stanford's coming to dinner.'

'Surely you don't have to bother for him. He'd think you marvellous whatever you looked like – even first thing in the morning.'

'Don't be silly,' she said, rather snappishly. 'David, now look; are you coming without a fuss? I've had just about enough of you today. You've absolutely worn me out. I do think you're an unkind little boy, when I've got so much to do.'

She made a great mistake, Oliver thought, in appealing to his better nature. It never worked. As David's face began to go red again, he said: 'Why don't you go up and leave him here to keep me company? I'll send him up when I get sick of him.'

'If you're sure he won't be a pest. I wouldn't have said that David was the ideal company for someone with a bad heart.' She picked up the mug and carried the stool and chair back to their place under the wall table where the drinks were. 'There's a piece of apple pie here for Evelyn – if and when she deigns to come in. If she wants anything else, there's some cake in the big green tin. Tell her not to dare touch the fruit salad; it's for tonight.'

As she was going out, she heard David say in what was meant to be a whisper: 'Can I look under the sheet *now*?'

'If you're going to pester Uncle Oliver, you'll have to come up with me,' she told him.

'Once,' he said, ignoring her, 'I looked under Evie's sheet, and there was a little dog in there, and a kitten.'

'How cosy,' Oliver said.

'Revolting,' said Heather, and went out.

While he was reading to David, Oliver let his mind stray and thought about his younger sister. What would John think of her when he came home? He had not seen her for more than a year, and before that, only in infrequent snatches since they were married in the first year of the war. Oliver had seldom seen them together. It was an accepted thing that they were very much in love, so he supposed they were. When Heather was touchy, people nodded at each other as much as to say: 'We must make allowances for her. She misses John.'

John had not seen his wife in the full tilt of motherhood. He had never seen this baby that she overdressed, overwashed, overfed, and generally overdid. The war had changed everybody, but Heather more than most. She still looked the same: baby-faced, a little too fat, primrose-coloured hair so curly that she pretended she would prefer it straight, always something jingling at her wrists – and now, of course, that little gold crucifix round her neck as well – plump calves and small feet, but she never used to be so reckless and excitable. She was inconsistent too, fickle to her own personality. Sometimes, she was almost liquid with motherly love; at others, she was as shrill and exasperated as a slum mother boxing her child's ears in the street. David never knew where he was with her. Sometimes she treated him like a grown-up, sometimes like a baby in arms, sometimes like a showpiece, sometimes almost like a juvenile delinquent.

She seemed permanently wound up, as if she had lost the ability to relax, even after the children were in bed. She would sometimes come and sit in Oliver's room with her mending basket, but she fidgeted all the time; jumping up because she thought she heard the baby crying, putting down a sock half finished and starting on a vest, hopping from subject to subject, not interested in anything Oliver had to say and too distrait to say anything interesting herself. She had been lively and high-spirited enough in the days when her biggest worry was in which dress to go to what with whom, but she had usually been good-tempered and she had punctuated bouts of terrific energy with sudden periods of inertia, when she would fling herself down and fall asleep wherever she happened to be. She could dance all night in London, drive up to Shropshire through the dawn in somebody's sports car, drive off with somebody else to swim in the Severn, play tennis all afternoon, and then suddenly, when there were people in for cocktails, she would be missed and discovered unconscious on a sofa, pretty in sleep as a child.

She never cast herself down to sleep now, and did not appear to sleep much at night, for Oliver, lying awake, could often hear the floor of her room creaking as she moved about overhead, doing probably quite unnecessary things to the baby.

Any comment on Heather's behaviour usually ended with: 'I expect she'll be all right when John comes home.' He had been a Japanese prisoner of war for nearly a year, and since his release was waiting in Australia for a passage home. Oliver had not been at home during John's last leave before he went to the Middle East, but it was always spoken of as a halcyon time. He and Heather had left David with Mrs North and gone up alone to a tiny fishing hotel in the Western Highlands. 'Whatever happens,' Mrs North used to tell Heather, 'at least you'll have that fortnight to remember.'

It was after Heather came back from the nursing-home where Susan was born that she started this business of going to church. Religion was a subject not often discussed by the Norths, but they gathered that Heather had made friends with another patient, a Roman Catholic, who had persuaded her to go to Mass. Mrs North had written to Oliver in alarm, telling him that Heather had taken to going off on her bicycle before breakfast – even on weekdays – that she had mysterious appointments after dinner in the evening, known as 'going out to coffee with someone', whom Mrs North suspected of being the priest, and that she had bought a Madonna, and a crucifix to hang round her neck.

'I believe she thinks of Turning,' his mother wrote. 'Can you imagine Heather, who never seemed to give religion a thought! Still, I shall try not to mind, even though I was raised as a good Presbyterian, if it's going to make Heather happy.'

Heather did become a Catholic, announcing her intention defiantly, and almost disappointed at the lack of opposition, but it did not seem to be making her happy. Being a convert, she kept more strictly to the laws of the Church than if she had been born to it, and she went about the whole thing in a strenuous, besotted way that seemed to disturb her peace of mind rather than restore it. On the mornings when she was going to early Mass, her strident alarm would wake everyone at six, and she would rattle the handles of her drawers and make no attempt to hush the children, as if she did not see why, if she was awake, anyone else should be asleep. She would leave the house in a tearing hurry and bicycle off tense-faced, with a scarf over her head, and would invariably return cross, tear off the clothes her mother had put on David, and dress him in something else.

She had written to John of her conversion, but she had told nobody what he had answered. It would be interesting, Oliver thought, to see what happened when he came home. He hoped they would stay at Hinkley for a bit so that he could watch how they adjusted their lives to each other. Being in bed had given him a profound interest in other people's behaviour which had not felt before. He had never taken much notice of his family, except in relation to himself. He was far more aware of them now that he was a spectator rather than a participator in their lives, and liked to think that he understood them better. Certainly he had not made much attempt to understand them before.

His mother came in, wearing a heliotrope apron with a row of pockets across the front labelled 'Scissors – Hankie – Specs – String – Cash', each of which, like the rice, sugar, tea, coffee, and currant jars on her kitchen dresser, surprisingly held the right thing. Under this, she wore a lavender dress which accentuated the tints of her hair rinse. As she turned her back to pour herself a glass of sherry, Oliver saw that she was wearing her best corsets. Oh yes, of course, Stanford Black was coming.

'Where's Nurse Gray?' she asked.

'She said she was going to help you.'

'I expect she's laying the table. She offered to help in the kitchen, but we're only having cold and I said, "My goodness, I've prepared dinner on my own so often, I can do it once more." She said she knew how to make mayonnaise, but you can never be sure, and I know you like my mayonnaise.'

'Best I've ever had,' said Oliver obediently. His mother took a

25

sip of her drink and put it down on the beam that formed the mantelpiece of the old Tudor fireplace. 'I'd better go and see how she's getting on,' she said. 'She may not know where things are. She seems a very nice person, don't you think, darling? Is she all right with you? You're quite happy with her?'

'She's fine,' said Oliver. 'Far better than Sandy.'

'Oh, now isn't that just grand. Has Violet been in yet? Really she is the limit. She'll never be ready for dinner. I'll send Evelyn out after her, though I suppose she's not in either. That child's absolutely running wild, you know. I can't think what Bob will say.'

'With all due respect to your brother, he doesn't seem to take much interest in her.'

'Now that's unkind, dear. You know he can't have her over in the States until he gets a proper home. He's much too busy. If Violet does come in,' she said as she went out, 'remind her that someone's coming to dinner. I won't have her coming in in those trousers and muddy shoes like she did last week when Mrs Ogilvie came. Tell her she's to wear that blue dress with the white collar.'

'Surely she's old enough to decide what she'll wear.'

'She doesn't act as if she was.' Mrs North got as far as the door, paused, retraced her steps for a nip of sherry, smiled dotingly at Oliver, and went out.

Surely no more inappropriate name than Violet could have been chosen for Oliver's eldest sister. But who could have foreseen at the christening that the baby was going to turn out like this? Mrs North as a girl was dumpy and plump already, but her bulk was all sideways, and Mr North had had no bulk in any direction. Violet, however, had gone steadily upwards like a fertilized cornstalk. At twelve, she was the tallest girl in her school, with teeth like tombstones and joints which were always bruised and scarred from being so prominent; at twenty she was nearly six foot, flat as a board, but solid and sinewy; now, at thirty, she could do a man's work without tiring, and had, so the shoemaker in Shrewsbury assured Mrs North, the largest lady's foot in Shropshire.

She came into the room in a khaki shirt and tie of Oliver's, a

26

green pullover, riding breeches, golf stockings, and shoes like bull-dozers. With her came an old Labrador and a red-setter puppy who made a wild dash for Oliver, scattering the rugs, and bounced by the bed with little yelps, his hind legs quivering as if he were going to spring up.

'Vi – for God's sake! If he jumps on my leg – –'

Violet plunged forward. 'Dalesman, you ass – come here!' She caught hold of his tail, and as he circled round she clasped his neck, for he had no collar, and knelt on the floor holding him, while he set on her with ecstatic tongue, leaving shining chestnut hairs among the hay seeds and barn dust on her jersey.

'Awful to be scared of a dog, isn't it?' said Oliver. 'But if you had my stump. . . . It jumps about two feet when it sees anything like that coming. He's a bit uncouth though, isn't he, Vi? I thought Ma had forbidden him the house.'

'He's young,' said his sister in her deep, abrupt voice. 'Come on and lie down with Poppy, show how you can behave.' She dragged the dog over to the corner where the Labrador was lying like a sphinx, and Dalesman resisted her, skidding over the floor with front legs spread wide. 'Down!' she commanded him, and he grinned at her, with a yawn that nearly split his head in two. 'Down, blast you!' She pushed him to the floor, and he lay where she had pushed him, uncomfortably, with his front legs still spread and his hindquarters half raised, ready to spring up again.

'Better put the rugs straight, Vi,' said Oliver. 'Ma'll be in for a nip in a minute.' She kicked at them carelessly with the side of her shoe and went over to the table to get a drink. She came back, spilling some of it on to the floor, and flopped into a chair by the bed with her legs stuck out, passing a large brown hand through the cropped hair which emphasized her masculine features.

'Tired?'

'Oh, I don't know. Been thatching all day. The stack in the bottom field's done now, and the two in Waker's. Fred's got a new man, just demobbed. He's a lazy tyke.' Dalesman had left a wet streak along her cheek, which she did not bother to wipe off. If she were a man, she might have been called handsome, with that high-bridged nose, firm mouth, and heavy chin. Her skin, although powderless, was not red and shiny, but tanned to quite

27

a mellow shade, like a weathered saddle. Because she was short-sighted, and could not be bothered to wear her glasses, her eyes were usually screwed up under the thick brows.

Mrs North came in for a sip at her sherry. She was in a hurry and did not notice the dogs. 'Will you just look at these rugs!' She bent down to straigten a corner. 'Violet, what do you do to a room when you come in to it? And don't forget Stanford's coming to dinner. You'll have to change.'

'Oh hell.' Violet slumped lower in her chair.

'I've told your little Nurse Gray to come and get herself a drink,' Mrs North told Oliver. 'She's folded all the table napkins into mitres, with a piece of bread in each. You never saw anything so cute.'

'She doesn't drink, Ma.'

'Well, she can come in and have some fruit squash or something. It's seven o'clock, Violet.'

'It's not, it's five to.' Violet peered at her watch, which had a thick leather strap and a metal guard over the face. On the other wrist she wore a buckled leather support.

'It's two and a half minutes to. Where's Evelyn? Didn't she come in with you?'

'She went with Jack to turn the horses out.'

'I'd better go and holler for her, or she'll never come in.'

'I'll go,' said Violet. 'She's probably gone up the hill to see Dandy, anyway.'

'You won't,' said her mother. 'You'll go and change.' She took another sip and left them.

'Doesn't she love to know where everybody is?' said Oliver. 'It must be quite a relief to her to have me in bed. At least she knows where I am. Oh look, here's Elizabeth. You've met my sister Violet, haven't you?'

'Yes,' said Elizabeth, standing just inside the door. Violet made some gruff noise at her. Anyone small and neat and quick always made her feel larger than ever.

'My mother thought you might like some fruit squash,' suggested Oliver unhopefully.

'No, thank you, Major North.'

'Well, come and sit down, anyway. This is everybody's off-duty time. We relax.' Elizabeth came forward and sat on the edge of the high-backed armchair by the fireplace. She had changed into a green dress with a drawstring neck and a full skirt. She had put a little lipstick on; not too much the first night, in case Mrs North did not like it.

'You look like a salad,' said Oliver. She smiled politely. 'Cool, I mean.' He wondered what to say next. Violet was still slumped with her chin on her chest, frowning at her glass.

Elizabeth looked at her stuck-out legs calmly for a while and then asked: 'Are you in the Land Army, Miss North?'

'God, no. Why? Oh, you mean this.' She plucked a piece of straw off the front of her green pullover. 'I pinched this off the last L.G. we had. Left in a hurry.' She let out a sudden guffaw. 'Sybil, Ollie. You remember.'

'Perfectly. I watched her haymaking in the hill field all the last week in July. That ugly old scoundrel Dick, wasn't it?'

'Yep. That new stud bull we had gave 'em ideas.' She guffawed again and Oliver giggled. Elizabeth looked neither shocked nor amused.

Oliver cleared his throat. 'Your room all right?' he asked politely.

'Yes, very nice, thank you.'

'Good view of the Wrekin from that room,' grunted Violet.

'The Wrekin?' Elizabeth turned to her puzzled. She had never been in Shropshire before.

'That minor mountain over there in the distance.' Oliver nodded out of the window. 'You can just see the corner of it from here; it goes purply-black at this time in the evening. It's supposed to be the earth some old giant dug out of the bed of the Severn. There's a smaller hill behind it – Ercal – that's where he shook his spade.'

'You're quite wrong, Uncle Ollie,' said Evelyn, appearing suddenly on the lawn outside and resting her chin on the window ledge. She was ten years old and just the right height for this.

Oliver had given an exclamation and jumped, and Elizabeth started up out of her chair and went to him.

'You mustn't do that, dear,' she told Evelyn in a professional voice. 'It's bad for your uncle's heart. Are you all right, Major North?'

'Lord, yes. Don't fuss. I'll get worse shocks than that before

I'm done.' She straightened his sheet without looking at him and went back to her chair. He thought: She's not worrying for me. It's her own responsibility she minds about.

Evelyn's pale, triangular face, half hidden by a lock of nasturtium-coloured hair with a bow dangling at the end, still hung on the window-sill.

'What d'you mean, anyway, I'm wrong?' he asked it.

'He wasn't digging up the Severn. He'd brought that earth there to dam it, 'cos he had a down on Shrewsbury. But when he had one foot in the river the Bore came rushing along, and he lost his balance and dropped the earth in the wrong place.'

'Is that a fact? Then how do you account for Ercal?'

'Oh, wormcasts,' she said casually. 'What's for my supper?'

'Apple pie, I think.'

'Jeepers. Look out – I'm coming in!' Two thin hands like a fledgeling's claws appeared on the ledge and there was a scrabbling noise as she sought a foothold in a crack of the yellow sandstone wall.

Elizabeth started forward again. 'Be careful,' she called. 'Whatever are you doing?' But Evelyn had pulled herself up, shifted one hand to the timber of the window and crouched in the opening like a goblin on a toadstool. 'Keep your hair on,' she said, 'I always do it like this.' With a spring, she was over the bed and cradle, skidded on the rug which Mrs North had just straightened, picked herself up and went straight to the side table.

Elizabeth turned to Oliver. 'She oughtn't – –'

'Oh, she always does that. She's quite safe.' He smiled at her. 'You needn't fuss, Elizabeth. You'll get used to our family in time.'

'Yes,' she said, and he wished again that she would give some hint of what she thought of them.

Evelyn came over to the bed, holding the wedge of apple pie in both hands and talking through it. She wore a skimpy pair of trousers, more like old-fashioned cycling knickers than riding breeches, boy's socks, gym shoes, and a grubby Aertex shirt. Round her waist was a boy's belt with a snake buckle. 'I've been up to see Dandy,' she said. 'He's filling out beautifully on the grass in that top meadow. Vi and I are going to start breaking him next week, aren't we, Vi?'

'If he's fit enough.'

'Oh, he will be! He must be if I'm going to ride him at the Pony Club rallies at Christmas.'

'You certainly wouldn't think he was that shrimp I paid a quid for at Dunster market.' Violet suddenly shot out a large hand and pulled Evelyn between her legs, gripping her with her knees. She picked something out of the mesh of the Aertex shirt, examined it and said severely: 'You've been giving him oats.'

Evelyn fidgeted. 'Honest, Vi, I haven't, truly. Well – perhaps just a teeny handful tonight, just to get him used to the taste, you know.'

'Oats are precious. That pony's got to work before he gets any. And if you think you're going to get him all corned up for me to break – you can do it by yourself.' She pushed the child away, tossed off her drink and stood up. Evelyn let a piece of apple fall on the floor. 'Vi, you know I couldn't, not without you!' She slid an appealing look at Oliver. 'Oy, *make* her be nice, Uncle Ollie,' she said in agony.

'How are you going to start him?' said Oliver casually. 'Saddle him first, or wait till you've lunged him a bit?'

'Oh, we're going to saddle him,' gabbled Evelyn, 'next week, and then lunge him with all the tack on – –'

'We are not,' said Violet, putting down her glass on the seat of her chair. 'That pony's going to stand on pillar reins for two days, with a snaffle in his mouth and a pad on his back, before I take him a step outside.'

Evelyn gave Oliver a grateful glance. 'D'you think the jointed snaffle, Vi, or that bar thing with the little wiggly bit for his tongue to play with?'

'Not sure,' said Violet, and they moved away, talking gravely, like people at diplomatic lunches.

Stanford Black came in soon, in a uniform that did not look like six years of war. He was a Squadron Leader, who had been stationed near Shrewsbury for the last year. He was not very tall, with a slight crinkle in his hair and a little moustache like two light strokes of a paintbrush. He had wandered in alone, for the front door at Hinkley was always open, but Mrs North was hot on his heels, without her apron, fussing round him, pressing him to things, enquiring after the health of himself and his people, whom she had never seen. Her American blood was always stimulated by visitors. He chatted cheerfully and easily to Oliver, liking the sensation of looking down instead of up to a man.

'When are they going to let you out, Stan?' Oliver asked.

'Oh, don't call him that,' said Heather, coming in with an effect of colour and distant sleigh-bells. 'It sounds so common.'

Oliver thought he was rather common. He did not like him very much, but he seemed to have a certain illicit glamour for Heather.

Mrs North spied first Violet, then Evelyn, then the dogs, and was horrified three times with increasing intensity.

'But I'm still hungry, Aunt Hattie,' Evelyn protested.

'Come and have some chocolate.' Oliver called her over and gave her a thick bar.

'Not your ration – –' she breathed, awestruck.

'No fear. I'm not all that generous. It's what your father sent from New York. You should have it.'

'I hope he brings a lot over when he comes to fetch me. That'll be the only thing I shall like about going there. Chocolate and chocolate all day long. And banana splits.'

'You're not old enough to remember banana splits.'

'Aunt Hattie told me about them. She used to have Knickerbocker Glory, too, in the olden days. I think that's very rude.'

Violet had been shy with Stanford when he first came in, but she was even shyer when she came back, after an interval that was evidently not long enough for her to wash her face or comb her hair, in a badly fitting blue dress and low-heeled brown shoes. She felt wrong in skirts and she knew she looked wrong, and she sometimes stood in front of the mirror and wondered why, but there seemed to be nothing she could do about it. Mrs North had done her best with her when she was first grown up. With shrugging dressmakers, she had planned campaigns on Violet's hulking, flat-chested figure, but she had ruined all her clothes by screwing them into balls when she flung them off, which was as often as possible, to get into the comfort of slacks or an ancient tweed suit with leather on the elbows. She had once had a permanent wave, but the result, when modishly set, was so like Douglas Byng that it had never been tried again.

When the war came and she started to work for Fred Williams

at the farm, she felt justified in having her hair cut short, and it was obviously not worth wielding the powder-puff with which she had sometimes floured her face to please her mother. Heather had occasional spasms of trying to 'Make something of Violet', and the elder sister would stand patiently like a horse being harnessed while the younger tried clothes on her and hauled at her waist as if she were strapping up a suitcase. She would purse her lips while Heather applied lipstick, and lower her lashes to be mascaraed, peering in the mirror without being able to see the result.

'Oh, Vi!' Heather would meet her half an hour later. 'You've washed your face.'

'Had to, before anyone saw me.'

'But that's the point. I want people to see you like that. Oh, what's the use?' she would moan, and leave her alone for another few months.

Stanford Black looked with interest at Elizabeth and made a few knowledgeable remarks about hospital. He always knew something about everything, and always had a friend who had done whatever anyone was talking about. Oliver was quite glad when they all went in to dinner. He looked forward to the evening gathering, but he still found that more than one person in the room at a time soon made him tired.

His mother came in with his soup, on a lacy tray-cloth with a few wild orchids in the little cut-glass vase. He held it under the lamp to admire them. 'From the wood?' he asked her.

'Mm-hm. I had Heather pick me some when she was down there with the children this afternoon. I know how you like them.'

'I do. Much better than the hothouse sort pinned upside down on a black-velvet bosom.' He grinned. 'Remember that huge spray you had for Heather's wedding? Green ones. Foully opulent in war-time.'

She clasped her hands in her waist and narrowed her eyes to see into the past. Her pince-nez glinted as she shook her head slowly. 'You bought me them. It was your first leave. I planned the wedding round that.'

'Not round Heather, of course,' Oliver murmured, beginning to drink his soup.

'Well, she could get married any time, couldn't she – with John safely at home? I remember his father kept trying to make me have it earlier – some nonsense about the boy's grandmother going to Scotland – but I won.' When she smiled, the corners of her mouth disappeared up into her fat cheeks. 'She didn't leave John much money, anyway, which was a score off old Sandys, though they could have done with it. Heather might have been able to have a Nanny. I get very worried about her, darling, d'you know it?' She said this about every five days. 'She's so jumpy and excitable. I've been wondering lately if it might not be her glands. Too much thyroid or something.'

'Not with her chubby shape.'

'Don't be silly, dear. Heather isn't a bit too fat. She's just right. I know you like 'em skinny, though. How is Anne, by the way?'

'Oh, all right, I think. I heard from her the other day, but she writes such scatty letters, you can't tell what she's up to.'

'Mm.' Mrs North considered him, shifted her gaze six inches beyond his head and in her mind's eye pictured Anne's non-chalant face on the pillow beside him. 'Well, I must go, or my dinner will be all haywire. I'm not taking soup these days, so I left them to it.'

'No soup? This is something new.'

'I sometimes get scared of putting on weight as I get older. It runs in my family, you know.' The old boards creaked under her as she went out.

Elizabeth brought in his next course. 'Mrs North's carving, so she let me bring this in,' she explained. He looked at her to see whether she were making a joke, but her face was quite impassive. She watched him ladling salt on to his plate. 'Are you allowed so much salt?' she asked briskly. 'Dr Trevor said there was a slight tendency to oedema.'

'Oedema, my foot,' said Oliver. 'The one they threw into the pig bucket at that.' He relented when she was half-way to the door and said: 'How's the dinner? Enjoying yourself?'

'Very much, thank you.'

'Think you'll like being here with us?'

'Yes. I'm sure I shall, thank you.'

It was going to be hard going if she did not relax a bit. The girl was buttoned up as tightly as a leg in a gaiter. Shy, probably, like that chap at Aldershot whom they all thought so rude until he confessed to somebody after the fourth gin that he nearly died every time he had to come into the Mess. But Elizabeth seemed too self-possessed to be shy.

*

After she had kissed him good night, his mother came back again in her dressing-gown, as he knew she would, to ask him what he thought of Elizabeth. It was an apricot-coloured dressing-gown, very smart, with satin lapels, full skirt, and wide sash belt. When she leaned forward you could see the dark expensive lace at the top of her nightgown. The clothes she used to buy before the war were good and most of them had lasted. She wore a pair of mules with swan's-down pompons, rather shabby because she wore them for cooking the breakfast, and a length of pink tulle was tied in a bow round her head. She had finished doing her hair. She had been figuring for quite a long time before she came in.

'She certainly does seem a very nice person,' she said again and waited, as if half expecting him to contradict her. 'Don't you think so, darling?'

'Oh yes, awfully. Takes a bit of getting to know, I should think.' Elizabeth had put on her white overall again when the washing up was finished and had made him very comfortable before she left him for the night. *Persuasion* leaned open against his crooked-up knee; his heart was beating quietly and unobtrusively, instead of in perceptible jerks, which made him gasp, as it sometimes did; a half-eaten bar of 'ZAZZ, the Health and Energy Giver, made from finest milk chocolate, maple syrup, condensed milk, pecan nuts, and 1% Dextrose, at our model Sweeteries in Detroit, Mich.' lay in its paper ready to hand.

'She's a good nurse? Tell me honestly, if there's any little thing – –'

'She seems perfect so far.'

'Yes, so she does about the house. I must say it's going to be a great blessing to have someone who's quick and efficient. Of course, I only let her do the routine things. I wouldn't trust anyone but myself to do the cooking and things like that!'

'You think no one but you can boil an egg, don't you, Ma?'

'Well, you know I like to think that.' She smiled indulgently at

35

herself, and then, seriously: 'And honestly, I sometimes wonder if they can. Remember that time Sandy hard-boiled all the breakfast eggs when I had migraine? If the hens hadn't been laying so well at the time I'd have killed her.'

'Why don't you get yourself some proper domestics?' Oliver asked. 'Pension off old mother Cowlin and get a decent cook and a maid, instead of half killing yourself to run the house?'

'You know I don't mind what I do to keep this house going. And we've got to save a bit if we are going to live here, until whoever decides the income tax comes to his senses. It's not a cheap house to run – bless it.' She laid a caressing hand on the ledge of strap-work carving which ran round the dark panelling. 'And we have to have Cowlin and the boy for the garden. I'm not going to let that go to seed. Anyway, you can't get cooks or maids, so what's the use of talking? We shall get on fine as we are, if it isn't going to be too much for Elizabeth. I asked her tonight if she thought she could manage, and she just said: "Perfectly, thank you," in that funny, prim little voice.'

'She's not very communicative, is she?'

'There's something about her I'm not quite happy about.' She fidgeted with things on his bedside table. 'She seems perfectly content and she's very polite – a bit too polite for this house – but she's so kind of – detached. Doesn't seem to want to make friends.'

'Perhaps she's shy,' Oliver suggested, taking a bite of ZAZZ.

'I don't think so. She has a lot of poise. No, I asked her to come and play Vingty in the drawing-room after she'd finished settling you, but she said she'd rather go to her room. I thought she was probably tired, but when I went in quite a while after to see if she had everything she wanted, she was just sitting in the dark looking out of the window. I thought we might have a little chat, but she wouldn't. Just stood up and answered me yes and no, so I gave up.'

'Funny girl,' said Oliver.

'I think perhaps I'll just go in once more before I go to bed and see if she's unhappy about anything. I like everyone to be happy in my house.'

'I should leave her alone, Ma. After all, she's only just come. She's probably asleep by now, anyway.'

'Would you, darling? Well, you're usually right. I think I'll go to bed then. I haven't read the paper yet. Oh, Oliver, must you eat that sickly stuff after you've done your teeth?'

'Yes, I must, I'm afraid.'

'I shall write Bob not to send you any more. Let me get you the toothbrush and mug then, before I go.'

'Oh, *Ma*.'

'All right, don't say it. I'm not going to fuss.' She gave him one of her scented kisses. 'Don't read too late, dear,' she said from the shadows by the door. She could as soon have left him for the night without saying this as a priest could have omitted the *Ite, missa est* at the end of Mass.

Half an hour later, he had just thrown out the two top pillows and turned out the light, when she opened the door, and was going out again when he called: 'It's all right. I'm not asleep.'

She saw the white shapes of the pillows on the floor. 'Oliver! Your pillows – you know you're supposed to have them all in.' She came and propped them behind his shoulders, not very comfortably, but he would throw them out after she had gone.

'You're very bad. I'm glad I came in. I just wanted to tell you that I did look in on Elizabeth after all and she's sleeping quite quietly. So sweet, with the moon on her face. She's really rather a pretty girl, isn't she?'

'Oh, I don't know. So-so,' murmured Oliver. He knew that if he said yes she would lie awake half the night planning what would happen if he fell in love with his nurse.

He could not get to sleep for a long while after she had gone. He saw the light on the lawn from her window click out, and much later, Heather's light went on and he heard her moving about overhead, while he lay with the breeze on his face, breathing the faintly scented air and turning his mind over idly. He did not worry about not being able to sleep at night. He had all the day to sleep in if he wanted to.

CHAPTER 3

HINKLEY was a small manor farm, four hundred years old in places. Oliver's room, like most of the ground floor, was panelled in dark oak, with two blackened old beams crossing in the centre of the ceiling. It was not self-consciously period; it had never been restored or preserved or quainted up with spinning-wheels and wrought-iron lanterns. Since Tudor times, people had lived in it and furnished it according to the fashion of their day, but incongruities, as long as they were comfortable, did not spoil the atmosphere of the dark little parlour. Its chief charm was its air of sheltered relaxation and it could stand any furniture that was content to do its job without calling attention to itself. That tall tapestry armchair by the fireplace, for instance, looked nothing until you sat back in it and found yourself in a nest, coddled against draughts and disturbances. The footstool to which you instinctively raised your legs was a square of tough red leather, stretched tightly between stubby trestles. It was not beautiful, but the fact that it had stood up so well to the weight of the hundreds of feet which had scarred its brass studs had earned it its fireside pitch.

The fireplace itself, a Tudor arch of the sandy Shropshire stone, with an iron basket inside and a chimney in which David could see the sky as through a telescope, was the only part of the room that had been tampered with. It had been half the size when the Norths came to Hinkley, with a painted mantelpiece, and a black hooded grate baring its teeth between glazed tiles. Mrs North, far more attuned to Old England than her husband, had done a lot of tapping and listening and prodding her cushiony thumb into the plaster. When he came home from work one day, Mr North found that she had torn away a whole panel of wood and crumbled off enough plaster and hairy felt to make it simpler to go on with the demolition than patch it up again. With cries of triumph, she had encouraged the men who pulled the Victorian camouflage down on to dust-sheets, and when at last the wide hearth was exposed, wrote many letters to the States and one to the local paper in strains that would have done justice to the finding of a Roman bath, complete with skeletons. Mr North did not say that it used twice as much coal, nor that he had pre-ferred the wide mantelpiece to the ledge of beam which was too narrow to hold his photographs. When the fire was first lit, he did not complain of the smoke, but opened all the windows and sat in a draught, hoping that it would escape before it disappointed

Hattie. Eventually, a lead cowl was fixed inside and the fire now burned well, consuming great quantities of logs from the osier basket, the refilling of which gave Cowlin an opportunity to see Oliver. One of the times when Oliver longed most to get out of bed was when the fire needed poking and he wanted to kick the logs and send a fountain of sparks up the chimney.

On the left of the fireplace was the door into the hall, which had heavy iron hinges and an old wooden thumb-latch. On a little shelf above it rested two Quimper peasant plates which were only taken down at spring-cleaning and never failed to surprise Mrs Cowlin with the amount of dust they had accumulated in twelve months. On the other side of the fireplace, the room ran back into a shadowy little corner with cupboards built into the panelling and shelves for Mr North's sober textbooks which nobody opened now. Oliver's books stood between the Dolphin book-ends he had had at Oxford along the back of the solid refectory table under the east window.

All the features of this room combined to make it dark. Oliver's bed itself held the light until the end of the day, but his pillows and the hump of the bedclothes cut off some of the daylight from the room; the small-paned east window was low and shadowed by the roof, which came right down at this end of the house like an overhanging eyebrow. The ceiling was low and, for no apparent reason, on two levels, which corresponded to the fact that you had to go down two steps from the corridor above into the south bedrooms.

But there was nothing gloomy about the darkness of the room, nothing sinister about the shadows which gathered there. It was a darkness like the cosiness of a cottage parlour, with a little window made even littler by lace curtains and potted plants. Oliver loved the sun, but he almost resented the freak summer of this October, which was postponing the time when his room would be lit every evening by his lamp and the fire, and he would go to sleep to the jigging pattern on the ceiling of the old nursery guard which Mrs North insisted on putting there at night.

Oliver liked his room. He had always liked this room, long before it became the cocoon inside which, like a grub, he must stay until his body was ready to try its wings in the outside world. As a boy of ten, when they first moved to Hinkley from London,

39

his bedroom had been the odd little room up its own short flight of stairs, halfway between the first floor and the attics. It had the only west window in the house above the ground floor, a miniature oriel, supported outside by sloping timbers. House-martins used to nest in the angle between the joist and the wall on one side. They would never build in the other side, although he used to climb up the pruning ladder to bait it with bits of wool and felt. Back to this little room he had come from school and from Oxford and, not quite so regularly, when he was feeling his feet in London and Paris as the cocksure young representative of a firm who made wireless sets that looked like clocks, bookcases, cigar boxes – like anything, in fact, but wireless sets.

This ground-floor room that was now his bedroom had been his father's library and study then. Mr North had been a house agent. He had always been a house agent; he was a man who stuck like glue to anything on which he once embarked. Someone had told him that nobody could be a success who had not studied Real Estate in America, so, as he was a modest man who was always ready to believe that other people knew better than he did, he had gone to America. There he had met the plump and smiling Hattie Linnegar, best waffle maker for her age in Philadelphia, who had known quite soon that they ought to get married and had no difficulty in bringing it about. Soon after Violet was born, the two years' grace which his English firm had allowed him being expired, he had come back to London to go on being a house agent in exactly the same way as before he went to America.

He was a man who did not easily assimilate new ideas. He was non-porous to the changes of the world, and lived among them without absorbing them. Being country-bred, he had never absorbed London, and so, when the manager of the North Midland branch died, it was Mr North who offered, without pushing himself, to go to Shrewsbury.

The Norths had never worked the land at Hinkley. They had always rented the farm buildings and most of the property to a bad-tempered man who had a stroke in the rick yard, and after him to Fred Williams, who had been to an agricultural college and had progressive ideas. As a boy, Oliver had wanted to be a farmer, but he grew away from the desire. Mr North was quite ready to believe that his son knew better than he about not wanting to be an estate agent and had remained until the day of his death uncomprehending and slightly dazed by the job into which Oliver had slipped through one of his Oxford friends.

'Do you remember, Ollie, when this room was Daddy's study? What did he study, I wonder, when he shut himself away in here? He can't have been writing his book on Shropshire Seats *all* the time, because there was hardly anything to show for it when he died.'

'He probably wanted to get away from us.'

The two sisters were sitting in Oliver's room after dinner. Heather, in one of her qualms that she was not doing enough for Oliver, had brought in her mending, and Violet, looking in for a dog she had mislaid and sensing a promise of intimacy and comfort in the lamplit room, had stayed. She had put a cushion on the floor and sat with her head resting against the bed, her legs in a trousered position that was not doing the shape of her skirt any good.

'His desk was under that window.' Heather bit off a thread, nodding towards the east window which looked out on to the rose garden, with the yew hedge and tennis-court beyond.

'Wasn't,' scoffed Violet. 'It was between the fireplace and the wall. That table's always been under that window.'

'Don't be more ridiculous than you can help,' said Heather, whose opinions were not tempered by the fact that she was invariably wrong about things like this. 'I can *see* his desk under that window. And he had all his little pots of cactuses and acorns and things on the window-sill above it.'

Violet snorted. 'You are a futile ass.' Like her old clothes, she clung to the epithets she had acquired when schoolboy magazines were her favourite reading. 'That was in London, in the dining-room. He never had his pots indoors here. What d'you think greenhouses are for?'

'He *did*.' Heather, getting cross, sewed faster, pricked her finger, said 'Damn', and shook it, saw a spot of blood on the baby's nightgown, said 'Damn' again, rolled up the nightgown and stuffed it in the work-basket, took out a vest, and made a face at it, selected a piece of wool and a needle that was too small, sucked fiercely at the wool, scrabbled for another needle, threaded it, sighed, and started to darn with jabs. The mutter with which she had accompanied these actions rose to the surface. 'How could you know, anyway?' she asked. 'You hardly ever came indoors except when you smelled food. He had his desk under that window. When you came in at the door, you could see the back of his head, with that bald patch he used to brush the hairs across.' She darned in silence for a moment and then added challengingly: 'That table was in this window where Oliver's bed is now.'

Violet let out a loud hoarse laugh, kicked her heels in the air, and thumped them down on the floor. 'That's a good one! That table – this window – – Oh, that's rich!' Her tanned face became suffused with convulsive mirth.

'What's so funny about that? Don't rock against Oliver's bed like that, you jackass, you'll hurt him. I don't care what you say, that table was in this window, wasn't it, Ollie?'

'It wasn't even in this room,' said Violet, prolonging her laughter beyond the limit of her amusement, and coughing. Sometimes, if she were having a good time with a joke, she would laugh until she became black in the face and choked. 'Tell her, Ollie.'

'What? Oh, I don't know.' He had hardly been listening to what they were saying. He was lying looking out of the window, letting the familiar crescendo act as a background to his thoughts. His sisters' arguments had been a background to his life ever since Heather was old enough to say 'shan't' and 'isn't'.

They were both wrong about the table. He knew quite well that it had stood in the middle of the room, because he used to sit at it occasionally to fill in the stamp album which it pleased his father to see him keep up, but he had learned long ago not to interfere or take sides. It only prolonged the argument, which would otherwise peter out eventually in favour of another which one hoped would be less boring. His sisters' squabbling dated from kicking the furniture nursery days. It had increased in intensity and shrillness as they reached adolescence and dropped off slightly as Heather grew up, acquired more interests outside the family and came to accept Violet as something that could not be helped, like an act of God. Either because she was at home less, or because she said it less, her exasperated cry of 'Oh, *Vi!*' rang less frequently through the house. Lately, however, she had reverted. The sight and sound of her elder sister was like a rash which she had to scratch. And like a rash, the more she scratched it, the more it irritated. Mrs North had to resurrect her nursery voice: 'Let your sister alone!' because when Violet was goaded she became *farouche* and moody and would not come to meals and it was inconvenient to have her raiding the larder of tomorrow's lunch after everyone had gone to bed.

After the argument about the table had died down, Violet said (it was not always Heather who provoked the quarrels): 'Why do we have to have that Black man to meals so often? Dinner on Monday and tea again today. Don't they feed him properly at Ockney? He gives me a pain.'

'You give him a pain, more likely,' retorted Heather. 'You hadn't washed your hands for tea and that horrible dog of yours slobbered all over his trousers. I thought he was very good about it, considering dog-spit never comes off.'

'He's pansy,' said Violet.

'You don't know the meaning of the word.'

Violet guffawed again. 'That's a good one!' Heather darned faster than ever, her kissable mouth clamped like the two halves of a shell. Violet lurched upwards and sideways, took a book at random off Oliver's table, and began to read, holding it an inch from her eyes.

Heather kept darting irritated glances at her and eventually burst out: 'Why don't you wear your glasses? No wonder your eyes are getting worse.'

'They're not.'

'They are. That's why you knocked over that glass at dinner, and upset the salt. Even you can't be as clumsy as all that. I know you hate yourself in them, but what's it matter what you look like? If they're helping your eyes, I mean,' she added in a half-hearted attempt to disguise what she obviously meant. 'Don't you think she's silly, Ollie?' And when he refused to be drawn, she rounded on him. 'Oh, don't be so *mild*. You lie there so serenely, like some blasted saint – it's enough to drive anyone mad.'

'I thought you liked saints,' Oliver said. 'Catholic ones, anyway.'

'Not in the home.'

'What would you like me to do?' he asked. 'Shout and scream and have a heart attack?'

43

'I'm sorry, darling. I didn't mean that. Forget it. I'm a pig.' She put down the vest and fumbled in her sleeve for a handkerchief, sniffing. Violet looked round, interested, and Heather was able to recover her equilibrium by saying: 'You've got cigarette ash all down the front of that blouse. How on earth do you manage to get in such a mess?'

When Elizabeth came briskly in, it looked like a peaceful family scene. 'Excuse me, I'm so sorry to disturb you,' she said, and was going out, but Oliver called her back. When she switched on the centre light, the family scene was disclosed as both sisters looking cross and Oliver with shadows under his eyes and his pillows slipped down so that his head looked as if it were dropping off.

'I've been hoping you'd come in,' he said. 'I'm damned uncomfortable.'

'Why didn't you ask me?' said Heather, reproachfully. Violet did not say anything. It was an accepted fact that she was no good in a sickroom, and she would sooner wash up the glasses than touch her brother. Once when she had come in by mistake when Elizabeth was doing his dressing, she had been invited over to have a look. She knew they had thought her churlish for taking one glance and hurrying away as if she were not interested, but she was ashamed to let them see what the sight of his stump did to her.

She was still very shy of Elizabeth, who was so deft with her hands that she made Violet drop more things than ever. She would have liked to make friends with her, for she had no real friends except Evelyn and Joan Elliot, the square and hairy dog girl at the kennels in the village, but she did not know how to begin. She had shown Elizabeth round the farm, and Elizabeth, although she had obviously lived all her life in towns and thought a heifer was a breed of cow, had seemed to like it and had shown a polite interest in the workings of the grass-drying plant, made incomprehensible by Violet's explanations. Oliver had heard her offer to take Elizabeth riding.

'Thank you very much, but I'm afraid I don't know how.'

'Teach you if you like,' Violet had thrown at her. Elizabeth had said that would be very nice, thank you, and there the matter rested until Violet could find the words to suggest it again. She was not sure whether Elizabeth wanted to be taught to ride, and on thinking it over, she was not sure whether she herself wanted to risk Brownie's mouth.

She scrambled up now as Elizabeth approached the bed, mumbled good night to her brother and went off with her skirt rucked up at the back, to see if there were anything in the biscuit tin.

Heather also wanted to be friendly with Elizabeth. She welcomed anyone new. But, as she had said to Oliver: 'She's so unapproachable. You feel if you could chip off some of that polite plaster casing she walks around in, you *might* find a real girl underneath, but honestly, I'm beginning to doubt if there's anything there. I've tried to get together with her, but she won't let her stays out one notch.'

'No girls' gossips?' asked Oliver.

'Gossip? She doesn't know the meaning of the word. I've been into her room and asked leading questions about all her photographs, but she shut up like a clam as if she thought I were being nosey. So queer. Most people will talk for ever about their relations – especially nurses. Remember Sandy's cousin Arthur in the Merchant Navy? God, how I suffered.'

She picked up her work-basket and stood now, feeling useless, watching Elizabeth critically as she pummelled pillows and drew sheets taut. 'You must think us an awfully helpless family,' she said, 'not being able to look after our own brother ourselves.'

'I don't see why,' said Elizabeth. 'Acute heart cases need very special treatment. They should really be nursed in hospital.' This was the first time she had vouchsafed even so indirect a criticism since she came to Hinkley. Oliver and Heather exchanged glances. 'That's one for you, my lad,' said Heather, her crucifix swinging forward against his chin as she kissed him on the forehead, and went out.

'Oh, dear,' said Elizabeth. 'I do hope Mrs Sandys didn't think I meant to be rude. I didn't mean it like that.'

'All the same if you did,' said Oliver cheerfully. 'You're quite right in theory. But you reckon without people like my mother. Hasn't she ever told you how she snatched me from out of the jaws of hell? It was one of her finest achievements. What are you going to do now – not my dressing again?'

'You know you have to have that cod-liver oil on four-hourly. It's not been done since six.'

'I wonder you don't get up in the night and do it,' he grumbled.

'I suppose I should really,' she said seriously.

'If I didn't know you so well already,' said Oliver, 'I should think you were my devoted slave, but I'm forced to admit it's my stump you cherish, not me.'

'Tell me about your mother and the jaws of hell,' said Elizabeth, 'and perhaps you could wind this bandage at the same time.'

*

'As you know,' said Oliver, 'I was wounded at Arnhem. The same shell that smashed up my leg left a bit of itself in my chest as well. We'd been in the attic of a house in the main street for four days, potting at a mobile gun that used to come up the street on and off to try and blast us out. Quite a lot of the chaps got hit, and I was sure I would soon – I was stiff with fright all the time I was in that attic. I should love to be able to tell you that I fell at my gun, firing to the last, and falling back with a cry of encouragement on my lips, but I'm sorry to say that I fell simply through greed.

'There were twelve of us in that house. Those who weren't working the gun or sniping used to live in the cellar – the old man who'd owned it was a specialist in Hocks, but his red wines were like prickly ink. We lived mostly on stew, made in a bucket by an absolute wizard who'd been a cook at the Savoy or somewhere. He used to have the thing simmering all day and throw in everything he could lay hands on. We'd scrounge a chicken sometimes and once someone out on patrol sniped at a Hun and got a rabbit. This particular day, when I came down from the attic, I went over to the bucket and had a taste out of the ladle to see what the lunch was going to be like.

'"Not enough onion," I said to Willie. He was the man who made the stew.

'"I haven't been able to get any today," Willie said. "Every time I start out for the kitchen garden, a Heinkel comes over and drops something down the back of my neck."

'I said we couldn't eat the stuff without onion. We'd become rather eclectic about that stew. I told him what I thought about the service in his hotel and went out myself to get some onions.

46

'The house had one of those long, narrow gardens, with flower-beds and what had once been a lawn first, then a kind of arbour and then the kitchen garden. I found the onions and put about a dozen inside my blouse. I was just turning to go back when I saw a little bay tree in a corner by the end fence. I remembered Ma and her bay leaves. She planted that tree in the tub by the front door, and when we lived in London, there was one in our Square and she used to send me out to pinch some while the gardener was having his tea. Willie, being a professional cook, would appreciate them.

'"Willie will be pleased," I thought, and that was the last thing I did think, because the shell got me half-way to the tree.

'Willie must have found me when he came out to see what had happened to his onions. I don't know. When I came to, I was being gently rocked; I thought I was a baby in my cradle. I swear it. I'm not just making that up because I've read that you get a subconscious mother-craving *in extremis*, though I did read that afterwards and was gratified to think I'd run so true to form. Actually, I was in a small boat. Our advanced dressing station was on the other side of a branch of the Rhine, and we had to take our seriously wounded across at night. There was a stiff wind blowing along the river and the boat was rocking against the little jetty. I was lying in the bottom, wrapped in a blanket like a cocoon. I thought at first that was why I couldn't breathe properly. There were some hoarse attempts at whispering going on and a lot of muffled oaths. People kept stepping over my head in muddy boots. It was damned cold and I couldn't see anyone I knew.

'I knew one of the doctors at the dressing station though, a Scotsman with a little black moustache and a soft voice. He told me they were going to take my leg off before they moved me to the clearing station. I can't remember minding very much. I think I thought it was a good idea if it was going to make it hurt less. Everyone was frightfully amused when they bared my bosom to listen to my heart and found a dozen large onions nestling in there. Then, of course, they found the hole where the bit of shrapnel had gone in, so they took that out, and ever since I've heard nothing but heart, heart, heart, and you mustn't do this and you mustn't do that, and what a miraculous escape and you're a fool to chuck it away just because you won't do what you're told.

'That was in the base hospital in England mostly. I was a bit of a pest there. The ward sister was very frank and man-to-man. She was the one who kept calling me a fool and promising me death. She favoured the direct rather than the humouring technique, and when they realized that my stump was not going to heal properly, told me so with great pride as though she admired her bravery in being so honest. When my dressing was being done and the nurse called her over to have a look, she would say: "What did I tell you? You'll be here a long time yet," as if it were all my fault and served me right.

'I was in one of those temporary huts, a sort of annexe to the main hospital. There were twenty beds in it, lockers that looked like soap boxes turned on end, and an iron stove in the middle which always had a few unshaven men sitting round it playing cards. It certainly was rather a bleak spot, but I'll never forget my poor old Ma's face when she first came to visit me. I think she expected to find me in a private room, surrounded by beautiful cooing nurses and flowers and exotic fruit.

'She was horrified to think that anyone should have put her son – *her son* – into a place where the backs of beds were not high enough to support the pillows and the bread and butter for the whole day was cut the night before. Because she was too sympathetic, I, out of cussedness, was too cheerful. Actually, I hated the place. We all did, and used to work each other up by grumbling until gloom hung in the struts of the tin roof like a cloud of cigarette smoke. If an optimistic new patient came in, prepared to make the best of everything, we took a lugubrious delight in schooling him to our way of thought. My mother, of course, sensed the atmosphere, but I told her she was imagining things, not because I was noble, but because I couldn't stand pity from anyone just then.

'She had taken rooms in the town, and was back again the next day. It wasn't visitors' day, so of course she was not allowed to see me. I could hear the argument going on in the passage outside the hut. I knew who would win, and sure enough, the old lady sailed in presently, followed by Sister, scarlet in the face. It was winter then and the windows of the hut were low, but we

48

were not allowed to have the lights on until five. On this particular day, a leaden, soaking afternoon had made it twilight in our hut by about four o'clock. A hideous man called Stringy Salter was making up the stove with a lot of noise. He wore a red blanket round his waist and a filthy white sock over the plaster on his foot. Two other up-patients, very decent chaps really, but not prepossessing, were playing cards. One had a hacking cough and the other had a patch over one eye. We had had our tea, but I had been slow with mine because I didn't want it, and the orderly had not cleared it away. A plate with a great hunk of bread and butter and a cup without a saucer, half full of tea which I hadn't been able to drink because it was too strong, stood on my locker beside the old tin lid I used as an ashtray. The man in the bed next to me had died the night before and the springs of the bed were bare, because his mattress had gone to be fumigated. My mother sat down on the black iron and looked at me.

'"This is just terrible," she said. "You can't stay here."

'"Oh, it's all right," I said airily. "It's fine. You see it at its worst today. Come on a sunny morning when we're larking about with the V.A.D.s —" At that moment, the most horse-faced of all the V.A.D.s, a brave old relic of the last war, chose to come pounding down the ward with a bucketful of dirty dressings, like a swineherd going to the sties. The orderlies were supposed to take them from the sluice out to the bins, but they usually forgot.

'One of the men called out to her: "Annie — " That was her name, Annie. Annie Rooney they used to call her. "Annie, for Christ's sake, when are they going to turn these bloody lights on?" Only he didn't say bloody, unfortunately. He had to lie flat on his back and couldn't see I had a visitor.

'Annie answered him tartly: "You shut your noise, young Bobby Combes, or you won't get any light at all tonight." That was her idea of a joke. She was a cheery old soul, but to one who didn't know her finer qualities, she must have sounded a bit grim. She had a voice like a nutmeg grater; she smoked like a chimney off duty and would do anything for you if you gave her a packet of cigarettes.

'I could see my mother getting more and more worked up. "Why hasn't this bed got a mattress on it?" she asked. I told

49

her and she got up quickly, and Sister, thinking she was going away, came up and said: "I shall have to ask you to leave now, Mrs North. The ward is closed."

'"It should never have been opened, in my opinion," said Ma, showing a ready wit. She squeezed my hand in the gloaming and whispered that she would be back tomorrow. I must say, I never thought she would get in. Sister had redoubled her defences by having screens round the bed and saying I had had a bad day and was too ill to see anyone. I could hear them at it on the other side of the screens. I found out afterwards that the men were laying bets on the pair of them and Scotty Macrae won half a crown and a rubber air cushion when my mother came triumphantly through the screens. I don't know how she managed it, but she came every day after that, visiting hours or not, and Sister pretended not to notice her or arranged to be off duty when she came. She used to talk to me about my mother, of course, and would lay the cold end of her stethoscope on my chest and tell me that my heart was worse. "And no wonder," she gloated.

'My first hint that Ma was being active behind the scenes was when the M.O. said one morning: "Pity that stump of yours is playing us up. You might have been able to go home soon otherwise."

'"*Home?*" I said. I had not expected to be discharged for weeks yet. That was one of the things that was getting me down, not having any sort of definite date to look forward to. Stringy Salter knew when his plaster was coming off and he used to notch the days off on it with a penknife.

'The M.O. looked uncomfortable. He was young and guileless and I suppose he had been having quite a rough time with my mother. "Yes," he said. "When a patient's people are prepared to take a lot of responsibility – but I'm afraid in your case, it's impossible at the moment."

'When my mother asked me who was in charge of the hospital, I wanted to make a bet myself, but no one would take me. They had all got to know her pretty well by this time. She never would tell me exactly what had taken place between her and the colonel. I knew she got at him through an uncle of mine who was at the War Office, but I'd love to know what they said to each other. Anyway, the upshot of it was that I was suddenly attacked one day with blankets and hot-water bottles and a small swig of diluted brandy – the night nurse used to help herself and fill the bottle up with water – and borne away on a trolley to the accompaniment of cheers from the multitude.

'When I arrived here, in the smartest private ambulance ever seen, I found Sandy already installed and the best bedroom crowded with flowers and books and log fires and hysterically welcoming family. I had no sooner hinted at this room than Ma got a builder to stop doing bomb repairs in Birmingham and fix up this window bed for me. A remarkable woman, my mother.'

*

'I expect you think I'm spoiled,' Oliver said.

'Not at all,' said Elizabeth, tucking in the last blanket and bending to pick up her dressing tray.

'My sister Heather,' said Oliver, 'says I lie here like a blasted saint. Do you think I'm saintly, Elizabeth? Am I a good patient?' He had been mildly tormented for some time now by curiosity to know what she thought of him.

'Of course,' she said. 'But you must be quiet now. You've talked too long; you'll never get to sleep.'

'Anyway, I know you think I shouldn't have been brought home,' he pursued. 'You said so.'

'Did I? That was silly of me, seeing that it gave me a nice job,' she said brightly and escaped before she could commit herself further.

Did she mean that it was an easy job or that she liked being with them? Or was it just one of the polite, meaningless remarks with which she always warded off attempts at intimacy? Trying to understand Elizabeth made you feel like an archaeologist trying to probe the centuries-old secrets of a fossil. Perhaps Heather was right, and there was nothing there to understand.

He thought of ringing the cow-bell, to call her back and ask her what she meant. He looked at it, then picked it up, holding the clapper with his finger, and examined the Swiss cow with a leg at each corner painted on it against a background of the Rosegg valley. Having decided what he was going to say, he rang it, hating its imperious jangle in the quiet of his room. She did

not come, so he rang it again, and Heather burst in wearing a
rubber apron and looking as though she had no time to spare.

'What is it, Ollie? You've woken Susan.'

'I say, I'm terribly sorry. I wanted Elizabeth, actually, but I
suppose she's outside burning my dressings.'

'Well, surely she can hear it from there. Why doesn't she
answer it? That's what she's paid for.'

'Don't be horrid, Heather.'

'I feel horrid. We've all been jolly nice to her, and she won't
even be friendly. If she wants to be so stand-offish, at least she
might do her job properly. I don't think I'm going to like her
very much. Just listen to that little pest upstairs. D'you want anything, before I go and murder her?'

'No, thank you,' said Oliver meekly.

When Elizabeth came in later to say good night, he did not talk
to her, but waited quite impatiently for her to go. He could feel
approaching one of the waves of weariness and depression that
attacked him from time to time, and until it passed over he could
not be interested in anybody except himself. He turned out the
light, and making a peevish face to himself in the darkness, settled
down to indulge in a little self-pity.

CHAPTER 4

WHEN Oliver was depressed, the whole house knew it. As he was
usually quite happy, he made heavy weather of these fits of
weltschmertz, like a robust man who thinks he is dying if he has
a cold. He did not think himself into his moods; they just arrived,
and that they left him was due to no exercise of will-power on
his part. He had no more control over them than a sunbather
waiting for a cloud to pass away from the sun.

Since, apparently, he must suffer them occasionally, he made
the most of them and did not attempt to disguise his weariness
of soul. If he felt cross, he was cross. If anybody bored him, he
showed it. If he did not like some dish of his mother's, he left
it on his plate, instead of throwing it out of the window as he
normally did. Cowlin, the gardener, had a fox terrier who had

found out Oliver's meal-times and used to stand with his hind legs on the lawn and his front paws against the outside wall, head on one side, jaws slightly parted, eyes lustrous.

When Oliver was depressed, nothing could be done for him. He was determined to savour his melancholia to the dregs. No book that you produced was readable, he did not want the wireless, no food tempted him and he would admit to no appetite, any visitor you offered him was a bore. In fact, he used to put down his book and hastily pretend to be asleep when the doorbell rang. He wasted a lot of time doing this for the postman, the laundry, Joan Elliot, Evelyn's local cronies, and Mrs Dalrymple, who collected half-crowns for the Hinkley savings group. When Hugo Trevor, who was his friend as well as his doctor, came to see him, Oliver would tell him not to order his artificial leg. He would never walk again and did not want to. Dr Trevor, an imperturbable man with short limbs, who looked as though he had been carved out of one block of stone, would sit by him and talk about anything and everything but his health, which was the only thing Oliver wanted to talk about at these times. In the end, he would get up, tell Oliver harshly that he was neurotic and go in search of Mrs North, who was also his friend, leaving Oliver to wallow in the pathos of being misunderstood.

Then one morning, for no reason at all, he would suddenly feel quite different. He knew it before he was properly awake. A lightness over his eyes, a vitality in his limbs, even in the one that was not there, a tingling in his scalp, as if he could feel the very hair growing, an urge to hop out of the window and across the lawn all told him that the mood had passed. He would try himself out by thinking of all the most irritating things he knew: Mrs Cowlin's creep, Heather's charm bracelet, Violet's habit of standing in front of the fire with her legs straddled, Fred Williams' Sunday suit, his mother's transatlantic habit of saying '*mm*-hm', and '*mm-hm*' when she meant yes and no, Elizabeth's prim little mouth if she thought you were being too familiar. If he could contemplate all these things with equanimity, he would look at the day before him to see whether it seemed full of possibilities, or a dragging cortège of ticking minutes. Then he would think about breakfast. If he could pass all these tests, he would pick up his shaving mirror, see how his face adapted itself to a smile,

53

and then, if it were not too early, reach for the bell. This was the one time he did not mind ringing it. He could not wait to announce the glad tidings to the household.

This was the most amusing part of the whole business. Whoever answered it would not know, of course, that they had been liberated and would come in with a patient expression, resigned to whatever treatment they might get, perhaps with an excuse on their lips, expecting to be cursed for taking so long to answer the bell. The relief in their faces and the tactful way in which they said: 'You're feeling better, this morning, aren't you?', as if it was his health and not his temperament that had been ailing, caused him great glee. Swift as fire, the news would run round the house: 'Oliver isn't bloody-minded any more!' and long before breakfast-time each member of the household would have made a sightseeing trip to his room.

He had not had the mood for more than three months, and the one that overtook him now coincided with Elizabeth's week-end off, which meant physical as well as mental discomfort. Elizabeth went to London, and while she was away the district nurse did what she called 'stopping by' twice a day to do for him those things which his family could not manage. If she were not so busy, she would have come more often, for she was in love with Oliver.

She had always been in love with him, ever since she was the stocky, red-haired child at the Hare and Hounds at Burnell Heath, and he was the boy who came on his pony to buy stone ginger beer. The inn was on the edge of the heath, a yellow toy house with a garden divided into neat segments, completely surrounded by a privet and elder hedge against which lapped the gorse and bracken of the common. Oliver, a weedy, fair boy in a red polo jersey and jodhpurs, used to stand outside the hedge drinking the ginger beer with his pony's reins looped over his arm. Mary Brewer would swing on the gate in the short faded gingham she wore in all weathers. She never felt the cold and would go without stockings or gloves all the year round and glow when other people were pinched and blue.

She swung on the outside of the gate, so that she did not have to face Oliver, and threw remarks at him over her shoulder in a gruff manner which was meant to show unconcern. Mrs Brewer, in a butcher-blue pinafore and a hair net, would view the scene from an upstairs window and think what a pretty pair they made. Pity the boy was so skimpy, but he might fill out later if he took after his mother and not his father. Her mind would run away with her and she would rest her arms on the window-sill and dream just as mad, romantic dreams as Mary did. She had bequeathed to her daughter a star-gazing soul in a homely exterior. If Oliver looked up, she would shake out a yellow duster, half in salute, half as justification for being at the window. When he handed Mary back the foam-crusted glass and rode away, she would swing on the other side of the gate so that she could watch him cantering over the common, his pony's quarters switching from side to side as it avoided gorse bushes which he meant it to jump.

Oliver had barely noticed Mary in those days, except as a girl who asked silly questions about his pony. The Brewers were London people and Mary, when she grew up, had gone back to London to learn to be a nurse. Oliver's New Forest pony became a retired polo pony and then a small hunter and then a man-sized horse, and his ginger beer became cider and then a pint of mild. Mary, being older than he, had gone away during the cider stage. He used to ask after her when he remembered, and then, when he had been having pints of mild for about four years, he stopped his car at the Hare and Hounds on one of his infrequent visits home and found two gaunt, swarthy strangers in the little toy house behind the privet and elder hedge.

'The Brewers?' said the woman indifferently. 'I dunno. I never heard of such people.'

'But surely you took over from them. You must know them – a fat woman and a little man with white hair. They had a daughter too – what was her name? – didn't you buy this pub from them?'

The woman laughed cynically to think that he should imagine she had that much money. 'This place belongs to a company. Me and Mr Stark works it for them. I can't tell you about no Brewers or Stewers or what is it,' she said, and went out of the bar as if she resented being asked to do something which was not in her contract to the company.

Not long afterwards, Oliver, driving Heather home from a tennis party and wanting a drink, took her into a stuffy little hotel on the main road near Shrewsbury. They rang the bell in the lounge and a short, strong-looking red-haired girl with a plain face redeemed by a broad grin came in, reeled on her solid legs, clutched the edge of the door for support and said: 'It *is*, isn't it?'

'Is what?' asked Heather.

'Oliver North,' said the girl wonderingly. 'I haven't forgotten you, you see.' Heather raised her eyebrows.

Oliver raked his brains desperately. 'My God!' he said suddenly, 'Mary. Mary Brewer from the Hare and Hounds. You used to bring me ginger beer. Where have you been all this time?' He knew that Mrs Brewer had told him, and that he ought to remember.

Mary, still rather overcome by the sight of Oliver in white flannels and a striped silk scarf inside his open-necked shirt, told him in the same off-hand manner with which she used to throw remarks at him from the garden gate. He asked her to have a drink with them and she went away to get the drinks and came back with Mrs Brewer, still apparently in the same hair net. Yes, she told them, while Mary stood by and admired Oliver, Mary was a State Registered Nurse now, giving her old folks a hand while she was at home on holiday. Done her midwifery and going to start as district nurse here next month. Oh, she knew the business all right. Hadn't she nursed Mr Brewer good and proper last week when he cut his hand on a broken hoop?

Heather, who was rather a snob at this age, said, as they drove away: 'I never knew you were so democratic, Ollie.'

'Brewers and I? Bosom pals – must make that one of my ports of call,' he said, and forgot all about them until Mary turned up nearly five years later on a bicycle in a round hat and a long blue coat to wash him on Nurse Sanderson's first day off. She had not changed at all. Her work was very hard, but it satisfied the rapt, idealistic qualities in her, and because she loved it, it left no marks of wear and tear. Her capacity for service was infinite, and for Oliver, of course, she would have died. He did not notice her devotion at first, but once Heather had gleefully pointed it out, he was embarrassingly aware of it all the time. That explained, of course, why she was unnatural with him, although quite at her ease with his mother and sisters. She could laugh and joke with them, and order them about or turn them out of the room with the self-confidence born of proficiency and ten years of handling all sorts of people. With Oliver, however, she was awkward. She was too polite, too apologetic if she hurt him, she laughed too much at the feeble jokes with which he tried to leaven the strain of their sessions.

These half-hours twice a day were delicious agony to her. She was in heaven and hell at the same time. The time was all too short and yet it was a relief when she could relax from the terror of saying or doing the wrong thing. As she pedalled away misty-eyed down the drive between the paddocks, she went over and over the things that Oliver had said and pondered what he meant by them. She lived for his nurse's week-ends off and wondered whether they would give Elizabeth a holiday at Christmas.

She never told Oliver any of this, of course, but now that he was on the lookout for it, he saw it written all over her face every time she came in. It was bad luck on her that Oliver should be having a mood this week-end, but he thought it was worse luck on him that Elizabeth should go away just when he needed her most.

She washed him and did his dressing before she left early on Saturday morning and either did not or pretended not to notice that he was in a bad temper. He did not say 'Have a good time' when she said good-bye. Why should she have a good time when he was trapped here, tied to his bed at the mercy of women?

At lunchtime, Cowlin's terrier stood like Tantalus, smelling the cooling meat on Oliver's plate. When Mrs North came in with his pudding her concern for his appetite was aggravated by the memory of her long, sycophantic conversation about the butcher's family, and the care she had taken over cooking that piece of liver, and the staleness of the fish which she and the rest of the family were eating.

'I thought you loved liver, darling!' she exclaimed. 'It does upset me so to see you leave your food. Let me get you something else. Would you like an egg?' She would never learn that if she would just take his plate away as if she did not care whether he starved to death or not, he would have found more satisfaction in eating his food than in leaving it.

'I'm not hungry, thanks,' he said.

'Oh, darling. You've been eating chocolate, I suppose. You ought to have more strength of mind.'

'I finished my chocolate *long* ago,' he said, aggrieved.

'Perhaps you should have had a drink before lunch,' she pursued. 'It might have given you an appetite. You'll enjoy your pudding, anyway. It's apple charlotte, with the top off the milk; it was quite creamy today.'

'Oh, Ma, not apples again. Is there nothing else in that damned garden of ours? What's happened to all the pears?'

'Why, I thought you were so fond of apples! You always say you can never get enough of them. I can open a bottle of fruit if you like, but I wasn't going to touch them till later in the year.' She had not yet realized what state he was in. Later, when the mood had become an accepted factor of the household, she would know that if she had brought pears he would have wanted apples.

'Well, just try and enjoy this, dear.' She put the plate down on his tray. 'The crust is so nice and crisp, and I put a lot of sugar in the apples, but just taste it and see if you want any more.' He ate a spoonful of apple in a martyred way. 'It's all right, thanks,' he said listlessly. When she came back, he had pushed the bed-table as far away from him as the cradle would allow, with the pudding half uneaten. She could not help thinking how the children had asked for more milk on theirs when there had been no more to give them.

'Would you like coffee today, dear?' she asked. He wished she would not pronounce it cawfee.

'I don't mind,' he said. He knew he was being impossible, but he could not help it when he felt like this. Once he had gone over the edge and given himself up to depression, he seemed unable to struggle back to civilized behaviour. He was even beyond being ashamed of having so little will-power.

When his mother produced the last two ounces of her chocolate ration and, laying it lovingly on the bedside table, went away without referring to it, he was a little ashamed, but not enough to prevent him eating it during the afternoon.

Oliver cheered up a little at cocktail time. David always made him feel better. Heather had come in first without him to ask: 'Are you sure you want the kids in tonight?'

'Of course I want them,' he said. 'Dammit, I see little enough of them as it is.' So he had read aloud to David from an astonishingly dull book about trains which consisted mostly of statistics about the total mileage of rails, numbers of passengers carried and meals served, and pictures of trains in acute perspective and women in low waists and cloche hats. Although David seemed to know it by heart, he could never hear it often enough and listened rapt, correcting Oliver if he skipped anything, and forgetting his milk and biscuits.

'Drink up,' Heather kept saying, until Oliver stopped in the middle of a description of Euston station to complain: 'Must you keep using that dreadful expression?'

'What on earth do you mean?'

'"Drink up" and "eat up". It's the sort of thing people say who call their children the Kiddies.'

'Well, what's wrong with that?' Heather would not have dreamed of calling David and Susan that, but if Oliver wanted to be argumentative, she could be too.

'Common. Sorry, David – "In the sorting office, the mail sorters divide the bags into the various postal districts – –"'

'Well, really, Oliver. You are impossible.' When she was annoyed, Heather would jerk back her head with its forelock of curly fringe, like a pony tossing at its bit. 'You always say *I'm* a snob. Why don't you practise what you preach?'

'If you must natter, for God's sake don't natter in platitudes – all right, Davy, I know – "Before loading on to the red mail vans with the monogram G.R. entwined on the side." Why on earth do they use such ridiculously long words in kids' books? I could write a better book than this myself.' Heather did not answer. Oliver decided to improve David's education. 'G.R. stands for George Rex, you know. That means King George.'

'"All is bushle on number ten platform,"' droned David, unheeding. '"The Flying Scotsman Expresh from Invernesh and Perth is due. Porters with troyies – –"'

Oliver felt better after David had gone to bed and reflected that only children and dogs knew how to treat you when you were irritable. He chatted quite cheerfully to his mother and sisters and then Mary Brewer arrived, accepted a drink and said: 'Now I'm going to turn you good people out. There's work to be done!' She rolled up her sleeves over thick, freckled arms whose white skin showed up the redness of her hands, bluntfingered as if they had been planed off at the tips. She wore a grey-blue dress of a material which bore some relationship to sacking and kept on her crushed little blue hat. Under it, her strong red hair, square cut, stuck out at the angle to which her bicycle ride had blown it. What she had to do for Oliver, she spun out longer than was necessary and succeeded in dispelling his flash of good temper. He missed Elizabeth and wondered what she was doing. What did she do in London? She did not divulge much more about her week-ends than 'I stayed with a friend' and 'Yes, I had a lovely time, thank you'. She never seemed to go home, although he knew that her father lived in London. Her mother was dead. She had told him that much in a manner that discouraged further inquiry.

Violet was so excited. After dinner, something happened which would cheer Oliver up, and she was going to be the one to break the news. He heard her coming all along the passage from the drawing-room, clattering across the tiles of the hall with a change of sound like galloping hooves crossing a road, and then the latch of his door crashed up and she was upon him, her body coming faster than her feet so that she lurched and almost fell across his bed. He put up a defensive arm as she lurched to a standstill against the step of the window recess.

'Ollie, what do you think – what do you *think*?' Her gruff voice rose to a sudden squeak, like a clarinet inexpertly played.

'Spill it,' said Oliver.

'Jenny's coming back!' Jenny was Oliver's horse, requisitioned by the Army four years ago. He had never expected to see her again. 'Some man rang up from Chester. Fancy, she's been quite near us all the time and we never knew. Some Captain Something-or-other – decent, he was. He says they're moving on and don't need her, and if we want her we can have her back.'

'If we want her! What about keep, though? Can she go out to grass?'

'I asked him that. Bit of a snag; she's been in, apparently, since September and not got much of a coat, but Fred would have her in one of his boxes and we can scrape up enough corn.'

'Think she'll eat dried grass?'

'Have to. Oh, Ollie, isn't it super? This Captain bloke said he'd run her over tomorrow in a horse-box. I'm going to clean her tack tonight when I've bedded that sick cow. I can't wait to get on her and see what the Army's done to her manners. You are pleased, aren't you, Ollie? Are you excited?' She was like a child wanting confirmation of the success of a birthday present.

'Rather.' Violet's pleasure was tremendous. She might be no use in a sickroom, but at least she had done more for Oliver to-night than anyone else. When she came back late from the harness room, she went whistling into the larder and then whistled on the stairs and in her bedroom, where, as she got ready for bed, she appeared to be holding a steeplechase over the furniture.

She was so excited that it was not until the next day, when the bay mare arrived in charge of an amiable young captain, that she realized another side of the situation. When the horse-box had driven away, Violet brought Jenny round to the lawn so that Oliver could see her from his window. Her years in the Army had done her no harm. She had lost some of the youthful abandon with which she had gone away, but she was fighting fit on Army rations and shone like copper on Army grooming.

'Isn't she a grand mare?' said Violet, tugging at the halter to try and make her come nearer the window. 'She's filled out and muscled up a lot. She never had those quarters on her when she went away before. Remember that post and rails she made such a mucker of the last day you hunted her? She'd clear it with a foot to spare now. Oh, Ollie, isn't it sad?'

'What is?' He was devouring Jenny with his eyes, loving every line and every movement of her.

'To think you'll never be able to ride her again. Oh, isn't that awful, when you broke her and schooled her and everything. She never went so well for anyone else as for you. Remember that handy hunter finals at Shrewsbury?' She might have gone on for ever, plugging this depressing theme, had not Mrs North appeared in Oliver's room and cried out in horror at the thought of iron-shod hooves on the lawn.

'Take her off at once, Vi! How can you be so thoughtless when Cowlin takes such a pride in that lawn?'

'I had to show her to Ollie. She won't hurt. Look how light she is on her feet,' as the mare wheeled round, churning divots out of the grass. 'Isn't it ghastly to think that Ollie won't ever be able to ride her again?'

Oliver saw his mother making faces at her, which Violet could

not see. 'D'you remember, Ma,' she pursued, 'when he first got
her, and she took charge of him down the hill field and you got
so windy, and when he came back she'd jumped the gate into the
spinney and he'd fallen off – sorry, Ollie. I know she came down
– and he had a lump on his head like an egg. We used to have
some fun in the old days. Remember when we rode up the Wrekin
in that gale and nearly got blown off the top. Oh, it *does* seem a
rotten shame – –'

'Be quiet, Violet,' said Mrs North sharply. 'And take that
horse off the lawn right now. I don't expect to have to ask you
twice at your age.'

'Thirty-five next week!' sang out Violet. 'And I can still vault
on to a sixteen-hand horse. Watch me, Ollie!' Jenny trampled
the lawn in circles as Violet leapt, thrust down with her arms
braced on the mare's bare back and with a convulsive heave of
her whipcord behind and a fling of her long legs was astride the
mare, hopped her over a box hedge and clattered round the
flagged path at the side of the house.

'That girl,' said Mrs North despairingly, straightening up from
the difficult position she had adopted to see what Violet was
doing without touching Oliver. 'Never mind, darling, I'm sure
you'll be able to ride again one day.'

'Oh, sure,' said Oliver. 'On a nice safe old plug, and get my
cork leg caught up on every gatepost. Jolly.'

'Don't talk like that, dear. What's the matter with you? It's
not like you to be so bitter. Anyway,' she brisked up and gleamed
her glasses at him, 'I came to see what you'd like for lunch.
We're having stew, but I could make you a Welsh rarebit if you
like, or scrambled egg?'

'Oh, anything, Ma,' said Oliver. 'I don't care.'

'There's a piece of corned beef, if you'd like that. I could hash
it for you if you don't want it cold.'

'Not that stuff,' he said, 'I'm sick to death of it.' She knew he
liked corned beef. He had loved it since he was a boy, so there
was no reason why he should suddenly stop now. She sighed.
So he was not out of his mood after all.

He was still in it when Elizabeth came back on Monday
morning. She went upstairs at once to change her grey flannel
suit for her overall and cap and slipped into work as uncon-

cernedly as if she had never been away. When she had remedied the defects which she fancied she detected in Mary Brewer's careful arrangement of him, she asked him how he had been.

'Low,' he said. 'You've been lucky to be out of the house. Why do I get so depressed, Elizabeth? I know all the time that underneath it I'm perfectly content, yet somehow I can't shake it off. It's like a great weight sitting on my head and then suddenly it moves off and I'm quite normal again. Thank God, it doesn't happen often now. I used to get it a lot in hospital. "Got the blues, dear?" one of the nurses used to say. "I can see that little black doggie on your shoulder." Promise me you won't ever say that.'

'I'll try not to.'

'Perhaps it was because you weren't there. I missed you a lot. Perhaps I need you.' He tried sometimes, experimentally, to flirt mildly with her, but it slid off her unheeded. 'Tell me what you've been doing. It might cure me to take an interest in somebody else. I've been brooding on myself all week-end. Did you have fun?'

'Yes. I stayed with a friend of mine, a girl I trained with. She's married now, but her husband's still in the Army, so there's room for me at her flat.'

'Go on.'

'Well, let's see. She met me at the station and we had a late lunch, then we went to the cinema.'

'What did you see?'

'The new Lauren Bacall.'

'Never heard of her. Lord, I'm getting out of the world, aren't I? What did you do in the evening?'

'I went out to dinner,' she said, as if that were all she meant to tell about it.

'Who with – your friend?'

'Elspeth? No.'

'Another friend?'

'Yes.'

'Man or woman?' It was hard work, but he persevered. Elizabeth did not seem quite so reticent as usual. She had a ruminating, slightly distracted air, as if she were not giving her

whole mind to resisting his curiosity. He might catch her out yet.
'Man or woman, I said.'

'Oh, a man.'

'Ah. Your boy friend.'

'Just a man I know.'

'What's his name? Don't think I'm being nosey, but you never tell me anything off your own bat, and, oddly enough, I am interested.'

'Arnold Clitheroe.'

'Oh. What did you do? You had dinner – –'

'Yes, and we danced.'

'Does he dance well?'

'We dance quite well together.'

'You enjoyed yourself, in fact.'

'Yes, I always do with Arnold. He – –' She was about to add something and then stopped.

'Go out with him on Sunday?' asked Oliver casually.

'Yes.'

'He is your boy friend. I know it. Tell me something about him, Elizabeth. Why are you being so coy?'

'I'm *not* being coy.' It was the first time he had ever seen her angry. 'And I don't see that it's any of your business. What's the idea of this stupid cross-examination? If you're trying to make fun of me, I'm afraid I can't see the joke.' She banged out of the room. She had never banged his door before. This was interesting, most interesting. Oliver leaned back, tapped his finger-tips together, and smiled. He was feeling better already. This was how it always was. Suddenly, between one sentence and the next, for no particular reason, the heaviness of his mind and body would lift and take itself right away. He imagined it sometimes as a shutter, rolling back inside his head; it was like someone coming into a darkened room full of stale sleep and pulling up the blind and opening the window to let in a sunburst of morning air.

Already his room, instead of being the prison it had seemed for the last two days, empty of consolation, was filling with its own warm, comfortable atmosphere. He could almost imagine he heard the furniture creaking as it relaxed. Outside, the pale November landscape was beautiful. The orange sun was like a woolly toy. Far away on the side of the hill, he could see Evelyn leading down her half-broken young Exmoor pony. Soon she and Violet would start struggling with it in the meadow at the bottom. He would watch that; it was always good fun.

He could smell onions cooking and found that he was looking forward to lunch. He picked up his shaving mirror. It had always been a bony, angled face, but since he had got thin his cheekbones seemed higher and his forehead more knobbly and prominent. His hair, ungreased for months now, seemed to be getting fairer and softer and kept trying to grow in the childish, untrained way of twenty years ago. It wanted cutting too. He smiled at himself. Ugly, grinning devil. Presently, he would ring the cow-bell for something and let the glad tidings spread through the house.

CHAPTER 5

MRS NORTH often said to Elizabeth: 'I don't know what we should do without you.' She certainly was a most useful person to have about the house. Besides looking after Oliver and ful-filling to the letter the duties which Mrs North had worked out for her, she was always doing little extra things which might have been taken for kindnesses if she had not done them in a manner that implied that this was what she was paid for. Mrs North was often tired in winter, because the cold weather did not agree with her. Elizabeth would urge her into bed, professionally rather than solicitously, and appear later with a tempting tea-tray, just when Mrs North was wondering whether to pander to her legs by staying in bed, or to her stomach by going downstairs for tea.

Sometimes she would take her rest in Oliver's room, with her feet on the red leather stool in front of the fire. Lying back, the sides of the high armchair hid her face, but Oliver could tell when she was asleep by the steeper rise and fall of her chest, although she still held her book up on her lap. She would read for a while, then a long time would go by without a page being turned and her chest would start to appear beyond the sides of the chair. Waking for a few minutes, she would go on reading as if nothing had happened, until she dozed off again, to wake and read and doze and wake all through the afternoon. Sometimes, when they had been talking, she would throw out an idea on the instant of waking, as if she had been planning still in her dreams. She was napping thus one November afternoon, while Oliver played the wireless softly and watched Evelyn and a pig-tailed friend, in scarves and gum-boots, raking the leaves on the lower lawn under a red and rayless sun.

'Perhaps, after all,' said Mrs North suddenly, 'the little green room might be better. It's warmer, being over the kitchen.'

Oliver could not remember what they had been talking about half an hour ago. 'Sure,' he said.

'Of course, there's a better bed in the big spare room. She's probably used to a good bed.'

'You mean Anne? Oh, don't worry about her. Put her in a loose-box.'

'Where do you figure she'd like to sleep?'

'In here, I should think, judging by the tone of her letter. Look at those silly kids out there. They haven't a chance in this wind. Evie!' he shouted. 'You'll never do it! Why don't you give up?' Evelyn turned towards the house, spilling most of her armful of leaves. 'We can do it,' came her shrill, breathless cry. 'We must. Cowlin said – –' The rest was smothered as the wind blew the leaves she held into her face and away before she could put them in the wheelbarrow. She grabbed the rake from her friend and began to work with desperate energy. She was always pitting herself against tasks that were far beyond her, convinced that she could do them, and battling on to the point of tears before she would give up. Oliver had watched her yesterday, building a jump in the hill field with Violet, struggling to get a heavy pit-prop into position across the uprights and thrusting Violet away when she ambled up to help.

'Sweep them with the wind, not against it!' he shouted, making passes which she could not see, as people make gestures while telephoning.

'You oughtn't to shout, darling,' said Mrs North, waking up. She read for a moment, and when she woke again Oliver asked: 'Good sleep?'

'I wasn't asleep.'

'You were – ten solid minutes.'

'I can't have been. I'm reading. I maybe just nodded for a

66

second. I'm not crazy about this book, but the girl at the library said everyone was reading it, so I suppose I should.'

When Elizabeth had brought Oliver's tea, she came back again in a few minutes with another tray for Mrs North.

'Isn't that darling of you!' she exclaimed, taking her feet off the stool with a grunt so that Elizabeth could put down the tray. 'You shouldn't have bothered; I was just coming along. What about the children?' She always thought everyone would starve if she were not about.

'Heather and I are having it with them in the nursery.'

'Hot scones!' Mrs North lifted the lid of the muffin dish. 'Did you make these? You are a dear.' Elizabeth was a disconcertingly difficult person to thank. She simply said: 'You said this morning you wanted the sour milk used up.'

'Yes, but I don't want you to cook in your off-duty time.'

'Oh, I've been out,' said Elizabeth. 'I went down to the village. I got your stamps and envelopes, and I took your shoes to Mr Betteridge. He says they'll take a week.'

'You shouldn't have bothered. I could have taken them. But it was darling of you to think of it.' But Elizabeth would not have it so. 'I had to go down, anyway, to get some toothpaste,' she said, and Oliver wondered whether she liked his mother and did these things to save her, or whether she were really as detached as she seemed.

'Oh, Elizabeth!' Mrs North called her back as she was closing the door, with the lilting cry with which Americans call up the stairs. 'I've been wondering whether I won't put Miss Frith into the little green room after all. We might make the bed up presently.'

'I did it this morning,' said Elizabeth.

'In the green room? But how did you know I – –'

'You suggested it last night, before you decided on the other, but I thought you'd probably change your mind again.' She said this not rudely, but as a commonsense statement.

Oliver laughed when she had gone out. 'How well she knows you already, Ma.'

'Better than I know her, I'm afraid. I can't seem to get near her at all. And she's such a good little thing, I would like to be fond of her, but if you show her any affection she shies off as if

67

she were afraid of it. She certainly can make scones, though. I
taught her that.'

'I thought she could when she came.'

'Mm-*hm*. Didn't rise properly. She had her dough too wet,'
said his mother with her mouth full. 'I showed her.' Oliver saw
Elizabeth go out through the drawing-room on to the lawn to
call the children in to tea. The wind blew her white overall close
to her body. She put her hand up to her head, but her thick corn-
coloured roll of hair stayed neat. It was too neat. It made an
effective frame to her composed little features and it showed off
the clean line of her chin and nose and forehead, but sometimes,
wondering what she would look like with it tumbling in disorder
round her shoulders, he had to repress an impulse to pull it down
when she was bending over him with the serious expression she
used for nursing. Heather had taught him at an early age the
folly of tampering with a woman's hair.

'Evelyn and Nancy!' she called. 'Evie! Tea!' But they could
not hear her. She did not often shout, and when she did, her voice
had no carrying power. The children had got the barrow full of
leaves and Evelyn was trying to lift the handles to wheel it away.
It was too heavy for her, and Nancy tried to help, but Evelyn
pushed her away. Oliver could imagine her scarlet, furious face.
Eventually, after a little scrapping, they took one handle each,
but they had only trundled a few yards when the cumbersome
old barrow toppled over, taking Evelyn down with it because she
would not let go and spilling out the leaves which they had taken
two hours to collect. It was Evelyn who hurt her wrist, but it was
Nancy who bellowed. Elizabeth ran, jumping nimbly down the
steep bank between the two lawns instead of going by the steps,
and when she reached the children, Oliver was surprised to see
Evelyn fling her arms round her waist. Elizabeth dropped on one
knee among the leaves and did not seem to notice that Evelyn,
clutching at her, knocked her little white cap off while she was
examining the wrist.

'Will you look at that?' said Mrs North, who was peering over
the bed in frustrated anxiety because she could not go across the
lawn in her bedroom slippers. 'The girl looks quite human.
Funny – Evie never hugs anyone, even when she's upset.'

Elizabeth picked up her cap and stood up and Evelyn aimed

68

a vicious kick at the overturned wheelbarrow and then took her hand and they came towards the house, Nancy wiping her nose on her scarf. The light was failing as they came across the top lawn and Oliver could not be sure whether it was his imagination or whether Elizabeth's expression was really softer and friendlier than any of them had yet seen it.

*

Somebody had to go and meet Anne at the station, because she chose to come on a train that did not connect with any bus.

'Blast her,' said Violet. 'We're short of petrol. *I* haven't got time, anyway.'

'I'd go,' said Heather, who had been Anne's friend before Oliver appropriated her, 'but I'm supposed to be taking the children out to tea with that woman with no roof to her mouth.'

'Let me go,' suggested Mrs North, but they rounded on her. Cars were precious these days.

'I'll go,' said Elizabeth, 'if you don't mind me driving the car.'

'But it's your off-duty time, dear, and I do like you to stick to that. It's not fair otherwise.'

'I want to get some things in Shrewsbury, anyway,' Elizabeth said. 'How shall I know Miss Frith?'

'She'll be the only person on the train in sheer silk stockings,' said Heather. 'She works at an American Army club.'

'She's a skinnymalink,' said Mrs North, 'with eyes like saucers and beautiful clothes.'

'Look for dark rings under the saucers.' Violet guffawed at her own wit.

'Last time I saw her,' Oliver said, 'her hair was scraped up on top of her head, with a kind of diamond hatpin stuck through it. It's probably hanging down her back by now, or bright yellow with a fringe – sorry, Ma, I mean bang. She'll be wearing highly unsuitable clothes in which she'll manage to look exactly right. I remember once she came to a point-to-point in a sort of black swishy thing and a hat made of one ostrich feather and a veil, and had all the other women in the party chewing their tweeds in mortification. God knows how she does it.' His mother looked at him sharply. If he wanted Anne to stay, of course he must

69

have her, but Mrs North had not wanted her to come. She had once made Oliver very unhappy.

It was clear from the start, however, that this time she was out to please. Elizabeth had had some difficulty in finding her at the station, because she was wearing a tweed dress and coat and flat-heeled shoes. She had brought two bottles of gin and some expensive fruit, American chocolates for Mrs North, cigarettes for Violet, and a pre-war bottle of scent for Heather.

Oliver had only seen her once since he spent the whole of one leave in London with her nearly three years ago.

'I like your hair,' he said. It was cut short all over her head and arranged in hundreds of crisp little curls, all turning up from her fine-drawn, alert features. He could never get used to the fact that she was not as intelligent as she looked.

'Do you like it, darling? I did hope you would. It takes hours to do, and I should hate to think it wasn't worth it.'

'Last time I saw you, you said it didn't matter a twopenny damn whether I liked your hair or not, remember? You said you didn't care if it did look like William Tell's son.'

'Did I, darling? I don't remember.' She apparently did not mean to remember any of the other things she had said on that occasion. She was very thoughtful and solicitous, and fussed over him, pouring out his tea, and giving little pats to his pillows. If she had had any eau-de-Cologne, she would have dabbed it on his forehead. She wanted to spread his jam for him, so he let her.

'I'm not quite paralysed you know,' he said.

'Oh, but you are! I mean – you know what I mean. Your mother pounced on me as soon as I arrived to tell me not to excite you.' She giggled. 'You're not allowed to do a thing for yourself, they tell me, and I'm the girl that's going to see you don't.' After dinner, she insisted on reading to him. He tried to dissuade her, but she knew that reading aloud was one of the things you did to invalids. She found an old book in Mr North's bookcase called *Rambling in Shropshire's Byways*. It made her laugh. Her idea of reading it aloud was to skim through whole paragraphs saying 'Mm-hm-mm-etc. etc. – this wouldn't interest you, darling,' and then, 'Oh, this is a scream, you must listen to this: "Treegirt Trafford Hall, a favourite subject of brethren of the brush, lies *perdu* until we come upon it round a graceful bend of the carriage drive." Is there any more like that? Let's see. . . . Mm-mm-mm. . . .'

Oliver lay and watched her as she sat below him, curly head bent into the lamplight, her lovely hands turning the pages, very careful not to touch the bed, her tall body in a red dress looking at the same time relaxed and ready for action. The scent that came to him from her hair was disturbingly familiar and her presence still had the galvanic quality that made you feel that life was more exciting than it really was. He felt that the old emotions might be only just round the corner, but he did not want to bring them any nearer. He had got over Anne two years ago and he did not intend to let her spoil his peace of mind. He did not need her in this new life; there was no place in it for passion and jealousy and ecstasy and despair.

He wondered what her idea was in breaking their two years' silence with the affectionate letter which had brought her here. At the moment her attitude towards him was sisterly. She was not enticing him in any way except by just being Anne. She couldn't help that.

She was being very sweet to everybody this week-end. She tried not to stare at Violet when she came in in a dress with a dipping hem and a belt made from an old canvas girth. She played charmingly with the children after tea. She was friendly to Elizabeth, once she had satisfied herself that there was nothing between her and Oliver. She and Heather, who had drifted apart, converged again and stood with their arms round each other's waists and tried on each other's clothes. Mrs North came into Oliver's room in her dressing-gown to say she had been wrong about Anne and came back again ten minutes later to try to find out how she affected Oliver.

On Sunday morning he asked Anne what she thought of Elizabeth and Elizabeth what she thought of Anne. He enjoyed hearing what women thought of each other.

Elizabeth said politely: 'She's very attractive.'

'You like her?'

'Yes. Give me your other hand, please.'

'I haven't seen her for two years, you know. I've been wondering why she suddenly came down here now.'

'Your nails are filthy. To see you, I suppose.'

Elizabeth had been at her most maddeningly reserved this week-end. Oliver decided to try and shock her out of it. 'She and I had a terrific affair once,' he said, watching her face while she dug at his nails with an orange stick.

'How nice,' she said.

'We had a flat in London for three weeks. Captain and Mrs Oliver North. It was rather fun.'

'It must have been.'

'I thought we were really going to be Captain and Mrs Oliver North, but it didn't come off. Ever felt like throwing yourself in the river, Elizabeth?'

'Hundreds of times,' she said shortly, giving him back his hand. 'Your mother wants to know how you want your egg done.'

*

Anne said: 'I think she's sweet, poor thing. It must be awful.'

'I don't see why,' said Oliver. 'I don't think I'm so revolting.'

'I didn't mean that, darling, you know I didn't. I mean living in other people's houses and being neither one thing nor the other. Bit trying for the family too, always having someone around. When I had my tonsils out at home, Mummy used to make the nurse have her meals up in her room. Then, of course, the maids struck.'

'I wonder the nurse didn't,' Oliver said.

'But, darling, she was such a crashing bore. You must admit this one isn't exactly scintillating. Is she always so *piano*?'

'She has hidden depths.'

'Poor Ollie, why are you so sweet about everyone nowadays? You have changed. You used to be so divinely malicious. Remember how we used to lie in bed and pick everybody we knew to pieces?'

'Heather says I'm getting saintly.'

'Well, you are rather, you know,' Anne said sadly. 'You'd better look out. Poor Ollie!'

'Why are you looking at me so tragically?' he asked, and she went on looking at him for a moment and then suddenly burst into tears.

'What on earth – –? Here, Anne – Anne – what's up?'

'It's so sad! Oh, it's so sad.'

'Don't be a chump. Here, blow your nose; you know you look awful when you cry. Stop it, Anne.'

She stopped, and holding her handkerchief to her mouth, looked at him with enormous, swimming eyes. 'But, darling, it *is* so sad. I can't help crying for you.'

'Is that why you wrote and came down, because you felt sorry for me?'

'Of *course* I was sorry. Oh, I know we'd bust up and everything – that was my fault – but when I heard about you I was dreadfully upset. I cried and cried.' Her eyes took on a faraway look, seeing herself doing it.

'Listen here, Anne, I don't want pity from you or anyone.'

'Don't be horrid to me, Ollie. You don't know how awful I felt, remembering how I'd done you dirt.'

He laughed. 'I got over that ages ago.'

'Oh, I'm sure you did, darling,' she said quickly. 'But you were in love with me, weren't you?' she added a little wistfully. 'I kept remembering how vile I was that last time we met, when I broke it to you that we weren't going to be married.'

Oliver took her hand and put a kiss into it. 'Little Annie,' he said. 'No one would ever suspect what a nice person you really are. And to think I thought you'd only come down because you'd just finished off a boy friend and looked through your little red book to see who else you knew.'

'*Ollie!*'

He knew quite well now why she had come down. Anne was always either dramatically unscrupulous or dramatically noble. He must stop her saying what she felt she had got to say. He could not tell her that he did not need her now any more than she really wanted him, but he must wean her from the idea that had sent her down to Hinkley in a sacrificial cloud.

'Good thing we didn't get married two years ago,' he began.

'Why? Oh, I wish we had.'

'No. I don't want to be married to anyone now. Not ever, I think. I suppose having this sort of thing makes you a complete egoist; I seem to be absolutely self-sufficient. I don't need a wife, and I shouldn't be any good to anybody as a husband.'

Anne looked embarrassed, which was an unfamiliar expression

on her insouciant face. 'You mean – – Ollie, can a man who – –'
He knew what she was dying to ask him and he laughed and
laughed. 'Oh, Anne, I don't know,' he said weakly. 'I haven't
tried. I didn't mean that, anyway. I just meant that I'm happiest
like this, on my own. I feel fine.'

'You really mean,' she said incredulously, 'that you're quite
happy, lying here like this?' Her eyes threatened to fill again.

'I shan't always have to stay here, of course; but at the
moment, yes, I believe I am quite happy.'

'D'you know, I really believe you are,' she said wonderingly.

'You are sweet, Anne,' he said suddenly.

'Why?'

'Oh, I don't know. You just are.' She was sweet because she
was so transparently relieved.

'Would you like me to read to you, Ollie?' she said presently.

'Why should you bother? Look, the sun's out. Go for a walk
before lunch; do you lots more good.'

'I'd much rather read to you, Ollie dear, if you'd like it. Is
there anything you want before we start?' Now that he had let
her off dedicating her life to him, she could not do enough for
him. There must be something she could do to make up for all
the things he had lost. She thought of his loss in terms of all the
things they had enjoyed together, and knowing how she would
feel in his position, she marvelled that he had said he was quite
happy.

'You have changed, you know, Ollie,' she said again, looking
up at him. Her mind had been no more on the book than his.

'I suppose I have. For the better, would you say?'

'I don't know. We did have such fun. . . . I used to know you
so well, and now – –' She gave a little laugh. 'It's silly, but I feel
I hardly know you at all.'

'Don't you love me any more?' he teased her.

'Darling, of course I love you, you know that. I always shall.'

'*That's* good,' he said comfortably.

'In quite a special way,' she added, to avoid having to say:
'like a sister.'

He could not resist interrupting her reading a moment later to
say: 'By the way, Anne, you haven't told me a thing about your
love life yet. Who is it at the moment?'

She gave him one of her candid looks, eyelashes fanned out along her upper lid. 'Actually,' she said, 'there isn't anyone at the moment.' And then she looked down and her mouth twitched. 'And my address book isn't red, it's blue,' she murmured.

On Sundays at Hinkley, everyone had lunch in Oliver's room. He often had to take two Veganin afterwards and sleep it off. Even Heather's baby Susan was brought down in a wicker basket and mulled on a stool in front of the fire. She was growing too big for the basket and she was getting beyond the age when lying down and making faces was enough amusement. She would struggle to sit up and lean over the side, and lunch was constantly interrupted by someone jumping up to stop her falling into the fire.

While Anne was reading, Elizabeth, in the flowered overall she wore for housework, came in with a tray to set the table. She glanced at the *tête-à-tête*, and when Anne offered to help, said: 'Please don't let me disturb you,' and started trying to manœuvre the refectory table from the window to the middle of the room by herself. Anne jumped up and took the other end, and Oliver watched them laying the table, Elizabeth so quick and neat, and Anne slinging the knives and forks about, and sitting down to read the rhymes on David's mackintosh mat, while Elizabeth finished the work. Sometimes, if Elizabeth were cooking the lunch, Heather laid the table on Sundays, which put Oliver in a draught for half an hour, because she made so many trips to the pantry for things she had forgotten that it was not worth opening and shutting the door each time. Elizabeth, of course, had brought everything she needed, and when she had set the chairs round and put a cushion and one volume of Mr North's Oxford Dictionary on David's, she went out, shutting the door quietly.

Anne, going out soon after to get some more cigarettes, came back and said: 'Darling, there's a most attractive man in the hall. The front door was open, so he walked in, and he wants to know if you're visible. Are you?'

'Depends who it is. If he's wearing a Gunner's tie, and a moustache the same colour as his plus-fours, no, because he keeps trying to sell me a Ford station wagon to convert into an invalid car.'

'No moustache, no plus-fours.'

'Not Colonel Jukes then, thank God. I hope it's not old Fothergill. He'll expect to be asked to lunch and I couldn't stand those castanet teeth now that we've got water biscuits.'

'Sweetie,' said Anne gently, 'I *said* attractive.'

'You have some odd ideas about men, though. Has he got suède shoes and a face like Oscar Wilde? I couldn't bear to have Francis explaining the country customs of Shropshire to me this morning. Oh, I tell you who it might be – that awful man who gets up the local plays.'

'I don't think it's any of those,' Anne said. 'I wish I'd asked him his name. I can't very well go out now and say: "If you're Colonel Jukes or Old Fothergill or Francis or a man who gets up plays, go away; if not, come in."'

At that moment, there were cries of hospitable pleasure from the hall and Mrs North came in, bringing a tall, dark, well-fed young man, whom Oliver greeted with: 'Toby! How grand to see you. Why didn't you come straight in? Anne's been making me sweat thinking of all the people you might be.'

'I didn't know whether you were allowed to see anyone, or which your room was and so on,' said Toby. He had a way of holding his head very erect, with the chin tucked into his collar, and speaking in a clipped, half-strangled voice. He had the assured look of a man with an easy life, but his movements were rather formal and ungraceful.

'He's just been demobbed,' said Mrs North, patting his arm, 'and he came straight along to see us. Now wasn't that nice? You'll stay to lunch, won't you, Toby? We have a family party in here on Sundays.' Her eyes roved the table, seeing whether it was properly laid. 'Will you be too cold if I open the other window, Oliver dear? The atmosphere's just terrible. You shouldn't smoke so much in here, you know, Anne.'

'Sorry.' She threw the cigarette she had just lit over Oliver's bed on to the lawn, where it smouldered, sending up a stalk of smoke.

When Oliver introduced her to Toby, he laughed inside himself to see them appraising each other. It made him feel very old, remembering the days when he himself had always been on the lookout for new material. How peaceful to be out of the restless, shifting game. Standing by his bed and talking to him, they both

76

centred their attention on Oliver, but he could see that they were very aware of each other. He looked at the scene objectively, seeing it as a triangle of which he formed the apex and they the base. Although he knew both of them well, the lines of contact which they sent out to him were weaker than the line which already joined these two strangers. They stood in another world, the old world of drinks and parties and affairs and the extremes of fun and *ennui*. He was in his own new little world, a vantage-point like a crow's nest, in which there was only room for himself.

Seeing Toby eyeing the hump under the bedclothes, Oliver talked about his leg. He found that new visitors were usually afraid to mention it unless he did.

Heather and David came down at one o'clock, both red in the face from a battle about washing hands. Heather went back for the baby and to powder her nose and do her hair again because she found Toby there. Toby said the correct things about Susan, and Heather fussed because the fire was too high. 'You needn't have made such a furnace, Elizabeth,' she said crossly.

'Put the child farther away then,' Oliver suggested.

'Oh, don't *interfere*, Ollie,' said Heather, straightening up and pushing up her fringe, and Toby looked at her, turning his neck round inside his collar like a turtle. He had already noticed the difference in her.

Mrs North kept pottering in and out of the room to see whether Violet and Evelyn had come in yet, wondering whether to wait or start without them. 'It makes such a schemozzle with everyone coming in at odd times,' she said. No one had ever done anything else at Hinkley, but she had never given up trying to make her family as clock-conscious as herself. She had two watches, one on her wrist and one on her chest on a thin chain that got tangled with the chain of her pince-nez. She was always looking at one or the other and she could never pass a clock without glancing at it. As well as the travelling clock on her dressing-table, she had an alarm clock by her bed, which she took downstairs every morning, because she could not see the kitchen clock from the scullery. When she went for a walk, even just down to the village, she timed herself there and back as if she were a train, and sometimes went half a mile out of her way to see the clock in the church tower.

Violet and Evelyn came in just as she had decided to start without them. They brought with them Fred Williams, whom Mrs North had forgotten she had asked to lunch. He was always ill at ease in the house, like a yard dog brought into the drawing-room, and he was not helped by the commotion of someone having to lay a place for him and going out to run another plate under the hot tap. He was a short-legged, long-bodied little man with a big head and a face saddened by a tremendous nose, red and shiny as a lobster's claw. His ears stuck out and his hair had been cut like a footballer's, clumpy on top and almost shaved round the back of his head. He was not fascinatingly ugly, he was just ugly. He wore an unfortunate suit of emerald-green tweed, which his uncle had sent him from the Outer Isles several years ago and which would last for several years to come. On ordinary days, he wore breeches and gaiters and polo jerseys, which suited him, but this green suit was the uniform he wore for sociability and for business in Shrewsbury that involved going into offices. He also wore it on the rare occasions when he went to London, where it must have startled case-hardened waitresses and shone like a spring leaf in outer offices at the Ministry of Agriculture.

People like Anne and Toby paralysed him. They paralysed Violet too, so she was no help to him. She left him stranded in the middle of the room and went and straddled in front of the fire, biting her nails.

While everyone was charging in and out with plates and food, and arguing about who should sit where, Fred stood awkwardly with his hands hanging, lunging forward to take a tray from a woman or put a mat under a hot dish just a second after Toby had already done it. Oliver called him over to talk about the farm. Since he had been ill, Oliver had reverted to his boyhood's inclination towards the land. When he was first grown up, his one idea had been to get away from Hinkley, up to the towns where life moved quickly and there were people to be met and money to be made. Now, his one idea was to keep away from pavements and alert young men in city hats. Fortunately, for his heart would probably never stand a London life again, his enforced tranquillity had given him an appetite for peace. He would have liked to become a retired country gentleman and potter through the Shropshire seasons, if he had any money to retire on. The thought that he ought soon to be earning a living was one of the few things he worried about, particularly when he was depressed. When he tried to talk to his mother about working again, she changed the subject, or told him how well her shares were doing, or what she had read in the paper about Service pensions. She would keep him a drone for the rest of his life if she had her way.

Fred told him about his new fertilizer, of which he was as proud as if he and not I.C.I. had invented it.

'Tell you what,' Oliver said, 'I wish you'd lend me some of your books on soil and fertilizers and that sort of thing. If I could learn something about it now, perhaps I might be some use to you when I get up.'

'That would be fine.' Fred looked uneasily over his shoulder at Mrs North.

Oliver laughed. 'My mother's been talking to you, hasn't she? I believe she thinks I mean to go straight out and push a plough. No, but I thought perhaps I might be some help behind the scenes, take some of the bookwork off your hands and learn more about the job as I go along.'

Fred's nose and the line on his forehead where his hat pinched it flushed with pleasure. 'That would be grand,' he said. 'You could be the brains behind the organization. I'm planning big things for this next year or two, if only I can get the men and some more machinery. I'm already after that land between here and the Wrekin. It would be a fine help to have you working with me.'

'Steady on, old boy,' said Oliver. 'Don't forget I don't know much about the business. I should probably be more of a hindrance at first.'

'Oh.' Fred looked down, and Oliver, following his gaze, saw that he was wearing brown boots under the emerald-green trousers. 'Oh no, it wouldn't be like that. After all, you've been decently educated and that. If chaps like me can pick it up, there can't be so much to it.'

He said this without any irony or sense of grievance. He always maddened Oliver by his blatant insistence on being an underdog. He was just going to tell him pithily about his public school and Varsity and explain why Fred was undoubtedly so much better educated than he, when Heather called from the table: 'Do come and sit down, Fred, and let's get on with lunch. It's always the same in this house; the minute you bring in the food, everybody disappears.'

'Sorry, sorry.' Fred grinned nervously at Oliver and hurried over to the others. Mrs North was carving at a side table and he hovered by her, wondering whether he were expected to hand things round.

'Oh, do sit *down*!' said Heather. 'Everything's on the table. It's so silly if everyone jumps up and down all the time waiting on each other. Don't be neurotic, David, that isn't gristle.' Fred's nose came round like the beam of a lighthouse as he turned.

Evelyn patted the chair beside her. 'Come on,' she said. 'You're supposed to sit here by me.' Violet, holding her knife like a pencil, was at the end of the table on his other side, but she hardly took any notice of him. On the farm, although he was her employer, he never gave her any orders. She usually knew what had to be done, and if not, he would throw out suggestions rather than commands. He had not liked the idea of her working for him, until it was explained to him as patriotism. Five years of labour and vicissitudes had made them able to work together without words. They were never heard to talk to each other about any subject unconnected with the farm, and then it was mostly in grunts and chin-scratchings. Fred had a slight Norfolk tang to his speech, a suggestion of Oi for I and a reversal of words like move and mauve. His accent was pleasant but slow, and it took a long time for him to tell you anything. He came to these Sunday lunches prepared with a few stories, but he seldom got more than halfway through any of them without interruption. Today, Toby shot a polite question out of his collar at him about the herd, and Fred put down his knife and fork and leaned across the table to tell him about the milk yield, but almost at once David spilled his lemonade, Elizabeth jumped up and scooted round the table to stop Susan falling into the grate, and Mrs North went out to see whether she had turned off the oven.

Violet took advantage of the general commotion to help herself to the last three potatoes. Back from the kitchen, Mrs North went over to inspect Oliver's plate.

'Enjoy your lunch, darling?' she asked, beaming to see it clean.

'Always do on a Sunday. Whatever else they may say about you, Ma, you certainly can roast beef.'

'As a matter of fact, Elizabeth cooked the lunch today,' she said. 'I was doing out my larder.'

'Well, I expect you taught her.'

'Oh, sure I taught her. Won't you have a little more, darling? It's cutting so rare now.'

'Couldn't.' Then, as her face fell: 'All right, I'll have another potato if you like.' She hurried joyfully back to the table and halted, crestfallen, as Evelyn sang out: 'Vi's just pinched the last three!' She was a silent and businesslike child at meals, but she never missed a thing. Her pale, well-bred little face concealed a mind quite Cockney in its observation.

'Oh, Violet, *really*,' said Mrs North. 'You are – –' She was going to say greedy, but she altered it to thoughtless. It was bad enough to have a daughter who behaved childishly when visitors were there, without calling attention to it by treating her as a child as well. To cover her, she tried to turn it into a joke by saying with a smile: 'I suppose you couldn't ask whether anyone wanted any more, hm?'

'Thought you'd all finished,' said Violet, putting down the gravy boat so that it dripped on to the table. 'I was starving. Didn't have any breakfast.'

'Not much you didn't,' said Heather. 'I saw you in the kitchen with a great hunk of bread, *and* some of the children's milk *and* the golden syrup tin out, *and* you were dipping your buttery knife into it.'

'Saves the washing up,' retorted her sister.

'As if you ever did any,' said Heather bitterly. David gave a scream of laughter and knocked over the salt. He loved quarrels; they excited him. Oliver had heard this kind of conversation a thousand times since his childhood. It was very dull. He saw Anne and Toby exchange amused glances. Fred was looking embarrassed. He kept clearing his throat as if he were going to say something and then being unable to think of anything to say. When he saw Heather, still muttering, begin to clear away the plates, he jumped up so quickly that his chair fell over backwards and nearly decapitated the baby. Heather gave a little scream and the knives on top of the plates she held clattered on to the floor.

81

Violet's old Labrador inched her way out on her stomach from her hiding-place between Violet's spreadeagled feet and began to lick the knives. When Heather had picked up the chair and moved Susan farther away from the table, she looked up flushed from her kneeling position by the basket and worked off her shock in anger at Fred.

'Terribly sorry, terribly sorry,' he stammered, hovering on the outskirts of the circle that was trying to jolly Susan out of her fright. 'But it didn't touch her, did it? Is she all right? Ah, there's a good little girlie!' She screamed louder as he bobbed his great nose down at her. In desperation, he tore off his wrist-watch and held it to her ear, as he had seen people do.

Heather knocked his hand aside. 'Don't be a fool,' she said. 'She's much too young for that. I do wish you'd be more careful, Fred. You might have killed her. You're as clumsy as Vi.'

'Oh, shut up,' said Violet from the table, where she was leaning back, cleaning out her mouth with her tongue. Toby had risen to help, but Anne pulled at his sleeve and told him to sit down. 'She won't feel any better if she sees that yellow tie,' she said, and he laughed his austere, choked laugh. He thought her amusing. They talked to each other while they waited for the Norths to settle their troubles and get on with the next course, and then Anne remembered Oliver and went over to the bed to see how he was getting on.

'Gives one a bit of a head, you know, this kind of thing.' He nodded towards the group at the fireplace.

'Poor darling,' she said vaguely, 'it must do.' She played a scale down his pyjama sleeve, watching her fingers, and then looked up at him with one of her sudden rippling smiles. 'Did you really mean it, darling, what you said before lunch about being perfectly happy?' She wanted to make quite sure that she had done all she could to fulfil the obligation which had sent her down here. She felt she had got off too lightly. Oliver laughed at her, kissed her hand and sent her back to Toby. Mrs North saw the hand-kiss and stood for a moment in thought, turning her pince-nez from one to the other of them. Anne had certainly seemed much nicer this time. 'A very sweet person,' she had told Oliver last night when she came in to try and find out whether he were still in love with Anne. Oliver should not love anyone just now, but

82

if he had to, it could be worse. Prepared to make the best of anything that would make him happy, she gave a little shrug and set herself in motion again to organize the next course.

Oliver's headache was becoming worse. 'Take it away,' he said, when Elizabeth brought him his treacle tart, but seeing his mother looking anxiously over her shoulder at him from the serving table, he changed his mind. Elizabeth laid a finger on his pulse for a moment and went away without saying anything. She seldom asked him how he felt or told him what she thought of him. She formed her own judgement and acted on it without comment. If she had been Mary Brewer and had thought the lunch party was tiring Oliver, she would have said matily: 'Now, I'm going to ask all you good people to bolt your dinners and let my patient settle down to his rest.'

Elizabeth, however, particularly when outsiders were there, gave the impression of 'knowing her place' far too well ever to say anything like that. She would simply be so brisk about the serving and clearing away, whisking up people's plates before they had a chance to ask for a second helping and brushing off crumbs while they were still wondering whether to have cheese, that they would find themselves finished and on their way to the drawing-room where she had firmly taken the coffee tray. Oliver thought that it was not so much for his sake, as a relic of her hospital training of 'only two visitors to each patient and kindly leave the ward when the bell rings', that she disapproved of these family gatherings in his room. She had been very brisk and efficient today; she always was when there were visitors, managing, by her politely impersonal air, to convey that although she was among the family she was not of it.

Her back view, where she sat at the table between Anne and Violet, looked a little constrained, as if she were the parlour-maid who had unwillingly accepted an invitation to sit down with the family. Yet she was not so much ill at ease as deliberately not at her ease. She looked like someone whose bags were ready packed upstairs and who would at any minute get up and go away, leaving no mark of her stay either in the house or in her own heart. It was extraordinary that after three months at Hinkley she still was so little at home. She seemed quite content, but it was as if she purposely refrained from making a niche for herself

83

or forming any ties which she could not break at a moment's notice. Although she followed a routine, she had not formed any habits. She had no favourite chair, never spoke of a favourite walk. She had established no harmless little personal indulgences, nor did she seem to have attached herself to any one member of the family. Mrs North was friendly and appreciative and would have liked to be affectionate, had not any attempts at affection slid off Elizabeth's oiled surface. Heather was as casual and inconsiderate as if she had been a sister; Violet made clumsy gestures of friendship, warily, like a large dog bouncing round at a distance, afraid of reproof if he jumps up with muddy paws, yet ready to knock you over at the slightest encouragement. The children liked Elizabeth and trusted her. She could be relied on not to smother them with love one minute and with curses the next. She never gave them curses, but neither was she ever seen to give them any demonstrations of love. Towards Oliver himself, in spite of their inevitable intimacy, she was still detached. She was the first nurse he had met who had no grating mannerisms, but she often annoyed him by her refusal to accept gratitude, praise, or criticism. Sometimes, feeling cosy and comfortable after she had settled him for the night, he would give her a warm sentimental smile and put out a hand to squeeze hers and tell her she was a darling, but she invariably put on that maddening air of 'what I do, I do because it is my duty'. It piqued him to think that she took so little interest in him as a man and expected him to take no interest in her as a woman. He did not want to make love to her, or enter into a kind of 'Farewell to Arms' liaison between nurse and patient, but her behaviour was a challenge to his technique, which had been considered quite good in the old days. It would be interesting to see whether he could break her down.

He lay and toyed with his treacle tart, and watched the group round the table. Since they were there for his benefit, they kept trying to include him among themselves by glances and smiles, or questions thrown, or remarks repeated that he had not heard, yet he felt withdrawn from them, and looked at them objectively. He found it less tiring not to try to follow a conversation which he could only hear imperfectly. Odd remarks and exclamations, free of their context, reached him as titillatingly as snatches of talk from passers-by in the street.

By half shutting his eyes and ears, he made it seem like someone else's family lunch, more remote, but more interesting, like other people's domesticity seen from the street. From his bed, he saw the nine people round the table as on a stage set. Under the centre light, which had to be lit even in the morning in this low, dark room, their hair shone: his mother's with its blue-mauve iridescence, Toby's jet and sleek, the filigree fairness of Heather's curls so different from the pure polished gold of Elizabeth's head.

Here were all the ingredients of a happy family picture. The benign mother, smiling fatly to see everyone enjoying the food she had cooked; the pretty young matron, bending to the bright-eyed little boy in the high chair; the ruddiness of outdoor health on Fred's and Violet's skins; Evelyn, the little befriended waif with the blue bow on the end of a lock of ginger hair dangling over her plate. Anne and Toby to keep the comedy sophisticated, looking as if they might at any moment speak a line by Noel Coward. The clatter of knives and forks, and the murmur of conversation, highlighted by laughter.

Then someone called to him, another turned in her chair and asked him a question, and by drawing him into the scene they broke the spell of their own charm. He was aware now that his mother was still annoyed with Violet, that Heather was nagging David to eat his pudding, that Fred was being a bore, that Violet ate with her mouth open, that Evelyn was not pathetically thin, but just naturally skinny, and that Anne and Toby were discussing someone called Puffy Bates of whom nobody else had ever heard.

Is it something humdrum in oneself, Oliver wondered, that makes a scene lose its glamour the minute one steps inside it, that dulls Someone Else's family lunch as soon as it becomes One's Own family lunch? In the same way, a village on the side of a hill, seen from a train, may look like the perfect place to spend the rest of your days, yet if you were to get out of the train and go into the village you would find that the magic had escaped from it to settle on the tail of the departing train which had so bored you as you sat in it and yearned towards the village.

'I knew a man once,' Fred was saying, 'who kept a pig in his kitchen, tied to the leg of the table.'

'Now say, isn't that interesting,' said Mrs North. 'Don't you like your pie, Oliver? I could get you something else. . . . Do go on, Fred, I didn't mean to interrupt.'

'And at every meal he used to feed it off his plate, all the best bits, until in the finish the pig got so fat – –' Mrs North half rose. 'Would you like an apple, darling? Or some cheese – a piece of cake?' Toby had half risen too, and been pulled down again by Anne, and Fred had got up, holding tightly to the back of his chair.

'Can I fetch anything?' he asked. He would love to do something for Oliver, and his story was not coming off; he did not want to finish it.

'If you wouldn't mind, Fred. There's a green cake tin in the larder. You know where that is.'

'Oh, Ma, I don't – –' began Oliver, but Fred had already gone. He was away quite a time and returned empty handed, as flushed as if he had been burrowing for the cake in the boiler.

'Oh God.' Heather pushed back her chair. 'Much quicker to go oneself. Eat up, David.' She pushed a spoonful into his mouth on her way out.

'Sit down then, Fred, thank you all the same,' said Mrs North kindly. She was always particularly kind to him, because she felt bad about not liking him. 'Do go on with your story.'

Fred, who had just picked up his spoon, put it down again, gulped and said: 'Oh yes, what was I – –?'

'About the pig.' Anne smiled at him charmingly.

'Oh, it was nothing really. It doesn't matter.'

'Say about the pig,' said Evelyn remorselessly.

'Pig, pig, you pig,' shouted David, beating with his spoon. Everyone except Violet, who ate steadily on, was concentrating on Fred. He looked round in a trapped way, hitched his finger under his collar and said unhappily: 'Where had I got to?'

'The pig got so fat,' prompted Anne.

'Oh yes, and – er – well, the man got so thin, you see.' They waited politely for a moment to see if there was any more. Fred, taking refuge in treacle tart, made a loud squeak with his spoon on the plate.

Heather came back with the cake tin and said: 'You can't have looked very far. It was on the bottom shelf. Oh, sit *down*. I'll cut a piece for Ollie.'

'But, Heather, I don't want any.' Oliver had been trying to say so for some time.

'Well, of all the – –' Heather bit her lip. Mrs North looked at her. Surely, in front of visitors, she was not going to commit the cardinal sin of being unkind to Oliver?

'Does anyone want any more treacle tart?' Violet asked.

'Oh, take it for heaven's sake,' said Heather. Violet took it.

*

Although Elizabeth had taken the coffee into the drawing-room, Anne and Toby drifted back with theirs to talk to Oliver. Toby, in his new grey suit which was just a little too smart, like clothes on the stage, told him about mutual friends he had seen in London. 'A lot of the old gang are back. If you sit in the Berkeley for long enough, you see everyone you know. Peter and Betty have got their flat again. Bob's bowler-hatted. The Horse is still at the Air Ministry; he's been leading a squadron from there for the last four years, the intrepid fellow. And Nigel – remember the parties he used to give with his father's money? They've lost most of it and the old man died and so on. Sobered the poor chap up a bit, you wouldn't know him really. Still, he did get into a fight with a Yank in Denman Street.'

Anne laughed. She knew all about Yanks in Denman Street. Oliver still had that feeling of being in another world. He could picture Toby and the crowd having drinks at the Berkeley, dancing while their dinner cooled on the table, fighting Yanks, getting sentimental round about two o'clock in the Four Hundred, and discovering inner meanings to life and depths of soul which vanished with the daylight, but he could not see himself there, although he always used to be there.

When Toby said: 'Tell you what, we ought to get you back to town as soon as they let you up – give you a bathchair, or a stick or an Alsatian or something – and I'll organize one hell of a party, do you all the good in the world,' Oliver agreed hollowly, secure in the knowledge that he would not go.

'I must get cracking,' Toby said, shooting his cuff back from a gold wrist-watch. 'It's the last day of a film in Shrewsbury I simply must see. Why don't you come along?' He looked down at Anne, throwing out the invitation casually, as if he did not care whether she went or not.

She patted the bed. 'Thanks very much, but I'm going to stay with my little Ollie. We're going to play chess.'

'No we're not. You go to the cinema, Anne. I shall be quite happy. I'm supposed to sleep, anyway.'

'Not really. You're just saying that.'

'No, honest. Do go.'

'Oh, but I said I would – –' She looked from one to the other of them doubtfully. Oliver looked sleepy and owlish, the room was stuffy and she did not much care for chess. Toby was attractive in a restrained way, with possibilities, and he had a Lagonda. They would probably go and have drinks somewhere after the cinema.

Fortunately, Elizabeth came in at that moment in her white overall and cap, and said: 'I'm so sorry, but I'm afraid I have to do Oliver's dressing now, and then he ought to have a sleep.' Anne and Toby went off like children let out of school and Anne came back in a few minutes looking like a *Spectator* sports advertisement in a chunky tweed coat and a bright yellow scarf. She came no farther than the door, as Elizabeth was already busy with Oliver's leg. 'Sure you don't mind if I go, darling?' she asked, leaning on the latch and swinging one leg.

'Not a bit. Much more fun for you than being cooped up in here with me all the time. Be nice for Toby, too. How d'you like him?'

'Oh, all right,' said Anne cautiously. 'He's rather fun really.' A horn pipped outside. 'My God,' she said. 'The arrogance of these males.' She lingered a little longer deliberately, and when she had gone Oliver said to Elizabeth: 'Poor Anne.' She went on bandaging him in silence.

'I said, "Poor Anne",' he repeated.

'I heard you.'

'You're missing your cues. You're supposed to say: "Why poor?" so that I can let the audience know what I'm thinking. I'm getting so old and stuffy, Elizabeth, that it rends my heart to see the wretched girl off again on the old roundabout. You know how it goes – attraction, pursuit, capture, intimacy, familiarity, boredom, rows, and then all the bother of disentangling oneself. To think she's got all that to go through, and then after this time another and then another, always looking for something you never find.' He yawned. 'It exhausts me even to think of it. Funny, it used to be the breath of life to me, but I doubt if I could cope now.'

'I thought she was in love with *you*,' said Elizabeth bluntly, tucking in the sheet.

'Which shows, my darling, either that Anne is a better actress or you are less intelligent than I thought.' He suddenly got tired of this kind of talk. 'My God, I'm weary,' he said. 'I say, Elizabeth,' he looked at her seriously, 'I don't seem to be getting much better, do I?' He quickly held up a hand as she opened her mouth to answer. 'No, don't say: "Of course you are!" brightly, because I'm not. I know how I feel.'

'I wasn't going to,' she said. 'I was going to say you're not really fit yet to have so many people in here all at once.'

'I know,' he said. 'I love my family, but – Sunday lunch. . . . However, there's no stopping a habit like that once it's been started, is there?' They looked at each other for a moment, linked by a common appreciation of the delicacy of family relationships. 'D'you know,' he said suddenly, 'I believe if I could go somewhere with you, quite alone, I should get perfectly well. And that's not a compliment, just a tribute to your professional qualities.'

'Thanks,' she said, and picked up her tray.

'But I expect I should get awfully bored really,' he said. 'Go away, I want to sleep.'

*

Anne came back after dinner in a highly excitable state, with profuse apologies and explanations about where they had been and whom they had met. 'Darling, I do wish you'd been there,' she said, sinking into the chair by his bed and lighting a cigarette. 'We had such fun. But it's mean of me to say that. We'll have some fun tomorrow, shall we, you and I? What shall we do? We could play some game – backgammon or something, or whatever you like. What does one do with a man in bed?'

'You should know,' said Oliver, and Mrs North, coming in

with his hot milk and finding that her infectious giggle had set him off, reproved Anne for exciting Oliver at bedtime. He could remember her using almost the same words to an uncle who used to hurl him up to the ceiling in his childhood.

'We were just talking about playing backgammon,' he told her.

'Not now, dear,' she said. 'Tomorrow it would be nice.'

The next day, Anne dutifully got out the backgammon board and had just found the dice when the telephone rang for her.

She came back looking rather sheepish. 'That was Toby. He's going over to Bridgnorth to see some hunters and he wanted me to go with him.'

'Well, you're going, aren't you? You'll love it; you might get a ride. Borrow a pair of Vi's trousers.' He looked at her shape from the waist downwards. 'No, perhaps not.'

'I'm not going, anyway, darling. I wouldn't dream of it. I told him I was spending the morning with you.'

'Don't be a chump. Ring him up again and tell him I say you're to go.'

'He's hanging on, as a matter of fact.'

*

Gradually, Oliver saw less and less of Anne. She stayed on at Hinkley, using it as a base for outings with Toby. On Thursday morning she asked Oliver: 'Would you mind awfully, darling, if I went back to town today instead of tomorrow? Toby's going down this afternoon and it seems silly to go in that fearful train when I might go by car.'

They parted affectionately, each pleased to think how satisfactorily they had got the other off their hands.

CHAPTER 6

'CAN you *believe* it?' Mrs Ogilvie asked Oliver piercingly. 'Can you *believe* it?' Oliver waited patiently to hear what was to test his credulity this time. Mrs Ogilvie, who dropped in now and again to keep him *au fait* with local gossip, had already asked him this question about the pepper shortage, a strike of bus conductresses, the engagement of two of the dullest people in Shropshire, and the colour of Francis's new bathroom curtains.

'Of course, I don't want you to think I'm criticizing your sister, but really, Oliver, Heather is queer in some ways. She's not a bit like she used to be. Oh, I know she's tired and all that – what she'd do if she had six children like I had, I can't imagine. But can you *believe* that she's written to that poor John asking him to bring back butter and chocolate and rubber hot-water bottles from Australia?' She strode up and down in a blue gabardine mackintosh and her son's Commando beret, filling the room.

'I mean, when the poor man's been literally starving for nearly a year, it seems so heartless to think of that when all she should be thinking of is getting him home and getting him well.'

She paused just long enough for Oliver to say: 'I don't see why. He's not starving now. He's living off the fat of Australia, probably doing much better than we are.'

'No, but it's what I call the idea of it, the – –' She snapped her fingers for a word, '– the indelicacy, don't you see?' Unable to make him agree with her, she said: 'Well, in any case, it's high time he did come home. Heather is getting so irritable and nervy, she's spoiling herself completely. If she goes on like this, he won't like her when he does get here.'

'Perhaps she won't like him,' suggested Oliver.

'Nonsense, my dear boy, of course she will. What she wants is a man.' Mrs Ogilvie prided herself on not caring what she said. 'What do you suppose is the reason for this Papist craze? It's a well-known thing, my dear – look at any adolescent girl. She doesn't seem to be getting much out of it, though, does she? What a rash step to take. If she wanted to go to church, why couldn't she have gone to Hinkley? Poor old Mr Norris would have been delighted; he gets such tiny congregations. Why drag the Pope into it? And all these vows and things they have to take. Why not be a nun and have done with it?' Her questions were all rhetorical and her conversation ran itself. All you had to do was to lie back and be sapped by her vitality. If you volunteered any remark, however insignificant, she seized on it with such a strenuous '*Really?*', and so much more excitement than it warranted, that you wished you had not spoken.

91

Violet barged in to get her cigarette lighter. 'Oh – hullo,' she grunted and went out.

'First time I've seen that girl in a skirt for ages,' said Mrs Ogilvie 'And indoors at this time of the morning too. What's wrong with her?'

'Perhaps her trousers have gone to the cleaners,' Oliver suggested.

'Oh, do you think so? Is that it? Yes, that might be it, mightn't it?' The Commando beret nodded vigorously. 'Or do you think she's becoming a bit feminine at last? No, I don't think so,' she answered herself. 'Not at her age. She's been like that for too long now. Can you *believe* that any girl could take so little trouble with herself? Tell me if I'm tiring you, won't you, dear boy?'

'Not a bit,' said Oliver faintly.

If Mrs Ogilvie could have seen what Heather saw that evening, she would have found it even more incredible. Heather burst into Oliver's room, giving a fair imitation of his morning visitor.

'Can you believe it?' she cried. 'Can you *believe* it? I've just caught Vi in front of the long glass in my room – with the light on, of course, waking up the children – and would you *believe* it – she was putting on lipstick!'

'Nonsense,' said Oliver.

'I swear it. True, she was wiping off as much as she put on – *with* one of my precious face tissues – but the fact remains she was trying.'

'By the way,' he asked. 'Did she send her pants to the cleaners?'

'Not she. She likes them encrusted. Why?'

'She was wearing a skirt this morning. Mrs O. saw her and nearly burst a blood-vessel. You know how she goes on.'

'Oh Lord, has that woman been here today? I suppose she came to let off steam to you about what I'd written to John. I met her in the village when I was posting the letter. I wish I hadn't told her about it. I thought it was a good idea, but she was horrified. Told me that it was things like that ruined a marriage.'

'You know what she is,' Oliver said. 'Just because her own husband walked out on her, or, rather, had himself wheeled out in his bathchair, she can't bear anybody else's marriage to be a success.'

'Mm – yes,' said Heather thoughtfully, frowning under her fringe that was like a little straight-clipped hedge. Then she took a deep breath and said in a rush: 'Ollie, I'm rather dreading John's coming home.'

'Why? D'you think he'll have changed so much?'

'It isn't that. After all, he's been a prisoner less than a year, and he's not the sort of man to be changed.'

'I know what you mean. He's stable. Outside things don't alter his character.'

'No,' she said. 'Other people come back bitter, or irritable, or broody; but you'll see, Johnny'll come back with just as nice a nature as he went out.'

'It must take some living up to.' Oliver had spoken idly and was surprised to see by the quick turn of Heather's head that he had hit the mark.

'And you know,' she said, 'you just can't quarrel with him. He won't. That's what makes it all so difficult. It's maddening when you feel like having a row and someone just sits there making bubbly noises with his pipe and saying: "Steady, old girl."' She looked at Oliver propitiatingly, wanting him to condone. He said nothing and waited to see how much she would tell him.

'When I said I was dreading John's coming home,' she went on, sitting down and carefully pressing in the front pleats of her skirt so that she could talk without looking at him, 'I meant that I didn't know what it was going to be like to be married to him again. It's all very well for people who are madly in love. Everyone pities them when their husbands go off to fight, but really they feel quite smug because they're sure of what it's going to be like when they come back. But if you're not sure – –'

'For heaven's sake, Heather,' interrupted Oliver, 'don't try to tell me that you and John aren't madly in love. The whole of Shropshire knows you are. It's a kind of creed.'

'Oh, we are, of course – as much as two people can be when they start discovering things about each other. I'm not sure it's a good thing to be in love before you marry; it gives you the wrong ideas.'

'Such as?'

'Oh, you know. You've been in love with people. You know how they give out a kind of glow for you, which makes them

93

more exciting than other people. You can spot them coming a mile off, and if you see the back of a head rather like theirs in the street, that glows too, a bit, until you see the face.'

'I know what you mean,' Oliver said. 'It's a sort of enchantment they have for you. It colours everything they say and do and wear. It even comes through on the telephone, I used to find.'

'Yes, that's what it is. That's what being in love is, isn't it? But listen, Ollie,' – Heather began to wail a little – 'how can someone go on being enchanted when you live with them day by day and hour by hour? It's when you start letting yourself notice things that you were too dazzled to see before, that's when it starts to go.'

Oliver was surprised by the sadness in her tone. 'You shouldn't talk like this, darling,' he said. 'It doesn't get you anywhere. You're probably exaggerating, anyway. You're tired, you've got the responsibility of the kids all on your own, you've had five years of war, and the worry about John.' All the old facile arguments.

She brushed them aside. 'It's nothing to do with that. It's something that happens to every marriage. I know that now. I've watched other people. No one's given a perfect marriage; you have to make it for yourselves out of some very unpromising situations. The point is not what you've got, but what you make of what you've got. Lord, I sound like someone preaching, don't I? I'm the last one to preach, because John and I just haven't been able to make it. That's what's been so disillusioning, to find out how inadequate we are. Are you bored, Ollie?'

'Of course not, go on.'

*

'I've never talked to anyone like this,' said Heather nervously. 'Least of all John. That's been one of our big mistakes: we don't admit things. I've never been able to make him have anything out, even that silly business about Hugh Aitcheson – remember? – when we were engaged. John was so damnably tolerant. I was just spoiling for a colossal row, but John simply refused to talk about Hugh, and then when Hugh had drifted out of the picture, John and I just drifted back together again with everything unsaid and me feeling rather a fool.

94

'I was a fool too. Lord, what a fool I was to think that all you had to do was to marry someone you loved and you could sit back and be happy ever after, amen. I was quite nice in those days too; at least, I felt nicer than I do now. But as John started to get on my nerves, I started to get irritable, and then, of course, he wasn't liking me any better than I was liking him. He never showed it, but I could feel him getting disappointed in me. He can't have loved me for my brain; I believe – but that was one of the things he never talked about – I believe he loved me for my sunny little nature and the air of artless youth which I detect in photographs of myself before marriage. But when the sunniness went, what was there behind it? He'd married a wife with no depth. I suppose I haven't got any, though God knows I try. I'm not quite sure what depth is.

'Oh, the first year wasn't too bad really. A lot of it was lovely, as a matter of fact, with everything new and exciting. John was in Dorset, and I used to dash down there when he wasn't dashing up to London. We really were happy in that ridiculous little flat up there, which used to sway if anything dropped too close. I remember the warden used to batter on our door to try and make us go down to the shelter at night, but we wouldn't, until there was that terrific blast and the flat sucked in its teeth. I was expecting David then, you see.

'They say children bind a marriage together, like glue, or the egg you put in rissoles, don't they? They're dead wrong. I can date the beginning of our discord from the beginning of David – at least from the time when he began to affect me. I used to get tired and cross and hot and sick of myself, and I was getting pig-faced, but John would insist on treating me as a sort of Madonna. I used to stick my feet up on a sofa and wail at him to fetch me things, and, silly ass, he used to fetch them instead of tipping up the sofa and telling me what the doctor said about exercise. But he's so good, you see, John is, so much too good for me, besides being cleverer, and all the time I was getting to feel inferior.

'Where were you when David was born? Of course, you were in Scotland, weren't you? I don't suppose I've ever told you anything about it. It was just another instance of the very thing that should have brought us together sending us farther apart. I don't mean the actual having David, but the adversity we both went through. You're supposed to come together in adversity, aren't you?

'I don't know whether you know anything about that nursing-home, Burley House. I expect some of your friends' wives have been there. A lot of Service people do; they get reduced rates – and, my God, reduced amenities. I'll never forget arriving there. John took me. He was at home at the time, taking a course. Things started to happen about two o'clock in the morning. He was marvellous then, of course, just what I wanted, rushing about with rugs and a wrinkled face and conjuring a taxi out of somewhere – I didn't care where. When we got to this place, just outside London, he wanted to come and see me safely into bed. They laughed at that, of course, but I remember, while I was almost passing out in the hall, I remember being disappointed to see how meekly he obeyed them. He's always had a holy fear of rules of any kind, no matter who makes them. He's the sort of man who always walks on the right in the Underground, so, of course, when the nurse said: "We never allow anything like that," he just blew me a despairing kiss over her head and faded away.

'Oh, Ollie, I did have an awful time. It's all right, don't get nervous. I'm not going to give you any grisly details. I just want to tell you about the night sister they had there. She was the same shape in front as behind, with yellow hornrimmed spectacles and a nose like a boathook. Before I'd even opened my mouth, she said: "Now we don't allow any fuss. People have babies every minute of the day and night, so you needn't think you're anything extraordinary. I don't want any fuss." I wasn't going to fuss. I had thought of asking her to get my night things out of my case, but I changed my mind. I was practically collapsing, but she just stood over me and watched me undress, looking at my underclothes in a sneering sort of way though I'm sure they were better than hers. When I'd turned down the bed and got in, I discovered I hadn't got a hankie, so I had to crawl out again and get one. D'you know, that bloody woman watched me drag myself all the way to the dressing-table and back. God, if she ever has a baby, I wish they'd do to her what the Germans did to pregnant women; but she won't, of course, until they come in test-tubes.

'Need I say that she didn't send for the doctor in time? That's a favourite trick of theirs. They love to be able to greet him with the baby already arrived when he turns up. Not that the nurses didn't manage me and David all right on their own, but I was paying for that doctor, and he might have stopped the night sister slapping my face at one crucial moment.

'They wouldn't let me see John the next day. I heard him whistling outside the window until they chased him away. I whistled back, but of course he couldn't hear me, and I didn't dare get out of bed even if I could have. When they did let him come, I was having my tea. He'd had quite a day, and no lunch, so I rang the bell and asked humbly if I could have another cup. The nurse wasn't exactly rude, but she didn't bring the cup, and when I was going to ring the bell again, John wouldn't let me. Rules again, you see. However, when she came to tell him he must go, he was rash enough to ask if she could bring in his son. Into the room? She was appalled. He could go with her and look at David through glass if he liked. He told me next time he came that they had brought a baby to the other side of a hatch and shaken it at him for about half a minute, and from his description of it I'm sure it wasn't David.

'Those were just a few of the things wrong with that place, but the most wrong of all was that John sat down under it. I kept on at him to make a row, and really it was pathetic to see the struggle between his two very decent emotions – chivalry towards me and the hatred of giving any trouble. A lesser man would have raised hell. John just did his Blessed-are-the-Meek act. That was when I started to realize his inadequacy, and he realized mine when I came home and he saw what an inefficient mother I was. I'm pretty good now. I know you think I make a fetish of it, but honestly, Ollie, don't listen to anyone who tells you you can look after children and do anything else besides, and that's one of the reasons I'm worried about John coming home. I made a pretty good hash of being a wife as well as a mother when I only had one baby. What'll it be like with two? He was always wanting me to go out, you know, and as soon as I'd got my figure back I wanted to as well, but I wouldn't pay anyone to come and sit with David, even if we could have found somebody. At least I said it was the money, rather righteously, but really I wouldn't have trusted anyone alone with David. I would hardly trust John.

If I left them together while I went shopping, and David was crying when I got back, I'd make out it was John's fault, which wasn't fair, because he was better with the baby than I was. He was silly with him, though; he used to put on an inane face when he talked to him and waste his energy playing all sorts of games that the wretched child was far too young to understand. That was why I was so annoyed when Fred tried to make Susan listen to his watch – I don't know if you noticed – because that was what John used to do to David when he was only about a month old.

'Well, there you have us. John at the War Office, upset because he hadn't been sent abroad yet, but determined to do his duty where it lay, coming home every night to an unenthusiastic wife and strings of wet nappies hanging in front of the sitting-room fire. Our life was drab. That was what made us decide to go on that holiday to Doraig, when John got his embarkation leave at last. Although we never admitted it to each other, I know we were both thinking that if we could get away on our own, we might get back some happiness.

'A second honeymoon, and everyone thought it so wonderful. "You'll always have that to remember," Ma said. She was right. I don't think I'll ever forget it. To start with, it rained all the time. That was nothing. We could have been blissful in the rain. Ridiculous – the first thing I can think of that annoyed me was the sort of water-chute cape on the back of John's raincoat. It shows how neurotic I was getting. It was a perfectly ordinary Army one, I suppose, but it annoyed me in the same way as those little woolly hoods on golf clubs. Frightfully practical, but somehow old-maidish. We used to walk a lot in the rain – there was nothing else to do up there if you didn't fish. I was still feeling tired, but I never gave myself a chance to be anything else. Instead of taking it easy at first and gradually working up to longer walks, I forced myself on for the masochistic pleasure of being able to feel resentful with John for having dragged me all those miles, although he spent most of them urging me to turn back. In the evenings, long, long evenings they were, he thought he'd read to me while I knitted. Cosy idea, but he chose something above my head and was disappointed that I didn't appreciate it. I tried to pretend that I did, but he knew, because I never remembered where we'd got to, and I'd interrupt him in what was apparently a key passage to go upstairs for more wool.

'That's another thing – he's so polite. I mean, I'm his wife and we'd been married more than a year, yet he'd still leap up like a scalded cat if I got up and dashed upstairs for something I could have found much easier myself. It's rather nice, but somehow in an Englishman it isn't normal, and I can tell you, it makes a girl feel uncomfortable.

I was worrying about David, of course. John was worrying too, but I used to make out I was the only one.

'Of course, we did have some happy times up at Doraig. I was still in love with him – I am now, only somehow it doesn't work. I loved him for being so good with the Scots. The old boy who ran the hotel was a real Highlander. You know – cinnamon-coloured tweeds an inch thick and photographs of clan gatherings all over the walls, and very courteous. John knew just how to talk to him and they used to spend hours standing outside the hotel in a drizzle discussing life with people who came along driving cows. I was proud of the way he looked too, and thought we made a nice pair in the dining-room. Oh yes; that was another thing, so silly really. The food was lovely, but they only knew one way of cooking potatoes – in their jackets. The first meal, we both said: "What nice potatoes"; the second meal, we said: "Ah good, those nice potatoes again"; the third and fourth meal I didn't say anything, and after the fifth I never ate one, but John was still bravely saying: "Ah, baked potatoes!" for the benefit of the waitress, who was deaf, anyway.

'On the way home, I tried to talk to Johnny. There we were, shut up in our little coffin of a sleeper, rushing through the night eating venison sandwiches and oatcakes. One could have got very close, but each time I approached the subject he sheered away, patted my hand and told me I was tired. I thought him obtuse at the time, but I see now it was because he'd longed so much for this holiday alone with me that he wouldn't admit, even to himself, that it hadn't been much of a success.

'Well, then he went away, and my God, I missed him. I got to thinking about myself, and how it was all my fault and I was just ripe for meeting someone like Blanche Aubrey, who seemed to have such peace of mind.

'She was in the nursing home where I had Susan – *not* Burley House. She was up, and she used to come into my room and talk and talk, and she was such a sweet person herself, I thought perhaps it made you like that, being a Roman Catholic. Well, you know the rest. I thought I might find the answer to everything. As you've probably gathered, I haven't, so it's made things worse. I can tell from his letters that John doesn't like the idea; its only excuse for him will be if it has made me easier to live with, but he'll find it hasn't. I haven't had time. I haven't understood it properly yet, or got it straight in my mind, and I need to be on my own to do it. I'm not ready for John to come home. I'm a wretched creature, Ollie. I do all the things you're supposed to do, and I pray, and I struggle and struggle to find what Blanche has found, but nothing happens.'

*

'Perhaps you try too hard,' said Oliver.

Heather suddenly regretted her confidences, went red in the face and stood up. 'You don't understand. What do you know about it, anyway? No one likes me being a Catholic. You're bigoted, the lot of you. Sorry I've bored you so – I don't know why I did. You and Elizabeth can have a good laugh about it.'

Elizabeth, who had come in as Heather banged out, asked: 'What can we laugh about?'

'Nothing. We can cry if you like. I feel just ripe for a good howl.'

'Save it for tomorrow, then. It's my week-end off.'

'So it is. Oh Lord, two days of Mary Brewer in that dreadful little hat.'

Elizabeth looked slightly superior, as she always did when Mary was mentioned. 'There's really not much need for her to come twice a day,' she said, 'now that your leg's so much better.'

'Poor girl,' Oliver said. 'Don't deprive her of her only fun.'

'She can't go on nursing you for the rest of your life,' said Elizabeth quite acidly, 'any more than I can. Don't forget to ask her where she put the surgical spirit; I can't find it anywhere. If she's taken it, she must get us some more. There was exactly half a bottle. And tell her not to change that dressing. I don't want all my good work undone.'

'You certainly have done a good job of nursing on that leg,' Oliver said. 'If only Hugo would let me up, I'd be able to get fitted for a cork one. I must say it would be nice to be out of here by the spring.'

'Don't count on that too much,' said Elizabeth, 'after what he said last time he came. I wish I had a stethoscope like his,' she mused. 'I could hear all sorts of tiny little things in your heart when he let me listen.' She went over to the fire to warm her hands, for it was cold by the bed with the window open. Oliver wore a sweater and a brightly checked lumber jacket, which his mother had brought back for him years ago when she last visited America. He had worn it for winter sports and then forgotten about it until Mrs North had fished it triumphantly out of a trunk in the attic when he scorned her offer of a shawl to wear in bed.

'Ah,' he said gallantly, 'no wonder my heart said all sorts of little things with you bending over it.'

'Don't be silly,' Elizabeth said coldly, leaning with one arm laid along the mantelpiece, and kicking gently at a log. 'That's the kind of thing senile old men say in hospital.'

'Sorry. It was rather. I feel a bit senile tonight, though. Life seems to be passing me by.'

'I thought you were quite happy here,' she said. 'You always say you are.' She had taken lately to talking at him in rather a defiant tone. He wondered sometimes if she were getting sick of him and tired of the job.

'I am really,' he assured her. 'It's just that one gets to feel a bit static sometimes. You see people in here and they talk to you and you think you know them. Then you realize their existence only begins when they get outside this room, and you want to follow them and meddle in their lives; but because you can't, you lie here and give sententious advice, which they never take even if they've asked for it.'

'So long as you don't start meddling in my life,' said Elizabeth defensively.

'I'd love to. I'm sure you're running it all wrong, but I don't get a chance because you never tell me anything. What are you doing this week-end? Meeting your boy friend?'

'I might.'

'Going home?'

'I don't think so.'

'Your father doesn't see much of his only daughter, does he?' Oliver said experimentally. 'You know, don't you, that you could have him to stay here any time you liked if he'd care to come.'

'Oh no,' she said quickly, 'he wouldn't. I mean, he wouldn't be able to, thank you all the same.'

'It was Ma's idea. She's very fond of you, Ma is, for some reason. I believe she imagines you're the kind of girl she'd like to have had for a daughter. Satisfactory, you know – turns out right every time, like a blancmange. I don't know what she'll do when you go. What will *you* do, by the way?'

'Oh, I don't know.' Elizabeth turned and looked into the fire. 'Take on another case, I suppose. Unless I get married.'

'To Arnold Clitheroe? Don't kid yourself. You'll never marry him.'

'What do you mean?' He enjoyed seeing her get angry. Although she controlled her features, her forehead became bright pink and her eyes opened very wide.

'You don't love him.'

'You don't know what you're talking about.'

'I do. If you loved him, you'd want to talk about him. You couldn't help yourself. Simple. Anyway, he's too old for you.'

'You don't even how how old he is.'

'I can guess from the kind of places he takes you to dinner. I bet he often says he wishes he could take you to the dear old Kit Kat, doesn't he?'

'I haven't the slightest idea where the old Kit Kat is.'

'There you are!' said Oliver illogically. 'That proves he's a different generation. What's he look like?' he asked, and then, as she did not answer: 'As bad as that? You must give him up, Elizabeth, and find some nice young man with less money and less paunch.' He knew he was being horrid, but when he got wound up like this he could not stop. 'Elizabeth Clitheroe. How would you like saying that in shops?' She was very cross with him. He was suddenly smitten by the narrowness of her shoulders as she stood with her back to him, kicking the brick kerb of the hearth.

'Don't do anything foolish, Liz,' he said gently, 'just for the sake of being married. It might be even worse than being a nurse.'

She turned round and put up a hand to tidy her tidy roll of hair. 'Please don't bother about me,' she said. 'I can look after myself.'

'Ah, but can you? That's just the point. Just because you know how to look after me, Liz, you think – –'

'And please don't call me Liz.'

'What does Arnold Clitheroe call you? I bet he calls you Liz when he's being bearishly affectionate.' She went out without answering. People who were not bedridden had the unfair advantage of being able to break off any conversation that was getting too much for them. He rang the cow-bell, but Elizabeth did not come back. He didn't blame her.

*

On the following day, Violet was seen to have powder on her nose. Even Mrs North, who needed a new prescription for her glasses as soon as she could find time to go to her oculist in London, noticed it. The powder was not clinging very well, because there was no vanishing cream underneath, and Violet, who had a cold, had soon blown and wiped a clear area round her nostrils, so that there was a line across her nose between the chalky top and the red tip. Heather had probably remarked on this at breakfast-time, because Oliver noticed when Violet came to take away his tray that she had rubbed off the rest of the powder and looked normal again.

'Hullo,' he said. 'Where's Elizabeth?'

'I said I'd do it so she can get on with the washing up and catch her train – ouch!' Everything on the tray slid down to one end and the coffee-pot fell to the floor, its lid rolling away under the furniture.

'Good job you'd drunk all your coffee,' said Violet with satisfaction as she picked up the pot.

'But I hadn't quite. Look, there on the rug.'

'Where?' Violet stooped and peered. 'Oh, cripes, Ma'll think it's one of the dogs.' This made her laugh. She rubbed the little pool into the rug with her foot. 'Good for carpets.'

'That's cigarette ash. Aren't you working today?'

'Not with this filthy cold.' She sniffed juicily at the thought of it. 'I thought I'd take a day off.'

'Well, that's a change,' Oliver said, 'considering last time you had 'flu it was all Ma could do to stop you going harrowing in an east wind with a temperature of a hundred and one. What'll Fred say?'

'Oh, he can manage,' she said casually. 'I told him yesterday I wasn't coming. They're whitewashing the cow barns this weekend.'

'But, Vi, I thought whitewashing was one of your favourite sports. How can you bear to miss it? It wouldn't hurt you, you'll be indoors.'

'Oh, shut up, Ollie,' she said in her cold-thickened voice. 'I've said I'm not going. Why does everyone keep on so?'

At lunchtime, Evelyn, looking like a skewbald pony, with whitewash on her hair and clothes, reported that she had just seen Violet making her bed.

'She was turning the mattress,' she told him in an awed voice. 'She *never* does that. She never does more than just pull the clothes up usually. I know because of when I've slept with her when there's been visitors in my room.'

'Say, whatever's bitten your eldest sister?' asked Mrs North, coming in with Oliver's lunch. 'I've just seen her shaking her bedroom rug out of the window.'

'There, you see,' said Evelyn darkly. 'D'you think she's ill, Aunt Hattie? Fred wasn't half wild she didn't come down to the farm this morning. D'you know what he said to me? He said women are the devil. I think that's rude.'

'She should have gone,' Mrs North said to Oliver. 'After all, he does pay her. Go and wash for lunch, Evelyn.'

'I have,' she said cheerfully. 'It doesn't come off.'

'There's some turpentine in the coal shed. Try that.' She automatically picked up Evelyn's dangling forelock and slid the bow back into place. 'I shall have to wash your hair tonight, childie.'

'Oh, not tonight.' Evelyn pulled away. 'What's the use? We shan't nearly have finished the whitewashing, specially if Vi doesn't come this afternoon. Fred's wild, you know, because the cows have to go in the old sheds till the stink's worn off and you can't use the electric milker in there. Fred says he reckons to lose five gallons over this week-end. He says I can do some milking tonight, though; that'll help.'

'We're going to tea with the Fosters,' Mrs North reminded her.

'Aunt Hattie, I can't!' she wailed. 'Fred said I could milk. He said I could milk Bonny and Alice and Serene – Serene's difficult, but he said I could try her – –'

'Stop telling me what Fred said,' her aunt told her, 'and go and use that turpentine. I've ironed your red dress. You can wear that this afternoon. You'd better put it on after lunch and not go out again, or I shall never get you in.'

Evelyn kicked a chair. 'Don't be that way,' said Mrs North. 'It isn't pretty. You'll have to start learning to act like a lady soon. What are they going to think of you in New York?'

'Not going there,' Evelyn said sulkily. 'Daddy's going to buy a ranch. He said so in his last letter.'

'I wouldn't count on that too much, dear. Grown-ups make foolish promises sometimes that they don't always keep.'

'Daddy doesn't,' retorted Evelyn fiercely. 'He's going to buy a ranch and live there and I'm going to have a horse and a three-speed bike and a heifer calf of my own to breed from, and a pair of chaps. I think that's a kind of trousers,' she told Oliver.

'Oh dear,' sighed Mrs North when she had gone out, 'I do hope Bob doesn't let her down, but I don't think he means it. I'm sure he'd never live anywhere but in the city. We shall have to spruce Evie up a bit before he comes for her. She's been too much with Vi.'

'I shouldn't worry about her,' said Oliver. 'She'll be all right.'

'I'm not worrying about Evie,' said his mother. 'Right now, I'm worrying about Vi. I can't think what's bitten her. It's so unlike her to take any account of a cold, but she's just been hanging around the house all morning blowing her nose on those enormous khaki handkerchiefs you gave her. I do hope she isn't sickening for anything. You might catch it.'

Oliver laughed. 'It wouldn't matter about poor old Vi, I suppose.'

'Oh, she's all right. She's as strong as an ox; she'd weather anything. Look, dear, I want you to start with soup today, and I've opened a bottle of stout. It won't do any harm to try and build up your resistance, just in case.'

*

'How comes it, then,' asked Cowlin, when he limped in with a bucketful of logs in each hand, 'that Miss Violet idn't down to the farm today? I seen 'er in the hall just now, so I thought I'd see what she talks about, and – – Ha!' He had a way of giving a staccato, toothless laugh in the middle of his sentences. 'Didn't she bite my yead off!'

'She has a cold,' said Oliver patiently. 'She doesn't feel well.'

'Ha! If you ask me, I'd say her and Mr Williams 'ave 'ad words.' Having put down his buckets, he bent to transfer the logs carefully, one by one, to the log basket. His breeches were very baggy at the seat and his legs, in leather gaiters, spindled into enormous boots.

'What about?' shouted Oliver. Cowlin had been deaf for years. Indeed, not one of his five senses was intact, for he had lost an eye in the last war, had no feeling in four fingers of one hand, and untreated sinusitis had left him unable to taste all but the most strongly flavoured food. Mrs North seldom let his wife help with the cooking because a pinch of salt to her meant a fistful, and a few drops of essence was half a bottle. Occasionally, if the wind was right, Cowlin could smell decaying cabbage stalks, but he could smell none of the flowers he grew so lovingly, nor could he even see them properly, for his one eye was colour-blind. Having acquired all these infirmities by the age of sixty, he looked forward to an old age in which there could be no further decay. He was already half crippled with rheumatism.

You could sometimes make him hear by saying the same thing in a slightly different way. Oliver tried: 'What were they having a row about?' and 'Why were they fighting?'

'Dunno. I couldn't year. But I seen 'em, going at it out there in the rick yard, in a nasty old wind too. Then there was quite a time when they wasn't saying nothing – just kickin' at the ground.' Oliver could picture it. 'Then Miss Violet she goes off one way and Mr Williams 'e goes off another and I says to myself: "Ha!"' He straightened up and gazed at Oliver impressively with one misty eye and one puckered socket. Oliver nodded. It was the easiest thing to do.

Cowlin always lingered as long as possible when he brought the logs. He stood with his back to the fire, trying out his knees like a policeman. 'Well, I'll be getting along,' he said, making no attempt to go. 'That ought to last you till tomorrow. That's apple wood, that is, you won't get no better.'

'I know,' shouted Oliver. Cowlin cocked his head inquiringly, so Oliver nodded. Cowlin stood happily on, his fallen-in lips spreading in a slow smile as he felt the warmth creeping into his back. Oliver offered him a cigarette. This made Cowlin laugh.

'Ha!' he said. 'I can't taste they. I can't hardly taste my shag now that they've made it so austierity.' He would have been quite content to stay there all afternoon. Oliver knew he must have a lot to do, for he managed the whole garden and the kitchen garden on his own, with the occasional hindrance of a nephew known as Sloppy Joe. He never seemed to be in a hurry, yet he got through an astonishing amount of work and always had time to knock up a garden seat or mend a puncture or skin a rabbit. Oliver had often wondered how country people managed to do as much work as London people, although going at half the pace. A country cook could amble about her kitchen and inconvenient passages and sit for hours in a creaking wicker chair and always have time to help a small boy make grubby pastry balls, while a London cook flew irritably about a labour-saving kitchen, at her wits' end if there were suddenly one more to dinner and ridiculing the idea of finding time to make cakes or jam which could perfectly well be bought in the shops.

Mrs North and Heather and the children went off in the car to their tea-party, after a great deal of horn-pipping and: 'For heaven's sake, if we don't go soon, it'll be time to come home directly we get there. You know what David's like if he's late to bed.'

'My goodness, Heather, if I can't even say goodbye to my own son! You'll just have to wait two more minutes while I fill his hot bottle. He says it's warm enough, but that's only because he hears you yelling.'

Mrs Cowlin did not come on Saturday afternoons, so Violet had been commissioned to give Oliver his tea. Mrs North had left his tray quite ready; she had even put tea in the teapot, but she would be uneasy all the time she was out. She would have been still more uneasy if she could have heard Violet, after telling Oliver what was on his tray, saying: '*But* there's a scrummy bowl of dripping in the larder. Should we have dripping toast, like we used to on Sundays with Father? I could make the toast in here, like he used to. Do let's, Ollie.'

'What about my tea, though? Ma'll create if she thinks I haven't had it. Don't forget I'm supposed to be on a diet now.' Violet gave it to her dogs, watercress sandwiches, sponge cake, buttered Marie biscuits and everything, mixed up in a tin bowl.

'And I tell you what,' Oliver said. 'Let's have the tea frightfully strong, just the way I'm not allowed it. Know how to make tea, Vi?'

'I think so.'

'Look, when you've boiled the kettle, bring me in the tea and a tin jug and some condensed milk, if we've got any, and I'll show you how we make tea in the Army.'

'What a lark.' Oliver could hear her crashing about in the kitchen, dropping more things than usual in her pleased excitement. Her day indoors had bored her beyond endurance, and ever since lunch she had been wandering in and out of Oliver's room saying: 'I can't think of anything to do.'

'Read the paper.'

'*Horse and Hound* hasn't come this week.'

She came back with the children's enamel milk-measuring jug, the kettle, which she wedged crookedly, hissing, on the fire, several doorsteps of bread, the bowl of dripping, two kitchen knives and two mugs with nursery rhymes on the sides. 'I found these in the cupboard,' she said. 'D'you remember them? This was yours – Old King Cole – and the Simple Simon one was Heather's. Mine's broken.' Although she had not been a particularly happy child, always left out of her brother's and sister's schemes, she often harked back with an unfounded nostalgia. 'This was Daddy's toasting fork, wasn't it?' she said, taking it off the hook by the side of the fire. She and her father had not been especially fond of each other, but at least he had left her alone and had not seemed to notice when she got bad reports or was stupid with visitors.

She hummed throatily as she made the toast. She was very happy. She was never allowed to do anything for Oliver. There was never anything she could do, but today she had given him a tea which he enjoyed and they had had a lot of laughs. When they had finished, and the kettle was black all over and the milk jug black all up one side where Violet had stood it near the fire to keep hot, Oliver, licking greasy fingers, said: 'This is nice, Vi. Thanks for looking after me. You're getting quite domesticated.'

Violet, lying on the hearthrug with her feet under the arm-chair, her third mug of tea cradled in her hands, said: 'Oh, rot. I'm no good in a house and never shall be.'

'I can't see that it matters. It's better to be like you than those women who rush at the table with a rag and a tin of polish before you've even finished your dinner.'

Vi grunted and took a noisy swallow of tea. 'It's all right *now*, Ollie,' she said presently, 'with Ma and everyone to do things, but I mean, suppose one had to do it, if one were looking after a house, or some rot like that.'

'What, you mean if you were married?' People had stopped talking about Violet marrying a long time ago, when it became quite clear that she never would.

She guffawed. 'Me married! Don't make me laugh.' But there had been something a little forced and unnatural about her guffaw. An insane idea came to Oliver, but looking at his sister slumped on the hearthrug in a pile of lumpy chunks, he put it aside.

'Ollie,' she said suddenly, 'shall I tell you something?'

'Anything you like.' But her impulse had already passed and she mumbled: 'No, it's nothing. Don't think I will.' He turned on the wireless and a cinema organ began to sob quietly that roses were blooming in Picardy, with every note a tremolo.

'I like that thing,' said Violet, humming it off key. She put down her mug and lit a cigarette, then heaved herself over on to her back, where she lay with her head propped against the footstool and her feet on the seat of the arm-chair. 'It was really why I didn't go out today,' she said. 'Not because I had a cold.' While she was coughing, Oliver turned down the wireless, only a fraction, in case she should be put off by his too obvious attention.

'It's so silly, really,' she went on, when her paroxysm was over, putting her hands behind her head and mumbling through her cigarette. 'I don't know what to do. Never had to cope with this sort of thing before.'

'Anything I can do?' Oliver suggested.

'Gosh, no. You see, what makes it all so difficult is that nobody likes him.'

'Likes who?'

'Fred, of course. That's what I'm talking about.'

'But I like him. I think he's a grand chap.'

'Oh, you. You'd like anybody. You've gone soft since you were wounded. Nobody else does. I didn't even think I liked him much myself. He's not so bad, though. He's been jolly decent to me.'

'What's he done, then, that makes it all so difficult?'

'Asked me to marry him,' said Violet in her grimmest, gruffest voice.

'Good God!' said Oliver before he could stop himself.

'Go on,' she said, 'laugh. I know it's damn funny.'

'It's not as funny as you think,' he said. 'I think it's a jolly good idea.'

She squinted round at him, but could not see his face at that distance, so she turned her head back again, wriggled her feet farther on to the arm-chair, and said: 'You make me tired. You're as bad as the rest of them. That's what they'd all say – jolly good idea to get old Vi off, even to Fred.'

'What am I supposed to do then? Register horror and say that no Williams is good enough for a North?'

'Don't be wet.' She threw her cigarette on to the fire and suddenly laughed, relaxing in relief at having got it off her chest.

*

'I say, Ollie, you know, it was damned funny really,' she giggled. 'Fred of all people. You could have knocked me down with a boathook. But he was so decent about it, and I felt such an ass. It's supposed to be the high spot of a girl's life, isn't it? Not girls like me, though. I did feel a lemon.

'It was a couple of days ago. I'd been having tea with him in his cottage. I do sometimes, you know, when we've finished work. I rather like it there; dogs all over the place, a nice smell of horse blankets drying, and it doesn't matter where you put your feet. Homey.

'Fred always makes the tea, and gets the buns out and all that. He's awfully good at that sort of thing. He'd have to be, wouldn't

110

he, if we – – Keep your hair on; I'm not going to. It's too *mad*.
Old Fred and I, we get on pretty well. After all, I've worked for
him for five years now, and we can be together without having to
gas. That's one thing I do like about Fred, I must say. He's almost
as good company as a dog. Well, this particular day, we were
both dead beat. We'd been a couple of men short or something –
oh yes, and I know – something went wrong with the drier and
Fred spent about three hours messing about inside the works.
When we'd had our tea – Eccles cakes it was – we both dropped
off. He's got a rocking chair. I do like a rocking chair. I woke up,
feeling an owl, and honestly, Ollie, I thought he was ill or something. He was leaning forward, half out of his chair, staring at
me, bright red in the face. He did look funny; his eyes were all
bulgy and he kept opening and shutting his mouth like a fish.
I thought he was going to have a fit or something, and I was just
wondering whether I ought to go for Elizabeth, when he suddenly said, in the most odd, squeaky voice: "Violet, I'd like you
to marry me." That was exactly what he said; I'll never forget it.
D'you know what I did? I laughed. Wasn't it awful? I felt sorry
afterwards, because he was hurt, but, honestly, I couldn't help it.
It must be my perverse what-d'you-call-it that Miss Driver always
said I had. When I'd come to a bit, I asked him why, and he
talked a lot of rot, you know, about being lonely, and us getting
on together, and couldn't we make a go of it. It's all right, there
wasn't anything about love. It wasn't quite that funny. He would
keep calling me Violet, though. I mean, he *never* calls me anything
but Vi.

'For a moment, I almost said yes, because I was sorry I'd
laughed, but then – you know how dumb I am – somehow I
couldn't. So I biffed off as quick as I could, and when I got home
and looked at myself in the glass, I was darned glad I hadn't,
because I knew he obviously couldn't have meant it. I felt such a
sausage having to see him the next day, but, thank God, he'd forgotten about it. At least, I thought he'd forgotten, but in the
afternoon the silly ass suddenly clutched me when we were going
across the rick yard to look at that barley that Tom said was going
mouldy, and said: "I'm still waiting for my answer." Just like
someone in a book. I told him not to be wet – I mean, how could
anyone marry me? I'd be as much use as a wife as a sick cow.

111

He got quite cross. You ever seen Fred cross? Of course that made me laugh again, and he got madder than ever and said I was being coy. *Me* coy! I hopped it then, and I haven't seen him since. Thank God this cold gave me an excuse not to go to the farm, but I can't keep it up for ever.

'Ollie, what shall I do? I can't face him again, much less go on working with him like we did before. I had an awful thought in bed last night. I thought perhaps he'd only asked me because he was sorry for me not getting off.'

*

'Ollie, I think I shall have to go away. What shall I tell Ma?'

'Tell her you're going to marry Fred.'

'Shut up. I'm serious.'

'So am I. If you want to, of course, I think he'd make a pretty good husband myself, far better than most.'

'How could I?' She had rolled on to her side to look at him, her hips an enormous mound in the air. 'I don't know whether I do want to. I haven't the foggiest idea what it's like to be married. I couldn't dither round the house all day making tasty dishes and putting out his slippers and kissing him when he came in from work. Can you see me?'

'Other women do it.'

'Yes, but I'm not other women. I don't like doing the things that women do. I like doing the things that men do. I have tried, Ollie, these last few days; you know – a bit of powder here and there and trying to do my hair nicely, but it doesn't work, and it's a hell of a bore.'

'Look here, Vi,' Oliver said eagerly, 'if he asked you to marry him, he obviously likes you as you are. And if you did, why shouldn't you go on working at the farm, the same as you do now? It would be a very good partnership.'

'And him go on paying me?'

'No, you ass, not if you were his wife.'

She laughed. 'Perhaps that's why he asked me, to get a spot of free labour.' She let down her feet with a thud and got up. 'I think I'll go and put some pants on. It's damned draughty in a skirt and these suspenders are giving me hell. Why does this dress look so funny, Ollie?' She tugged at it. 'I've tried putting a different belt on it, and wearing a scarf the way Heather does, but it doesn't look right. No, I'm afraid if Fred wants a wife he'll have to find someone else.'

'He doesn't want anyone else, he wants you. And he wants you as you are,' he repeated. 'I'm sure he wouldn't expect you to try and make yourself different.'

'Couldn't, anyway, if I wanted to, old bean.' She stretched and yawned. 'Heigh ho! Well, I've got that off my chest, anyway. Ollie, if you ever tell a soul, I'll shoot you in your bed with that rook rifle you gave me. The old spinster will now clear away the tea-things before Ma comes back and finds out what we've been up to.' She clattered about in the hearth.

The cinema organ was now playing a curly version of the *Blue Danube*. Oliver said: 'Oh, Vi, do marry him. It would be very unkind not to. He's frightfully keen on you.'

She turned round, scarlet with stooping, embarrassment, and her cold. 'That's the best joke I've heard yet,' she said without laughing.

'No, honestly, I mean it. He practically told me so one day, hinted like anything,' he lied.

Violet came slowly towards the bed, dangling the dripping jug from one hand. 'I wish I had my specs on; I could see whether you were lying.'

'Cross my heart,' said Oliver, crossing his fingers under the sheet.

Violet looked past him out of the window, her rugged face softened and shadowed in the failing light. 'D'you know what the Min. of Ag. want Fred to do?' she said. 'They want him to plough up the hill field and grow crops on it. Have you ever heard of anything so mad, even with tractors?' She listened. 'There's that bull calf shouting again,' she said. 'He's been at it since Thursday. I remember hearing him when I was in the cottage though I didn't take much notice; I was in too much of a stew. It would be rather nice in a way,' she went on thoughtfully, 'to have my own house to do what I liked in. I could have Poppy and Dalesman indoors, and we wouldn't ever have to have visitors. D'you think everyone would laugh if I said I was going to marry Fred?'

'Hullo there!' Mary Brewer burst in at the door, carrying her little fibre attaché case. 'Soft lights and sweet music, eh? *Oh Danube so blue . . .*' She waltzed across the room and fetched up giggling by Oliver's bed, not looking directly at him. Violet picked up the rest of the tea-things from the fireplace and went away.

*

He was bursting to tell someone. He even wanted to tell Mary Brewer. She would have thought it deliciously romantic, but of course she didn't know Fred. He told her about the surgical spirit instead and she put on rather an uppish voice and walked with dignity to the cupboard in the panelling in the little recessed corner of the room. 'I was always given to understand this was where it lived,' she said and put it prominently on a table. 'I'll leave it here so she'll be sure to see it when she comes back.' Mary and Elizabeth, who had never met, always spoke of each other as She.

Mrs North and Heather got home late, and Oliver heard both David and Susan crying in the hall. There had apparently been some trouble at the party about presents. The hostess had muddled them up and given David's to another child who would not part with it and David had made a scene. Heather would not let him come in to see Oliver, but took him straight upstairs, wailing. No one came in at cocktail time that evening. Heather was too busy, Evelyn had gone out with a torch to see how much whitewashing had been done without her, and Violet had disappeared.

'She's gone out,' Oliver's mother told him. 'Isn't that just like her? After hanging around the house all day being a pest to everyone, she goes out as soon as it gets cold and damp. She can't be so ill after all.'

'She's all right.' Oliver was longing to tell her. He wondered where Violet was. Could she have gone to see Fred already? The thought that he might have influenced her was most gratifying.

'If she's able to go out, she could have got me some more coke,' said Mrs North, who looked tired and had a smudge on one side of her small, squashed nose. 'I told her to make the boiler up, but of course she's let it go nearly out. I've had a terrible job to get it going again.'

'I wish you'd try and get a maid,' said Oliver. 'I hate you

114

having to do these dirty jobs. And I can't do anything except just lie here like a parasite – –'

'Hush, dear,' said his mother. 'You know I wouldn't let you do it even if you were up. I can manage fine. It's only at week-ends when the Cowlins don't come. We should be quite all right if only everyone would co-operate. It is a bit depressing to come back to a cold house with no curtains drawn and the back door swinging open. I shall be glad when Elizabeth gets back.'

'So shall I,' said Oliver, whose back was still sore from Mary Brewer's zealous rubbing.

'I can't find the children's milk jug *anywhere*.' Heather came in wearing a damp flannel apron with her hair dishevelled, the fringe parted in the middle and standing up on either side like two little horns.

'Why, I've just found it in the scullery, soaking in the floor bucket. I thought you'd put it there.'

'I? Why on earth should I – –'

'Well, it's black, you can't use it.'

'That's Vi,' said Heather bitterly. 'She doesn't care a hang about anyone else's things. Honestly, Ma, it's a bit thick. She can't even be trusted on her own for an afternoon. What's she been doing with my jug, Ollie?'

'Search me,' he said.

They kept finding things that Violet had or had not done. As they got more and more irritated with her, the chances got less and less of her news being received sympathetically, if and when she chose to break it.

When his mother told him that he did not look well, Oliver realized that he did not feel so well tonight. His eyes felt heavy and he was conscious of his heart beating. He took his pulse. The rate was all right, but he did not think the slight irregularity was purely imagination. Was the thing never going to right itself? There were times when he despaired of ever being anything more than a bathchair nuisance.

His box of heart pills was empty. The new box was in the cupboard, but he did not want to ask his mother to get it, because she would fuss about him needing them. The longing to get out of bed and walk across the room was almost unbearable. If only he could do just that, he would ask nothing more, would stay in this room

115

for the rest of his life. Just to be able to walk across the floor to the corner cupboard. Imagining himself doing it, he could actually feel the floor under the sole of the foot that was not there. His stump twitched. With the weight of the leg removed, the big nerves in it were too powerful. It was always making involuntary movements, even in response to no conscious thought, as readily as an eyelid blinks.

He began to realize that one of his moods of depression was hovering over him. Either because of this or because he had eaten too much toast and dripping, he could not eat his supper, which made his mother anxious and his mood worse. His head started to ache and the dressing on his stump, which Mary Brewer had insisted was loose so that she could rebandage it, was now too tight.

Violet had not come back to supper. His mother kept coming in to ask if he thought she had gone to see Joan Elliot, or had taken her bicycle out and had an accident, or had gone to the cinema, and should she ring up Joan and find out?

Perhaps she had thrown herself into the pond in an agony of indecision. As the self-absorption which always accompanied his fits of depression grew, he began to lose interest in Violet's *amour*. The idea, which had seemed so promising this afternoon, began to pall. He tried to see it as he had before, as the best thing for Vi, her one chance of being married to a man with whom she could be happy, and who seemed quite satisfied with her as she was, but he could not make the affair seem anything but dreary and rather squalid, nor Fred anything but a bore and a prospective blot on the family. This afternoon it had not seemed to matter that he spoke with a Norfolk accent, was paralytic in company, and a head shorter than Violet. Oliver wished now that he had not tried to persuade her. Sentimental, meddling fool. Heather made him feel worse by saying cheerfully: 'I hear you're having a mood.'

'Who says so?'

'Ma told me in confidence.'

'Well, I'm not,' he said crossly.

'Please yourself,' she said, 'but I would like just to know what Vi's been doing with the kettle. She boiled it up on the fire in here, didn't she?'

'Why ask, if you know she did?' said Oliver.

When his mother came in to say good night, she stood by his bed, folded her arms and said: 'Violet's back, and where do you think she's been? Having supper with Fred. I was very cross. People will talk, you know, even about her. You know what she is, she's got no idea of what one can and what one can't do. Darling, you don't think she's running after that dreadful little man, do you?'

'He's not a dreadful little man,' said Oliver.

'Don't get me wrong, dear, you know I'm very fond of Fred, but he's not quite – I mean, one couldn't – –' Mrs North had been in England long enough to know beyond what point democracy was impracticable. 'I mustn't imagine things,' she went on. 'Violet never thinks about men; I often wish she did. And the way she treats this house like a hotel! I'd kept her supper hot and you can guess how mad I was when she came in and said she'd had ham and eggs at Fred's, although, needless to say, she ate her own supper as well later on. No wonder we got so few eggs from the farm. All this about the hens not laying.'

'Ma,' said Oliver, 'you're tired. Go to bed.' Violet was certainly making things very difficult for herself.

An hour later, when he was lying in the dark wondering whether, if he did eventually go to sleep, he would wake up feeling as bad as he did now, the door opened an inch and Violet said in a raucous whisper calculated to wake anybody up: 'Are you asleep?'

'No,' he said resignedly. She came into the room, and by the dying glow of the fire he could see that she was wearing her Jaeger man's dressing-gown and plaid felt slippers. She came up to the bed and stood with her hands in her pockets looking down at him, her cigarette end glowing in her unseen face. 'Thought you'd like to know,' she said. 'I took your advice.'

He did not know whether to be pleased or sorry. Six hours ago he would have been genuinely enthusiastic, but so much had been said and thought since that he had to whip some conviction into his: 'Oh, Vi, I'm so glad. You mean you're going to marry him?'

'Mm-hm.' She had caught that expression from her mother. 'I'm awfully bucked I did, Ollie. I believe you're right; he really did mean it. I didn't know what I was going to say. I just charged in before I could change my mind. He was sitting there looking

117

awfully browned off, and I thought: "Oh hell, I'd better get out of here," but, luckily, he seemed to know what I'd come for. I didn't have to say anything; he just sort of took it for granted. We've been making loads of plans. It's going to be rather a lark really, but gosh – the thought of telling Ma!'

'She won't jump at the idea,' Oliver warned her, 'but you'll probably bring her round.'

'*I* never will. You've got to help me, Ollie. After all, it was you made me do it.'

He groaned. 'Oh, Vi, I can't.'

'Rot. Look, be a sport, break the news for me tomorrow after I've gone out. I'll stay out to lunch and they'll have simmered down a bit by the time I get back.'

'I wish you'd do your own dirty work.'

'Don't be a swine. I thought you were on my side. I do think you're a twerp, Ollie, honestly.' She had started by whispering, but her voice had risen by now to its normal pitch. He was afraid his mother or Heather might come down to see what was happening.

'Oh, all right,' he sighed.

'Thanks loads. That's got that off my mind.' She sank into a chair and lit a cigarette from the stub of her last one. 'Gosh, I don't feel a bit sleepy, do you? I could talk all night. D'you know what Fred's going to do? He's going to register half the herd in my name, and let me do what I like with them. He's going to buy me a bull, as good as Tartar. He's – –'

'Tell me about it tomorrow, old girl. I've got a headache.'

'Oh Lord, you're not going to have a mood, are you?' That would upset the household, upset her chances.

'Of course not. It's enough to make me, though, the way everybody keeps asking me if I've got one. Go away now, there's a good girl, and let's get some sleep.'

'O.K.' She got up and tightened the dressing-gown cord, which she wore round her hips, like a man. 'Never mind, you'll have your Elizabeth back tomorrow, that'll make you feel better. Night, night.' Half-way to the door, she turned with a giggle. 'Tell you what, I wonder me and Fred don't give you ideas. They say one wedding makes another.'

Oliver was sickened. 'Go away,' he said.

118

''Sfunny,' mooned Violet, 'I do feel bucked now that I've taken the plunge. You ought to try it. I feel as fit as a flea. I could go out and take Jenny round the National course. I feel just as if I'd had a couple.'

Violet's engagement was going to be a little trying if it was going to make her moonstruck. Oliver had not bargained for this. And to compare her happiness with Fred to anything that he would wish for himself – it was fantastic and presumptuous, it was almost profane. Violet swam blissfully out. Was it his imagination, or was there already an increased assurance in her walk and manner? As she went upstairs, he heard her singing adenoidally about roses and Picardy. Did she want to wake the whole house? Anyway, if she were going to get above herself, the family would soon take her down.

He heard her door bang, then he switched on the light and began to read, but he could not concentrate on the book. He could hear Vi moving about, although she was two floors above him. He pictured her in her attic room with the cistern, their old playroom, which she clung to because it had a trapeze swinging from the centre beam. She could only walk upright in the middle of the room, and after all these years she still sometimes came down to breakfast with bumps on her head where she had sat up unguardedly in bed. Oliver hoped she was not wearing his old striped pyjamas tonight. It would be too incongruous to wear men's pyjamas on your engagement night. But there was something so incongruous about Vi getting married at all that his imagination sheered away whenever he tried to picture it. And this air of gay girlish rapture was going to be the most incongruous thing of all. Poor old Vi, he would try and put her case as well as he could tomorrow to make up for the things he was thinking about her tonight.

He thought of Fred, going to bed in his little stone, slate-roofed cottage, furnished with throw-outs from the house. He had been into Fred's bedroom and knew that he slept in a sagging brass bed with one knob missing and did his footballer's hair at a mustard-coloured dressing-table with a mirror that swung itself back to front. He knew that he kept the green suit behind a curtain hung across one corner and his other clothes in a tallboy with huge knobs and sticking drawers, and that he washed his vermilion

119

face in an enamel basin at a washstand that smelt of wet wood. Fred did not seem to notice any of these things, and neither would Vi, although her mother would want to have the cottage done up for her. He pictured Fred lying neatly right in the middle of the bed, with his gaudy nose outside the sheet. Although he knew it was unlikely, he imagined him in a night-shirt and when he got out of bed he would look like someone in an unfunny farce. Oliver wondered whether he were feeling elated or nervous or proud, or simply dazed at having brought the thing off. If he had been scared of coming to the house before, what would he feel like now? Oliver wondered whether he intended to get married in the emerald-green suit.

Susan was crying. After a few minutes he saw the square of light from Heather's window appear on the lawn and heard Heather get out of bed. Susan went on crying. Why didn't she give her a dummy or something? Why did women get married, anyway? Vi didn't know what she was in for. The thought of Vi with a baby was so comic that it made him feel better.

He went to sleep with his book open and the light on, and woke in a panic from a dream of terror, thrashing about and hurting his stump. He was sweating and his heart was thudding. Hugo was right in what he implied, though the soft-voiced old devil would not say it right out. He was not getting any better.

Chained to the bed. If only one could get up and have a walk on the lawn, or heat some milk or make a pot of tea. Better almost to be in hospital; at least there was always a night nurse about. He believed he would even welcome that horrid girl with the teeth who used to try to wash him at five o'clock, pretending it was six, as if she did not credit him with the sense to look at his watch. At least she had sometimes made tea for him – if she happened to want some herself. If Elizabeth were here, he might have rung the bell and asked her to make some. She would not mind; she would take it as all part of the job to be woken at two o'clock to make tea for a melancholic. But she would not sit with him and drink tea and talk to him. She would give him his tea, ask briskly if there were anything else he wanted, and go back to bed in her neat blue-and-white spotted dressing-gown.

He saw Heather's light go out and heard her get back into bed. He wondered if she had said her prayers to the Being whom she seemed to regard more as a sparring partner than a God, and whether they had done her any good. He wondered whether they had made her feel holy enough to make him a cup of tea. If he rang the bell, it would irritate her as much as it irritated him. He ought to have a long stick, so that he could tap on the ceiling.

Five and a half hours before anyone would come near him. Desperately, although he was not hungry, he ate a bar of chocolate, as an act of bravado to his stomach, which retaliated by feeling sick. So, to take off the sickness, he had to smoke a cigarette, which made him thirstier for tea than ever. He drank some water and fell into a light doze, waking every hour to look at the clock and sigh and punch the pillows and blow out his cheeks and try out a moan or two to see how it sounded.

CHAPTER 7

WHEN the cable came from John to say that he had sailed from Australia, Violet's first remark was: 'Goodo, he'll be here for my wedding.'

It was a trait of the female Norths to run things to death. Heather ran Susan, Mrs North ran Oliver, Violet had always run horses and dogs, and now she was running her engagement. The day fixed for her wedding was the only date on the calendar and all other time was referred to it. If someone remarked idly on the warm weather, Violet would say: 'Bet you it's grilling at my wedding. I shall sweat like a pig.' When Mrs North talked about scrubbing the deck-chairs before the summer, Violet said: 'What a scream, to think of you sitting out in the garden, just like every year, and I shall be married.' When Elizabeth repeated Dr Trevor's half-promise to let Oliver sit out of bed in a month's time, Violet said: 'Three weeks before my wedding. He'll be able to give me away.'

'He'll hardly be fit for that, I'm afraid,' said Elizabeth in her professional voice, making a little pursed mouth. 'He might be allowed to come to the service in a wheel-chair perhaps. We'll have to see.'

Violet frowned towards her brother. 'Not if he's going to pass out in the aisle or anything. We don't want a flap like when George Adams was sick at his old man's funeral.'

As Violet's daily quota of conversation was so small, she used it all up on her wedding and had few words to spare for anything else. When not talking about what she would insist on calling 'getting spliced' she would subside into blank-eyed, vacuously smiling comas, from which she only emerged at the smell of food or the sound of plates and cutlery. As far as she was concerned, no one had ever been engaged before, and certainly very few girls can have gone about it in her way. The basic fact of getting married was enough for her. Plans and details she swept aside as irrelevant, and cheated Mrs North of cosy discussions on clothes and curtains and women to do the rough. 'Do what you like, Ma,' she would say, and leave the room before she could be pinned down to a day for going up to London to get at least one presentable suit. She scoffed at the idea of new underclothes. 'Waste of money and coups. Who's going to see 'em?'

Mrs North cleared her throat. 'Well, dear, Fred – –' But Violet did not seem to have envisaged the intimacies of married life, or, if she had, saw no need for such refinements as nightdresses when she still had the two pairs of pyjamas bequeathed to her by Oliver, whose taste in stripes differed from that of the aunt who had given them to him. Perhaps it was just as well that the bathroom at the cottage was only a dark and mildewy lean-to shed off the kitchen, for Violet's sponge was fit only for car washing and her toothbrush looked as if she had been rubbing up curb chains with it. She probably had. Her mother planned to give her a dressing-table set for a wedding present, in the hope that her brush and comb would be relegated to the dogs, for whom they had apparently been designed. Now that she was certain of her destiny and no longer subject to spasms of thinking that there was something wrong with herself which she ought to put right, Violet made no more attempts on her face and figure. 'Fred doesn't like make-up,' she would say complacently when Heather shaded her eyes from the shine on Violet's nose, or: 'Fred doesn't like fancy bits on clothes,' when her mother asked whether it was absolutely necessary to wear a luggage strap round her waist. Heather was determined that she was going to make her up on her wedding day if she had to tie her down in a chair to do it.

She took no part in the wedding plans. She would not even go to see the vicar, and when Heather bullied her into helping with the invitation cards, she made such a mess and objected to so many of the guests that they were glad to let her slouch whistling away to the farm and finish it themselves. Oliver, who had the neatest handwriting, filled in the cards, while the others checked lists and looked up addresses.

'Look here,' said Heather, 'we simply must ask Toby and his parents, whatever Vi says. And the Gibsons, it'll look so queer.'

'I daren't ask Francis, after what she said about him. Her language is just terrible, you know; it's all this farm work,' said Mrs North, who was sitting at a table covered with envelopes, cards, the blotter, letter rack, and inkstand from her desk, ashtrays, cigarette boxes, and cups of tea.

'Oh, ask him,' said Heather, 'she'll never notice. He'll only make trouble if he doesn't come, because he's sure to hear all about it.'

'What about Lady Salter? Vi's still sore about that rat poison one of the dogs picked up. I should die of shame if she was rude to her.'

'Risk it,' Heather said. 'She probably won't talk to a soul, anyway. If we had only the people Vi wants, the place would be like the farmer's tea tent at an agricultural show.'

'Joan Elliot I bar,' put in Oliver.

'We must have her,' wailed his mother, 'she's Violet's best friend. She talks about her being a bridesmaid.'

Oliver groaned. 'In corduroy knickers and a leather waistcoat.'

Violet did not really care whom they asked. All that concerned her was that she was going to marry Fred Williams. Someone would see that it came about; they had always seen to things for her. She was not so much selfish as like a child who takes it for granted that cooked meals and clean clothes appear and that his toys get put away and his socks mended. Domestic details are none of his business, and they were none of hers.

'But, Violet, you must have a bed at least,' said Mrs North despairingly, after fruitless attempts to make her discuss furniture. 'You can't sleep on the floor, even if you do insist on wearing those terrible pyjamas.'

'Fred's got a bed, hasn't he? What's wrong with that?'

'But, dear, that ugly old bed – not really a proper double – –' Mrs North looked helplessly at Oliver and he made a face. The thought of Fred Williams and Violet in that sagging brass bed was impossible, but no more impossible than the thought of them sitting up side by side in little twin divans from Heal's with reading lamps and chintz flounces.

Mrs North changed the subject. 'Say, how would it be, Violet, if you let your hair grow a little before the wedding? It would be much more becoming.'

Violet ran a hand through her bristly crop and snorted. 'Heck no, it wouldn't grow now if I tried. Fred likes it all right like this, anyway.' She fell into a rumination and came out of it with a hoarse chuckle. 'Coo, fancy me being married, you know.' This was one of her stock remarks, which she produced at intervals during the day.

'Fancy,' Oliver said.

'Violet has quite come out of her shell,' announced Mrs Ogilvie after a Sunday lunch during which Violet's conversation had consisted mostly of Fred says and Fred thinks, while Fred, who always had to come to Sunday lunch nowadays, had sat looking like a Punch doll when the Punch-and-Judy man's hand is not inside, saying, and apparently thinking, nothing. 'I suppose you're very happy about it, Hattie?' This was not one of her rhetorical questions. She had been trying for a long time to find out what Mrs North felt about her prospective son-in-law.

'Why, surely. I think Violet and Fred will be very happy.' Oliver recognized his mother's acting voice. 'He's such a – –' She searched in vain for something she could say about Fred.

'Yes, isn't he?' cried Mrs Ogilvie with automatic enthusiasm. 'I can't tell you how glad I am you're having the wedding here and not at Shrewsbury, like the Gibson girls did. You'll never believe what they had to pay for the reception, with those bogus cocktails and the sandwiches obviously cut the night before and curling up at the corners. I ate something bad there, too, I was terribly ill next day. I didn't want to hurt Sybil's feelings, but I had to tell her, so that she could make a complaint. Poor Mr Norris will be so pleased. He hasn't had a wedding in the church for years. I shall cry, of course; I always do. You mustn't think I mean anything by it, but it's just the idea of the bride all in white, you know, so sacrificial.'

'Violet doesn't want to be married in white,' said Mrs North. 'She couldn't, anyway. She's spent all her coupons on a new riding-coat and a pair of boots.'

'But she can't get married in those!' shrieked Mrs Ogilvie.

Mrs North did not mention that she had only just weaned Violet from the idea of going to the church on horseback and coming out under an archway of riding-crops and hoes. 'They're having a riding honeymoon,' she murmured, but Mrs Ogilvie was not listening. 'She positively must get married in white. My dear Hattie, it's the one day in a girl's life – the one day in yours too, really, since Heather had such a quiet wedding. Let me help you with the coupons. I know a man' – she glanced hastily round, although there was no one in the room but Mrs North and Oliver – 'who sells them at two shillings each. Can you believe such a price, but what can one do? I got this that way!' She plucked at a dun-coloured jersey suit, which could have saved at least one coupon if the skirt had not dipped six inches at the back.

'I don't know that I care about black market – –' began Mrs North, but Mrs Ogilvie cracked her fingers like a stock-whip. 'Nonsense! It's the duty of people like us to diddle the Government all we can. They're doing it to us. I happen to know for a fact that they've got bales and bales of cloth stored in that American depot near Reading. You can see it from the train, six hangars full of it. Socialism gone mad.' This was her latest battle-cry, applicable to everything from bus strikes to no more dried eggs.

She continued to pace the room. She seldom sat down, and conversation with her was tiring to the eyes as following the play at Wimbledon. 'That's settled then. Violet shall be a white bride, and I'll get Lady Salter to lend her that lace veil that's been in their family for generations. It'll cover up her hair. Who's going to give the girl away?' She drew up opposite Oliver. 'You going to get this young man out and about by then? High time he was off that bed, if you ask me. One of these days, old chap, I'm going to take you in my two hands' – he flinched as she lunged at him – 'and pull you out of bed' – she strained backwards with stiffened

125

arms – 'and hop you into the fresh air. That's all that's wrong with you now. You're coddled.'

'I get plenty of air,' said Oliver sourly. 'I haven't got T.B.'

'You will have if you stay here much longer,' said Mrs Ogilvie cheerfully. 'Let's see what your chest expansion is. Got a tape measure, Hattie?'

'No,' lied Mrs North. She manœuvred herself protectively between them and remained there until Mrs Ogilvie puttered away on her bicycle with a little outboard motor fixed to the rear wheel, on which she went everywhere, even to London, wearing A.R.P. overalls and a leather helmet.

'She's still talking about coupons,' said Mrs North, coming back from the front door. 'I couldn't get a word in to say we don't want them. If she does get them, I shall use them to buy a new dressing-gown and slippers for you when you get up. And Lady Salter's priceless veil! I saw it when her grandchild was christened. Can you see her lending it? And can you see it after Violet had worn it half an hour? It's just as well she doesn't want to wear white; she wouldn't look well in it, and I should never get her to go for fittings. I can't even get her as far as the linen cupboard to look at sheets.'

'She's worse than ever she used to be,' said Oliver. 'She's forgotten all about training Evelyn's pony while the kid's at school. He's simply running wild up in the top field, half broken, and she's fused my electric razor, doing the hairs at the back of her neck.' There were times when he regretted having given the advice which had helped to put Violet into her present state.

'So long as she's happy,' sighed his mother. 'I should have hated her not to marry, but oh dear, if only it had been anyone but Fred. Do you suppose I shall have to go on making conversation to him for the rest of my life? I wish your father were alive, dear. He could have taken him into his study sometimes and it wouldn't matter Fred not talking because your father never cared to talk much either. Only this wouldn't have been his study now that you're in here. How should we have managed? Your father could have had the telephone room, or you could have had my bedroom and I could have had the spare room. I've always liked those built-in cupboards in there. We could have had the electric fire in my room changed for an open grate. The chimney may be blocked up, though; I don't know.'

'Stop making hypothetical plans,' said Oliver. 'You've got trouble enough with real ones.'

'But at least your father could have saved me that awful interview with Fred, when he came to tell me he wanted to marry Vi. I knew what he wanted to say, because she'd already told us, and I wanted to help him, but he *would* say it by himself, although he just couldn't get it out. I've never been so embarrassed. Poor Fred, I was in the kitchen baking, and he came to the front door and rang the bell as if he were a formal caller. I had him come into the kitchen, because I thought it would make him feel more homey, but it didn't seem to. He tried to shake hands with me; and when he realized mine were all doughy, he pretended he'd only been holding out his hand to look at his watch, although it was on the other wrist.

'He wouldn't sit down. He would wander around the kitchen, always between me and the stove when I wanted to get to the oven, poor little man. He couldn't get to the point. He started off by telling me there were three new calves, which I knew, although I didn't say so, then he got round to the farm, and from there to saying how much he liked it and how he appreciated knowing us and what a pleasure it always was to come here because we made him feel so at home. At home! Did you see him at lunch? If that's being at home, my goodness, what's he like with strangers? I daren't think about the wedding. I tried to help him out, but each time I thought he was coming to the point, he'd shy off and go back to something safe like the weather, or the state of the hedges, and he warned me a dozen times he'd put rat poison down in the big barn, as if I was in the habit of pecking around in there for something to eat.'

'Why didn't you say: "I hear you want to marry my daughter"?'

'I couldn't, dear. He wanted to say it himself. Besides, suppose he really had only come about the rat poison? Violet's so funny, it might have been her idea of a joke when she told us the day before. He went and fiddled with the curtains, and of course he pulled that one that's always coming down. I let him fix it, although I was itching to do it myself, because I thought it might help him to have something to do with his hands, as he never knows where to put them, and while he was doing it, with his back to me and the curtain draped round one ear, he kind of mumbled: "I want to ask you something." I haven't much of an ear for English brogues, but his accent does seem a bit strong sometimes, doesn't it? That shows you how English I've become; a good American wouldn't even think about it.

'I told him to go ahead, and he was just starting to mumble again when I smelled my scones burning and had to rush to the oven, and he came to help me, letting the curtain fall down again, and of course made things worse by setting fire to a tea-cloth. I must say he and Violet are well matched. By the time the excitement had died down he'd lost the courage to finish what he was going to say. He was too busy apologizing for the tea-cloth, anyway, and for the burned scones, which he seemed to think must be his fault too. It was one of my best tea-cloths, although I told him it was only an old rag. No one can say I'm not good to that man.

'He couldn't get out of my kitchen fast enough. I guess he was scared to think what he'd nearly done, like a man who works himself up to shoot someone and then runs a mile screaming when the gun doesn't go off. I tried to ask him again what he wanted, but he pretended not to hear. He muttered something about having an appointment and ran for it, and since then he's scared to death every time he sees me in case I should reopen the subject. I suppose they really are engaged? For all I've heard about it from him, it might be just some crazy invention of Violet's.'

'He's given her a ring,' Oliver reminded her.

'Oh yes, of course. Poor Fred, I wonder where on earth he got it. I really ought to talk to him about money, I guess, though he seems to be doing all right with the farm. I will say that for him; he knows his job.'

'If I work in with him later on,' Oliver said, 'I'll be able to check up on all that. The place may make quite a bit of money in a few years. Fred's got all sorts of ideas, if only we could get the labour and materials.'

'Yes, well, we'll have to see how you are before you commit yourself, darling,' said Mrs North in the soothing voice which she always turned on to his suggestions of working. 'I don't know that farm work will be very suitable.'

'I've told you a hundred times,' he said exasperatedly, 'I'm not going to do manual labour. I'm going to potter. What else do you suggest I should do, anyway? I'm not trained for anything, and if I'm not fit to farm, I'm certainly not fit to prop myself on a wooden leg in the gutter all day, selling matches.'

'Don't be bitter, dear,' said his mother. 'Why don't you try and write something? I've often thought since you were wounded that would be a nice career for you, to be an author.'

'All right,' said Oliver, 'go and buy me some paper and a pencil with a hard point and I'll lie here and write a nice long novel and the first publisher I send it to will fall on it, baying.'

'You might be a free-lance journalist,' she said, still hopefully.

'I might,' said Oliver, 'if I could write.'

'You don't have to worry about earning money, anyway, darling. I've got plenty for both of us, and when I die you'll have even more.' He knew she wanted him to say: 'Don't talk like that. I can't bear it,' but instead he asked: 'What if I want to get married? I suppose you support my wife as well?'

'Oh well – no need to think about that just now.' It was plain she never considered the possibility. To her he was out of the running, finished with the things that everyone else did. He must always be kept apart, protected from the world like an idiot child, nurtured in cotton-wool like china too fragile to be used. Later, when he was up and about and able to argue without his head splitting open, he would have it out with her.

'Anyway,' his mother said brightly, 'Fred's gotten himself a cheap wife. Violet doesn't need much to live on; I believe she's a throwback to my pioneer ancestors. She asked me the other day whether Fred had come to talk to me, and I hadn't the heart to tell her how hopeless he'd been, because she really does seem quite fond of him. Oh dear,' she sighed, and the folds of her face sagged sadly. 'I only hope she's happy.'

'She's happy all right,' Oliver said. 'It's running out of her ears. She was like a two-year-old the day it was fixed up, don't you remember? To please me, she took Jenny out and went over and over the jump in the pouring rain for me to see, and all the time I was asleep.'

'She's never got rid of the catarrh that settled on her that day,' said Mrs North.

Evelyn was disgusted with Violet. 'It's a good thing Dandy's got me,' she said, 'for all the interest *she* takes in him now.' Violet did not even do much work on the farm nowadays. She mooned about with a cigarette or a straw or sometimes both between her lips, giving a lazy hand here and there with one of the hundreds of jobs into which she had once thrown herself so strenuously. She drove with Fred when he went out in the lorry or in the dilapidated little car upholstered with dogs' hairs and corn seeds, sat about waiting for him on walls, drumming her heels, and plodded after him about the farm like some faithful domestic animal that does not need a halter. Sometimes, she came and sat in Oliver's room, but she never stayed long. They never recaptured the isolated intimacy of that afternoon over the dripping toast. Oliver had been of use to her then, but she had progressed now beyond quiet sickrooms and invalid brothers. She had soared into a wider sphere whose shadow eclipsed everything else. Oliver found her very boring and he gathered that she was as bored with him as with everything else not directly connected with her marriage.

Heather did a lot of rather ostentatious church-going over Easter. On Sunday, Mrs North and Elizabeth visited Mr Norris's cold little Gothic tabernacle, where he bleated like a sheep in its pen, narrow-faced and docile, from the pulpit. But Heather went to Mass every morning, and to *Tenebrae* on Good Friday and Benediction on Sunday, and left her missal lying prominently on the hall table in between. She told Elizabeth at least three times that she would not be wanting early morning tea, and became righteous when her mother protested mildly at the third request for late breakfast and someone to dress David.

'Send him in to me,' Oliver said. 'I'll see he gets dressed,' but when Heather came back from Mass, David was still sitting on the hearthrug wearing a vest and one sock, with the rest of his clothes scattered on and under various bits of furniture. Heather was very cross, then remembered she had been to church and was cross with herself for being cross. Oliver often wondered what she was getting out of her strenuous search after Christianity, and wanted to ask her, but although she liked to parade her religion before the family, she resented discussion of it. He was interested in Roman Catholicism, but he knew nothing about it, and Heather had either forgotten most of what she had learned at the time of her conversion or would not answer his questions because she thought he was mocking her.

John was expected home within the next fortnight. There was naturally a lot of talk about this, and, in the end, allusions to him began to affect Heather in the same way as allusions to the Catholic Church. She would flare and flounce and bang doors and cause her mother to say: 'She's all het up. It's a nervy time for her, after all these months of waiting.'

Elizabeth, who had less to do for Oliver now that his stump was healing and his heart strengthening, began to give Heather more help with the children, which she did on modern hospital lines, uncuddlesome, but extremely efficient. Heather, who was full of theories of her own, at first would not let her touch Susan. Now she let her do dull things, like pushing her out in the pram, but she would not admit that Elizabeth was good with the children.

'Listen!' she cried triumphantly, when everyone was saying how quickly David had got settled one night when Elizabeth had put him to bed. 'There he is crying now. I knew it; it's the minute you turn the light out, and the poor darling must have wondered what had happened to me tonight.'

David was not crying, but soon after she went up to him he was. His wails were still coming down through the ceiling when she came back to Oliver's room, where they were having drinks before dinner. She held a saucer out before her in a disgusted way. 'I *told* you I didn't want him to get into the habit of a nightlight, Ma,' she said.

'I haven't – –' began Mrs North, and Elizabeth broke in calmly: 'I put it there; it seems the only sensible thing when he's so nervous of the dark. It can't be good for either him or the baby when he screams like that.'

'I wish you wouldn't interfere with the management of my children,' said Heather pompously. 'He's only trying it on. He's got to learn to settle off quietly, and he never will if you spoil him.'

131

'Now, Heather,' said her mother, 'Elizabeth was only being kind. You know I never interfere with your children, but I've always thought he was too sensitive a little boy to be treated so strictly.'

'Oh, go on,' said Heather, 'side with her against me. She's always right; don't think I don't know that by now.' Oliver looked uncomfortably at Elizabeth, who, in trying to look as if she did not care, was only succeeding in looking prim. Heather glanced at her too, muttered something, and flung herself into an armchair and pretended to read a magazine.

On Bank Holiday night, however, she consented to abandon the children to Elizabeth, because she wanted to go to a dance in Birmingham with Stanford Black. Oliver heard the car come back at two o'clock in the morning, and when, some time afterwards, Heather came into the hall, he called her into his room.

'Disgraceful,' she said. 'You ought to be asleep.'

He switched on the light. 'Disgraceful yourself,' he said, noticing the state of her lipstick. 'You've been kissing Mr Black.'

Heather giggled. 'My last fling. I *have* had a good time, Ollie. We went on to the Malt House after the dance and met heaps of people. I haven't been so gay since I was a girl. Stanford's awfully good fun. I know you don't like him, but everybody else does, and he really is rather sweet.' She giggled again. 'What an innocent fling. D'you think John'll believe how faithful I've been to him all this time? If not, what waste of effort.'

'He ought to beat hell out of you if he thought you hadn't,' Oliver said.

'Oh no, not my little Johnny. He'd just forgive me sorrowfully like a father confessor. He'd never beat me. Some women like to be beaten, don't they, Ollie? I wonder why. Is it nice?'

'Go to bed.'

'I couldn't. I feel merry. I'd like to start the evening all over again.' She stood and thought for a moment, pouting, swaying slightly in the long flowered dress that hugged her plump bosom and spread into a stiff skirt, making her waist look smaller than it really was. 'I say, do you suppose I ought to go to confession tomorrow and say I let Stanford kiss me? They don't have it on weekdays, though. Still, I could ring the bell, couldn't I – but I never know whether the priest minds coming. He might be having his supper. After all, they've got to eat, though one never imagines them doing anything so worldly.'

'Look, Heather,' said Oliver, feeling the depressing effect produced by someone who has had a drink on someone who has not, 'I don't know much about your religion, but you seem to have got hold of the wrong end of the stick if you think you can do what you like and then wash it out by confessing it. John will never stand for you being a Papist if you talk like that. It's too childish. I don't suppose you mean it, though, when you're sober.'

'I am sober,' she said. 'I didn't have much to drink. I'm out of practice, though, with the dreary life I lead. And please don't lecture me about religion, because you don't know anything about it.' She looked flushed and bright-eyed and very pretty, with her fringe tangled and one ear-ring missing. 'Besides, you're smug,' she said, giving his hair a tweak.

'Don't jangle that damned bracelet in my eye.'

She ran it up and down her arm, smiling. 'It's a lovely bracelet. I adore it. Look, Stanford gave me another charm for it tonight, a little leering faun; isn't it sweet? He said I made him feel the way this faun looks, if you see what I mean. Think I ought to confess *that* tomorrow?' She was trying to goad him.

'Oh, shut up,' he said, 'and go away. You're bottled. And don't bother to ask whether your children are all right.'

'My babies!' she gushed, with clasped hands. 'The darlings. How are they?'

'David's fine. He was in here till half past seven. The other creature's been giving Elizabeth an awful time – screamed till about one o'clock.'

'Pooh,' said Heather. 'She can't be such a wonderful nurse as she thinks if she can't manage an angelic baby better than that. She's probably made her uncomfortable. I'll go up and see.'

'No you don't,' he said. 'You're sleeping in Elizabeth's room. She's looked after your brats for you, so you might at least give her some peace.'

'But, Ollie,' she wailed, 'I must go and kiss them good night.'

'And anaesthetize them with gin fumes and Stanford Black's faun-like breath? Not if I have to get out of bed to stop you.'

Presently, she fell asleep in the chair by his bed. He watched her for a while, seeing in her again the young, untroubled girl who

133

used to fall asleep wherever she happened to be when at last her vivacity was exhausted. Then his eyes closed too and he went to sleep with the light on, to wake again at five o'clock and find her groaning and stiff and shivering. She left her shoes where she had kicked them off and crawled upstairs, cursing him for letting her go to sleep.

'You thought I was tight last night,' she told him when she came to see him later in the morning.

'I hope you were,' he said. 'I should hate to think you talked such rot when sober.'

'I was only pretending, you know, like I used to sometimes when I was young and feeling excited, and Ma used to say: "You're either plastered or plumb hysterical," remember? I don't feel very young this morning, though,' she added, rubbing her forehead until her fringe stood on end, 'or excited. How is it that you can go to sleep feeling wonderful and wake up to find nothing's any fun any more? I thought sleep was supposed to do you good.'

'Never heard of a hangover, I suppose,' he said. 'Go on, you'd better go off and confess it, if you're going, or the priest will be having his lunch.'

'Don't be blasphemous,' she said primly.

'That's what you said last night.'

'I didn't, you said it. I remember wondering why people who haven't got any religion themselves always have to jeer at someone else's.'

'How do you know I haven't got any religion?'

'You never go to church.'

'How can I?'

'No, of course not; but would you, if you could? You never used to unless you were dragged.'

'I wouldn't unless I knew why I was going and what I hoped it would do for me. Do you know why you pedal off to Mass so earnestly every Sunday? If you don't go, you feel as uncomfortable as if you walk under a ladder without crossing your thumbs, isn't that it?'

'Oh, Ollie, don't let's have a religious argument at this time in the morning, I don't feel up to it. Why can't you leave me alone?'

134

'Well, you'd better be prepared with a few arguments before John comes home. You know what he is; he never accepts anything unless he's sure he understands it. Look what he was like with that radiogram – charts and diagrams and most of its inside strewn about all over the place, when the thing was doing perfectly all right on its own. He'll want to thresh this out with you, and you've got to justify yourself.'

'And I suppose everyone will back him against me,' she said, 'the same as you all do that prig Elizabeth. I'm sorry, Ollie, because she belongs to you, more or less, but I do not like that girl. I can't think why Ma's so keen on her. I'm sure she doesn't like any of us; she's too damned aloof. Look at her, she's been here nearly eight months and she still goes about as though she didn't belong. She wouldn't think twice about walking out whenever it suited her, without consulting us. You wait; she's just the type to disappear suddenly in the night, and I must say I wouldn't be sorry if she did.'

'You would,' said Oliver, 'considering how much she does for you.'

'Only because it suits her. It's part of her game to make people think she's indispensable. It's no good being saintly at me, Ollie, I don't like her. I don't like anybody this morning. Oh God, look, there's Vi, going for a jolly tramp with the dogs. Look at her going all across that wet plough instead of going round by the hedge. Doesn't it infuriate you? Fred must have some sort of perversion, I think, to want to marry her.'

'You're vile,' he said.

'I glory in it,' she told him, and went out, jingling her charm bracelet round until she found the faun and making an affectionate grimace at it, looking at Oliver to see if it was annoying him.

What was John going to make of her? Having no guile himself, he took everyone at their face value and he would never understand that Heather said half the things she did for effect, to liven her tedium. Oliver could picture her in her present restless, dissatisfied state making rings round a bewildered John. Perhaps there was more hope for them now that she was play-acting so much. If she wanted to, she might play-act herself into being sweet with John. Or she might be poisonous.

People sometimes said to Oliver: 'You must get bored to death lying here all day,' and when he denied it they only thought he was showing fortitude. But he was only bored when he did not feel well enough to take an interest in anything that went on outside his own body. Mostly, the days passed so quickly that night was sometimes upon him long before he was ready for it. With all the day in which to write letters, he would find that he had not had time to write one, or to finish his library book, or a plasticine animal he was making for David. One of the charms about being an invalid, however, was that you could go on doing things far into the night without suffering for it next day. His nights had been revolutionized since an Army friend of his, a simple youth called Teddy Beare, who had probably never done anything so opportune in his life, had brought him a large Thermos flask. This was filled with tea every night by Mrs North, who trusted no one else to screw the lid down tightly enough, and it lasted for two wakings at two cups a time. As he dozed off in the evening, he almost hoped he would wake again soon, and on nights when he slept right through and woke to find Elizabeth replacing the untouched Thermos with a freshly made cup, he felt quite cheated.

Having lost his dread of wakeful nights, he scarcely ever had one, and when he did, instead of tossing and fidgeting and sighing and turning the light on and off and wondering who would feel worse, he or Elizabeth, if he rang the bell, he could sit up calmly, drinking scalding tea with no regrets for the horrid night nurse with the teeth and her stewed tepid cups. Refreshed, he would read or write letters until he fell asleep again, the Thermos standing by his bed like a guardian angel with two more cups of tea in it.

If he woke within waiting distance of half past seven, he did not drink any more tea, because it would spoil the cup Elizabeth brought him. She made better tea than anyone, even than his mother, who claimed to have become so Anglicized that she could make better tea than the English. Elizabeth did not turn the light on when she came in, so that, against the darkness of the rest of the room, the light from the window showed up the spiral of steam rising from the cup. A Spode cup in a deep saucer like a bowl, with a grey and white cow and a farmhouse on one side and a woman feeding hens on the other, it stood steaming there like a tempting advertisement for something that could not possibly taste as good as it looked.

Outside in the garden the birds were liquid with song, squandering all their music on this immaculate hour. As the freshness of the day wore off they would lapse into chirps and monosyllables, unless it rained and washed them a clean page of air to trill on again. Two or three thrushes – he liked to think it was always the same ones – were hopping on the lawn with a capricious air of not looking where they were going that was belied by sudden stabs into the grass. Working both legs together, they might just as well have had only one; and Oliver thought that if he were out there hopping with them, his action would be very much the same. Just as when he imagined what the floorboards would feel like if he could cross the room, the naked sole of the foot that was not there curved itself to the tickle of the wet grasses that were springboards for the clammy little feet of the birds.

Curiously, unless he were having one of the increasingly rare moods of depression in which he longed to be anywhere except where he was, it never irked him that he could not get out into the singing, pearly morning. He had been a spectator for so long now that he thought he could enjoy the garden just as well by looking at it as by taking part in its early-morning life. This room and his bed were the only tangible world. The garden outside, with its lawns stepping down to the bottom of the meadow that rose opposite in the hill with the clump of trees on top, obscuring half the hazy Wrekin, was a picture no more tantalizing than a landscape on a wall. One might trifle with the fancy of getting inside a picture, as Alice got into the looking-glass, but one's enjoyment of the picture was not spoiled because this was impossible.

So when people said: 'How dreadful for you to look at that lovely view and not be able to get out, especially in the spring,' he did not feel a pang. He did not try to explain, because he realized that nobody who had not been in bed for a long time or in prison could understand how one grew used to the egocentric shrinking of one's habitable world.

'I hear you may be up and about soon,' they said. 'How

137

wonderful that will be.' He did not try to explain that the wonder might be offset by the insecurity of being jolted out of cloistered habits. It was habits that made the day pass so swiftly, handing him on from event to little event like a bucket at a fire. His day was posted with landmarks. Meals, of course, always on time, thanks to his mother's clock mania; three pipes a day, after breakfast, lunch, and tea; the papers, the postman, the family to say good morning, Elizabeth in a white overall to rebandage his leg, David darting in after his walk instead of going to wash his hands for lunch, clattering across the floor in the clumsy shoes which Heather's latest doctor had built up to correct his pigeon toes. Elizabeth in a flowered overall and a cooking apron that never showed any traces of cooking, bringing and fetching trays; Cowlin with logs, for it was still cold enough for a fire, especially when your bloodstream had been short-circuited; David for his supper, the six o'clock news, the family for drinks, Evelyn for halma, a recent passion strong enough to lure her in from the farm. Black coffee after lunch and white after dinner, in accordance with his mother's convictions about caffein and sleep; his hot milk, his heart pills, his ginger biscuit, his washings, his bed-makings, his back-rubbings, all the little paraphernalia which keep an invalid too busy to lose his grip, which bolster his self-importance as a solace for the loss of his liberty.

Elizabeth's own love of routine and order made her pander to his habits. He had become so much attached to them that he wondered how he was going to shed them when he started to get up. Even if he did shed these, he would probably never shed the habit of having habits. As a young man, who thought nothing such fun as things arranged on the spur of the moment, who switched his tastes on impulse, who would not be pinned down to dates and hours and never came to a meal on time, he had despised old men who built themselves a protection of habits against the increasing precariousness they found in the world.

He knew that he would never go back to being a young man. His illness stood like a wall at the end of his youth. Ahead, at thirty, lay a quiescent maturity. He would probably become very soon an old man who walked the house like a rumbling lion if his meals were not on time, who changed his underwear at the same date each season, who lunched every day at the same table in the same club off an identical mutton chop and scoop of Stilton, who would not go anywhere abroad where he could not have bacon and egg for breakfast, by the sounds of whose morning toilet you could set your watch, who slit his letters with a paper-knife, who read *The Times* in the same order every day and would not allow himself to put pencil to the crossword puzzle before lunch, even if a solution leapt at him from the page.

Besides the trivia of his day, of course, there were bigger landmarks to keep him going, seeming disproportionately large in the confinement of his existence. There was Violet's wedding, more of a menace now than a landmark; there were visitors to see him, occasionally friends to stay. There were Elizabeth's week-ends, with the disruption of Mary Brewer, and the fun of plaguing Elizabeth when she returned clam-like from the arms of Arnold Clitheroe. Larger than anything at the moment, because it was exciting not only him but the entire household except Violet, loomed the homecoming of John. Oliver was very much looking forward to seeing him again, although he had never known him well. He had played golf with him and drunk beer with him and talked about things which put no strain on the mind, and had accepted him, as everyone else did, as 'suitable', without more than a passing wonder as to why Heather was in love with him. Oliver, at the time of their engagement, had been preoccupied with himself as an officer in the Shropshire Yeomanry. As he had been a Territorial, he got his commission at the beginning of the war and went early out to France. On his last week-end at home, Heather brought John Sandys to stay at Hinkley. John was still a civilian and did not count in those gallant days when Oliver thought it was all going to be like what one had heard of the last war. He was posing about fatalistically and planning a few last riotous days in London teeming with girls eager to let him drink champagne out of their slippers before going out to mud and blood. He had been in camp near Blackpool for a few months, and Blackpool was gay. He had brought a girl from there to stay at Hinkley, a curving blonde in what was then the fetchingly new uniform of the A.T.S. Heather, as always when she had an admirer around, was at the top of her form and it had been a gay week-end with barely time to notice John as more than an inoffensive chap so madly in love with Heather that he laughed

139

at everything she said. Oliver remembered how nice John had been to his mother. He had put it down at first to strategy, but realized afterwards, when John went on standing up for her and fetching things and asking her what she had been doing all day, to which she was not accustomed, that he was really like that. Oliver, excited, on the verge of something new and tremendous, who had never in his life known what it was like to be left behind, jollied his mother along for fear of a sentimental lapse, but she was gallant and corseted and self-possessed. She had not been so fat at the beginning of the war, which proved, she said now when they told her not to eat chocolates, that it was glandular.

On Oliver's last night, John and Heather had come in from a drive hand in hand and Heather had said: 'Don't laugh, folks, I'm going to marry this.' Mrs North had cried and Oliver had felt a little jealous, not understanding that this was her reaction to the strain of not crying over him. The curving blonde, her thoughts turned to matrimony, had made large eyes and provocative remarks at Oliver, souring slightly when he did not rise to the bait.

Oliver went to France; and soon after John joined up, Heather and he were married. What with their leaves never coinciding and John being sent out East when Oliver came home for good, he had hardly seen his brother-in-law and knew nothing of his life with Heather until she had told him a few weeks ago.

As a repatriated prisoner of war, one had expected John to look wasted, or worn and seedy, or at least slightly yellow. Mrs North had made elaborate plans about feeding him up and had saved her own butter ration for weeks. She had abandoned her scruples about never asking Fred Williams for anything, because he always gave it her, however inconvenient, and had laid in two hams, a duck, and a boiling fowl. She had bought a magnum of cod-liver oil and malt and told Heather that she was going to force John to have a milky drink in the middle of the morning and last thing at night.

'You won't have to force him,' Heather said scornfully. 'He loves milk.'

'We must be prepared to find a great change in him,' Mrs North kept saying, but when he arrived the only change was that he was slightly fatter and ruddier than when he went away. His waiting time in Australia had repaired the ravages of what had been one of the better Japanese prison camps. Violet wanted horror stories from him, but all he could offer were blurred photographs of jungle vegetation and unknown, bearded men with enormous knees and skinny calves emerging from shrunken shorts. Although he spoke of boredom and hunger and of brewing the same tea-leaves a dozen times and then tossing for who should eat the leaves, he made none of it seem uncomfortably real. Oliver thought that if he had had to suffer several months in a Japanese prison camp he would have made a much better story out of it than this.

John talked much more of the wonders and delights of Melbourne than of the horrors of the Malay Peninsula. Heather was justifiably aggrieved to find that he had brought neither the butter nor the sugar nor the chocolate for which she had so scandalized Mrs Ogilvie by asking.

'But Heather Bell darling' – Oliver had forgotten that he used to call Heather that – 'we weren't allowed to bring food. They issued a special order.'

'I bet everyone else did.'

'I don't think so. They searched our gear pretty carefully at Southampton.' However, he had brought Mrs North a huge bottle of eau-de-Cologne, cigars for Oliver, impossibly advanced toys for his children, a bushranger's fly switch for Violet, and for Heather six pairs of silk stockings and a length of peacock-blue brocade threaded with gold which he had had made into an evening coat.

This evening coat did more to make John's homecoming a success than anything else. Heather was touched to the verge of tears, not so much by the coat itself, although it was a glorious thing, as by the thought of John, who had always fled in terror from hairdressers and dressmakers and anything connected with feminine mysteries, bargaining for the brocade with a tout in the hotel and solemnly seeking out a French dressmaker, describing Heather's shape and discussing how she might like it made up. Because he liked plump women, John had remembered Heather as slightly fatter than she had been when he left her, so it fitted her perfectly now. He was thrilled with himself about it. For

141

months he had looked forward to showing her off in it when he took her out, hardly daring to consider her not liking it. Having overcome a slight chagrin at her declaring that it was a housecoat and must be worn as that and not as an evening wrap, John sat back beaming his gratification while Heather paraded before them all, preening herself, kicking out the stiff skirt as she turned, gold clips in her hair, gold ear-rings, a big filigree brooch and most of her bracelets decking her to suit her mood.

'Johnny, you are sweet, you are *sweet*,' she kept saying.

'You look stunning. I'm awfully glad you like it. It's a shame about the butter and things, Heather Bell, but you do see, don't you?' A momentary frown clouded her face at his tactlessness in reminding her of what she had forgiven and forgotten, and she said quickly: 'It's not the coat so much, though I adore it; it's you thinking of having it made and taking all that trouble. You are sweet. Isn't he sweet?' she inquired of the room at large, her eye unfortunately lighting on Fred, who went scarlet, half rose, cleared his throat, opened his mouth and took a deep breath as if he were going to say something important, then let all the breath out on a 'Yes' and subsided deflated into his chair.

'It certainly was darling of you to bring something for all of us,' said Mrs North, who was settled beatifically over her cocktail, without her usual shuttle trips to and from the kitchen.

'Oh, that's all right,' said John in the deep, pleasant voice which was one of his best features. He never called Mrs North anything, not knowing what to substitute for everyone else's 'Ma', to which he could not quite bring himself. He was a hefty, blue-chinned, settled-looking man of forty. Most men retain something of the boy in their face or expression all their life, and can never be called a completely finished adult product. Oliver, after his months of illness, noticed that even at his worst he sometimes looked like a peaky adolescent, but John was one of the few people who could be accurately described as 'grown up'. He had been husband and son and supporter and adviser and saviour to a frittering widowed mother ever since he was twenty. By the time he met and fell in love with Heather, fascinated by the insouciance in her which he lacked, he had realized that life was a thing of serious substance; even its jokes and pleasures must be given a certain weight of consideration. That

142

was why he laughed louder and danced and played games more energetically than most people. He also worked harder and worried more and had meant every word of what he promised when he stood beside Heather in Hinkley church.

He was good-looking in a dark, square-jawed way, his face rather too broad for its length, as if a heavy weight were pressing the crown of his head too close to his chin and causing the permanent horizontal wrinkles in his forehead. He was solid and muscular, with huge feet and knobbly, practical hands. In the grey flannel suit he had bought in Melbourne, and a white shirt that emphasized his tan, he looked attractive enough for anyone to love.

Heather did seem to love him. Her doubts and fears had evaporated and left her blithe. On his first night, she followed John about the house in a fascinated way, tending to his wants, and he was just as fascinated and eager to wait on her. The deadlock caused by each one's insistence that the other should empty the cocktail shaker was only resolved by Mrs North making another drink all round with a lavish disregard of the gin shortage.

It was an evening of celebration. They all had dinner in Oliver's room, and everyone, including Oliver, had quite a lot of the champagne which Mrs North had been hoarding behind a padlock for just such an occasion. Fred burned like fire and held forth on race form, Violet went black in the face twice with laughing and fell off her chair. Mrs North, who had had a plastic hair set and a mauve tinted rinse the day before, wore her black watered taffeta with the juvenile bows in which she could be heard coming a whole floor away and was not devastated because the meat was overcooked and the apples sour. Elizabeth became quite animated and Oliver thought, as always, that it was a pity she did not spend more of her time smiling. The pure, balanced structure of her face was too composed as a rule, but when it curved and sparkled in a smile she was very pretty. He looked at her once when everyone else, even Fred, who felt safer making the same noise as the others, like a canary trilling to a sewing machine, was laughing at some family allusion unknown to her, and caught her looking rather wistful. But she gave herself a little jerk and, getting up, began to collect plates.

Evelyn, who had been allowed to stay up to dinner, sat on

John's knee afterwards and he told her about riding in Australia. He had an idea of applying for a transfer to the Australian branch of the shipping firm for whom he had worked before the war and transplanting his family out there when he was demobilized. When he mentioned it tentatively, Heather had been so enthusiastic that he had had to say: 'Steady, steady, old girl; it'll want a lot of thinking about yet.'

'If we go Down Under, as they call it,' he told Evelyn, 'you'll have to come out and stay with us. You can get all the riding you want there.'

'Too much wire,' said Evelyn knowledgeably.

'The kids are never off their ponies,' went on John, resting his chin on the top of her head so that she could feel his voice rumbling through her skull. 'The ones that live in the country ride into town to school every day.'

'So they do in California,' said Evelyn. 'Daddy's going to buy a ranch, you know, so I'll be going out there as soon as he comes for me. I shan't be able to come to Australia, thank you very much all the same, Uncle John. Perhaps you could come and stay with us. And Heather, of course,' she added politely.

Heather had gone over to Oliver, swaying self-consciously in the housecoat whose brilliant colour was reflected in her eyes. He held out a hand. 'Happy?' he asked.

'A new woman,' she answered with the smile that had settled on her face for the evening. 'Look, Ollie, I don't have to tell you – forget everything I said, hm? You were quite right. I was tired and worried and imagined things. Everything's fine.' She looked quickly round at John's broad shoulders and the short curly hair at the back of his head. 'You do like him, don't you, Ollie?' she said urgently.

'An awful lot. I always have.'

'No, but you never knew each other very well before, and he's a bit shy of you now, you know, I can see that. He's always been so healthy himself, he's scared of seeing anyone in bed.'

Oliver patted her hand. 'You don't have to sell him to me,' he said. 'I've always liked him. I'm going to get up and have a round of golf with him tomorrow.' As always, when he had had a few more drinks than Dr Trevor allowed him, he felt he could do great deeds. His head felt light as thistledown and his heart was

144

going like a clockwork toy in his breast, chasing the blood into his limbs and making them strong and active and craving for movement.

'You look lovely in that coat,' he said, and put his arm round her waist, feeling his legs sliding to the floor and moving into a dance. The wireless was playing a waltz and he could feel himself dancing; the rhythm was in his legs, he could feel the dip and sway of his hips and shoulders as he danced down the stretch of shining floor, with Heather's waist straining against his firm arm and her head flung back. The lighted walls and pale, staring faces flashed past them like the wheeling crowd seen from a roundabout. They were at the end of the room and the band was louder. Poised for a moment on one leg, that miraculous leg which was better than ever since he had last seen it smeared all over the stretcher in the dressing tent, he threw Heather into a smooth reverse. The wheeling walls went whirling round again and they were waltzing up the room, working harder against the slight slope. Panting, he opened his eyes to see the flat white counterpane in front of him and Heather standing uncomfortably within his arm.

She looked relieved. 'Golly,' she said, letting out her breath, 'you did give me a fright. I thought you were going to pass out or something, you looked so queer.' He felt queer. His head was swimming and his leg twitching and the clockwork toy in his breast had become a sledgehammer. He grinned and told her he felt fine, and when she had gone back to John he caught Elizabeth's eye, and bless her, she coped without making a commotion and gave him two of his pills and made herself unpopular by turning everyone out of his room, letting them think she was fussing unnecessarily.

Heather said: 'It's ridiculous, Ollie, she never lets you have any fun. All this Irma Grese stuff. Just because she's your nurse, she thinks she can treat you like a child.'

Even his mother said: 'Of course, you're in charge, dear, but I do think, Elizabeth, that now he's much better you needn't pamper him quite so much. After all, he'll be getting up soon.'

Oliver drew up the sheet as she came to his bed, so that she could not see the thudding of his heart under his pyjama jacket. Elizabeth was polite but firm. They all went away, and when

Elizabeth came back from taking Evelyn up to bed, Oliver said:
'Sorry to let you down. I couldn't spoil the party, though, and
have them all think I was going to peg out. I didn't know they
were going to round on you.'

'Don't worry about me,' she said, raising her eyebrows slightly.
'I don't mind what they think so long as they don't interfere
with my treatment of you.'

'I'm sorry, anyway,' he persisted. 'They were horrid.'

'*I* don't care,' she said, sticking a thermometer in his mouth
and picking up his wrist. 'I can take care of myself. You evidently
can't. One drink too many and your heart starts tachycardia-ing
all over the place.' She sounded quite cross.

He took the thermometer out to say: 'You've been here for
too long. You're getting sick of me. Why don't you chuck it
up? I'll never get any better.'

'When I take on a case,' said Elizabeth, without taking her
eyes from her watch, 'I like to see it through till it either gets
better or dies.'

'Doesn't matter which I do so long as it's one or the other?'

'No. Put that thermometer back and for heaven's sake let me
count. I've had to start again six times.'

Guiltily, after he was settled, his mother stole into his room
in her dressing-gown. He was lying looking out of the window,
not sleeping, hardly breathing, trying not to think, just keeping
everything as still as possible. His mother stumbled over something, so he switched on the bedside light. The plastic set was
carefully pinned into a myriad Grecian whorls, highlights of cold
cream larded her face, and she wore the cotton gloves in which
she slept after she had greased her hands.

'I know I shouldn't come in,' she said, 'because Elizabeth said
you were to settle early, but really I think I might be allowed to
judge what I can and can't do with my own son. You're perfectly
all right, aren't you, darling? The party didn't make you feel
bad?'

'Of course not, Ma, I'm fine,' he said. 'Don't *fuss*.'

'It's Elizabeth who fusses, not me. I was a little sore with her
tonight when we were all having such a good time. I thought
she was too, but she doesn't like to have your schedule upset;

146

I suppose it's what they teach them in hospital. Maybe she's right, but – I don't know – she's such an odd girl. She works so well in the house and she couldn't be more careful with you. She's good to me too, but – –' She laughed. 'It sounds kind of silly, but I don't even know if she likes me or not. It makes me nervous, d'you know it?' She suddenly gave a gasp. 'Well, for heaven's sake! What d'you think I've forgotten? Your Thermos, darling. Fancy me forgetting your tea! You can't think much of me as a mother, when a little bit of excitement goes to my head and drives everything out of it. Silly old fool that I am. . . .' She started to go out, grumbling to herself.

'Don't bother now, Ma, for heaven's sake,' said Oliver, who wanted peace more than tea. 'I don't think I shall wake tonight; I feel pretty sleepy.'

'You might, though, and then what would you think of me? It won't take long to boil the kettle,' she said from the door. 'I'll be right back.'

When she came back with the Thermos, she had remembered what she had originally come in to say. 'Isn't it lovely to see Heather so happy?' she asked, making vicious efforts to tighten the Thermos cap beyond its limit. 'It's just as I said all along, you see, when everything seemed to get in her hair. She was only that way because she was missing John, though she wouldn't let on to it. And I'm not surprised; he's such a lovely person. And listen, darling, he may look perfectly fit, but that time in prison has told on him. There's a strain behind the eyes, I can see. I'm going to insist on his resting up and eating properly . . . I've been wondering whether I ought to have him see a doctor.' She was determined that not even John's rude health should cheat her of her debilitated prisoner. 'I wonder what he thinks about her Turning,' she went on, untucking the bottom corner of Oliver's bed and retucking it. 'Have either of them talked about it to you?'

'Why should they?' he said languidly. 'It's no one else's business but theirs.'

'Except that Heather happens to be my daughter,' said his mother a little huffily, 'and I want to know that nothing's going to spoil her happiness.' Her eyes took on their far-away gaze. She looked through the pince-nez into a mother's paradise. 'I can't tell you how lovely it is to me to see them together. And those

147

children ... little David taking to his father at once, didn't you love it? He's going to look just like John, with those very black eyes. ...' She rambled on, while Oliver waited patiently. She would stop some time, but the unaccustomed wine had stimulated her to even more than her ordinary nocturnal volubility. She began to make plans about Heather and John in Australia: where they would live, whether they would be able to afford servants, how soon David could start school, whether she might not combine visits to them with visits to Philadelphia.

'Go to bed,' Oliver said, coming back from a reverie to find her still talking. 'You must be tired, Ma.'

'Don't worry about me, darling boy. You're the one we have to worry about. Can you imagine me forgetting your tea just because my son-in-law's come home? I can't get over it.' He knew she would come back after she had left him, but he did not know it would be to whisper in the dark: 'Listen, dearest Ollie, don't think because I make a lot of song and dance about John and Heather that any of it means a thing to me compared to you recovering. I suppose I ought not to say this, but I would almost wish John dead in Malaya if that could give you back your leg again and your strong heart.'

CHAPTER 8

PERHAPS the novelty of John would have taken longer to wear off if he had not been at home so much. He had three months' leave, and by the end of the first month Heather was beginning to feel like a mother at the end of the school holidays. She was heard to remark that it was unnatural for a man to be in to lunch every day. John was not discontented or at a loose end. He asked nothing better than to be about the house and farm all day, reading and smoking and making marginal notes in his books, chatting sociably to anyone who felt like it, taking long striding walks with Violet's dogs and leaving muddy boots in the scullery, or bringing in an earthy head of celery which he thought would be nice for lunch just when the meal was being dished up. When Heather mentioned the boots, and muttered something about

148

poor Mrs Cowlin and no wonder there was class warfare, he sneaked off to the scullery to clean them himself. He could not find the shoe-box and did not like to ask, as he wanted it to be a surprise for Heather, so he used a table knife and a nailbrush and scraped the mud into what he took to be a bucket of dirty water instead of his daughter's underwear in soak.

He was a large man and he moved slowly. He had a habit of standing in doorways when people were coming along with trays. Oliver noticed that Heather sometimes looked irritated when she came into his room and found John ruminating there, particularly when he levered himself up for her or tried to take from her anything she was carrying. She adopted Oliver's expression of 'I'm not paralysed', which he used on his mother when she wanted to fill his pipe or comb his hair or scoop out the inside of his baked potato. Oliver remembered, from the days when they used to go out, how John would fling wide a door for a woman as if she were twice the size, and how he would skip about so as always to be on the outside of the pavement. They had once taken a most unsettled walk along the grass strip between the traffic lanes of a by-pass. He used to put his hand under Heather's elbow to help her up steps or even up the gentle slope of a theatre aisle, and she would shake him off and tell him she was not a cripple, just as she did now, and he would laugh indulgently and do it again the next time, just as he did now. David had spilled cocoa over the housecoat and Heather had not yet sent it to be cleaned. She had begun to mention again the butter and sugar and chocolate, and after she had weighed John she mentioned it more frequently and frowned when she saw him plastering his bread unthinkingly with the butter ration. Oliver wondered whether John noticed the gradual waning of her first enthusiasm. He was never anything but amiable and pleasant and always ready to welcome the sudden impulses of either affection or compunction which caused her to fling herself at him declaring that he was sweet and she loved him. If she kissed him, he would hold up his cheek and screw up the side of his face to receive it. Oliver had never seen him kiss her on the lips in public.

When he went to London for the week-end, to see his mother and the manager of his firm, Heather tidied her room, which she and John now shared, the children being together in the spare room. Oliver heard her creaking about over his head all morning, opening and shutting drawers and cupboards, moving furniture, Hoovering, and he wondered how many of his things John would be able to find when he came back. Heather soon grew restless, however, and said several times: 'I wonder what John's doing,' or: 'Doesn't the house seem empty?' or to David: 'Daddy will be home tomorrow.' After tea on Sunday, she started to wander in and out of Oliver's room saying: 'Johnny should be here by six. I have missed him. Isn't it funny – in this short time I've got more used to having him about than I got used to not having him all those months he was away. Yet when he is here we don't seem to get on so well.'

'I never hear you fighting,' Oliver said.

'Of course not; he won't. You hear me snapping at him, though, and it just bounces back to me off him.'

'I suppose all husbands and wives get on each other's nerves at times,' said Oliver obligingly.

'But I don't get on his. At least, if I do, he doesn't show it. He doesn't show if he minds my snapping at him either, which makes me feel worse for doing it. It's just that I feel peevish, you know, Ollie, and because he's there he gets the brunt of it. But when he goes away I miss him. I feel I should have been charming all this week-end if he'd been here. I suppose that's the way love goes,' she said, without much conviction.

She lingered, balancing Oliver's tea-tray on one hip. She seemed to be in a tractable mood. You had to pick your moment carefully if you wanted to ask Heather things like: 'What does he think of your being a Catholic? I had a sort of tentative, abstract talk with him the other day, and I must say he doesn't seem to have been brought up to see much farther than the Thirty-nine Articles. I don't imagine he approves?'

'Obviously not. He wrote that from Australia, but the silly part is, I don't get a chance to try and explain, because now he simply won't discuss it. He looks like a hurt dog when he sees me going off to church, but if I ever try to tell him how I feel about it, or what made me want to be a Catholic, he cricks his jaw sideways like he does when he feels grim about something and says: "You must do what you think is right. One person can't interfere with another's religion." And though I'd bite his head

150

off if he did, I almost wish he would in a way, because then I could feel martyred. St Heather of Hinkley, persecuted for her faith. I should get a hell of a kick out of that. Heavens, is that the right time? I must go and make myself beautiful; he does like to see me done up.' She went away and Oliver heard her asking her mother if she had any Thawpit. She was going to try to get the cocoa stain out of the housecoat.

Six o'clock passed, and at seven Heather, who had been up and down the stairs countless times to look out of the front door, came into Oliver's room for a drink and said: 'I *do* wish he'd come. What on earth d'you suppose has happened to him?'

'Train was probably held up,' said Oliver. 'I shouldn't worry.'

'Good Lord, I'm not *worrying*. But I can't get David to sleep. John promised he'd see him in bed when he got home. I do think he might come.'

At eight o'clock David, struggling against drowsiness, fell asleep sitting up. Heather tucked him up and came downstairs to give them a pathetic description of David, white from exhaustion. 'It's too bad of Johnny,' she said.

'He probably missed his train,' her mother told her. 'Don't carry on so, Heather, as if no one had ever missed a train before.'

'He's not the sort of man who misses trains,' said Heather, 'and if he had he'd have telephoned. He always thinks of doing things like that.'

'Perhaps the car wouldn't start at Shrewsbury,' Oliver sugested.

'Cars always start for him. He understands them.' She fidgeted about tensely, swishing the skirt of the housecoat. 'Relax,' Violet grunted, but Heather became increasingly worried and soon infected her mother, who was always game for a spot of anxiety. 'I'm sure something's happened to him; I've got a premonition,' Heather said, leaning across Oliver to peer out of the window, as if she expected to see John's ghost materializing on the moonlit lawn. 'Fancy going through all that in Burma only to end up under the wheels of a London taxi,' she said dramatically.

'Don't be ridiculous, Heather,' said her mother, her mind instantly seizing and embroidering on the vision. 'Besides, the hospital would have let us know. I put his name on all his shirts only last week.'

151

'If only I could get in *touch* with him at least he'd know I was worrying about him,' said Heather ingenuously. 'Supposing there's been a train smash, Ma, or he got appendicitis, or lost his memory, from delayed shell-shock or something.' They discussed the ghoulish possibilities of John's fate until Violet asked with an enormous yawn: 'How much longer are we going to wait dinner?'

'Let's have it, shall we?' said Mrs North. 'I can keep John's hot for him. Come along, Heather, it'll pep you up. We're having the pheasant, pot-roasted.'

'I couldn't eat a thing,' boasted Heather. 'I think I'll go up and cuddle my babies.'

Violet snorted as she went out of the room. 'Golly,' she said pityingly, 'I wouldn't be put off roast pheasant because Fred was a couple of hours late. The other day, when he didn't come back for tea, I got sick of waiting and ate all the grub. When he came in starving there was nothing to eat; it was a scream.'

'I bet Fred didn't think so,' said Oliver.

'Oh, he didn't mind,' said Violet vaguely. 'He had some bread or something.'

By half past nine Heather was certain that John was dead, or at least dying. She switched from restlessness to wan courage. One had the feeling that she might go up soon and change the peacock-blue housecoat for black, with veiling. When her mother kept telling her that John's business had probably kept him another night in town, Heather shook her head with a sad smile and repeated: 'He would have rung up. He would never be so late without letting me know.' When her mother had gone out to satisfy herself that John's dinner was not drying up, Heather said to Oliver: 'This is judgement on me for not being nicer to him. I do wish I'd gone to the cinema with him yesterday when he asked me. I said I had to bath Susan, though I really could have left her to Elizabeth, and he went off so pathetically all by himself.'

'I wonder he didn't take Elizabeth,' Oliver said.

'She'd have gone with him like a shot too,' answered Heather, and Oliver looked up at the rancour in her voice. 'Don't think I haven't noticed how she makes up to him. She never produced that smile for any of us.'

'You're crazy,' Oliver said. 'Just because she likes him and feels friendly. You always complain she's too unfriendly. What do you want?'

'I don't want her to make passes at my husband, I know that.'

'You do say the silliest things when you're worked up,' Oliver said, annoyed. 'Anything less likely than John and Elizabeth having an intrigue.'

'Oh, I didn't say *John* would,' Heather said in an exasperated voice. 'He's never looked at another woman since we were married, and not many before that, I should think. He's almost inhumanly chaste. Oh dear, I do wish I'd gone to the cinema with him.'

'Never mind,' said Oliver cheerfully, 'it's very nice going to the movies by yourself. You can concentrate better without someone asking you whether you're enjoying it, or have you got a match.'

'Yes,' said Heather, sounding as if she were going to cry, 'but he didn't enjoy the film.' Her mouth trembled, her eyes were blurring and her face was getting red, when suddenly the well-known squeal of the family car's brakes, which not even John was able to mute, drained the blood from her face with a gasp and she rushed out without shutting the door, so that Oliver heard her rapturous greeting of John. He came in looking rather sheepish, with Heather hanging on to his arm, recovered enough now to start asking questions. 'But why didn't you ring up, Johnny? That's what I can't understand. Why didn't you let me know?'

'I couldn't get through. I tried several times, but I couldn't even get Toll. I'm terribly sorry, darling, I'd no idea you'd get so worried, or I'd never have stayed on for a later train when old George suggested it. Hullo, Onions, how've you been?' Onions was John's name for Oliver.

'Oh, worried sick about you, of course, old boy,' said Oliver, grinning. 'You really shouldn't do this sort of thing. It's bad for my heart.'

Heather had let go of John and was standing a little apart, scrutinizing him with a slight pucker, as if surprised to find him not looking quite the same as her anxious imagination had drawn him. 'George Hanbury,' she said with contempt. 'Fancy anyone missing three trains for the sake of playing billiards with George Hanbury.'

'I rather like him,' said John apologetically. 'I know you don't, but it's not his fault if he hasn't got any of the social graces. You've never forgotten that time he spilled his drink on your dress, have you?' he added, smiling his pride at her fastidiousness.

'Don't remind me of it,' she said. 'And just to make everything perfect, he trod on the dress when we were dancing afterwards, and tore it.'

'Trust old George,' John laughed. 'He damn nearly tore the cloth today. He will one of these days with that backhanded twist shot of his. You ought to see it, Onions; dangerous, but most effective when the angle's tricky. He gets his right arm cuddled round his waist and his left elbow somewhere up by his ear.'

'I think I'll go up to bed,' Heather said, and John leaped to open the door for her. 'By the way, old girl,' he said as she came towards him, 'did you know there was a colossal great mark on the skirt of that coat thing? You ought to do something about it.'

Oliver could not see his sister's face, but he knew she had worked on the stain for more than half an hour. Meeting her mother in the doorway, she burst out: 'Ma, *where* d'you think he's been? Playing billiards with that awful George Hanbury.'

'Who's George Hanbury, dear?' asked her mother comfortably, and patted John's arm. 'Your dinner's all ready for you, Johnny.' She disentangled her pendant watch from the chain of her pince-nez. 'Why, it's two and a half minutes past ten. You must be starving. Did you have a good time, dear?'

'Grand, thanks. I'm awfully sorry I'm so late.'

'I don't mind. I like you to get among your own crowd again, after being stuck down here in our rut for so long. You should get up to town more. Would you like to have your dinner in here? Heather will get it for you. She's been terribly worried, poor child, but you see now, Heather, I was quite right; he was with friends. You'll find everything in the oven, dear, and his soup's in the saucepan.' In the silence which followed Heather's slam of the door, they heard her footsteps going not to the kitchen but up the stairs.

'Well,' said Mrs North, with a nervous little mm-hm, 'well, I'll just go and see that she can find everything.'

When she had gone out, John pleated his forehead. 'Actually,' he said, 'I had some beer and sandwiches at Shrewsbury, because I thought I'd be too late for dinner. I don't really want anything, though as she's kept it specially . . .'

'You have it, my boy,' said Oliver firmly. 'You've caused enough trouble for one day. You may not think it, but Heather has honestly been awfully worried. You might have been one of the children, the way she was carrying on. Most gratifying. Don't pay any attention to all this.' He waved his hand up towards the rattling of the handles of Heather's tallboy as she banged drawers open and shut. 'Reaction.' He thought he was being a ray of sunshine, putting things right between them, but John stiffened and his face took on a stubborn, blindly loyal look. 'I'm sorry I've been such a nuisance,' he said. 'It was damn thoughtless of me.' He left the room before Oliver could try again to discuss Heather.

Oliver wondered where he would go now. Upstairs to risk apologizing to Heather, or politely to the kitchen to be plied with food he did not want? If he had any sense, he would go up and make violent love to Heather before she could say a word. How wise Oliver felt lying here knowing he could run people's lives better than they could themselves. He had visions of himself as the oracle and influence of the household, but it was difficult to be either an oracle or an influence when people kept going away and you could not get up and follow them and make them listen.

'What have you been plotting with my mother?' Oliver asked, when Dr Trevor came into his room nearly half an hour after he had heard his car on the drive.

'Plotting?' Dr Trevor hitched his trousers up his thick thighs and sat down in his Rodin attitude. 'What d'you mean? I've been having a glass of sherry with her, if you want to know.'

'The wall between this room and the drawing-room,' said Oliver sententiously, 'is quite thin. It was built much later than the rest of the house; about a hundred years ago in fact, when the owners decided that two rooms would be cosier than one big one. I can hear the tone of people's voices through it, if not the actual words, and after months of practice I am very good at spotting the indulgent note that means they're talking about me.'

'You're wrong this time,' said Dr Trevor, with the quirk that did duty for a smile on his granite face. 'We were talking about Violet's wedding.'

'And,' said Oliver, with a triumphant glance at Elizabeth, 'Ma was telling you not to let me up for it, because the excitement would be too much for me.'

Dr Trevor could look you in the eye and lie without moving a muscle. 'Whether you get up or not,' he said, 'has nothing to do with your mother. It depends entirely on the state of your heart. If you'll shut up for a minute, I'll tell you what I think of it.' Elizabeth, with her usual inconspicuous efficiency, had brought in the stethoscope which he had left in his mackintosh and she handed it to him while he was patting his jacket pockets. When he was there she automatically assumed her hospital pose: hands behind back, head slightly on one side, expression politely intelligent, standing perfectly still, yet poised to spring for anything he needed, a second before he asked for it.

Oliver had not particularly wanted to go to Violet's wedding, until he realized that his mother meant to protect him from it, whether he were fit enough to go or not. It then became an issue of independence. To appear at the wedding would be the first move towards the normal life which his fragile heart dreaded, but on which he knew he must embark some time. There were times when he felt he could lie here for the rest of his life, when he could not face the effort to stop being an invalid. There were other times when he felt he could not stay in bed an hour longer and fancied himself striding up the hill towards the clump of trees so vividly that he was there already, with the roofs and chimneys of the house below him, the unequal fields with double hedgerows marking the lanes, and beyond, before the hills rose again, the winding line of trees that congregated along the Severn.

He had been dreading the ordeal of Violet's wedding, but because his mother was determined that he should not go, he was equally determined now that he could stand it. It would be a test of how much he was fit for it.

Violet's head and shoulders filled the window before Dr Trevor had finished with Oliver. It was pouring with rain, and she was

156

standing in the flower-beds in gum boots with a sack over her head. 'Well,' she said, 'what's the verdict?'

Elizabeth raised her finger in a hushing gesture, and Dr Trevor just shifted his eyes slightly and went on listening, so Violet waited, whistling through her teeth, squelching her feet up and down in the mud with a noise like blancmange coming out of a mould.

At last Dr Trevor leaned back with his stethoscope dangling on his broad chest, glanced at Oliver, then at Violet, and gave his head half a shake. 'Wiser not, I think,' he said. 'It's going on fine, but it's early days yet to face a crowd and too much carting about. I don't want to risk putting you back months; it isn't worth it.'

'It is worth it!' Violet stamped her foot with a splosh that spattered her skirt. 'I'm sure he's well enough. He told me yesterday he was, when Ma was saying he wasn't. I do think it's a swizz. Who's going to give me away? Nobody cares about my wedding.'

'As far as I can gather,' said Dr Trevor, fixing her with a small, clear eye like a tortoise, 'the whole house is revolving round your wedding, but I don't see that it will make it extra lively if your brother dies of it.'

'Dies!' snorted Violet. 'Don't be such an old woman.'

'It's all right, Vi,' said Oliver. 'It's a conspiracy. I'm perfectly fit to come. They're just treating me like a kid that doesn't know when it's tired.' He had slumped down in the bed. At the back of his mind he was relieved, but he was not going to admit it.

'You're both being exceedingly childish,' said Dr Trevor, stuffing his stethoscope into his pocket. 'Run away now, Violet, because I want to look at Oliver's leg.' She scowled at him, said: 'Hard cheese, Ollie,' and went slouching away over the lawn, hunched in the sack, kicking up little spurts of water.

When Dr Trevor had finished and Elizabeth was rearranging the bedclothes, he said: 'Sorry about the wedding, old chap, but don't think I've been influenced by your mother, because I'm in the habit of making my own decisions. I tell you what, you can start sitting out of bed for five minutes every day. You can sit in that chair and dangle your leg. Later on, when the wheelchair comes, you can go out in the garden when it's warm enough.'

'I don't want to get up,' muttered Oliver.

'See that he does it regularly, Nurse, once he's started.'

'I will, sir.' She went out to get Oliver's pulse chart, and Dr Trevor said, with a jerk of his square head: 'Nice girl that. Reminds me of a Swedish girl I used to know, fresh and cool, like butter. She in love with you yet?'

'Don't talk tripe,' Oliver told him.

'Oh, I'm not flattering you. It's inevitable with any young male patient they nurse long enough. Same with the patient – natural reaction of dependence and gratitude, even with far worse lookers than this one. That's the way nurses get engaged. Disastrous sometimes, when he sees her out of uniform and she sees him out of pyjamas and they don't need each other any more.'

Violet was furious. She received most ungraciously the idea of John giving her away. She had wanted Oliver, and Oliver had wanted to do it. Nobody ever let her do anything for him, and now she was not even allowed to give him this bit of fun.

'Glad you think it's fun,' said Heather. 'I should say he was well out of it. You needn't think it's going to be any fun for John to stand up there in that depressing church with half the county criticizing his back view, and to try and make a convincing speech afterwards about how charming you are, which Mrs Ogilvie will take down in mental shorthand for the benefit of everyone we haven't invited.'

'Why do it then?' retorted Violet. 'I'm sure *I* never asked him.'

No one but Heather was allowed to slight John. She fired up in his defence. 'Because he's too good-natured to refuse, that's why. You don't imagine he's going to get a thrill out of delivering you over to Fred like a lamb to the slaughter? No, not a lamb' – she looked coldly up and down Violet, who was standing in front of her dishevelled, in the Land Girl jersey and stained grey flannels, a bandana handkerchief bulging the pocket in the seat – 'some old bellwether.'

'Cheek!' shouted Violet. 'Did you hear what she said, Fred. Hit her.'

'Hit me yourself,' grinned Heather. 'You're stronger than he is.' The most embarrassing part of this quarrel was that both Fred

158

and John were in the room. The sisters never cared who was there when they started on each other; in fact, an audience seemed to encourage them. Fred had been crimson since the beginning of the argument, but his nose now flushed to an even richer shade. It forced itself on your attention, dominating his face, yet so out of proportion to it that it seemed no more part of his anatomy than the lamp the miner wears in his hat. When he was very embarrassed he blinked his eyes rapidly, as if they could not stand the glare from his nose.

John had reddened too, a flush under the tan of his broad cheeks. 'You're making a fool of yourself, Heather Bell,' he said. 'Dry up.'

She immediately stopped championing him. 'I certainly will. I was only trying to stand up for you, since you're incapable of doing it yourself. Considering you told me you didn't want to give Vi away and wished Ma hadn't asked you, because you couldn't very well refuse – –'

'Well, I like that!' cried Violet, now suddenly on the same side as Heather.

Oliver butted in rashly with: 'He didn't mean it like that, Vi. It's only because he's scared of making a public exhibition of himself.'

'Oh, don't *you* interfere!' Mrs North started forward with a little horrified exclamation as Heather rounded on him. 'You lie there doling out wisdom from your bed like a Salvationist handing out tracts. How do *you* know what he meant or didn't mean? Everybody's too damned interested in everybody else's business in this house, if you ask me. And that goes for you too,' she said, gathering up David from the floor where he was wailing an accompaniment to the angry voices, and bearing him away with his trousers rucked up and his legs dangling.

When she had gone, Fred made everybody jump by clearing his throat with a noise like a bad gear change. He got up and stood with his right hand wavering in the air between himself and Mrs North. He never knew whether he were supposed to shake hands with her. 'Er – well, I must be getting along,' he said. 'Thanks ever so much for the drink.'

'Not a bit,' she said, and went with him to the door. 'Say, I'm awfully sorry the girls behaved so badly. I can't think what's

159

gotten into them lately. One's got her husband home from a prison camp and the other's just going to be married, yet they're as quarrelsome as a couple of alley cats. You'll have to knock some sense into Violet when you get her to yourself.' Fred looked shocked. Mrs North stepped back as Violet pushed roughly past her and trod on the back of Fred's heels to get him out of the doorway.

'If your sisters weren't so large,' said Mrs North, waving good-bye to Fred and dropping the artificial smile as she came back into the room, 'I'd spank them both.'

'Too late now,' said Oliver. 'They've been like this ever since they could speak.'

'Never as bad as this, dear. Not Heather, anyway. She just seems deliberately to say the most hurtful things she can think of to everybody. Only when she's tired and cross, of course,' she added, seeing John stiffen. 'But she oughtn't to get tired and cross, John. She hasn't all that much to do, now that Elizabeth helps her so much. Don't you think we should have her see some-one? She may not be well.'

'I did suggest it, actually,' said John, 'but she wasn't keen. Said she felt perfectly well.'

'I'm sure there's something wrong,' said Mrs North, 'but *I* can't do anything with her. I wonder you don't take her in hand. It can't be much fun for you to have her acting this way.' John had his hands on the arms of his chair and was looking round for an excuse to escape. He could not bear to discuss Heather.

'Why don't you try a bit of cave-man stuff, old boy?' suggested Oliver. 'She'd probably love it. One damn good hiding and she'll be licking your boots.' John fidgeted himself to his feet, and gave a hollow laugh, as if trying to pass off Oliver's bad taste as a joke. 'Well, I suppose I'd better go and change before dinner,' he mumbled to no one in particular.

Oliver pointed to where his hunting-crop hung with its lash neatly curled on two nails above the fireplace. 'Take that with you, and next time she lashes you with her tongue give it her back with that.' He raised his arm and brought it sharply down across his chest, flicking his wrist and imitating the crack of the thong with his tongue against his teeth.

John stood in the middle of the room, jingling the change in his trouser pockets, head poked forward between raised shoulders, chin jutting and accordion pleats forming in the loose skin of his forehead. He did not want to discuss Heather. He did not want to stay and hear them talk about her, yet he did not want to go away without saying something in her defence that would stop them criticizing her after he had gone.

'It's not her fault really, you know,' he began and stopped. This implied that he agreed that there was something wrong with their relationship, and his loyalty would not let him admit even that.

'Not her fault?' Oliver pounced. 'I suppose you're going to say that when she jumps down your throat it's your fault for opening your mouth wide enough.'

'Something like that,' said John, gazing out of the window and stretching the crease out of the front of his trousers by clenching his huge fists in the pockets. 'I know I can be jolly irritating. My mother always tells me that I'm the most annoying man she's ever met, bar my father.'

'I dare say it's six of one and half a dozen of the other,' said Mrs North, with the soothing sound of the English Nanny from whom she had picked up the expression. 'Run along now, dear, and change, or you'll be late for dinner. And don't let's worry about Heather; I'm sure she'll be all right when she gets a rest. You and she shall go off for a holiday somewhere, away from all of us, and enjoy yourselves. You deserve a little enjoyment after the terrible time you've had.' Even if he did not look like a small boy, he could still be quite successfully treated like one. He gave her one of his charming crushed smiles and ambled out of the room.

'I can't bear it,' said Mrs North, shutting the door after him and sinking into a chair with her tubby little legs stuck out. 'I can't bear him to be so humble. No wonder Heather feels sometimes she wants to stir him with a red-hot poker.'

'He's got no more idea how to treat her than my foot,' said Oliver. 'The mashed one.'

'Don't, dear.' She gave an involuntary glance at the flat side of the counterpane. 'I worry about them, d'you know it?' she said impressively, as if there were something unusual in her worrying about anything.

'Takes your mind off me, anyway.'

'Oh, you. You're the only one who doesn't give me any anxiety these days. This house was quite peaceful during the war. Now that we've got peace it's all haywire. There's Susan teething, Violet acting like a temperamental movie star and looking like a cowhand, Evelyn running wild as a mountain goat, and John and Heather right off key. Mrs Cowlin's always more lunatic in the spring, and Cowlin's sulking because I want some of the cockerels killed for the wedding.' She sighed. 'Even Elizabeth isn't the comfort she was. She's so quiet and distrait. And every time she comes back from her week-end I've noticed she's more distrait than ever. I don't believe she'll stay with us much longer. Maybe she's in love; I believe she's got some man in town. I have asked her, but she just went cagey on me, and it's not natural for a girl in love not to want to talk about it.' Oliver said nothing, and his mother swept on in the mid-stream of her woes. 'And to crown everything, that poor, mad creature will be here next week, and you heard what John said about his annoying her? The poor man will be torn to shreds between his mother and Heather, and so will my nerves.'

'Mine, too,' murmured Oliver, and wished he had not, for she changed her mind about not worrying over him and decided that her biggest worry of all was that the unsettled atmosphere of the house was bad for him.

'I'm going to make new rules about people coming in here,' she said. 'Not too many at a time, and if they fight they'll be thrown out on their ear. I have it all planned about the reception. It'll be in the drawing-room, with the doors open on to the garden if it's fine enough, and just the people you want to see will be allowed in here, a few at a time. I'm not going to have a whole mob barging in and wearing you out.'

'But I like seeing people,' objected Oliver. 'I shall want to see them all, especially tricked out in their best. I want to see all the women's hats.'

'You can see them through the window if it doesn't rain. Anyway, you don't like having people in here who bicker, I'm sure of that.'

'I quite enjoy it if I don't have to take sides. It's like having a seat in the stalls at *Private Lives*.'

'Darling boy. Remember when you took me to see that, years before the war, and we went on to the *Sa*voy? You were such a personable young man,' she gazed at him misty-eyed, and then the clock by his bed suddenly came into focus through the mist and she plumped her little feet on to the ground, and bustled away, with her head full of dinner.

*

The poor mad creature was John's mother, Lady Sandys. She was not really mad, but suffered from spasmodic attacks of kleptomania, which had increased under psychotherapy, so were now left untreated, and politely ignored. She had been to stay at Hinkley once before, at the time of Heather's wedding, so everyone but Elizabeth knew the rules of the game. If you missed anything, you kept quiet about it and waited patiently, referring to your loss, if necessary, as having gone astray in the post.

Lady Sandys had a companion called Miss Smutts, a pear-shaped little old bore with a moustache, who had become adept at retrieving alien goods from the ingenious places where Lady Sandys hid them when the fit was on her. If she did not know to whom they belonged, Miss Smutts would put the watch, or the glove, or the bracelet, on the half-moon table in the upstairs passage, and all you had to do was to help yourself. Everyone automatically glanced at the table whenever they passed it, as hotel visitors glance at their pigeon-hole for letters every time they pass the porter's desk. Lady Sandys herself could pass the half-moon table with its array of personal knick-knacks without more than a fleeting surprise that anyone should leave a shoe or a toothbrush there, for once having taken the things, she lost interest in them and seemed quite unaware of ever having taken them. She might take them again, however, if the fit came on her, so it was wise to retrieve your property as soon as possible.

She never took money. She was theoretically honest but criminally vague. Since the death of his father, when he was only just grown up, John had always managed her affairs, and while he was away she had got into intricate tangles, for she kept Miss Smutts on a low plane and would not trust her to do the accounts. Lady Sandys would pay some tradesmen six times and others not at all, making it up to them just in time by having

163

them to tea, squandering her entire butter ration on crumpets in a silver dish and paying them not only what she owed, but a bit extra to buy something for their wives and children, in whom, after chat over the crumpets, she was passionately interested. If they lost anything while they were there, Miss Smutts would return it with a formal little note cramped into the top of the notepaper, to say that their gloves, or their handkerchief, or their umbrella, had been found behind the hat-stand in the hall.

When John came home he had considerable trouble in straightening things out. Some of the local tradesmen were getting blasé about tea-parties, and the manager of the bakery had actually heard Lady Sandys taking his stick out of the umbrella stand while he was washing his hands in the gents' cloakroom. There was quite a boycott consolidating round her in the Ebury Street neighbourhood, and Miss Smutts had to make constant trips to the town hall to re-register them. It was not good enough, John was told, when he went the rounds of his mother's creditors. They would like to oblige her ladyship, but what with having to make up their accounts weekly and send returns to the Ministry, she put their books right out. Then, too, she would insist on ordering things by telephone; and although they could never be delivered, it was a nuisance having her ringing up several times in a morning, when there was a queue of people in the shop waiting to draw their rations. When she could not wait any longer for the non-existent errand-boy, and went down to the shop herself, she could never be made to understand about points, although she liked to gamble with them daringly, as if they were roulette chips. She had once caused quite a disturbance in a small dairy by trying to buy baked beans with clothing coupons.

On top of this, the landlord of her flat did not want to renew her lease at the end of the month. She had managed to buy a whole range of enamel paints, and he had agreed to let her touch up the paintwork, without knowing that she meant to do it herself and that she was colour-blind. After much difficulty, John had found fresh fields for her in Maida Vale; and although she objected to it at first as being the wrong side of the Park, she was mollified by the proximity of Lord's, for she had loved cricket ever since she had been one of the belles of the Varsity matches in a lace hat and dress with thirty buttons. As John could not find them an hotel while windows were being put into the new flat, Mrs North had impulsively offered to have Lady Sandys and Miss Smutts at Hinkley, and had been regretting it ever since.

Before they arrived, having explained the situation to Elizabeth, who suggested Pentathol therapy, Mrs North gave a little lecture to Evelyn. 'It's just a funny game she plays, dear, to take your things. You may take them back off the table upstairs, but you must never say anything about it, because that's part of the game. It's a secret, isn't that fun?' She watched Evelyn's face doubtfully.

'It's wicked to steal,' said Evelyn righteously. 'Once I stole a mangold-wurzel for Dandy out of Mr Grainger's field. I prayed to Jesus and He told me to put it back. What does Jesus tell Uncle John's mummy to do?'

'I've told you, dear,' said Mrs North wearily, 'it's not stealing. It's a game.'

Oliver heard Evelyn telling David in a corner of his room at supper-time: 'There's a new game, called Thieves. We can all play it. You take things out of people's rooms, and they can't be cross with you, like Aunt Heather was that time I took her lipstick for Red Indians.'

'If only she goes before the wedding,' Mrs North prayed, when Oliver warned her what they were in for. 'She may not be having a fit, of course; but if she is, Heaven knows the trouble she'll cause. Maybe we could shut her up in her room? But that's unkind to John, and she's such a charming woman, in spite of it all, that she'll be quite an asset to the party. Lady Spicer was all over her at Heather's wedding, but of course she never did find out what happened to her spectacles.'

Lady Sandys and Miss Smutts arrived in a hired car from Shrewsbury, having taken a much later train than they had arranged, and kept John waiting fruitlessly half the day at the station.

Oliver heard shrill noises in the hall. 'Well, I did think you'd have met us, darling,' John's mother was saying; 'but as you didn't, *n'importe*. We found this delightful man, and he's been telling me all about the difficulty he has to get enough petrol, so I've promised to write to old Harrison about it. He's the fuel *king*, you know, and he'd do anything for me. Come in, Mr

Steptoe. Oh, the bags – thank you very much. Hattie, dearest, how are you? I've promised him he should have a cup of tea; he tells me he hasn't had time for a meal all day. Isn't that dreadful?'

Oliver was sure Mr Peploe would like bothering anyone for tea at seven o'clock as little as they would like to make it, and when after: 'And where is Oliver? I can't wait to see him. I've heard so much about him, he's quite a hero to me,' the door burst open, he saw Mr Peploe in the hall making embarrassed protestations to his mother.

Lady Sandys was tiny and bright and brittle, insubstantial as a humming-bird. She had been exquisite, and was exquisite still, until you got close enough to see the lines like little bird tracks running all over her face, and the bones too close under the skin, as pathetically miniature as those of a quail on toast that you can hardly bear to eat. No food ever had a chance to fatten her, because she was always on the go, even during meals. Oliver's mother, who seldom sat still for more than five minutes at a time, was stagnant compared to Lady Sandys. She tripped into the room in a slickly cut tailormade with a skirt no bigger than a pocket handkerchief. A doll-sized Edwardian hat was tipped over one eye and the other sparkled at Oliver through a fine veil drawn tightly over her pointed chin. Barely touching the floor, she crossed the room, both hands in long suède gloves held out to him.

'At last,' she said in her high, clear, musical voice. 'I've heard so much about you. I feel you're almost like my son. I've come all this way, you know, really just to see you. Oh, this *is* nice. I am so delighted to meet you! How are you? You're even better looking than they told me. It's that pale, fragile look, you know; it's absolutely becoming.' Her hand in his was as light as a leaf, and when she touched his arm she did not even press the pyjama sleeve against the skin. Oliver was not very substantial himself, but she made him feel quite hulking and clumsy. He grinned at her, and suddenly into his mind came the absurd fancy that if he opened his mouth wide enough he could take her whole head inside and snap it off the brittle stalk of her neck. Surprised at his thought, he realized that she had the same insect friability that arouses the sadist in small boys who tear the wings off flies.

166

She chattered and sparkled at him, and although she was effusive, it was not the overpowering effusion of people like Mrs Ogilvie, because it was not forced. The warmth of her greeting was sincere. She really was pleased to see him and as interested in him as she said. He could see why people were attracted by her.

Behind her into the room came John, whom no stretch of imagination could believe to be her son. 'What about the taxi, Mother?' he asked. 'He's waiting to be paid.'

'Oh, but he's got to have his tea!' She whipped round in concern. 'I promised him his tea. Do you know,' she turned back to Oliver, 'that poor Mr Steptoe hasn't had a thing to eat all day. I think it's scandalous. He was telling me how his wife always wants to make him sandwiches out of her cheese and corned-beef ration, but he won't let her, because she's anaemic, you see, and has to be fed up. I think it's quite haunting really, the lives some people lead. I wake in the night sometimes and worry about them; do you? Shall I go and put the kettle on, John, and do delicious buttered toast? I wonder if your mother-in-law's got any cinnamon. The poor man must have his tea. He's been looking forward to it ever since that village with the hump-backed bridge, where I suggested it.'

'It's all right, dear,' said John. 'Elizabeth's getting it'

'Elizabeth?' she asked, always interested in any new name.

'My nurse,' explained Oliver.

'Oh, yes, of course. I look forward to meeting her. Nurses always appeal to me, especially young ones. Is she young? They have that fascination of being experienced beyond their years, like French girls.'

'If you'd give me the money for the taxi, dear,' repeated John patiently, 'he could go straight out by the kitchen when he's had this famous tea. Smutty doesn't seem to have enough on her.'

'I never let her carry too much money about. She's so careless about it, poor old thing. You pay it, darling; I haven't any change.'

'Neither have I,' said John inexorably. He never gave up trying to train his mother.

'Let me.' Oliver reached into the drawer of his bedside table. 'Here you are, Jonathan; it'll be six bob with the tip, unless there was a lot of luggage.'

'There was,' said John. 'But I won't let you do that, old boy. I'll nip up and see what I've got in my other suit.'

'Oh, take this,' said Oliver, tired of holding it out.

'Thank you *most* awfully,' said Lady Sandys, with the butterfly touch on his arm again. 'I'll pay you back tomorrow.'

The extraordinary thing was that she did. Oliver seemed to have some stabilizing influence on her. She had taken to him immediately; she was fascinated by him and spent as much time as possible in his room, behaving more calmly than she did with other people. She even settled into a chair for half an hour and read him some new Walter de la Mare poems, which she had brought him as a present. When, three days after her arrival, Mrs North lost a new box of handkerchiefs, and Heather lost a scarf, and the half-moon table came into play again and everyone knew, without saying much about it, that the fit was on, nothing ever disappeared from Oliver's room.

Miss Smutts was most impressed. 'I can't understand it,' she told him in her mourning voice. 'You can do more with her ladyship than I can after twenty years. You mean that screw pencil I found really wasn't yours?'

'Nope,' said Oliver. 'She never takes a thing from here, even though I've tried shutting my eyes and pretending to be asleep to see what she'd do. I believe you're making the whole thing up.'

Miss Smutts folded her arms on her bosom which was the shape of two peardrops in a bag. 'Oh, no,' she said, shaking her head with a sad, superior smile. 'Indeed not. Twenty years she's been like this, poor lady, off and on. I've been with her since it started. It was her husband's death that did it, as I've no doubt you've heard. He was a very fine man; not that I ever saw him, except in his coffin, of course, when I first came to her ladyship, but the lid was on by then. Twenty years ago. . . .' She rocked herself slightly. 'Twenty years of trouble. I could tell you some tales. Whoo-hoo!' She threw back her lolloping head with a dingy imitation of an American soldier's love-call. 'I wish I had a shilling for every time I've saved her from the Law.'

'Smutty!' came an amused voice from the doorway. 'Get out of here and stop boring the invalid with tiresome stories of our past. She's always talking about me,' she told Oliver cheerfully.

'I listen sometimes when she has friends to tea in her room. Most entertaining.'

'One of these days,' said Miss Smutts sombrely, 'you'll hear something that'll make your eardrums rattle. That'll teach you to listen at keyholes.'

'Quaint old character, isn't she?'

Miss Smutts sniffed, stretching her pendulous lower lip up over the moustache.

'Do go and iron my nightie, Smutty, there's a pet. It's all rumpled, because I had such a sleepless night thinking of that poor postman having to bicycle up and down all those hills, and you know how I like to be *soignée* in bed.' She twinkled at Oliver. He was always amazed that there was nothing arch about her conversation, which was frequently of the variety that makes raddled old ladies so horrible. But it was not put on for effect. Her talk and her whole behaviour simply bubbled from her naturally as water out of a hill-side.

Elizabeth came in with Oliver's tea. She seemed to like Lady Sandys too. It was one of the few things she and Oliver had in common, and they enjoyed talking about her. It did not make her immune, however. Oliver noticed that she was not yet wearing her State Registered badge, which she had been waiting two days for Miss Smutts to find.

'Here's your lovely nurse,' said Lady Sandys, her eyes travelling admiringly over Elizabeth. 'I've been meaning to ask you: what do you put on your face, my dear, that gives you that dewy, rosebud look? It's quite enchanting, isn't it, Oliver?'

'Not bad,' he said guardedly.

'Nothing much,' Elizabeth said. 'Just the usual creams and powder and things. Would you like your tea in here, Lady Sandys?'

'I wish you wouldn't call me that. I wish you'd call me Muffet, like everyone else does. You'll have to, when I've adopted you. Did you know I was going to adopt her, Ollie? Not until you've finished with her, of course, but then I'll have her and I can pension off poor old Smutty. She gets more like the Frankenstein monster every day. This poor girl was telling me she's got no mother and her father's married someone she doesn't like. Did you know that?'

'What?' said Oliver. 'Oh – er – yes.' He looked at Elizabeth sharply. Lady Sandys had a way of getting things out of you by the sheer suction-power of her interest. She had certainly got more out of Elizabeth in seven days than Oliver had been able to in as many months. Elizabeth was looking very nonchalant, which meant she was embarrassed. 'Oh, I didn't mean that really,' she said; 'I made that up for fun. I'll get your tea.'

'Funny girl,' said Lady Sandys, gazing through the closed door as if she could follow Elizabeth with her eyes as well as with her thoughts. 'I thought she told me that, but I may have imagined it. I am a bit vague sometimes, you know. Why is she so quiet and buttoned up? I'm sure there's something behind it. She should have more effervescence at her age; she should let herself go.'

'Oh, no,' said Oliver. 'She's just made like that, with no great enthusiasms or affections. Some people are. They probably save themselves a lot of heartbreak.'

'They lose a lot, too,' said Muffet. 'But this girl's not naturally like that. She's putting on an act. I know it. I've got an instinct for people, you know, probably because I'm so interested in them. You are too, aren't you? I've noticed that. That's why you don't fret at having to lie here all the time. I should like to change places with you for a bit and have the opportunity of a detached view. I bet after a week of it I could tell you some astonishing things about the people in this house.'

'Lend me one of your legs, then,' said Oliver, 'and a slice of healthy heart muscle, and I'll swop.'

'I bet I'd do better with Elizabeth than you. If I were a man, I'd have the girl in bed with me in a week. Oh no, I mustn't talk to you like that, must I? That's the sort of act I put on to impress people I don't know very well, and then they go away and tell their scandalized friends what an old rip I am. I've led the most pure life actually. Sad, really, when you think of it.' As she put up a hand to pat at her upswept hair, which was still black like John's, with a silvery streak artfully incorporated in the front wing, Oliver recognized his mother's cameo ring.

Lady Sandys did not get on so well with everybody. She was at her best with Oliver, because she liked him, but with those

170

whom she did not like so well she was much odder and more unpredictable, altering her behaviour according to the effect different people had on her. She seemed quite fond of Oliver's mother, but Mrs North did not understand her. She did not realize that Lady Sandys was intrigued by anything that anybody did and mistook her passionate interest in herself and her running of the house for inquisitive interference. Sorry as she was for the little creature, she was not going to have her nosing about in her store cupboard and kitchen, dipping ladles into the soup to see what was in it, and squandering eggs and butter and milk on making uneatable pancakes as a surprise for tea, as she had done one day when Mrs North was out. Poor Muffet yearned after domesticity, but Mrs North did not credit her with enough intelligence to fill the mustard-pots. She took quite the wrong line with her; instead of treating her as a rational person, she humoured her with elaborate tact, transparent to everybody, including Lady Sandys, whose resentment manifested itself in more eccentricities than usual.

Violet made Lady Sandys laugh. Mischievously, she liked to tease her, and to see Violet congealing into increased boorishness. Heather had abandoned all interest in Violet's appearance, and Lady Sandys took over, coming down each day with some impossibly small garment or inappropriate piece of frippery. The fact that she was prompted by generosity, not malice, did not compensate for her delight in the ludicrous effects obtained, nor for making Violet appear ungrateful when she refused to try the things on.

'If that lunatic doesn't go before my wedding,' Violet threatened, 'I shan't get married at all, so there! D'you know what she wants to do? Stick a socking great bow in my hair with spangles on it or some damfoolery. I told her to put it where the sergeant put the pudding.'

'Violet, you didn't!' Her mother was aghast.

'Shall next time,' mumbled Violet, who, however, was always struck into dumbness by Lady Sandys' prattle, and revolved ponderously like a battleship, following with empty eyes the chattering, exclaiming little figure who pranced round her.

Fred ran a mile at Lady Sandys' approach, and made excuses not to come to a meal when she was in the house. He had spent three days in hiding, sneaking in and out of barns and peering from haylofts, because she had threatened to come and be shown over the farm. The children were attracted to her, as to all bizarre characters, from the bearded old tramp who sat on the pavement in Castle Street saying he was Christ, to the idiot boy in the village, with a head like a tombstone and a hyena's cackle. She doted on them, of course, but not suffocatingly. She took all their affairs seriously and never said: 'Run along' to a request for string, or to that kind of conversation, which begins with heavy breathing and: 'Shall I tell you something? D'you know, it was awfully funny; the other day – –' and never gets to the point. Her company made up a little to Evelyn for the loss of Violet and Fred, who, although they could hardly be called love-birds and seldom spoke to one another, made her feel an unwanted third. They had been Evelyn's hero and heroine, and she had been their mascot and slave. Now they seemed not to need her, and she did not want to be with them. When Fred said: 'Cut along, youngster, and put a head collar on Prince, and you can take him up to the smithy for me,' she still ran, from habit, but without that proud glow of a mission which had made her feel Joan of Arc as she perched on the rolling carthorse back, with her legs stuck out at right angles. She wished that Lady Sandys were more of an outdoors person. She was very good for indoors, but when Evelyn tried to make her come and see her jump, or visit the lambs, or the new fox earth, she would tittup along half-way in unsuitable shoes and then jib at some tiny obstacle like a drain or a stile and turn for home, saying that she had the wrong pair of legs on; these were only good for pavements and floors. Evelyn enjoyed the secret of the kleptomania game. Sometimes she would deliberately begin a forbidden remark, so that she could clap a freckled hand over her mouth and say sensationally: 'Coo, I nearly said something I shouldn't.'

'That's right, dear,' Lady Sandys would say innocently. 'The rude words can be left to men. Women are allowed to make the rude remarks.' It was fun, too, to see what appeared on the half-moon table, and to say: 'Anything in the post for me?' when anyone came down from upstairs.

John was patiently affectionate with his mother and tried to annoy her as little as possible. His ears were almost at right angles while she was at Hinkley, for he felt the responsibility of her as a great weight. He tried to protect her by laughing indulgently and saying: 'Nonsense, Muffet, you don't mean that' to cover her more extravagant remarks. He tried to protect the household by keeping her under his eye, which she took great delight in making as difficult as possible.

She knew that he was tracking her, although she did not know why he did it. 'Poor little Johnny thinks I'm going to have a stroke or something,' she told Oliver, talking to him through the window from the lawn where she was hiding while John looked for her in the house. 'He always wants to know where I'm going and what I'm going to do and why isn't Smutty with me? He treats me as if I were in my dotage, and it's enough to put me there. How did I ever come to have a child who took life so seriously?' Her swallow's-wing eyebrows drew together in a fleeting frown. 'It's an awful thing for a mother to say, but d'you know, I'm afraid he's got *very* little sense of humour. Look how silly he is with Heather. She'd soon stop being *difficile* if only he'd laugh at her instead of letting her wipe her boots on him as if he were a mat with Welcome written all over it.'

She did not like Heather, and Heather did not like her. She made no allowances for her mother-in-law's abnormality and would not be shushed away from making dangerously close allusions to it. She suffered more from Lady Sandys than anyone in the house, because although her kleptomania was unconscious, she instinctively took more from people she did not like, and the things she took were often symptomatic of her conscious feelings. John had learned his rigid Protestantism from her. Her disapproval of Heather's conversion manifested itself by the repeated removal of her daughter-in-law's prayer book or rosary. The blessed palm which Heather hung over her bed at Easter was never found again and Heather swore that Miss Smutts, who got to grips with Methodism every week in a kind of Nissen hut at Bornell Heath, had deliberately not looked for it. Once her crucifix disappeared, and even after it was found she muttered for a long time about sacrilege and blasphemy.

Her shoes were to Muffet like honey to a bee, but only one at a time, so that Heather was always hopping up the stairs to the half-moon table to complete the pair she had left in the scullery for cleaning. Her hand mirror and her brush and comb spent almost more time in the passage than in her bedroom. The doors at Hinkley had bolts on the inside, but no keys, but Heather found one in the tool chest that fitted and took to locking her door whenever she came downstairs, until John, returning late from a wet Sunday-morning walk, came like a dripping spaniel into Oliver's room, where the family were already at lunch.

'What's happened to the door of our room, Heather Bell?' he asked, treading up and down in his stockinged feet to try and get warm. 'It's stuck or something and I can't get in. I'll get pneumonia if I don't change soon.'

Miss Smutts nodded sagely, as one who, after twenty years, guessed what had happened. 'All the latches in this house want seeing to,' said Mrs North innocently. 'They're the original wooden ones, you know,' she told Lady Sandys proudly, 'nearly three hundred years old. Try pulling the door tight shut before you press the latch, John. No, wait, I'll come with you.' She put down her knife and fork and got up, sure that no one but she could do it, just as no one but she could poke a fire, or open a sticking window, or get the cap off a pickle jar.

'It's all right, Ma. Sit down and get on with your lunch,' said Heather impatiently. She took a key out of her cardigan pocket and held it out to John. 'Here, I locked it,' she said shortly, and turned her attention quickly away to David. 'Eat up,' she said, pushing a spoonful into his mouth without noticing that it was already full.

'You *locked* it?' said John. 'What on earth for? Oh – –' as Heather made a face at him. 'Oh yes, yes, yes; oh, I see,' he mumbled, looking chagrined.

'Well,' said Muffet brightly, 'I've heard of wives locking their husbands out of their bedrooms, but only when they were inside themselves. What's the game?' She looked round the table for enlightenment, at all the eyes that would not meet hers. David, who had been growing steadily blacker in the face while he bravely tried to deal with his mouthful, fortunately created a diversion, by opening his mouth very wide, putting in his whole fist and scooping everything out on to his plate and the table round it.

'Ma, we really must find his mackintosh mat,' Heather said,

as she cleaned up the mess. 'He can't be trusted to eat like a civil-ized being yet. I can't think what's happened to it. I remember washing it and hanging it up – – Oh Lord, you don't suppose – –? Oh no, really. That's just about the end: surely she – –' She glanced inquiringly at Miss Smutts, who swung her head in nega-tion like a pensive chimpanzee. John, not liking to leave the room until the atmosphere attributable to his mother had eva-porated, still hung about by the door, beads of water running down his nose from the damp little ringlets of hair on his fore-head.

'Did you have a nice walk, darling?' his mother asked him. 'You look like a suicide just fished out of the Thames.'

Mrs North swivelled round. 'John, for gracious sakes go up and change. You're shivering as if you had the *grippe*. Will you never learn to look after yourself? I don't know which is the greater baby, you or your son. If it's lunch you're after, you can't eat it in that condition, so hurry up and change before it spoils. I'll cut you some off and put it in the oven.' She got up and went to the side table, and Lady Sandys, who could not sit still while anyone else was in action, got up too.

'Let me take it, Hattie,' she begged. 'I always feel so useless in this busy house, and you never let me do anything.'

'No, dear, it's all right, thank you. You won't know how to light the oven.'

'Indeed I will; I'm not a mental defective.'

'Now you know it scares you when the gas pops.'

'Let me take it,' said John, through chattering teeth. 'I don't really think I want any, though.'

'Of course you do,' said his mother and mother-in-law to-gether, vying for custody of him. 'But you know you always say you can never find the matches in the kitchen,' went on Mrs North. 'All right, dear,' to Elizabeth, who was already at her side. 'You take it. Just put me on some vegetables then, Muffet, if you want to help. Not spinach. You don't know your son very well if you think he'll eat spinach.'

'Oh, is it spinach?' Lady Sandys giggled. 'I've been eating it thinking it was cabbage. You ought to look after me better, Smutty,' she said, going back to the table. 'You know I don't like spinach.'

'You want a keeper, not a companion,' grumbled Miss Smutts, pushing a bit of bread round her plate, and eating it with smacking lips.

When John had gone away, his shoulders hunched to his ears, Mrs North sat down, ate a few mouthfuls, got up again and said: 'I think I'll just go up and take his temperature. He did look awfully feverish, Heather, and I don't want him to be ill for the great day.'

'Don't *fuss*, Ma, he's all right.'

'You can't tell with John; he never says when he feels poorly. I think I'll just run up – –'

Lady Sandys jumped up again. 'Do let me do it,' she cried. 'I'm terribly good at taking temperatures. Where's the thermometer?' The thought of her rootling in the medicine chest was too perilous. 'I'll go up, shall I?' said Elizabeth.

'Well, after all, you are the nurse,' said Muffet, beaming at her. 'Thank you so much, dear; I know you'll look after him for me. She's very fond of Johnny,' she told them when Elizabeth had gone. 'They get on splendidly because they're both quiet people. Did you know he was going to take her up the Wrekin to see the sunrise? She's never been up. Neither have I, of course, and I don't intend to at my age, though they tell me it's well worth the climb.'

'You can take a car nearly all the way,' put in Oliver.

Lady Sandys turned round to smile and wave at him to make up for not having spoken to him for some time. 'Oh, but too prosaic,' she said. 'One ought to scramble up on hands and knees and cry "Excelsior!" at the top, with the world spread out before one.'

'That old view,' said Heather. 'I'm sick of hearing about it. If you tell anyone you live in Shropshire, they say how wonderful the view from the Wrekin must be. I've seen it hundreds of times, at sunrise, sunset, midnight – wild horses wouldn't drag me up there again.'

'Of course not, dear,' said Muffet gently. 'I wasn't suggesting you should. I said John and Elizabeth were going up.' She pushed out one side of her cheek with her tongue and smiled to herself, pleased at having piqued Heather.

In the silence that followed the handing round of pudding,

Evelyn, who had been pursuing the subject in her mind since it was first mentioned, shook back her hair and asked in a clear voice: 'But *why* did you lock your bedroom door, Aunt Heather?'

'Get on with your pie, dear,' said Mrs North.

'I am. I'm talking with my mouth full. Why did she lock her door?' Oliver saw that Heather, wanting to get her own back on Lady Sandys, was struggling against the temptation of dropping a bombshell. Feeling like the man who brought the good news to Aix just in time, he rushed in with: 'I'll tell you why. She's got your Aunt Violet's wedding present in there, only it's a secret.'

Violet woke up. 'Have you?' she asked. 'What is it, Heather? Do tell us.'

'Certainly not.'

'Come on, be a sport. I know, anyway.'

'Why ask, then?'

'Don't be a cow.'

'Girls, girls,' said their mother. 'What about my rule? No fighting in Oliver's room.'

'Don't be such a schoolmarm, Ma,' said Oliver ungraciously. 'They're not fighting, anyway. Oh cripes – –' He suddenly remembered that Heather's wedding present to Violet was a new bicycle, and saw, by Lady Sandys' puzzled eyebrows, that she knew too.

Evelyn, who also knew, said with interest: 'Well, what a funny place to keep it. There can't be much room. Where have you put it?'

'Oh, shut up about it, Evie,' said Heather.

'No, but where?' pursued Evelyn, who never gave up.

'Hanging on hooks,' said Heather grimly.

'Ye gods,' said Violet. 'I hope it's not clothes or anything, Heather. You promised you'd give me something I could use.'

'It's a parrot in a cage,' said Heather.

Violet took this seriously. 'How topping!' she shouted. 'Just what I've always wanted. Where on earth did you get it? I shall teach it all the swear words I know, and get some more from old Halliday. What a yell! Poor old Fred. I wonder if he likes parrots.' Heather could not be bothered to enlighten her, and Violet was still chortling when Elizabeth came back, looking important.

'I'm afraid you're right, Mrs North,' she said. 'His temperature's a hundred point four; pulse to match. Probably only a slight dose of flu, but I've told him to get into bed, and I'll take up a hot bottle and another blanket. He's shivering as if he were trying to go in for a rigor.' That was the end of lunch. Everyone started getting up and exclaiming, except Miss Smutts who sat sucking on a hollow tooth and intoning that these things easily turned to something worse. David beat the table with his spoon and shouted for more custard.

Violet pushed her chair disgustedly away from the table and leaned back as if she were going to tip over. 'Well,' she said, 'if he's not all right by my wedding day, Ollie will *have* to come. It is a swizz. Just one thing after another – everything goes against it.'

'It will be all right on the day,' droned Smutty, but no one was listening or paid any attention. They were all too busy trying to go up to John and trying to stop each other going up.

John's temperature continued to rise, and as an invalid Oliver became a back number. All the next day, he hardly saw a soul, except Lady Sandys, who kept coming in to complain that they would not let her do anything for John. He heard a lot of activity going on overhead, and after dinner they appeared to be playing general post with the furniture in John's room. It was later than usual when Mrs North came in to say her last good night to Oliver.

He told her she looked tired, and she said: 'I am a bit. Illness always makes extra to do.'

'But I thought Elizabeth – –'

'She's been invaluable, of course, plumb in her element. I dare say it's quite a good thing for her to have a bit more nursing to do. After all, it is what she's trained for, and I've sometimes wondered lately if she doesn't feel she's being wasted doing more of the household chores now that there's less to do for you. She doesn't complain, but it would be just too terrible if she suddenly said she wanted to leave.'

'I don't know,' Oliver said. 'You could get a proper maid. I shouldn't need another nurse.'

His mother did not allow him to talk like that. 'You'll have a

178

nurse just as long as Hugo and I say,' she told him sternly, 'but I should never get one I had such confidence in as Elizabeth. Although she's so young, I feel I don't have to worry when I leave the house. I never felt that with Sandy; she would have lost her head in a crisis.'

'Crisis!' scoffed Oliver. 'What crisis could I have?'

'Elizabeth's so level-headed, and she knows her job backwards. She knew just how John's illness was going to develop, and she knew just what to do for him to make him comfortable.'

'Then for heaven's sake,' said Oliver, 'why not let her get on with it, instead of wearing yourself out running round John in small circles?'

'Oh well, there are all sorts of fiddling little jobs I must do myself. I've been moving Heather's bed into the children's room tonight. John wanted it. He pretended he thought he'd have a better night if he was on his own, but really it's because he knew his coughing kept Heather awake last night.'

'That man's too good to live,' Oliver said impatiently. 'It's not decent to be unselfish when you're ill, especially with an embittering thing like flu.'

'He certainly has got a lovely nature,' mused his mother. 'I've never seen such a good invalid – except you, of course, darling. And don't talk about him as if he was prissy; he's very much a man – except in his unselfishness. I sometimes think Heather doesn't appreciate what a fine person she's married.'

'Too right she doesn't. His noble nature merely annoys her.'

'I don't see why it should. She has a crack at being noble herself, with all that churchgoing, even though it doesn't seem to have the right effect, poor little Heather.'

'And that annoys her all the more; to find that she tries so hard and gets up so early so often and bicycles so many miles and still can't make her peace with the world.'

'Why did she have to go the whole hog like that? She could still have gone to Mass, without tying herself up to something she may lose interest in, and as I know Heather, she always loses interest in everything she takes up. Remember her stage training? And that flower shop she and Veronica were all set to start? And look how quickly she used to tire of the people she was in love with. She was just as rash then – always getting herself tied up

179

and then having to wriggle out of it. How many times was she engaged – three or four?'

'Four, I think,' said Oliver, reckoning, 'counting that B.B.C. man who was always eating cough lozenges.'

'Well, she won't be able to wriggle out of this. It's considered a terrible thing, you know, to stop being a Catholic, even worse than never being one at all.'

'What do you know about it?'

'Oh, I just do.'

'You know a little about everything, don't you, like all Americans?'

'Of course,' she said proudly. 'That's what we mean by being cultured.'

Oliver said unthinkingly, 'She'd have to stop being a Catholic if she was divorced.'

His mother clutched at the front of her apricot silk dressing-gown. 'Darling, don't,' she cried. 'Even in fun. They may not get on very well at the moment, but it's wicked of you to talk like that.'

'Don't tick *me* off. It wasn't my idea. Heather mentioned it only this morning, as a matter of fact, admittedly in a fit of temper, but it shows it's entered her head.'

'I refuse even to think about it,' said his mother grandly, her brain obviously whirling with the subject. 'I never heard such crazy nonsense.' She did her last little jobs for Oliver, like shaking up his pillows, and straightening his eiderdown, and giving an extra turn to the cap of the Thermos, and putting her hand into the open window space to feel what sort of air was coming in on him. Having gone, she was back again within five minutes, under the pretext of returning a book he had lent her.

'And of course,' she continued, as if they had never left the subject, 'she wouldn't be influenced by that. She might be just as ready to throw over her Church as she was to enter it. I wish you hadn't told me she'd said that – no, I don't; I like to know what people are thinking. But how could she? Those lovely children, and John so devoted to her. . . . It would ruin her life. And mine too, I reckon.'

'I thought you were an American,' said Oliver cattily. 'You shouldn't get so worked up about a divorce.'

'Don't be cheap, dear. You ought to know better than to make silly sweeping statements about my country. Why, in the *old* places, like Philadelphia, and Boston, and Virginia, marriage is a lot more sacred than it is in England.'

'It couldn't be much less.' The giggling voice from the doorway make them both jump. In the shadows beyond the range of Oliver's lamp a little white figure glimmered, and came noiselessly towards them, like Elizabeth Bergner playing Lady Macbeth.

'Muffet!' said Mrs North. 'What on earth are you doing down here at this time of night? You went to bed hours ago.'

'I couldn't sleep, so I thought I'd come down and look for a biscuit. I do love bikkies.' Childish, in a plain white nightgown, a little jacket with a Peter Pan collar, and infinitesimal mules, she was matching her speech to her appearance. 'I heard you talking,' she said appealingly, 'and I've been so lonely all by myself up in that big room. You don't mind my coming in, do you?'

'Delighted,' said Oliver, wondering how much she had heard while she was listening outside the door.

'Do you know,' said Lady Sandys confidingly, 'there's a snake that lives under my bed, and sometimes he crawls up the angle of the wall and looks at me. Then there's that cupboard. I have to be sure and lock the door very tight so that the ape can't get out. I hear him rattling at the handle sometimes, when the lights are out.'

Oliver's mother looked at him in alarm. She had always known this would happen. She had known Lady Sandys would go over the top one of these days, but when it happened she did not want it to be in her house.

Oliver cleared his throat. 'Er – what kind of a snake?' he asked feebly.

'Oh, the usual spotty kind,' said Muffet vaguely, dismissing it with a wave of her hand. 'Do let's go on talking about marriage. It's a subject I could talk about all night.'

Mrs North took control of herself and the situation and laid a hand on the loose white sleeve. 'Don't you think we'd better go to bed, dear?' she said soothingly. 'It's very late, and you're supposed to be catching the early bus in to Shrewsbury in the morning, remember? Unless you'd like to stay in bed, as you don't feel so well tonight. How about that? I'll bring you up your break-fast quite late, and you shall have all the papers, and my electric hot bottle, and you needn't get up all day if you like.' This was just how she used to talk to Oliver when he was a small boy and had been sick in the night.

Lady Sandys shook off her hand and smoothed out the sleeve with a delicate little flick of her fingers. 'Who says I don't feel well?' she asked. 'Of course, I'm going to Shrewsbury; I promised I'd do your shopping for you, didn't I? Now don't take *that* away from me.' She was childish again. 'I was so thrilled to think that at last there was something I could do to help you.'

'Of course you shall, dear,' said Mrs North hastily, 'and Smutty shall go with you and help carry the bags.'

'That old creature. Must I always have her hanging around like a lunatic with its keeper?'

Mrs North looked embarrassed. 'I just thought it would be a nice change for her,' she amended. 'After all, she doesn't get much fun. You could take her to have coffee and cakes at Lawley's. They're making *mille feuilles* again now.'

'And have her being sick on the bus coming home? No, thank you.'

'Well, anyway, let's go up to bed now, shall we?' said Mrs North encouragingly. 'We can talk about it in the morning.'

'But I wanted to talk to my Oliver.' Muffet took a step forward into the lamplight. Her head was done up in a piece of magenta net, tied in an enormous bow on top. Being colour-blind, she presumably was not aware of what it did to her unmade-up face. Her eyes looked unreal and unfocused, glittering in the light like glass marbles. Was she acting, or was she really a little mad?

'Not now, dear,' said Mrs North. 'Oliver has to get his sleep, you know, or he gets tired.'

'And then you'll say I tired him,' said Lady Sandys quickly, peeking up at her with her head on one side, like a robin looking at a pigeon. 'I couldn't bear that. Good night then, my pet. We'll have lovely talks tomorrow.' She darted forward, gave him a but-terfly kiss and then skimmed away to the door, where she waited, like a little ghost, for Mrs North.

'Think she's all right to be left alone?' muttered Oliver.

'I'm worried,' answered his mother out of the side of her

mouth. 'But she'll never have Smutty in with her. Say, Muffet!' She raised her voice. 'If you feel chatty, why don't you come in with me tonight? That couch of mine is very comfortable, and it wouldn't take a minute to make up.'

'My dear, *no*, I wouldn't dream of it,' answered Lady Sandys. 'I whistle in my sleep, you know. Poor Arthur always used to have to sleep in his dressing-room. Still, it gave the servants something to talk about.'

'I wish you'd come in with me,' pursued Mrs North. 'I feel kind of lonely tonight. I'd be glad of company.'

'O-oh, don't be such a baby.' Lady Sandys chuckled. 'You're a big girl now, Hattie. You'll sleep in your room, and little me in mine,' she said in a sing-song voice, relieving Oliver's mind of its visions of his mother being found in the morning with her throat cut from ear to ear.

'Can't you lock her door?' he whispered.

She shook her head. 'Not from the outside. Oh well,' she looked suddenly very tired, and yawned. 'We'll risk it.' Nevertheless, when she had put Muffet to bed she did push a heavy chair up against the door, wedged under the handle, and Oliver was woken next morning, out of his best seven o'clock sleep by the uproar that was Muffet trying to get out to the bathroom.

She seemed perfectly normal next day, and Oliver and his mother wondered whether they had imagined her midnight oddity. She went gaily off in a tweed suit with a little round hat to match to catch the Shrewsbury bus at the crossroads, followed doggedly with the shopping bags by Miss Smutts, who refused to be shaken off.

Gaily she returned, without most of the things Mrs North wanted, but with a pile of books for Oliver, bath salts for dear Hattie, and an armful of flowers and a melon bigger than her head for John.

'How generous of you, dear,' exclaimed Mrs North, searching the bags in vain for the fish and soap and stamps and notepaper she needed. 'You have brought lovely presents. Where did you get them?'

'At Lawley's. I put them down to your account, by the way. I'll pay you back,' she said vaguely, concentrating on the letter she was reading. 'Well, doesn't this beat all! I thought the war was supposed to be over. Here's the builder tells me he hasn't even started on my windows, and he's so short of staff he can't promise them for another three weeks.' Oliver and his mother looked at each other over the little covered button on the top of her round tweed hat. 'Begging to remain, yours truly, etc., etc., etc. . . . Oh well!' She looked up and beamed from one to the other. 'I should worry, as you say in your country, Hattie. I wanted to stay for the wedding, anyway, so that I can help you with it, and of course I couldn't go back to London with an easy mind until Johnny's better. Are you *sure* you don't mind having me?'

'Why, of course not,' said Mrs North hollowly. 'I'm only too glad.'

'Yes, but it's Smutty. She's the most devastating bore, I know, and she will *eat* so much. She *was* sick in the bus, did I tell you? At least, not in it, but she had to hop out when it stopped at a village and go behind a sort of pigsty, and of course the bus started before she was ready and poor old Smutty had to run after it, pea green.'

Lady Sandys continued to be fairly sane and on her best behaviour. The half-moon table had been empty for a whole week, and Mrs North was even optimistic enough to replace on it the vases and pot-pourri bowl for which it was intended. The household kept its fingers crossed and prayed that the excitement of the wedding would not throw her off her balance.

Violet had kicked the furniture a bit and stuck out her jaw when she heard that Lady Sandys was staying, but as her wedding day approached she began to view it with less glee and more and more apprehension, until she finally became so depressed that she did not care whether Muffet were there or not. Nothing could make it any worse. She wished now, she told the family, that she had not let herself in for getting spliced. She croaked about the wedding like a carrion crow. It would be a flop; she would make a fool of herself; everything would go wrong. If she had to marry Fred, and she was talking about this now as if it was everyone's fault except her own, why couldn't she do it in a registry office, without a crowd of rubbernecking old busybodies gawping at her? The dark red silk dress which had been made for her in

184

London arrived, but she refused to try it on. 'I shall look a sight, anyway,' she told her mother, 'so why know it sooner than I need?'

Fred did not know what to make of her. She hardly went near him these days, and he took to coming up to the house, in spite of his terror of Lady Sandys. He did not come inside, but his face was sometimes seen for a moment at a window, shadowy and seeking, like one of the lost boys from the Never-Never Land.

'It's just nerves,' Mrs North told him. 'Girls are often like that before their wedding.'

'Women are funny cusses,' he said to Oliver through the window, standing on the lawn with his hands in his pockets, very man-to-man. 'I thought old Vi was perfectly happy, but now she's as broody as a sitting hen.'

'Love, old chap,' said Oliver. 'Takes 'em that way sometimes. You ought to be flattered.'

'No, don't muck about,' said Fred. 'I'm serious. Y'see, I've never been able to understand all along how she came to accept me. I just couldn't believe my luck, and, naturally, this sort of thing makes me think she's changed her mind.'

'Not she,' said Oliver. 'But why not have it out with her? Might clear the air a bit. How do you know she's not wondering whether *you've* changed your mind?'

'Oh, I don't know,' Fred looked down and made patterns in the flower-bed with the toe of his boot. 'Vi and I, y'know, we don't jaw much – don't need to as a rule. What's she doing now?'

'In the drawing-room, I believe, reading the paper.'

'Gee, is she? I might see her if I look through the window, then. I haven't seen her for two days.' His face, oppressed and saddened by the weight of his nose, looked wistful. It seemed that he really did love her. Oliver wondered what Violet looked like to a man who loved her. Did he see her as she was, or enhanced? How would she wear the magical aura, and how would her voice sound when, beloved, its most casual word was musical and full of meaning?

Fred slunk off and was back in a moment. 'Mm,' he said, 'she's there. She's got that blue thing on. I like her in that blue thing, but' – he laughed indulgently – 'she hates skirts, you know, can't bear 'em. Says she's only happy in trousers. And, I must say, she's

185

the only woman I've seen look well in 'em. See her turned out for hunting in a bowler hat and a white stock on that mare of yours – she can knock spots off the county ladies. Not that I don't mean she's not a lady,' he stammered. 'She's too much of a lady for me, that's the trouble.'

Oliver, who couldn't bear to see Fred growing redder and humbler, changed the subject. 'I wish I could be there to see you married.'

'I wish you could like hell, old boy,' said Fred. 'You'd back me up. Old Ken's all right – he's going to be best man, you know – but he's as scared of the whole business as I am.'

'Lots of whisky beforehand,' said Oliver. 'That's the secret.'

'You bet,' said Fred. 'We've planned that. And we'll chew tea afterwards,' he said solemnly. 'Sweetens the breath like magic.'

'And there'll be lots of booze afterwards,' said Oliver, 'to help you through the reception. It was a bit of luck Stanford getting hold of that champagne for us. It'll make it a much better party.'

'Mm,' said Fred without enthusiasm. Stanford Black was one of the people who made him blink and go sweaty in the palms. He hoped Vi would not mind his hands being sweaty. Hers never were; they were dry and rough and strong.

One of the few cheerful features of the wedding was that John would be able, after all, to give Violet away. He was out of bed now, although still rather feeble, and a nasty yellow colour where his tan had paled. He swore tactlessly that it was due to Elizabeth's good nursing that he had recovered so quickly from his severe attack of flu. He and Elizabeth had become quite friendly over it, and shared one or two jokes and allusions which no one else understood. Heather had all along taken the line of: If Elizabeth's there, there's nothing *I* can do, and had confined her ministrations to John to leaving him in a howling draught every time she went in and out of the room, and airing her grievances about his mother at him while he lay in bed, unable to escape. She was slightly revolted by illness, and had always made a great song about the children's disorders. She sprinkled eau-de-Cologne all over John, who hated it, and would ask him ten times in an hour how he could bear the room so hot and stuffy. If he coughed too much, she would say she was sure he could stop if he tried, and she left all his handkerchiefs for Elizabeth to wash, saying that if she wanted to have the kudos of nursing him she could have the dirty work as well.

Oliver, who was feeling rather jaded, taunted her with being jealous of Elizabeth.

'Jealous!' Heather tossed her head. 'What on earth for? There's no more between them than there is between her and you. It's simply this rather arch patient-and-nurse atmosphere. No, I'm afraid it's the most pathetically innocent relationship. I don't believe Johnny knows how to flirt; he never did with me. I remember the first time I met him, at the Strakers' dance, he stared hopelessly at me all evening and just sat looking miserable when I was dancing with anybody else. Poor Johnny, his technique was terrible, I'm sure it wouldn't work on Elizabeth after her London boy friend who sends her home with orchids on her coat. He wouldn't ask a girl if he could kiss her, like John used to. If I'd worn glasses, he'd probably have asked me politely if I'd like to take them off. There are men who do that, you know. I had a girl friend who wore glasses and she said it was hideously shaming, and when they did that she used to stop the taxi and get out.'

'What did you do when John asked you if he could kiss you?'

'Oh, I let him,' said Heather drearily. 'I was kind of in love with the poor mutt.'

'And aren't you now?'

'Oh, Ollie, I don't *know*. Don't keep on at me, I feel terrible.'

'You want a change of scene, my girl, that's what's the matter with you. You're as fed up with all of us as you are with John. Wait till you get to Australia; you'll feel quite different.'

'I'm not going to Australia.'

'Blast, I thought we were getting rid of you.'

'Muffet says if we go she's coming too, if you please. John wants to take her because he thinks he can't leave her behind to fend for herself. Oh, she says she'll have a separate house, or igloo, or whatever you have in the Bush, but I know what it would be. She'd be on our doorstep all the time, and so would her creditors.'

'How d'you feel?' she asked him suddenly, looking at him.

'I feel rotten today,' he admitted. 'I don't know why.'

'You look it. You look like I feel, pale yellow, with touches of blue.'

'Not about the lips, I hope,' said Oliver anxiously, reaching for the mirror. 'Oh God.' He thumped his chest cautiously. 'Why can't one change a dud heart like the dynamo on a car?'

'You haven't been having proper attention lately,' said Heather triumphantly. 'Miss Elizabeth's got a new interest in her cocky little head. She's paid to nurse you, though, not John.'

'I thought you weren't jealous,' he said. 'Anyway, it's not you who pays her. Nor me either,' he added glumly. 'God, Heather, it's awful to be so dependent. I shall have to get up and start earning money soon.'

'Let's you and I run away, Ollie, shall we, and live somewhere where you don't need to work because you don't need much money. You just lie around in shorts eating fruit and soaking up the sun, and at night you go to cafés, and gipsies come and play to you, and you put a glass of brandy on their violin.'

'You'd need money to buy the brandy.'

'It would be very cheap brandy.'

Oliver put his hand on his chest again. 'If I run away,' he said, 'it'll have to be with someone who'll push me around in a bathchair. I can't see you doing that, Heather, wheeling me on to the front and tucking in my rug before you settle down beside me with your knitting.'

'Good Lord, we're not going to Eastbourne,' she said. 'Don't be so damping. I'm offering you the tropics, and intoxicating wine, and music, and women with long brown legs, but all you want is Wincarnis in a South Coast town with Elizabeth. Yes, I mean it,' she said vehemently. 'Go on, admit it. You're as jealous as hell of Elizabeth and John – just as jealous as I am!' She left him triumphantly, and he picked up the mirror and made a *moue* with his lips. They certainly did look shockingly blue.

CHAPTER 9

As Violet's wedding day approached, inexorably and too rapidly, it was not only the bride who began to wish it need never come.

It was like all parties: fun to arrange and talk about at first, but less and less fun as the hosts begin to get cold feet, and to wonder whether the drink will hold out and what they will do if people stand about in lifeless groups, and to wish that they had some new clothes and had not invited so many people and, finally, that they had never thought of the party at all.

Even Mrs North, who loved to entertain, was depressed about it because she was so tired. She and Elizabeth had been cooking like mad things for three days before the wedding, and the family were getting tired of makeshift meals. 'It'll be worse after the party,' Heather said. 'We shall be eating leftovers for days. You never saw such a mountain of food as they've made. It's absurd. People are never going to eat all those sausage rolls and cakes and cheese straws in the middle of the afternoon.'

Mrs North, still flushed from her concentrated oven work, looked a little dashed. 'You never know,' she said. 'It's far better to have too much than too little. And some of them may not have had any lunch if they've come long distances. I'm sure Fred's friends will eat hearty, anyway.'

'Well, I mean to,' said Violet, who had just been inspecting the larder with a wetted finger. 'I can't wait to get my hands on that trifle. I shan't have any lunch tomorrow, I don't think, so I can enjoy myself at the reception.'

'Think again,' said Heather. 'The bride's supposed to be far too nervous and ethereal to eat. Ma hasn't half killed herself doing all that cooking for *you*.'

'You needn't be so snotty. I haven't noticed you helping much.'

'You're the last one to talk. Have you done a thing, just one thing, towards your own beastly wedding?'

'You know I can't cook,' said Violet, complacently.

'That poor Fred. But cooking's not everything. Who went to fetch the flowers? Who's decorated the church? Who sewed tapes on your dress so you won't keep twisting and wriggling to hitch up your shoulder straps all through the service?'

'You know you love doing flowers,' Violet said. 'And you didn't fetch them; your mother-in-law did.'

'And gave some away to the conductress in the bus coming home, so that I had to go and get some more. And who's spent all day telephoning Christie's about the cake? Jolly clever of you to keep out of the house all day, so you couldn't be asked to do anything. I almost hope the cake doesn't come in time, except that it would be a let-down for Ma. What are you going to cut it with, anyway – a hay knife? Ma, *look* at her! The day before her wedding, and a dinner party in her honour in an hour's time, and she just sits on the floor in those stinking trousers, burnishing a curb chain with your saucepan cleaner.'

'Most important,' said Violet, shaking metal polish into her hands and jingling the curb chain between them as if she were playing in a rumba band. 'It's going on my honeymoon with me.'

'I don't believe you'd notice if Fred got left behind,' said Heather scornfully, 'as long as the horses were there.'

'Yes, I should,' said Violet, 'because there'd be one horse too many, so sucks. I haven't shown you my new saddle yet, have I, Ollie?' She tilted back her head to look at him. 'Jully super of Fred, wasn't it? He wouldn't tell me what it cost.'

'Darned sight better than what you've given him,' put in Heather. 'I'd call off the wedding if my fiancée only gave me a set of new teeth for the clipping machine.'

'But it was what he wanted!' cried Violet in dismay. 'And it was an awful fag getting them; they're not making that sort any more. I had to go all the way to Birmingham in the end, didn't I, Ma?'

'Yes, dear, you took a lot of trouble. Don't be unkind, Heather, and if you two must bicker, as I've said hundreds of times, don't do it in this room. And don't do it anywhere where I am either because my head's going round and round.'

'Poor old darling.' Heather went over suddenly and kissed her on top of the hair-net that was preserving her elaborate hair-set for tomorrow. Mrs North loved to be kissed, and none of her children did it often enough. 'You do look tired. You almost look your age for a change. See what you've done, Vi? You weren't allowed to kill your brother over your wedding, but you've succeeded in wrecking your mother. Let me get the dinner tonight, Ma. You stay here with your feet up and talk to Ollie.'

Mrs North immediately sat upright and let down her feet at the idea. 'That's darling of you,' she said, 'but I have a soufflé to make.'

'You haven't got a monopoly in eggs, ducky. Other people can make soufflés, you know.'

'Not the way I make 'em,' said her mother. 'Not mushroom soufflés. You know how Violet likes my mushroom soufflés, and it is her evening.'

'She'd eat anybody's soufflé, even if it was flat in the dish. Though I shouldn't think she'd have any room after all that picking in the larder.'

'Violet, child, you haven't! I dared you – –'

'Keep your hair on,' said Violet. 'I was only looking. You're a mean sneak, Heather Sandys, and a lying swine. I shan't be sorry to get away from you.' Without getting up, she crawled over to the table by the side window, hauled out a dog by the scruff of its neck, skidded it over the rugs and went out with a slam of the door that rattled all the mullioned window-panes.

'I shall miss old Vi,' said Heather. 'She's fun to tease, because she always rises, like Ma's soufflés. It's going to be awfully slow having no one to fight with. She's not a bad soul either, you know. I'm very fond of the old bird.'

'No one would think it to hear the way you talk to her,' said her mother.

'That? Oh, that doesn't mean a thing. It's the only language she understands. She gets out of her depth if you give her polite conversation.'

'She must be fathoms under with Fred then,' said Mrs North. 'He's so darn polite it makes me nervous.'

'Oh, they get on fine,' said Heather airily. 'They just never talk.'

Contrary to tradition, Fred was coming to dinner on the eve of the wedding. John, who had had the correct night out with the boys before he married Heather, had offered to arrange a party for Fred at the local roadhouse, but Mrs North, who was getting a little oppressed by Muffet and Miss Smutts, begged him not to leave the women on their own. 'It makes it so dull for Violet if we only have a hen party,' she said.

'I shouldn't have thought it made it any more thrilling to have Fred,' piped up Heather, who never missed a cue, but her mother did not allow this sort of talk any more with the wedding so close. She herself, satisfied that it was what Violet wanted, was training herself to make the best of him. Besides being bad taste, she said,

191

to criticize Fred at this stage, nothing that anyone said could alter the fact that he was within days of being a member of the family.

The best man, Kenneth Saxby, who had been at the Agricultural College with Fred, was coming to dinner, too, and going back to sleep at the cottage. He was a nice-looking, serious young man, with pimples on his forehead and an incipient carbuncle on the back of his neck, which he had covered with Elastoplast. He was a vet, with a growing practice in Warwickshire, and the minute he arrived Violet cornered him for a free opinion on the canker on her old Labrador's ear.

He was brought in to see Oliver before dinner, and Oliver noticed how differently Fred behaved with someone whom he knew well. His nose was quite a normal colour. He wondered how long he would have to know the family before he would shed his burning self-consciousness. Elizabeth came in with a loaded tray to lay the table and both men sprang at her.

'It's quite all right, thank you; I'm so used to doing it, it doesn't take a minute,' she said, picking up the little coffee table that Fred had knocked over on his way to help her. Oliver saw that Kenneth was struck with her appearance and was obviously trying to work out whether she was a superior kind of maid, a friend, or a member of the family.

Moving neatly about his room, so much at home in contrast to the awkwardness of the two men, she did indeed seem one of the family. Oliver could not imagine his room without her moving about in it. What would it be like to be awakened in the morning by someone less clean and fresh? For no one could ever look as spruce as Elizabeth before breakfast. What would it be like to have no one to whom to say the things which other people did not understand? True, Elizabeth did not always answer, and when she did she was sometimes indifferent and sometimes disapproving and sometimes even rude, but at least she always knew what he was getting at. Somehow, without seeming to be particularly interested in him, she understood his mind. Hers was rather similar: detached, independent, unexcitable. He had long ago given up the idea of trying to woo her into tenderness. Any flirtatious attempts slid off her and left him feeling undignified. Arnold Clitheroe must have a better technique; he wondered how he went about it. It was difficult to imagine Elizabeth relaxing her guard. Perhaps she never did, and Clitheroe loved a poised and polished statue, without knowing what went on inside. Oliver thought he knew Elizabeth quite well by now, well enough at least to guess at what she was thinking. Since the wedding preparations began she had been quieter and more withdrawn than ever, getting on with a hundred jobs without being asked, yet not entering into discussions and plans. She only seemed interested in the wedding as far as the work it made. This she accepted calmly and performed efficiently. She had given Violet a really attractive brooch, which Violet had not appreciated.

' It was very generous of her,' Mrs North said, touched. 'That's an expensive brooch.'

'Probably one her boy friend gave her,' said Heather. Arnold Clitheroe seemed to give Elizabeth quite a lot of things. He seemed to be hot on the trail, from what Oliver could gather from Elizabeth's guarded answers to questions.

She was looking unusually warm and pink tonight, and her eyes were smiling as if she were excited inside. She had made the enormous concession of having two cocktails. Fred and Ken had been summoned to the drawing-room to be social. Oliver watched Elizabeth lay the table, and when she was looking it over, standing on one leg in a way she had when pensive, he said suddenly: 'All this wedding business – does it inspire you to thoughts of doing the same?'

She looked at him calmly. 'I imagine I shall get married one day,' she said. 'I don't mean to go on working for ever.'

'And you couldn't go home, of course. At least, I gather that from what Muffet said you'd told her.'

'Muffet,' said Elizabeth, moving a knife into exact alinement with a soup-spoon, 'is a lying old busybody. She'd say anything to make it look as if she knew more than anyone else.'

'You wouldn't really go and live with her, would you, like she's always planning?'

'I suppose one could do worse. Bit too insecure for me, though. I want to keep on the right side of the law if possible.'

'With someone like Arnold Clitheroe, for instance. No one could go wrong with a name like that.'

'I could do worse.'

'Liz, you're surely not considering – –? Why, the man must be at least fifty. Much too old for you, however nice he was.'

'I might. He's always asking me, but I haven't made up my mind. I tell him I want to see this job through first.'

'For God's sake kill me off and go to him, then,' said Oliver peevishly. 'Go ahead and ruin your life.'

'Why shouldn't I get married?' she asked. 'Other women do. In fact, it's considered a bit of a disaster if they don't. Look at Vi. I mean, without wanting to be rude, no one could say Fred was the ideal husband, yet everyone's glad, because it's better than marrying nobody.' Elizabeth never came close to you on the rare occasions when she spoke her mind. She stood now with the table between them, talking to him across the room.

'But good heavens!' Oliver ran his fingers through his hair. 'You can't compare the two. Of course, Vi isn't everybody's meat, but a girl like you – –'

'Yes, what about a girl like me?'

'Don't fish. I'm not going to tell you you're pretty, if that's what you want. John can do that.'

'Oh, he does,' she said smugly.

'Stop being coquettish,' he said. 'It doesn't suit you.'

'How dare you,' she said, colouring. 'You are the rudest, worst-tempered man I've ever known. You think that because you're the spoiled baby of this house you can say anything you like and get away with it.'

'That's a beastly thing to say.'

'You started the beastliness.'

'That's right,' said Muffet, who never entered a room without listening outside first. 'Having a little tiff. Won't do you any harm; then you can kiss and make up afterwards. How pretty you look, Elizabeth darling, when you colour up, but I expect Oliver tells you that.' Conscious of resentment, but not caring, she went on: 'I couldn't bear it a moment longer in the drawing-room, Ollie. I had to come in here to make sure I was normal. That young man of your sister's behaves as if I were the phantom of the opera. I strike him dumb. When I try to draw him out with kindly conversation he just opens and shuts his mouth like a fish, and never a word comes out. The other one, his friend, is quite

194

an interesting fellow – clever, too, he's been telling me about some of his cases. He finds it very hard to get the right instruments, he says. I'm going to look round when I get back to London and see what I can find for him.'

'Fred's very shy, you know,' Oliver said. 'You have to make allowances.'

'Shy? No one's shy with me; I can talk to anybody. But not to your future brother-in-law. I've never met such heavy going.'

Mrs North came in, untying the heliotrope apron with the labelled pockets. 'I'm all ready to dish up,' she said, 'if you are, Elizabeth. I thought I'd never be ready. My goodness, how we've got through it all, I don't know. I keep going into the larder to gloat over the food; it really does look swell. Those fruit jellies of yours are setting perfectly.'

'I was going to put some cream on top,' Elizabeth said. 'I thought they looked rather dull.'

'Couldn't be half as dull as that fellow in there,' said Lady Sandys in her clear, carrying voice, jerking her head towards the thin wall of the drawing-room.

That fellow in there did the wrong thing, of course, by turning up next morning and asking to see Violet.

'She mustn't see him! Don't let her see him!' Mrs North scuttled down the stairs when she heard his voice in the hall. 'It's terribly bad luck for the bride and bridegroom to meet on the wedding morning. Surely you know that?' she asked him crossly. She had been up since half past six, and, so far, everything possible had gone wrong, from a sulky kitchen fire and soured milk to a child sick on the carpet and Violet's petticoat showing two inches below her dress.

Fred was understood, through his stammering, to say that one of the horses was sick and Ken wanted some drugs. He himself must stay and help Ken with the horse, and the only other man who could drive had just put a load of grass into the dryer and could not leave the machine.

'Wouldn't you know it?' wailed Mrs North. 'Wouldn't you know something like this would have to happen? I wanted to keep Violet in the house all morning to be sure of her being ready

195

on time. If she goes jaunting off to Shrewsbury, Heaven knows when she'll get back.'

'B-but it's a matter of life or death, Mrs N-N-N' – gulp – 'North,' said Fred, who had a sense of the dramatic on occasion.

'Heather, I suppose you couldn't – –?'

'I couldn't,' said Heather firmly. 'I've got all the flowers in the house to do, and the children to dress. And you're not going to make John go in that draughty car.'

'What's all the rumpus?' Oliver heard Violet come thumping down the stairs. 'Oh, hullo, Fred,' she said casually. 'How d'you like my dress? This petticoat thing isn't meant to show; they're just pinning it up.'

'He mustn't see it! Fred, don't you dare look at her. Have you children got no sense of what's right? Violet' – as Fred started his stammering explanation again – 'I'm afraid you've got to take the car and get some drugs from Shrewsbury. One of the horses is sick. And if you're not back by twelve o'clock – –'

'Which one?' Violet was immediately businesslike. 'Colic? Marigold? Whee-ew!' She whistled like a man. 'When should she be foaling?' In a moment she burst into Oliver's room, her hair dishevelled from trying on and a flap of white silk hanging down at the back of the red silk dress in which she was going to be married.

'Can I borrow your trench-coat, Ollie?' she asked breathlessly. 'It's raining like stink, and I don't want to get this fancy dress wet going to the garage.'

'Now, Violet.' Mrs North followed her into the room. 'You're not going out in that dress. You just go upstairs and take it off before you go.'

'Can't, Ma, no time,' said Violet over her shoulder on her way out.

'The horse won't die for the sake of two minutes. You *can't* go shopping in your wedding dress! And I have to alter the petticoat.' Her mother pursued her at a trot.

'Do it when I come back.'

'I'll never have time. Take it off now.'

'Oh, *Ma* . . .' Oliver heard their arguing voices fading down the passage and presently his mother came back and lectured him for five minutes about his sister. She was rattled this morning.

196

The capable command which had borne her through the last few days had succumbed at last to the waiting accumulation of fatigue. Her round, creased face was quivering with near-tears.

'I shall never get through this day, Ollie, never. So many things have gone wrong already and I feel there are so many more to come. I can't face it. What shall I do? I can't face it.'

'Oh, rot,' he said, 'you'll sail through it.' It made him uneasy to see her crumple. He remembered his childhood's sudden panic of insecurity if he ever saw her tired or crying. Who could cope with life if she could not? 'Go and have a drink, old dear,' he told her. 'A good strong one, that's all you need.'

'At this hour in the morning?' She consulted her pendant watch and checked it with her wrist-watch. 'Oh well, it is three and a half minutes to eleven. Maybe I will, just to keep me going until the next disaster happens along. You know they haven't sent the cake yet? My goodness, why didn't I ask Violet to call for it in Shrewsbury? That shows you what kind of a state I'm in; I never thought of it. Darling, when this schemozzle is over I'm going to take to my bed for a week and rest up. I feel all to pieces, and I've tasted so many things I've gotten terrible dyspepsia. I've been taking bicarbonate all morning. I never thought I'd be envying you, but I reckon you're the lucky one today to be in here out of it all. Yes, Mrs Cowlin, what is it? Oh, my gracious, take it off the fire then, and find a rag to wipe up the mess. Not the teacloth – wait, I'll come and see.' Slightly restored by this new challenge, she gave Oliver an exasperated look and followed Mrs Cowlin out, nearly overbalancing in the doorway by aiming the pretence of a kick at the back of Mrs Cowlin's creeping black woollen stockings.

Oliver was by no means out of it all, however, even though he could not take an active part. People found him useful as an audience for grievances or an adviser on problems which they had usually already settled, but wanted corroborating.

His next visitor was Heather, in an overall, with her head tied up in Oliver's silk invasion map of Germany. 'I've just had a row with Ma,' she stated, taking one of his cigarettes.

'So what?'

'Well, Ollie, she really is exasperating. Got a match? I know

197

she's got a lot to do, and all that – incidentally, she wouldn't have half as much if she'd occasionally trust someone else to do some of it – but she really is *difficult*. I took David in to see her in his party clothes, because I thought it would please her, and she went off the handle about his boots. She knows quite well McNaughton won't let him wear shoes, and if she thinks I'm going to spoil the good work of months, not to mention the money I've spent on these flat feet – which he gets from John – just for the sake of Vi's tiresome wedding, which there's been more fuss about than the Lord Mayor's Show – –'

'I don't see that one day could matter.' Oliver had found that since he had been in bed, with his day made up of little things, he could take a genuine interest in trivial domestic affairs which before had been beneath a man's notice. 'Anyway, are the boots doing all that much good? Elizabeth says – –'

Heather blew up like a rocket. 'Elizabeth says! Don't quote that woman to me. What does she know about osteopathy, anyway? Isn't that just typical of all hospital nurses? Because they've had a few years' potty training they always think they know more than the doctors.'

'Elizabeth is a very knowledgeable girl,' said Muffet, coming in, also in an overall. No one in the house had thought it was worth while dressing properly before putting on their wedding garments. John had been sloping about in a spotted dressing-gown with a silk scarf, like someone in a Noel Coward comedy. Muffet's overall was of glazed chintz, with a bold design of peacocks' tails and a wide sash round her matchstick waist. 'You're wanted upstairs,' she told Heather. 'Your son has put bright red plasticine all over his face, and the effect, though striking, is un-English.'

Heather raised her eyes to Heaven. 'O, God,' she said, 'is there no peace in this house?' and went out, passing her mother-in-law like a gust of wind.

'Absolutely none,' said Lady Sandys cheerfully. 'I've been trying all morning to find somewhere to sit where they're not moving furniture. As they won't let me help, I thought I might at least read the paper so that I shall have something to talk about this afternoon. I came to ask you, darling, whether you think I ought to wear my orange, or my black-and-white? One doesn't

198

want to be overdressed in the country. On the other hand, one doesn't want to appear to patronize the country folk by dressing down to them.'

'Your orange? I've never seen you in an orange dress.'

'Oh, my pet – how like a man. Of course you have; I've worn it hundreds of time for dinner.' Oliver had seen her in mustard yellow, and in navy blue with brass buttons, and in bright blue with a Toby frill round the neck.

'You know, that orange dress I got at that shop where they were so unpleasant about the bill; I told you. I shall never go there again. It's got a ruff round the neck like Queen Elizabeth. I always think it looks as if one's head had been neatly carved off and dished up as a cutlet.'

'Oh,' he said, wondering what colour she would call an orange dress, 'you mean the *orange*. No, I should wear the black-and-white.' This would avoid the possible confusion of somebody telling her they liked her blue dress.

'That's got that settled, then, thank goodness. You're the only one that's any help to me. Everyone else is too busy to talk. I've been swept out of the kitchen, and dusted out of the dining-room, and Hoovered out of the drawing-room. Smutty's in one of her sombre moods, and when I ask her she just says: "Please yourself. All I know is I'm going to wear my wine." By which I suppose she means that bottle-green monstrosity. The poor old thing always was hazy on colours.'

'Uncle Ollie, Uncle Ollie,' called a breathy voice at the window. Evelyn's chin was on the sill, as she stood in the flower-bed in an unbuttoned mackintosh, with rat-tails of hair streaming from under a sou'wester. 'Uncle Ollie, isn't it dreadful, one of the mares is dreadfully ill. It's Marigold – you know, the one I told you about, that Fred took to be married to that horse at Culver. That man that came yesterday to be best man – he's a vet. I've been helping him. I just thought I'd come and tell you. Good-bye!' Her face disappeared suddenly.

'Evie!' He called her back. 'I don't think you should be down there. You – you might get in the way.'

'I'm helping them, I tell you. Oh, you mean because Marigold's going to have a foal. Pooh, that's nothing. I've seen stacks of calves born – lambs, too, but that's more dull.'

'Your Aunt Hattie's looking for you,' said Lady Sandys.

'Oh, blow. I'd better scoot before she catches me. She wants to get me dressed for the wedding. How can they have a wedding when Marigold might die?' She raised a tragic, rain-washed face to Oliver.

She had barely disappeared round the corner of the house when Mrs North arrived in an overall with horizontal stripes, and smocking stretched to its fullest extent at the waist. 'I told her not to go out this morning. She'll get soaking wet, and I shan't be able to do a thing with that hair. If I don't get dressed before lunch, we shall never get to the church on time. Oh – –' she said vaguely, 'good morning, Muffet.'

'I've seen you already,' said Lady Sandys, 'but only *en passant*. You were travelling too fast to hear me say good morning. What time is lunch? I'd better go and change, too.' She flung back the wide sleeve of her overall, and as she looked at her watch, Oliver saw with horror that she was wearing Heather's charm bracelet. So it had started again. After nearly two clear weeks, she must choose today to get acquisitive.

'Yes, you'd better go, or you'll be late,' he said nervously, wanting to get her away before his mother heard the familiar jingle. There was no point in adding to her worries by telling her now. This might be just an isolated aberration. Lady Sandys had got to come to the party, anyway, and it would be time enough to worry when she was seen walking round in Mrs Ogilvie's regimental brooch or Lady Salter's foxes.

'Thank the Lord she's all right,' said Mrs North when she had gone. 'I shouldn't have a minute's peace if I thought she were having one of her fits with all those people in the house. As it is, you never know what she'll do. I only pray she won't choose to make a speech. She might say anything.'

Violet was not back by twelve o'clock, nor by half past. Evelyn, who had been sent back from the stables by Cowlin, reported that Fred and Ken were still there, in their shirt-sleeves. 'The foal isn't born yet,' she said. 'At least, not properly. Do you know, Aunt Muffet, they wear little sort of slippers over their shoes so that they can't hurt – –' She saw Mrs North's expression.

'How extraordinarily interesting,' said Lady Sandys. 'Do go on.'

'You come upstairs with me,' said Mrs North, propelling Evelyn before her. 'What your father will say to you, I don't know. Child, look at your hair! It'll have to be pigtails, whether you like it or not. I'm quite resigned now,' she told the others, through Evelyn's wails of protest. 'I shall never get any of them to the church in time. Oh, a swell wedding it's going to be without the bride and bridegroom and best man!'

'Perhaps Vi will go straight to the church and get married in Oliver's trench-coat,' said Heather. 'Ma, I can't find my charm bracelet anywhere. Have you seen it?' It was so long since the half-moon table had been in use that people did not automatically connect Lady Sandys with any loss. 'What are you making faces for, Ollie?' asked Heather obtusely. 'Have you got a pain? For God's sake, don't say you're going to be ill now, just to make everything perfect.'

'Wind,' said Oliver, as his mother started towards him, all her other worries forgotten.

'And I had to go and finish all the bicarbonate,' she lamented. 'Go and see if Elizabeth has any, Heather.' Oliver did not get a chance of seeing Heather alone. He prayed that she would not notice the bracelet, because she would be quite capable of making a scene, and it had been said that if Lady Sandys were ever made aware of what her subconscious was making her do, it might upset her mental balance completely and permanently. Looking out of the window while he picked at the cold remains of last night's dinner, he saw Fred and Ken and Violet leaning in consultation on the rail of the stackyard. He shouted at them, but the wind was wrong. Finally, he rang his bell, and after a long time Elizabeth came in.

'Now what do *you* want?' she asked intimidatingly. 'As if we hadn't got trouble enough with David spilling gravy down his party blouse. If you've spilled anything down your pyjamas, it'll have to stay, because you haven't got another clean pair.'

'I only wanted to say that Fred and Ken and Vi are out there gossiping in the stackyard,' said Oliver meekly.

'They're not! Why didn't you say so?' Elizabeth was rushing out, but Oliver called her back.

'Just a second, Liz. Shut the door; I want to tell you something very private.' She shut the door and stood against it, looking

201

at him with interest, caught by the urgent, intimate tone of his voice.

'Muffet's got Heather's charm bracelet on,' he said earnestly. 'Don't let Ma know; it'll only worry her. Tell Smutty to get it off her somehow before Heather sees it.'

'Oh, yes.' Elizabeth's look of interest died. 'All right,' she said impatiently. 'I'll fix it. Don't get so fussed.'

It stopped raining after lunch and the veil of clouds drew away from a pale-blue sky and a mild May sun. Birds sang from everywhere with early-morning exuberance, and hopped on the juicy lawn. Miss Smutts, who had been saying at intervals during the rainy morning: 'Happy the bride the sun shines on,' now stopped saying it, and dwelt on the fact that it would still be too wet underfoot for the guests to overflow from the drawing-room into the garden, as Mrs North had planned.

The whole party came in to show themselves to Oliver before starting for the church, and lined up in a self-conscious row for his inspection. Violet, who had insisted on sitting down to a square meal when she was finally hauled in, had been dressed in half an hour, and Heather had done a few rapid things to her face and hair. She was passed from hand to hand like a lay figure, thinking and talking of nothing but Marigold's foal, which only Ken's skill had saved, until they began to wonder whether she would not rather be marrying Ken than Fred.

The others thrust her forward and she stood now helplessly before Oliver in the dark red silk dress and matching coat. Perhaps because she had not dressed herself, she had the air of not being inside her clothes. They hung from her square shoulders as if they were secured only by tabs, like a paper doll's one-dimensional wardrobe. They had buckled her belt tightly into her waist, to lessen her appearance of being the same shape all the way down, but she had loosened it surreptitiously on the way downstairs and had pushed it towards her hips, so that she looked longer-bodied than ever. She wore silk stockings on her muscular legs, and boat-shaped court shoes, low-heeled, because of Fred, in which she complained that she could not walk. A spray of gardenias was pinned to her coat and she carried a posy of the same flowers, clutching them doggedly before her like an

202

orphan presenting a bouquet to a visiting mayoress. The other hand hung uselessly, encased in a black kid glove, which, like the rest of her clothes, did not seem to be on her, but to be a separate entity, like a false hand. She had quite a successful hat, a red silk turban, matching her dress. Heather had coaxed a big curl up in front of it and fastened a diamond clip on either side. Violet had rejected ear-rings, and ever since Heather had tried them on had been rubbing at her ears until the lobes were red.

There had been a struggle, too, about Violet's glasses, without which she declared she would never see her way up the aisle. Even now, when she had been overruled by numbers, she kept taking them furtively out of her pocket and putting them on, pushing the turban up at the sides, so that Heather had to come in front of her and reach up to jam it down again. Last night, to the accompaniment of roars and kicks, she had plucked her sister's eyebrows, and powder, rouge and eyelash cream had made something quite pleasing of Violet's face. Brightened by lipstick, her mouth looked fuller and softer than usual, and the lower lip quivered slightly now and again from nervousness.

'Vi, you look grand!' said Oliver, glad that he could speak truthfully. He had been afraid they were going to guy her up like a pantomime dame. 'I've never seen you look so stunning.'

Somehow, one expected this different-looking Vi to speak with a different voice. 'Oh, shut up assing, Ollie,' said the old Vi, however. 'I look like something the cat brought in, and I feel an absolute twerp.'

'Honestly, Ollie,' said Heather, who was looking prettily over-dressed in a flower hat, a frilly blouse and every bit of jewellery she possessed, except the charm bracelet, 'the old horse doesn't look too bad, does she?' She stepped out of line to admire her handiwork and Violet stuck out her tongue at her, said 'Here, I'm sick of being a peepshow,' and retired to a corner to put on her glasses. The children, who normally wore dungarees and jerseys, were excited by their clothes and ran shrilly in and out of people's legs, showing off, making faces, and screaming with laughter at each other. Miss Smutts, heavy as a thundercloud in her braided wine frockcoat, said more than once: 'It'll only end in crying.' Susan, in Heather's arms, wore a stiff white dress like a fairy doll and a quilted satin jacket to match the Dutch cap which kept falling askew over her primrose-coloured curls, as she fought with Heather for the right to play tug-of-war with her pearls.

'The car's there! The car's there!' yelled Evelyn, streaking in from the hall and out again.

'Ve car! Ve car!' echoed David, streaking after her, falling down, waiting for a moment to see if he was hurt, finding he was not and bellowing all the same.

'Why, it's my dear Mr Steptoe!' Lady Sandys waved to him through the open doorway, and Oliver saw with a sinking heart that she was still wearing the charm braclet. He tried to catch Miss Smutts' eye, but she had gone to make sure of the front seat of the car, because she was always sick at the back.

After the others had gone, John and Violet waited in Oliver's room for Mr Peploe to come back for them. John, looking burly and handsome in a dark suit with a white carnation button-hole, his curly hair greased into little waves, seemed to be more nervous than Violet. She slumped, creasing her skirt, with her glasses on, in an arm-chair, ejaculating at intervals: 'God, I wish it was all over.' John moved his long legs about the room, talking jerkily about nothing at all. His forehead was like a harrowed field. He had cut his chin shaving for the second time that day and kept dabbing his handkerchief on a tiny spot of welling blood.

At last the returning car was heard, and Violet, with a 'Here goes, chaps!' pushed herself out of the arm-chair, pulled up her stockings like a schoolgirl and grasped her posy like a police-man's baton. ''Bye, Ollie,' she said gruffly. 'Wish you could come. Sure you're all right?'

'It seems awful leaving you,' said John anxiously. Oliver waved them away with his blessing and leaned forward with his arms on his knee to watch them get into the car. At the last moment Violet turned to wave to him, bumped her head on the roof turning back, and got in, rubbing at the turban. Oliver hoped that Heather would be at the bottom of the church to put it straight for her.

He watched the car go round the little green button of lawn and out of his sight and leaned back to explore the feeling of being alone in the house. Everyone in turn had volunteered to stay with Oliver, but he had resolutely refused, and to quiet them had even written to Dr Trevor for his permission to be left on his own. He had never been quite alone here since his illness and he was looking forward to the experience.

The Cowlins were at the church. So were most of the people who worked on the farm, although by leaning out of the window and twisting his neck, he could see a man with a tractor making patterns on a sloping field at the eastern boundary of the land. He was quite alone in the house and the stillness was so complete that he fancied he could hear all the clocks ticking, and even the kitchen range whispering, with a hiss now and then as the kettle lid lifted and a drop of water skidded over the hot old iron. All alone in the house. He felt perfectly well, so well that it was amusing to speculate idly on what he would do if one of his waves of dizzy faintness attacked him, or if he had the heart attack which Dr Trevor was always holding over him as a warning against doing too much.

For interest's sake, what would he do? The man with the tractor would never hear him. Could he get out of bed and hop or crawl to the corner cupboard where his pills were? He could never get to the telephone in the next room, and if he did, whom should he ring up? They would not be long, of course; they would be back before anything serious could happen to him. Elizabeth would be back. She would know what to do. But he was perfectly all right today. He had wanted so much to be feeling his best that it was quite surprising to find that he was.

He took up his book and began to read. Pity they were not going to be away longer, really. It was pleasant being on his own after the hurly burly of the last few days. He needed this solitary respite before the influx of the horde, who would all come in to see him whatever his mother said. Some of them did not know him very well and would be embarrassed because he had lost a leg and they did not know whether they ought to talk about it. He must make the most of this peace before they came, enjoy it consciously, as an active rather than a passive state.

The wind banged a door somewhere in the direction of the kitchen, then it banged again, more gently. Oliver cursed, and, listening for it to bang a third time, could have sworn he heard a footstep. Something bubbling on the stove probably. How easy it was to imagine things when you were alone in a house and helpless. There it was again, and a creak – that was the stairs, of course. They did that sometimes at night – creak, creak, creak, just as if someone was walking up, when really it was the old boards relieving themselves of the imprint of the feet that had trodden them down during the day. A different sort of creak, long drawn-out. That must be another door opening in the wind. Why the hell couldn't they latch the doors on a windy day? Had they no imagination? He was not nervous, but angry. How would they like to be left alone and unable to move in a house where all the doors were kicking up the shindy of souls in torment? He lowered his book – he had been reading the same paragraph for the last five minutes – and waited for the door that had creaked open to bang shut. Why couldn't it shut itself properly and have done with it, so that it couldn't open again?

It was because he had never been alone in the house before, that was why his imagination was so active. What *was* that noise that sounded like footsteps in the kitchen? It was not the scurrying of rats; he knew that sound quite well, and it was always overhead, and at night, quite comforting in its familiarity. No cats or terriers seemed able to get rid of the rats under the roof at Hinkley. He had often teased Violet about the inefficiency of her ratters, but really he was quite proud of the rats for not going. They were Hinkley rats; this was their home more than his, had been in their families for generations before the Norths came. People in whatever sort of nightgowns the Elizabethans wore – he pictured them full and long-sleeved, with a ruff at the neck like Muffet's blue dress – had probably lain and listened to just the same noise. At breakfast – steak, would it be? and three eggs each and buttermilk and parkin – they had said, as the Norths were to say, three hundred years later: 'We must get some more cats and keep them hungry. This house won't last fifty years if we let the rats overrun it.' Three hundred years hence, perhaps people would be still saying that. Unless an atom bomb had done what the rats had failed to do.

He tried to read again. It was odd that when he was alone and conscious of himself he could feel his heart beating. He almost fancied he could hear it, as, by straining his ears, he could hear the leisurely tock of the grandfather clock, swinging its pendulum like a censer in the hall. Supposing a burglar got in, having

heard that the house was defended only by a helpless crock –
what would the crock do? Unless his mother had secretly removed it, his revolver was in the drawer of the table by the
window. Would he be able to get to it, and having got there,
could he load it, and somehow, propping himself against the
wall perhaps, could he go in search of the man? He might surprise him among the silver in the dining-room, but would he
be intimidated by the pale, weedy figure, with one pyjama leg
flapping and an Army revolver wavering in one bony hand? He
looked at his hands. By Jove, they were thin, too. Made the
knuckles look knobbly; not attractive that. Hugo had promised
him he would lose that bluish tinge round the nails when he was
up and about.

Looking down at his hands, he noticed that his heart was
pushing his pyjama jacket gently up and down. So it had not
been his imagination that he could feel it beating. It was going
in for one of its obtrusive, laboured spells. The breathlessness
that he felt presently and the little gasp that he gave were not
caused by the fact that he thought he heard that footstep in the
kitchen again. It was just this darned heart. All the same, and he
felt the skin along his spine creeping as he admitted this to himself: there was someone in the house.

He had heard a stealthy tread in the passage. Was this a
dream? His imagination had become pretty vivid since it had so
often to deputize for actual experience. Had all this conjecturing
about what he would do if a burglar came made him unable to
distinguish between reality and fancy, as sometimes when he felt
himself walking across the room so vividly that he was quite
surprised to find, on opening his eyes, that he was still in bed?
Like the time when he had thought he was dancing with Heather,
and nearly had a heart attack? Supposing he was in for another
go like that, ought he to try and get out now, while he still felt all
right, and get his pills? Fool that he was not to have told Elizabeth to leave them by his bed, and fool she, not to have thought
of it. Dammit, she was his nurse; she should not have gone off
so gaily in her blue linen suit, looking very sweet, he must admit,
but caring so little what became of her patient. Oh, she had
offered to stay all right, but she had been easily persuaded to go.
If she was as uninterested in this wedding, in everything to do

with his family, as she had always appeared, why did she have to go jaunting off with them? He had at least thought she was interested in him as a patient. Had she not said: 'I mean to stay and see this case through?' If she was interested enough to put off getting married, one would have thought she was interested enough to forfeit the doubtful excitement of hearing Vi and Fred stammer: 'I will.'

He suddenly sat bolt upright and forgot about Elizabeth. Someone was moving about in the dining-room, and what was more, someone had coughed, a muffled cough, as if they did not want to be heard. He had read about people's hair standing on end and not believed it. Now he knew that it did happen. His scalp was creeping. His heart thumping in his chest felt enormous. It was like a melon there, hampering his breathing. How long would he have to wait before he heard the feet creep down the passage – nearer and nearer? How could he bear the fumbling fingers on the latch, not knowing what was on the other side of the door, like the old couple who waited in *The Monkey's Paw*? God, why did he have to think of that story now, of the Thing that waited in the street for its father to let it in, the Thing that never got in, so that you never knew what it looked like. How had Jacobs imagined it? Did he see it, as Oliver always did, as he had seen that soldier who fell back from the garret window in the Arnhem house, with the side of his face laid open and the jawbone and back teeth gleaming white under the running blood? Joe had lain still though, only twitching a little, but the Thing that waited outside the door in the street had walked down the street with half its grinning head blown away.

This, of course, was only a burglar. It had gone almost at once to the dining-room, as a burglar would. So they thought they could do what they liked in the house because it was only in charge of a cripple. Where the devil were the dogs? Of course, they were already at Martin's cottage, where they were to stay until Vi returned from her honeymoon. They might have left them in the house just while he was alone. Still, he could manage. This was going to be a pretty big thing, this getting out of bed when he had never done more than be helped into a chair a few inches away; this going to get his revolver, tackling the burglar singlehanded and keeping him covered until the others returned.

There they would find him when they came back, and he would be a hero, and they would all reproach themselves and each other with having left him alone. Elizabeth would fuss over him, but how guilty she would feel and how she would sweat to think of what might have happened to the patient under her responsibility.

Well, if he was going after that burglar, he must go before he got away with all the North family silver. Not that the silver was all that valuable, and perhaps not even worth the effort it was going to cost him, but how would it sound to bleat: 'I heard someone rifling the house, so I lay here and sweated till he'd gone away'?

Good thing he'd kept that revolver – more as a souvenir than anything else. Now that he had made up his mind what he was going to do he felt calmer, although as he lay in bed planning out each move, his heart knocked more at the thought of each impossible effort. Well, and if he never got there, and they found him stretched out on the floor in a faint, at least he would have done his best. Of course he could do it. He had not once felt faint sitting out in the chair; he was good for more than they gave him credit. Impulsively, because he knew that if he thought about it much longer he would not do it, he flung back the bed-clothes and paused, his mouth slightly open, as he heard the tiny cough again, nearer this time – definitely at the sideboard.

What was he going to look like? He pictured him like a cartoon burglar, scarf knotted round his throat, cap pulled down, a sack for the swag. A black mask perhaps? No, not an amateur like this, who came after small stuff and betrayed himself by coughing. Probably some old tramp who had got the cough from sleeping in hedges; he would be dirty and stubbled and ragged – rather a revolting figure. He would be easily cowed by the sight of a gun. Inch by inch, lifting his buttocks and his stump round on his hands, he got his leg over the edge of the bed, bent it, and stretched down until his bare toes touched the rug. Still keeping his hands behind him on the bed, he lowered himself until his foot was standing flat. His stump quivered as though it longed to help. He tried putting a little weight on the leg, but immediately he toppled, twisting round and saving himself with both hands on the bed. His balance was all wrong. The M.O. had said a leg weighed about thirty pounds. No wonder he was top-heavy with all that gone from one side. He pushed himself round again until his back was against the bed, leaning on it, He would never be able to hop, that was quite clear; it would have to be crawling. All fours would be best, so that his stump could swing clear of the floor – all threes, in fact. Bending his leg, he let himself down to his knee and then fell forward on to his hands. Testing this position and finding it satisfactory, he started off towards the table in the most ridiculous gait ever seen. He remembered that he was wearing a pyjama jacket and trousers that did not match. He had not thought it would matter, since the visitors would only see him from the waist up; he had not known then that he was going burglar hunting.

Painfully, yard by yard, pausing now and again to hear if the burglar were approaching, for he must get to the gun before that, he hitched himself towards the desk. He toppled over once and took quite a time to get up. The pain in his unsupported stump was considerable. Well, if he burst the wound and had to start his illness all over again, with transfusions and penicillin and all the trimmings, it would be their fault, and this time he would have a private room, please. He could never face a ward again after this solitary illness under the open window. They never had enough windows open in a ward, unless it was blowing a gale from the side where the windows were. When his head felt hazy and dizzy he had to stop and hang it down between his arms and shake the blood back into it. It had not been bad going over the rugs, but there was a stretch of boards on the last lap. When he reached the table, with his heart hanging in his jacket like the onions he had carried in his battle blouse from Arnhem, he let go of the floor with one hand, grasped the table top and, with breaking back, pulled himself up on his knee until his eyes looked along the bloom of the table top. He was at one side of the drawer; cunning that, because he could never have opened it otherwise. Holding on with one hand, he opened the drawer with the other.

He had not thought yet about what he would do if the gun was not there.

It was there. God bless Ma. God bless A-*mer*-ica, tum, tum, te tum. The gun was there, but where were the bullets? He rummaged about, in growing feverishness, but there was nothing else in the drawer but a ball of string, some papers and some packets of cigarettes he never knew he had. So that was Ma's game! Trust her to take the dangerous part of the gun away. He knew the bullets had been there, because he had seen Sandy put them in when she unpacked his things. He remembered the affected shudder with which she had dropped the gun and bullets into the drawer as if they would bite her and then looked round at him giggling, as if to say: 'Aren't I feminine?' Only he was much too far gone after that long ambulance ride to play up to the poor old horse.

Well, a revolver without ammunition was good enough. He would not have shot at the man, anyway, and he could threaten him just as well with an empty magazine. Criminals had been held up with pipes before now – or was that only in books? Feeling his way down the table leg, he got to his all-threes position again, and swivelling on his knee, started off on the long trek to the door. There seemed to be acres of carpet before him. Half-way across, he glanced at his bed and thought it had never looked so inviting. His head came round again quickly, as he heard the footsteps go stealthily across the passage into the drawing-room. As he listened, he realized he was making a point, like a gun dog, the hand that held the revolver slightly raised, head on one side, eyes fixed.

Thank Heaven the man had not come in here first. He was not ready for him yet. There was not much in the drawing-room, except his silver tennis cups, but it would take him quite a time to search round. Oh God, the party! All the food and drink would be laid out. By the time he got there at this rate, the man would be quite tight. He would join him in a glass of champagne, probably several after this trip, and what a charming picture that would make for the returning wedding party: a one-legged man in odd pyjamas and a dirty old tramp with a sack full of silver sitting on the floor with their arms round each other's necks singing 'The Red Flag'. Not that he knew 'The Red Flag', but the tramp would be sure to. Tramps were cultured these days, and wrote letters to the *New Statesman!*

Violet and John, glad to be released from the tension of waiting, had gone out in such a hurry that they had not shut his door properly. Good thing. He could never have coped with the latch, balanced on one quivering knee. He put his hand round the edge of the door, pulled it towards him, and started off along the passage. This was easier, because he could lean against the wall all the way, on the top-heavy side. He was travelling on the heel of his right hand, pushing the revolver before him along the carpet. Funny how he had never properly seen the pattern of this carpet until he got down to its level. The drawing-room door was before him like a challenge, five yards away. Could he make it? And if he did, would he have breath enough to accost the man? Surely he would hear him panting long before he got there. He stopped and tried to swallow down the dryness in his throat, that was as raw as playing football on a foggy November day. When he started again the panting started too, independent of his control, like something accompanying him down the passage. His face was running with sweat, and he could feel it trickling down under his jacket. He probably looked ghastly enough to give the man quite a shock.

'Hands up!' he was going to say, and find a bit of furniture – the seat of a chair or something – on which he could rest the gun. Unless they had moved it, there was an arm-chair just inside the door. Leaning on the arm of that, he could keep the man covered until the party returned. They couldn't be long now. He had been ages making this trip. They'd better not be long, because he could not keep going much longer. I bet my lips are navy blue, he thought with some satisfaction. Here was the drawing-room door at last. A creak sounded on the other side. Good, he could place where the man was – over by the window, probably at his mother's desk. He would not find much there except neat files of receipted bills and all Oliver's letters from the Army tied up in a bundle, and every photograph of her family that had ever been taken, because she had a lurking fear that people would die if you threw away their photograph. Well, he might die, after all this trouble he'd taken to live since he was wounded. God knows he felt like it.

He did not put his hand round the door, in case the man turned and got warning of his coming. He pushed it with his shoulder like a dog, crawled round the edge, saw the arm-chair, plunged forward, missed it and fell flat on his face with a feeble croak that no one would have taken for 'Hands up!'

Elizabeth, who had been doing something to the plates of food on one of the cloth-covered tables, turned, with her eyebrows in

212

her hair and her mouth open. He saw her, just before his face hit the floor.

Now that he was lying down he felt much better. He lay recovering his breath, with his face turned to one side so that he could grin at her. It was so damn funny. His chest shook, too weak to make the sound of laughter. 'I thought you were a . . . I thought you were a . . .'

'Don't try and talk,' she said, kneeling by him in the crisp linen suit that was the colour of cornflowers. 'Just lie there and rest. It's all right; I'll help you back to bed.'

'I don't want to get back to bed.' He could not tell whether it was hysterical tears or sweat pouring down his face. 'Prop me up against that chair so that I can laugh.' He had always been surprised to find that she was so much stronger than she looked. She was very strong now. He was a limp weight, but she hauled and turned him until he was sitting like a doll against the side of the arm-chair, with his chin on his heaving chest, his leg stretched straight out in front of him and his stump blessedly at rest on the floor.

'And now,' she said, sitting back on her heels, 'tell me what on earth you're playing at. And why the gun?' He raised his eyes without lifting his chin and saw that she was pale and that her hand was trembling slightly as she picked up the revolver. He had given her a scare. Serve her right for leaving him. Half a minute though, she hadn't left him. 'What are *you* playing at,' he said, 'when I thought you were at the church? Gave me the fright of my life. Damned inconsiderate.'

'I came back in the car that fetched Violet. Nobody knew. I didn't go into the church with the others, and I sneaked in at the back door here before John and Violet came out. I didn't like leaving you, and I see I was right. I might have known you'd get up to some crazy trick.'

'Crazy trick be damned. I thought I was a hero, saving the family silver. Why on earth didn't you tell me you'd come back, instead of creeping about like that?'

'I wanted you to think you were on your own. I thought it would be a good test for your nerves.'

'You planned this?'

'Days ago. That's why I didn't insist when you told me not to

213

stay. I knew what I was going to do. How on earth did you get here? That's what I'd like to know.'

'Oh, I crawled,' he said airily. 'It was nothing.'

'It was a pretty good effort. Shows you're fit for more than we think.'

'I'm not fit for much at the moment, Liz. How on earth are we going to get me back to bed before the others come? You swear not to tell? I should look such a fool.'

She got up, dusting her knees. 'How about a drink?' she suggested.

'Champagne,' he said huskily, licking his dry lips.

'There's none open yet. Whisky would be best for you, anyway.' She gave him a stiff one, and it lifted the top right off his light head, and he sang all the way along the passage in his wheelchair. As she was getting him into bed, they heard the first tyres crackle on the drive. She locked the door quickly.

To get back into bed and sink against the pillows was indescribable delight. He could not believe he had ever been away from this familiar softness pressing against him in all the right spots. 'Did I ever do that?' he asked her. 'Was I ever in the drawing-room pointing an unloaded revolver at you and saying: "Hands up"?'

'That reminds me.' She took the gun from the pocket where it had been dragging her suit out of shape and slid it quickly into the drawer. 'Now, are you *sure* you're all right?' she said, hovering over him.

'I feel fine,' he said.

'You shouldn't. You should be practically passing out by rights. I'll try not to let you see too many people, anyway. You would have to do this on the one day I wanted you to be specially fit.'

'I *am* fit,' he insisted. 'I say, Liz.' He caught hold of her arm as she was turning away to unlock the door. 'D'you think me an awful ass for doing that?'

She shook her head. 'I think you were pretty brave,' she said.

'I think it was pretty nice of you to come back from the church. Thanks, Liz.'

'Oh nonsense,' she said, frowning. 'I didn't want to see Violet marry Fred. Not enough to risk the health of my patient, anyway,' she added primly, with that maddening, withdrawn air, which she assumed like a cloak whenever the conversation began to get interesting.

'Thanks all the same,' said Oliver doggedly. He caught at her arm again, but she slipped away to open the door, behind which could be heard, two octaves higher than usual, the excited voice of Mrs Fred Williams. 'Must go and see Ollie first! Poor old Ollie, missed all the fun. Come on, Fred!'

Now that they were married, she was much more possessive. She no longer followed Fred about like a well-trained animal, but led him like a pig with a ring through its nose. It was 'Come on, Fred!' all over the house at the reception. The guests made plenty of noise, but Violet's noise rose above them all, and through the drawing-room wall Oliver heard far more of her hearty laughs than there could have been witticisms in that company. She was *exaltée*, beside herself. Her laughter burst from her under inward pressure – any noise would have done – shouts and whoops that children give from sheer high spirits. Oliver hoped she would not laugh while she was eating or drinking and choke herself black in the face as she sometimes did.

She was usually so shy and dumb with visitors, but today something seemed to have gone to her head, long before it could be the drink. It seemed that until the ring was actually on her sturdy finger and the momentous words spoken and the register signed in her rambling loops and Fred's neat squiggle, she had not quite believed in her marriage. Something would happen to stop it; it would never come off. That was why she had talked so incessantly about her wedding, to try and reassure herself. Since long ago, she had been accepted as the inevitable spinster, had accepted herself as that and planned her future accordingly. Even after her engagement, she still could not quite believe she was going to be married. That happened to other girls, not to her. Not to *her*, who had seen so many local young women grow up behind her and pass by her through the gates of matrimony, leaving her outside, an unchanging feature of the landscape – 'Good old Vi', whom one was told to be nice to at parties, who had always looked like that and probably always would.

But now that she was not 'Good old Vi' but Mrs Fred Williams, legally and inescapably, the lid of doubt had lifted and she bubbled over with exuberant pride. Elizabeth and Mrs North were trying to keep the noisier people out of Oliver's room, but they could not keep out Violet, because it was her day.

Nearly pulling Fred off his feet, she dragged him in to see Oliver directly they got back from the church. She had taken off her hat in the car and the front curl which Heather had created flopped forward unanchored, like an errand-boy's quiff. Her belt had got lower than ever, her gardenias were hanging upside down from her coat, she had splashed her stockings in a puddle outside the church and scuffed her new shoes kneeling before the altar. But her face, on which the make-up was wearing off in patches, was one vast grin, embracing all the world, including Fred when she remembered about him. Oliver was relieved to see that he was not wearing the emerald-green suit, but a neat brown pin-stripe, rather short in the trouser, showing the gaudy clocks which were his sole concession to wedding display. His shirt and tie were modest and his buttonhole the smallest carnation he could find. The hand that Violet was not clutching still held his hat, for she had rushed him in before he could find anywhere to put it down.

'Well – –' said Oliver. 'Congratulations!' He shook hands with them both, for Violet would not kiss him. Her handshake nearly took his arm out of its socket; Fred's was sticky and tentative. He was always afraid of touching any part of Oliver, as if he might break, like so many other delicate things he touched.

'Do we look different?' asked Vi eagerly. 'We're really spliced. Old Norris gave us the whole works; it was super. You should have been there. Look!' She stuck out her hand for him to see the ring. 'Eighteen-carat gold. I can't take it off to prove it to you, because it's a bit tight. Fred and Ken thought they'd lost it, of course – Ollie, you'd have died. There was I, waiting like a lemon, while they fished about in their pockets, each thinking the other had it. Old Norris's face was a scream; I didn't dare look at him in case I hooted.'

'Yes, I'm sorry I made a mess of that,' said Fred. 'It was a bad show. Still,' he added, with sudden quiet confidence, 'you've got it on now. You're really married to me.'

'Can't get it off, what's more,' said Violet, giving it an experimental tug against her brawny knuckle, 'so I guess I'll have to stay married to you, for better or worse, till death do us part and all the rest of it.' This seemed to her a tremendous joke, but Fred, who was looking very solemn, glanced at her fondly and said in an undertone: 'Suits me.'

The others burst in on them. Mrs North, with a tear glittering behind each lens of her pince-nez; David and Evelyn, riotously working off the restraint of sitting still so long; Muffet at the top of her form, standing on tiptoe to kiss Violet, who rubbed at her cheek and said: 'Oh blimey, I thought we'd got over all that in the vestry.' John, pleased that his ordeal was over, came in grinning with Heather, who was itching to get her hands on her sister.

'Come upstairs quick, Vi,' she said, a pin in her mouth as she rearranged Violet's flowers. 'The photographer's here and we must get that over before everyone arrives. Come on up and let me powder your nose. Where's your bouquet?'

'Gosh, I don't know.' Violet looked vaguely round. 'Must have left it in the car or somewhere.'

'Evie, run and see if Mr Peploe's still there,' said Heather. 'Oh, Vi, what *have* you done to your hair? It was looking so nice.'

Violet jerked away her head as Heather put up a hand. 'Don't muck me about,' she said. 'I let you before, so you might leave me alone now.'

'Just go up and let her tidy you for the photograph, there's a good girl,' said her mother coaxingly. 'She only wants to make sure you look your best.' Violet gave her a martyred look and suffered herself to be led out. Deep-throated cries from the hall indicated that Mrs Ogilvie was among the arriving guests who fell on Violet like a pack of hounds when the huntsman chucks them back their dead fox.

Oliver watched the photographs being taken on the lawn. The photographer, who was a tactful man, arranged Fred on the highest side of the slight slope.

Oliver could not see their faces, but he heard the photographer saying: 'A little smile from the bridegroom please! The bridegroom a little less serious, if you will. This is a wedding, not a funeral, you know!' This joke, which she had heard him make at all the local weddings, made Violet laugh, and he had to come out from under his cloth to say: 'Just close the lips a trifle more, Mrs Williams, and try to keep the face still. I shan't keep you a

moment. Don't lose the animation – yes, that's very charming.'
He pressed the bulb just before Violet doubled up in a fit of
giggles.

After several pictures had been taken of the happy pair, with
Violet's hands, as it afterwards transpired, looming exaggerated-
ly in the foreground, a family group was taken. Mrs North had
wanted Oliver brought out in his wheel-chair, but Elizabeth, who
was not going to get him out of bed again, pretended that one of
the tyres had come off and that the iron rim could not be wheeled
over the soggy lawn. The group was arranged on a carpet, with
David and Evelyn cross-legged in front, Mrs North in her chic
postilion wedding hat looking like the president of a Mothers'
Day congress, Muffet unable to be kept still, and Miss Smutts,
who had attached herself uninvited to the end of the row, brooding as if she were regretting having held her peace at the 'If any
man know of any just cause or impediment'.

'Well, what a day, what a day for you all!'

While he was grinning out of the window, Mrs Ogilvie came
in, unwinding scarves and flinging down gloves and bags all over
his room. 'I must say I give full marks to Violet for her appearance; I never would have believed it. She looks what my mother
would have called a handsome woman. It's a fine English type – a
lot of people admire it. And how do *you* feel about the whole
thing? Everyone's in the drawing-room, stampeding the food
and drink, but of course I had to come straight in to see my
wounded warrior.'

'I've brought you some champagne, Ollie,' said Muffet, coming in with a glass in one hand and a plate of sandwiches in the
other. 'There they all are guzzling away in there; it's a good thing
you've got someone to think about you.' She liked to think she
was the only one who really considered Oliver. As Mrs Ogilvie
did too, they eyed one another rather coldly as Oliver introduced
them.

'But I know you, of course,' said Mrs Ogilvie, casting off
another scarf and shaking her jacket out in front to give herself
air. 'I've seen you often in the village. I know your son *very* well,
of course. He's one of my pets – next to this boy. I must get him
along for another game of golf as soon as he's fit enough. My
dear, I can't tell you how shocked I was to see him looking so

seedy. When he came up the aisle with Violet, I thought: Well, you look far worse than when you came back from SEAC. Are you sure it was only flu he had?'

'Oh, quite,' said Lady Sandys airily. 'He opened the window and Influenza! I made that up.' She giggled. 'Good, isn't it?' Mrs Ogilvie looked at her sharply and then raised her eyebrows at Oliver. He pretended not to see, and said to Muffet: 'Why don't you go and get yourself a drink, Muff? I'm sure you need it.'

'Oh, I do, I do. And I want to go and study the local fauna in there. I just had to make sure you were quite happy before I could settle down to enjoy myself. I'll come back and drink your health in a minute, darling.'

On her way out she absent-mindedly picked up Mrs Ogilvie's crocodile pochette, which her son had brought back from Cairo. She studied it for a moment undecidedly while Oliver held his breath, then tucked it under her arm and continued on her way.

'Excuse *me*,' said Mrs Ogilvie, striding forward. 'I think you've taken my bag by mistake.'

'What?' Muffet turned vaguely in the doorway. Her eyes had the same blank, unfocused look as on the night when she had come pattering down in her nightdress.

'My bag,' said Mrs Ogilvie, enunciating as if Lady Sandys were deaf or a foreigner. 'I suppose you have one like it. Did John bring it home?'

'*John?*' said Muffet, as if she thought her daft.

'My *bag*,' repeated Mrs Ogilvie quite impatiently, snapping her fingers for it. Muffet followed her eyes and looked extremely puzzled to find the brown crocodile pochette, bursting full, like all Mrs Ogilvie's bags, under her arm.

'This isn't mine,' she said irritably, as if Mrs Ogilvie had put it there. 'Do you want it?' She offered it uncertainly, and when Mrs Ogilvie had snatched it away she held her hand for a moment to her eyes, pinching the bridge of her nose and giving her head a little shake as if trying to clear it. Then, with a lost look at Oliver, she turned and went out. He felt very nervous.

'Well, can you *believe* it?' Mrs Ogilvie blew off steam when she had gone. 'What an extraordinary way to behave! Is she a bit – you know?' She rapped her knuckles on her forehead.

'Lord, no.' Oliver forced a laugh. 'Just absent-minded.'

'I wouldn't ask, but you know what they say about her in the village.'

'No. What do they say?'

'Oh, I couldn't possibly repeat it. After all, she's practically related to you, isn't she?'

'How dare they gossip about our guests? A lot of ignorant bumpkins, gawping at somebody from London as if she was an aboriginal – –'

'Oh, forget all about it, dear boy. I shouldn't have said anything. You know what a lot of gossips they are; they make up stories about everybody. You ought to hear what they say about Francis. Have you seen him yet, by the way? You'd never *believe* his tie if I described it, so I'll let him spring it on you himself. Oh, look, here's your mother, bringing in some visitors. I'll go and do the polite next door for a bit.' She obviously wanted to go and investigate Lady Sandys.

It was Violet's idea that the cake should be cut and the speeches made in Oliver's room. His mother did not hear of it until the cake had been brought in and the guests were flocking after it, filling his low, shadowy room with smoke and gabble and bright colours.

Mrs North pushed her way through the crowd to his bed. 'This is just what I didn't want to happen,' she said. 'Are you sure you can stand the racket? I can't very well turn them out now; it looks so rude. That fool Violet – no, I suppose I shouldn't say that on her wedding day – but she's so thoughtless. Did you ever see anyone so over-excited? Will you just look at her now!' Violet was brandishing a large carving knife, making believe to cut off Fred's head, to the great amusement of a bunch of Fred's friends, weathered-looking men in tight best suits.

'*I* don't mind,' said Oliver. 'It's fun. So long as I don't have to talk to too many people. I get a bit breathless, that's all.'

His mother gave him a penetrating look. 'You look tired already,' she said. 'Oh dear, I do wish ... Where's Elizabeth? I *told* her to stay by your door and keep people out.'

'If I know anything about Elizabeth,' said Oliver, 'she's working like a beaver somewhere in the background. I haven't seen her since the party started.'

'She's been flirting with that Ken,' said Mrs North disapprovingly. 'He's gone quite daffy about her and I guess it's gone to her head. They're together somewhere now, I expect.' She looked round the room. 'I don't see him in here.'

'She's probably lancing his carbuncle,' said Oliver, and his mother said: 'Don't be disgusting, dear. I'm not pleased with Miss Gray today, though. She's let me down. You know she never came into the church at all? Simply sneaked off somewhere. She might at least show a little polite interest in Violet's wedding, even if she doesn't feel any. She's interested enough to drink our champagne, I notice, although she always pretends she doesn't drink liquor.'

'That's what it's there for, to drink, isn't it?' asked Oliver. 'And I'd like some more, by the way. It's doing me a power of good. It's the first I've tasted since we rustled the German H.Q. at Nijmegen. Hi, Toby!' He waved his glass at Toby, who was moving urbanely among the crowd. 'Fill me up, will you, before someone proposes a toast.'

'How's yourself, Ollie?' Toby asked, as he poured the champagne, holding an expensive white handkerchief round the bottle. 'I haven't had a chance to talk to you properly.'

'I'm fine,' said Oliver. 'How about you? I don't seem to have seen you for years.'

'I'm in town most of the time,' said Toby. 'Only get home for the occasional week-end. I'm in my uncle's office, you know – Ketch and Blackett, the solicitors.'

'Pretty good firm,' said Oliver knowledgeably, as if he had heard of them. 'Er – see anything of Anne these days?'

'Oh – we've done the town once or twice, you know,' he said casually. 'She's good fun on a party, isn't she? and I'll say one thing for her – she can dance.'

'I could say more than that for her, old boy,' said Oliver, grinning. 'She's a swell girl, Anne is.'

'She get down much to see you?' asked Toby, to satisfy himself that Anne was telling the truth when she said she never came.

'Lord, no. Our little romance ended long ago,' Oliver said. 'That time when you met her here, she was just coming to see whether perhaps I wasn't rather fascinating after all, now that I'd only got one leg.'

'And were you?'

'No, thank goodness. You can't heat up a thing that's gone as cold on you as our affair had. But I expect Anne's told you all about that. She always tells the next boy friend about the one before.'

'Does she?' Toby sounded rather uncomfortable.

'Rather. You wait. In a few months time some guy or other will be highly entertained by indiscreet details about you.'

'Well, as a matter of fact ––' began Toby, easing his neck in his collar.

'Oh – like that, is it? Well, I suppose you have pretty well had your run. Six months is usually about Anne's limit of endurance.'

Toby drained his glass and poured himself out another. He stood watching the bubbles, swirling the champagne gently round the glass as if it were brandy. 'I made the fatal mistake, you see,' he said, without looking at Oliver, 'of asking her to marry me.'

'Oh, she's used to that. People always want to marry Anne, for some reason – even I did. God knows why, because she'd make a hell of a bad wife.'

'Oh, but it was different with us.' Toby looked up quickly. 'It was the real thing. It was just that I rushed it, like an ass. I tried to pin her down, and of course she shied off. If I'd waited – –'

'Do-on't kid yourself, boy,' said Oliver. 'Anne wouldn't have married you. She won't marry anyone – not until she gets old and stodgy, anyway. She's far too scatty.'

'You just think that,' said Toby with some perception, 'because she wouldn't marry you.'

'Let's have a drink on it, anyway,' said Oliver hastily. 'To Anne!' He raised his glass.

'To Anne.' They drank. 'I say, old boy,' said Toby, suddenly dropping the rather stiff manner which he wore even in his own home, 'I'm awfully glad you're not sore about Anne and me. I rather thought you were, you know. That's why I haven't been around much to see you.'

'You poor idiot,' laughed Oliver. 'People in my situation don't get sore about other people doing things they can't do. They just send them off with their blessing and feel pleased they haven't got to go through the wear and tear themselves.'

'You're a funny fellow,' said Toby. 'I say, how about starting our needle chess contests again? I could come over whenever I'm at home.'

'I'd love it.'

'Could I come on Sunday? I'll be staying down over the weekend.'

'Any time you like,' said Oliver and was glad. He had always liked Toby, and he often thought he could do with a little more male company.

'Hrrm-hm!' Stanford Black, entertaining the company by pretending to be a hired M.C., banged on the table with a poker. 'Me lords, ladies and *gen*-tlemen! Pray silence for Major John Sandbag – I *beg* your pardon – Sandys!' Laughter.

'Who *is* that man?' asked Lady Salter. A tasselled stole of tired little martens' tails lay round her neck, and she smelled faintly of mothballs.

'Stanford Black. Friend of Heather's – friend of ours, that is. He's been stationed at Ockney for the last two years. Had to be taken off flying because he had a nervous breakdown or something – too much night fighting.'

'Ah,' said Lady Salter dreamily, 'one of the First of the Few. Nice-looking boy.' She had two daughters at home. 'Have I met his wife? Oh – isn't he? . . . What did you say his name was?'

'Black. His family are the Sidney Blacks – you know, the hotel people. Useful sort of man to know. He got us this champagne.'

'Very useful,' mused Lady Salter.

John had by this time been ferreted out from a corner and dragged into the middle of the room. He knew he had got to make a speech, and unnecessary cries of 'Spee-eech!' only hampered his starting.

'Ladies and gentlemen,' he began, squaring his shoulders, clenching his fists, and looking like Max Baer about to attack, 'it is my pleasant duty to propose the health of the bride and bridegroom.' People with empty glasses looked worriedly round in the hope of finding someone to fill them up. 'I believe it is customary to say a few words at this point.' Heather was standing near Stanford, looking bored. 'I can't say I've known the bridegroom very long,' went on John creakingly, 'but it has been my great pleasure to know the bride for – let's see – it must be nearly six years. Now, you all know Violet – –'

'Gosh,' muttered Violet, who had been standing by him with a vacuous smile plastered over her face, 'I didn't know he was going to gas about me.' She sagged slightly at the knees to make herself less conspicuous and looked about for escape, but the crowd pressed round her and said: 'Good old Vi!'

'We all know Violet,' persevered John, who had sweated over his speech during many hours of concentrated thought while he lay in bed with flu, 'and what's more, we all know her as one of the most genuine, kind-hearted, likeable people going.' Violet looked down and shuffled her feet; Fred's nose was aflame with pride. 'And I do feel,' said John, 'that I must take this opportunity of paying tribute to the untiring way in which she has worked for the war effort all these years.'

'Hear, hear,' said a few people gruffly.

'Fred will tell you' – John looked down at the bridegroom, who cocked his head on one side and tried to look informative – 'and I'm sure you will know that there's nothing more exhausting than working on the land. Vi's done a man's work, and more; in fact, Fred will probably tell you that he couldn't have kept the farm going without her through these difficult years.' More gruff acclaim. 'But then he's prejudiced,' said John, making his joke and getting his indulgent laughter. 'How fitting it is, then, that these two, who have worked together so successfully, are now teaming up to make it a life partnership.'

Muffet, standing on a chair to see better, was deeply moved. Lady Salter murmured to Oliver: 'Perhaps it isn't such an unfortunate match after all.'

'And I'm sure you'll agree,' went on John, tense in his efforts not to forget what he wanted to say, 'that the Land Army's loss has been Fred's gain.'

'But I wasn't in the Land Army, you ass,' said Violet, looking up indignantly and getting the ready laugh that wedding guests are always so eager to discharge.

'As for Fred, I haven't known him very long, but it's been long enough to see what a jolly fine chap he is, not to mention one of the best farmers in the district.' Fred nearly succumbed under the back-slapping that fell on him from his friends, who were bunched behind him like the chorus in *The Country Girl*.

John was beginning to look rather careworn. 'Well,' he said, taking a deep breath and coming thankfully to the end of his speech. 'I don't think there's anything more to say except that I'm sure we wish them all the good luck and happiness in the world. They certainly deserve it. So, ladies and gentlemen, may I ask you to raise your glasses' – he raised his champagne glass, which looked fragile in his huge fist – 'and drink to the health and happiness of the bride and bridegroom. Vi and Fred!'

'Vi and Fred!' echoed people self-consciously and sipped at their glasses like birds. Oliver suddenly heard himself call out in a squeaky voice: 'Three cheers for Vi and Fred! Hip, hip – –'

'Hooray!' yelled everyone, and one of Violet's dogs, which was wandering about with a blue bow round its neck, jumped, and scurried under a table. Some of the women looked sentimentally at Oliver and thought: How sad. His mother gave him a long-range beam from the other side of the room and raised her glass to him. Several people struck up: 'For they are jolly good fellows' in different keys and Oliver saw the Cowlins, standing in the doorway with the party from the kitchen, singing lustily, Cowlin without a tooth in his head, Mrs Cowlin nodding her head madly in a purple velour hat. Mrs Ogilvie made quite a performance of it, thrusting out her chest as if she had to fill the Albert Hall; Lady Salter moved her lips politely, as she did in church; Muffet caroled clear and true above the other voices; Francis, in an olive green suit and floral cravat, opened and shut his sea anemone lips in the least possible concession to so banal a performance.

Violet and Fred were standing hand in hand like babes in the wood, looking rather sweet. Fred kept moistening his lips and swallowing. He knew what he had to do.

Stanford Black banged the table again. 'Ladies and gentlemen,' he said, copying a joke which he had heard a real M.C. make at a London wedding, 'the bridegroom would *like* to reply!' More laughter and back-slapping. Fred was nearly pushed head first into the cake. Violet stepped back and made a face at him. 'Get on with it,' she urged.

Blinking with his whole face, Fred opened his mouth very wide, then almost closed it and let a few words trickle through. 'L-l-ladies and gentlemen,' he faltered. One or two people cupped their hands behind their ears, and Mrs Norris retuned her ear-box.

'On behalf of my wife' – he had been told that he must get that in – 'on behalf of my wife and I, a-tha – a-tha – a-thank you very much.' It came out in a triumphant rush, and as they applauded him he looked modestly down his nose. Calls for a speech from Violet brought forth a throaty 'Thanks *awf*'ly', and then Ken was seen to be swallowing his Adam's apple, preparatory to speaking up.

He spoke quickly and well. 'Ladies and gentlemen, it's customary, I believe, on these occasions for the best man to propose the health of the bridesmaids. As there aren't any, my friends Fred and Vi preferring to get hitched up in an informal kind of way, I'd like to propose a toast which I know you will drink with the greatest enthusiasm – the founder of this really magnificent feast: our hostess – Mrs North!'

She was pushed forward, shaking her head and protesting. 'Well, say – well, say, that's lovely of you, and I only want to say what a beautiful thing it is to me to see you all here in my house at my dear Violet's wedding. And I hope you won't think me a sentimental old fool if I ask you to turn around and drink the health of someone very dear to us all, someone – mm-*hm*, – who hasn't been quite as lucky as the rest of us.' She raised her glass. Oliver was terrified that she was going to burst into tears. 'My son, Oliver!'

He wished he might go under the bedclothes. Everyone was toasting him with great warmth and he did not like being the spring that touched off their fountains of sentiment. 'Thanks a lot,' he said, 'How about cutting the cake, Vi?'

'You bet,' she said, and picking up the carving knife, plunged it into the cake and bore down on it with token assistance from Fred at the extreme end of the handle. She wanted to slice it all up, but her mother would not let her. 'We must keep it neat, dear. Let Elizabeth take it out to the kitchen and cut it up on to plates. Where *is* she!' Elizabeth stepped quietly forward from the background and took the cake away, reappearing a few minutes later with plates of neat slices, which she offered round. Oliver heard people asking who she was and being told: 'That's Oliver's nurse,' and he could see that they were stimulated by champagne into thinking it romantic that he should have a pretty nurse. He saw her offer some to Mary Brewer, who was standing in a corner in a yellow dress and a fawn hat. This wedding was the first time they had met, and when he introduced them, Oliver had watched with glee their shrewd summing-up of each other. Now that he was better, Mary no longer came when Elizabeth was away. She was obviously asking after the patient, because Elizabeth raised her eyebrows and glanced across at him, before she said something in a clipped voice. Mary had taken the smallest piece of cake. 'Won't you have another bit,' Elizabeth asked, 'to put under your pillow?' Involuntarily, Mary glanced across at Oliver and he looked hastily away and met the concentrated gaze of Mrs Ogilvie coming through the crowd with the determination of the *Penelope* ploughing her way through the mines to Malta.

'My dear Oliver,' she said in an urgent, breathy whisper, 'I must tell you the most extraordinary thing. I've just been upstairs to the Fairies' – it was a form of bravado with her to announce her visits there – 'and you know that table in the top corridor? Well, perhaps you don't; it's such ages since you went upstairs, poor darling. Well, anyway, there's a table there where your mother keeps odd little decorative bits and pieces – the woman's touch, you know, that she's so good at.' Oliver waited with a sinking heart for her to come to the point. 'Well, today, it's positively littered with the most extraordinary collection, just like a jumble sale. I wouldn't perhaps have noticed anything, only, as I was passing, I saw among all the face cream and gloves and pincushions and bits of jewellery – this.' She held up dramatically a scarf of stiff and shiny green silk, which Oliver had last seen her discarding in his room. 'I can't think how it got there, because I haven't been upstairs till just now.' She laughed frankly. 'My family always tells me I must be an angel.'

'Oh well,' Oliver said easily. 'I expect one of the maids has put everything there that she found lying about, not knowing who they belonged to.'

'Oh, have you got a maid now? Mrs Cowlin? She doesn't go upstairs, does she? She's been in the kitchen all the time today; I've seen her downing beer in there when I've been through to the scullery to wash glasses for your mother. Or do you mean Elizabeth? But then, my dear boy, why a sponge? Don't think me curious, but it did strike me as odd when this house is usually so neat. I mean, why one bedroom slipper?'

Curse Miss Smutts and her fiendish tactlessness. He believed she enjoyed playing fence to Lady Sandys' pilfering. It was all very well to retrieve the goods, but why wasn't she, today of all days, doing her job and looking after her employer instead of letting her accumulate so much in such a short time? He would give the old fool a piece of his mind. As Mrs Ogilvie, firmly clutching her crocodile pochette, moved away to probe further into this intriguing mystery, Oliver said to Heather, who was standing near with Stanford: 'Seen Smutty anywhere? I want a word with her.'

Heather giggled. 'Probably passed out somewhere. She's been drinking like a fish.' Heather herself had not been doing too badly, or else the concentrated attentions which Stanford was paying her had elated her. She was pink and rather unstable, her fringe flopping as she threw her head about in the way she had when she was talking excitedly.

'Wasn't it a scream, the speeches?' she said. 'Stanny and I nearly burst ourselves trying not to laugh at Fred, didn't we? Darling Ollie.' She swooped round on him in a gush of affection. 'Are you enjoying yourself? I do hope you are. Can I get you anything – or a nice, pretty girl to talk to? I don't think there are any. Stanford wants us to go on to a party afterwards. I do wish you could come. Don't you wish he could come, Stanny?'

'Rather,' said Stanford. 'Wizard party at the Bartons'. They said bring along anyone I liked; they always have lashings of booze.'

'Is John going?' asked Oliver, feeling austere.

Heather frowned.

'Oh, we wanted him to, of course, but the old stooge says he feels too tired. He's getting quite an old woman about his health; God knows how long he'll go on trading on this flu.'

'What about Elizabeth?' Oliver asked. 'I'll be all right if you want to take her.'

Heather looked at Stanford. 'I don't see how she can really, because of the children. She said she'd put them to bed for me if I wanted to go out. She's upstairs now, as a matter of fact, starting Susan, because she was getting so cross.'

'Oh, I see,' Oliver said.

People were drifting about restlessly now, feeling the effects of champagne in the middle of the afternoon, thinking it was time

228

to go. But they could not go before Violet, and Violet would not go. She was still enjoying herself too much. She and Fred were going to drive to a hotel at Wells and on the next day to Exmoor, the horses having been already sent by train.

'Heather,' said Mrs North, 'I wish you'd take your sister upstairs, by brute force if necessary, and get her changed. If she doesn't go soon, the party will die on us.'

'Shall I get her, Mrs North?' asked Stanford obligingly.

'Thank you, I'm sure Heather can cope.'

'I'll fix her,' said Heather, finishing her champagne and putting down the glass. 'Come on Stanny, you come and help.' He followed her eagerly.

'Where's John?' Mrs North looked harassed. 'I haven't seen him for quite a while. Oh, my goodness, I wonder whether he didn't feel well and has gone to bed. I'll ask Elizabeth; she'll know, because he'd probably go to her. I wonder where *she* is.'

'Elizabeth,' said Ken, coming up behind her looking pleased with himself, 'is upstairs putting the baby to bed. I've been helping her wash it. Great sport,' he laughed. 'I'm rather good at it. Think I'll copy old Fred's example soon and go all domesticated.'

Oliver felt tired and flat and wished that the party were over. While they were waiting for Violet to change, one or two guests, as bored and tired as himself, wandered in and made desultory conversation. Francis sat down as if he would never get up and started to talk about a Morris dancing club he was organizing. His skin was puffy and waxy and his teeth yellow. He put his face very close to you when he talked, bending forward, right over Oliver's bed.

At last there was a clattering on the stairs and the familiar squeak of Violet's hand on the banisters, and a feeble cheer was raised from the hall by those who still had enough energy. The people in Oliver's room drifted out to see what Violet's going-away dress was like. Someone was hooting the horn of Fred's car, and Violet came into her brother's room like a tornado, with bits of her clothes dropping off and one shoelace undone. She wore a new tweed suit, the jacket cut with a flap at the back so that she could wear it for riding. On her head was a porkpie hat of the same material, which she had pushed back from the angle

229

at which Heather had placed it. A khaki handkerchief hung out of her sleeve, her stockings could have been tauter, and from one ungloved hand she swung, as if it were a stable lantern, the satchel bag that was meant to be worn smartly over her shoulder.

She looked radiantly happy. Happy too, but more soberly, in her wake came Fred – in the emerald-green suit. Oh well, people must have something to talk about after the wedding. The guests in the hall looked through the doorway to see the affecting sight of the bride's farewell to her invalid brother.

Violet charged up to the bed. 'Just off, Ollie,' she said. 'I feel a hell of a mess, all this changing clothes and mucking about. Do I look O.K.?'

'You look swell. So you did in the other thing, though. You've been grand.'

'Oh, stow it. Thank God it's all over. All this fuss just to get spliced. I've been in a blue funk about it, you know, but, 'smatter of fact, I've had a hell of a good time. I've never enjoyed a party so much before.'

The horn sounded again. Fred coughed. 'I think we ought to go, Violet,' he suggested. 'We've got a long drive, and it'll be dark before we're there.'

'Keep your wool on,' she told him without turning round. 'I'm not scared to drive in the dark, if you are.'

'Good-bye, old girl,' Oliver said. 'Have a good time. Write and tell me how Jenny's behaving.'

'You know I can't write letters. I'll tell you all about it when I get back. Wait till that mare gets her head on the moor, you won't see us for dust. Probably fetch up in a bog.' She threw back her head to laugh, then, as she brought it down again, said surprisingly, for she was seldom solicitous of Oliver's health: 'Hope you don't feel too fagged; you look a bit peaked.' As the horn sounded raucously once more, she held out a large friendly hand. 'Well, good-bye then, old thing.' She leaned forward, stumbling against the step of the alcove. 'And I say, Ollie, thanks awfully and all that. It was all your doing, talking me into it.'

'Rot,' he said. 'Happy?'

'You bet.' She suddenly lunged and kissed him, nearly over-balancing on to the bed. She straightened up, confused, and turned to her husband. 'Come *on*, Fred, for heaven's sake, or we'll never get there tonight.' He gave Oliver a conspiratorial look, which said: 'Aren't women illogical?', shook hands and trotted after Vi in his green suit, like a harvest bug.

'Well, they've gone at last!' Mrs North staggered in and collapsed into Oliver's arm-chair. 'My goodness, will you just look at the mess in here! I'll clear it up for you when everyone's gone – if they ever go.'

'Was there an old shoe on the car?' asked Oliver.

'There was.'

'And a notice saying: "Just Married"?'

'I'm afraid so, dear. Fred's friends put it on. No confetti or rice, though, thank goodness; that's one mercy about austerity. Say, my feet are killing me, d'you know it?' She put them on to the footstool, but let them down again almost immediately and stood up. 'Oh dear, there's someone wanting to say good-bye.' She went out into the hall, where Oliver heard her weary voice slide easily into practised sociability.

Elizabeth had made tea for the few remaining guests. Mrs Ogilvie, who believed in getting her money's worth, was still there, and Stanford Black was waiting to take Heather to the party. They sat jadedly in Oliver's room, discussing the guests with lazy malice, while Oliver lay back with his eyes closed and heard their talk coming from far away.

'I say,' said Stanford idly, in his flat Air Force drawl, 'most extraordinary thing, Heather, you know that charm bracelet your mother-in-law's got?'

Oliver opened his eyes. Heather sat up. 'Charm bracelet? She hasn't got a charm bracelet!'

'She has; I saw it. Haven't you seen she's got a little faun on it, just like you – –'

'John!' exploded Heather furiously, 'this is just about the limit. If that woman doesn't leave this house soon, I shall. Shoes and toothbrushes and hankies and things I can just stomach, though I'm getting pretty tired of it, but when it comes to jewellery and especially a thing I prize so much – –'

'What on earth – –?' Stanford looked puzzled.

'All right, old girl. All right, all right, all right.' John was painfully conscious that Mrs Ogilvie was sitting bolt upright in her chair, mentally slapping her thighs with glee at having happened on such a promising scene.

'It's *not* all right!' Heather tossed her head. 'I've been very good about it up to now, but this time I'm going to tackle her about it.'

'Heather, you know what Smutty – –'

'Smutty encourages her. I shouldn't wonder if they weren't making a racket of the whole thing, and Smutty only puts out a few valueless things as a blind. What about that ring of Ma's? That never turned up, did it?'

'Now, Heather Bell, you know she thought it might have gone down the waste pipe when she was washing.'

'Well, how do we know what your mother doesn't take from shops? You all pander to her and say she can't help it and let her pinch all your things – it makes me sick. I believe she knows perfectly well what she's doing.' Mrs Ogilvie's eyes were snapping like the shutters of a camera, as if she were trying to photograph every detail on her brain for filing in her library of gossip subjects.

'Did someone say tea?' The little black-and-white figure fluttered into the room like an innocent butterfly.

'No!' Heather jumped up and confronted her. 'But someone said charm bracelets! My God, you're right, Stanford.' She picked up Muffet's forearm, and held it out, to show the bracelet dangling down over the blue-veined hand.

'Heather, for heaven's sake!' John got up and went to them. 'It's all right, Mother; let's go outside. I'll bring you some tea in the drawing-room.'

Heather pushed him back. 'Don't you interfere. This is between her and me.'

Stanford and Mrs Ogilvie goggled. Oliver said uncomfortably: 'Oh, look here, Heather – –'

'And don't you butt in, either,' she flung over her shoulder. 'Now look here, Muffet,' she said grimly, while her mother-in-law stood with her arm still raised, throwing plaintive, puzzled glances at the others, as if appealing for help, 'where did you get that bracelet?'

'What bracelet, dear?' She looked at her hand as if she had never seen it before, and, with a start of surprise, picked up one of the charms and let it fall with a tiny tinkle. 'This? Oh, isn't it pretty? Someone lent it to me, didn't they? Who was it? I forget – I'm a bit tired, you know. The party – –'

'Someone lent it to you!' cried Heather scornfully. 'You stole it!' Mrs Ogilvie drew in her breath with a fascinated hiss. 'It's mine; and you took it from my room. And what's more, it's not the first thing you've taken, as you know perfectly well, although you pretend to be so innocent. You may flatter yourself you've fooled the others, but you haven't fooled me. I'm going to tell the police.'

Stanford had the decency to look very uncomfortable. Mrs Ogilvie was sitting on the edge of her chair, her legs planted like trestles.

'I don't know what you are talking about.' Muffet looked as though she were going to cry. She passed a hand across her forehead. 'It's all such a muddle. You muddle me so with your wild talk.'

'Oh, I give up.' Heather flung back her hand, as if disappointed that the result of her audacity had not been more spectacular. 'You deal with her, John; she's your mother. But I would like my bracelet back.' She held out her hand.

John put his arm round Muffet. 'Come on, old dear,' he said. 'Let's go upstairs, shall we? You ought to lie down and rest after all the excitement of the party. I'll bring you your tea in bed.'

She looked up at him coldly as if he were a presumptuous stranger. 'Please leave me alone. This girl wants this bracelet,' she said in a flat voice, fumbling with the clasp. 'I'm sure I don't know – –'

'Muffet,' said Heather sharply, on a sudden note of fright, 'do you know who I am?'

'No, dear,' said Muffet sadly, 'but I should be very pleased to if someone will introduce us.'

Heather was really frightened now, and even Mrs Ogilvie was beginning to look as if she would rather be somewhere else.

'John, is she pretending?' Heather stepped back and put her hand on his arm, looking at her mother-in-law with wide eyes. 'Oh, John, I don't like it.'

'Get Smutty!' said Oliver urgently. 'Or Elizabeth. Can't you see she's not well?'

'Anything I can do?' asked Stanford. He had got up and was standing embarrassed, hating to be at a loss when he was usually at home in any situation.

'Shall I phone for a doctor?' asked Mrs Ogilvie eagerly. Their suggestions hissed round Muffet, while she stood forlornly, fumbling with the clasp of the bracelet. They all stood a little back from her, as if they were afraid to touch her.

'Stay with her, Heather,' said John. 'I'll get Smutty.'

'No,' said Heather, giving Muffet a scared glance. 'I'll go.' She darted away and the others waited in the most uncomfortable silence any of them had ever known. Every time John tried to approach his mother she shook him off and gave him that blank, distant look again. 'Let me undo the bracelet,' he said gently.

'No, no,' she said, impatiently, pursing her lips like a cross old woman. 'I can do it, I can do it. Thank you very much indeed, all the same,' she added as an afterthought of studied politeness.

Heather came back with Miss Smutts, who had changed her best wine dress for her usual battleship grey and was intoning: 'I knew it. I knew it. I told you. Don't say I didn't warn you.'

'Shut up,' said John surprisingly, 'and be some use. My mother isn't well. Please take her up to bed.'

'Hoity-toity, young man.' She put a hand on Lady Sandys' arm. 'Now what's all this about? Why don't you come upstairs with poor old Smutty and let her put you to bed? You shall have some bread and milk later on, how will that be?'

'I loathe and detest the stuff,' said Muffet clearly. 'Oh – hullo.' She looked at Miss Smutts vaguely as if she were a distant acquaintance whom she knew by sight but not by name. 'Help me get this damned thing off. They keep bothering me for it, and heaven knows *I* don't want it.'

'Let's go where the light's a bit better, shall we?' Miss Smutts was able to shepherd her out, throwing a lugubrious glance of triumph at the others as she went. When she had got Muffet into the hall she stepped back into the room for a moment. 'This is a terrible thing you've done,' she told Heather in a voice like the clanging of the brass doors in the House of Usher. 'A terrible

234

thing. I'm not answerable for the consequences. You can't say I didn't warn you.'

'Oh, shut *up*,' shouted Heather and John and Oliver together.

Smutty sniffed, and withdrew. Mrs Ogilvie got up. 'I can only say – –' she began. They wanted to say 'Shut up' to her too, but it was unnecessary, because, for once in her life, she did not know what to say, and simply opened her hands in a helpless gesture.

'My mother hasn't been well, you know,' said John hastily. 'She had a nervous breakdown from war strain.'

'Oh, of course, of course,' said Mrs Ogilvie, grasping this soothing explanation eagerly, and Stanford mumbled: 'Of course. We quite understand.'

'Look,' said Heather. 'Stanny, why don't you be a dear and run Mrs Ogilvie home to save her walking and then come back for me? I'll be changing.'

'Heather, you're not going out?' John looked hurt.

'Why not? I can't do anything here, and I need something to take my mind off this. And don't say anything to me,' she said defensively. 'I know it was my fault; I know I'd been told, but don't say anything, or I shall scream.'

Her voice wobbled on the last word and she bit her lip and rushed out fumbling in her sleeve for a handkerchief.

'Well, good-bye, Mrs Ogilvie,' said John, with the false geniality of relief that she was going. He pumped her hand. 'Hope you enjoyed the party. Forget that it ended like this. I need hardly ask you,' he said pompously, 'not to talk about it. My mother doesn't like people to think she's not strong, you know.'

'But my *dear* John!' She raised her eyebrows at him. 'What *do* you take me for?'

'We take her for what she is,' said Oliver gloomily when she had gone. 'Can't you imagine how she and Stan are getting down to it now in the car? They'll probably call in on a few people on the way and tell them. Jonathan, why do you let Heather go out with that bounder?'

'Oh – –' John made a harassed gesture.

'Sorry, forget it. You don't want to be badgered now. I say, I – I'm most terribly sorry about all this. I suppose she'll be all right, will she? Has she been like this before?'

John shrugged his shoulders and turned away as if he did not

235

want to talk about it. He looked drawn and old, much older than forty-three. He didn't look like Max Baer any more. If he looked like a pugilist, it was a *passé*, retired pugilist, who had taken a lot of beatings and given up fighting.

Much later that night John wandered back into Oliver's room. Dr Trevor's partner had been, and taken Lady Sandys away to a Birmingham nursing-home where, he said with empty cheerfulness, he could get sympathetic nursing for her and arrange for suitable psychological treatment. Miss Smutts tried to tell him what had happened last time a psychologist had tampered with Muffet's libido, but the doctor, who thought Smutty was the old family nurse, had said: 'Yes, yes, yes, Nanny. Now don't you worry yourself; everything's going to be all right.'

Elizabeth had gone with him to Birmingham and had not yet returned. Heather had gone defiantly to her party with Stanford. Oliver noticed that she was not wearing the bracelet; she would probably never wear it again. Mrs North had gone to bed early with sleeping pills. She had cried when they told her what had happened and had insisted on blaming herself for not having been in the room to prevent it. Miss Smutts, too, had gone to her room early to pack. She was going to stay with her sister at Malden, until she should be needed again. 'And the dear knows when *that* will be,' she had prophesied gloomily, 'now that you've let the medicals get their hands on her. Much better have left her to me.' At about eleven o'clock Oliver heard her come downstairs again, and heard her shuffle along to the kitchen in her bedroom slippers to put the kettle on for peppermint water for her indigestion.

When she had creaked upstairs again all was quiet. A dead weight of fatigue hung over the house and it was difficult to imagine that the rooms had so lately been filled with noisy, happy people. Oliver was playing the wireless softly to keep himself awake until Elizabeth came back, so that he could hear about Muffet. John opened the door just wide enough to admit his shaggy head. 'D'you mind if I come and smoke my last pipe in here?' he asked. 'I saw your light on when I was in the garden. I can't sleep yet and the house gets on my nerves when it's so quiet. D'you mind? I won't talk if you don't want to.'

'Come in, old boy. We'll wait up for Elizabeth together, and hear how your mother's settled in. Get yourself a drink. There should be some whisky in the cupboard.'

'No, thanks. Oh well – perhaps it might pep me up a bit.' Oliver heard him pour a long drink, with only a splash of soda, which he took over to the arm-chair by the fireplace. When he leaned back behind the high side of the tapestry chair, Oliver could only see one trouser leg crossed over the other, and one slipper swinging from his toe. He remembered the first time he had sat out of bed in a chair, how funny it had felt not to be able to cross his legs.

For a while neither spoke. The only sound was the gentle strum of the wireless and an occasional bubbling whistle from John's pipe, which had been mended with sticking plaster after David had knocked it out of John's face, leaping up to hug him. Presently John crossed over the other leg and swung the other slipper. He stirred and gave one or two deep sighs and Oliver, who did not want to talk, took pity on him and said: 'If I was Mrs Ogilvie, I should say: "A penny for them."'

John was not sensitive to platitudes. He said: 'I was thinking about poor old Heather.'

'Oh, her,' said Oliver. 'I should have thought you'd got troubles enough without thinking about her. Personally, I'd rather not think of her floating ecstatically over the floor in the arms of Squadron-Leader Black.'

'It's different for you; she's your sister. I can't help feeling miserable for her. You see, this whole business is worse for her than anyone.'

'I don't get it.'

'But don't you see, Onions, it's worse for her because she thinks it's her fault. Of course it isn't; it would probably have happened, anyway, sooner or later. Nobody's blaming her, but she's got it into her head that we are. She'll hardly speak to any-one because she feels so sensitive about it. She wouldn't even say good night to me, and I heard her say to that Black fellow: "Thank God to get out of this house; they all look at me as though I was a criminal."'

'Poor old Heather,' said Oliver. 'She does love to see herself as the black sheep.'

John leaned forward and knocked out his pipe in the empty grate, a habit which always annoyed Heather. 'Who d'you think's going to clear it up?' she would ask. 'Or do you think it can be left there until the fire's lit next autumn?' He sat for a while with his hands between his knees, turning the pipe round and round, and then suddenly looked sideways at Oliver from under his puzzled brow. 'What can I do?' he asked helplessly. 'How can I get near her? She won't even let me try to explain that I'm not blaming her, just takes it for granted that I am, and shies off accordingly. God knows, we were getting far enough apart before; this'll just about finish it.' He put the pipe between his teeth again and leaned back again, hugging one knee, sucking gloomily on the empty pipe.

'D'you know what she told me once?' Oliver said. 'She said you made her feel inferior because you had a much nicer nature than she has.'

'Oh rot,' said John. 'What a damn fool thing to say. She's worth ten of me. And if it's a question of being pi – look at the way she's always rushing off to church. I never go more than once a week.'

'Perhaps why she rushes, why she took up this Catholic business in the first place, is because you made her feel there was something lacking in herself and she wanted to find it.'

'It doesn't seem to have made her very happy.' The evening's troubles seemed to have weakened John's loyal refusal to discuss his wife. Once having started, he unburdened himself now with relief. 'D'you know what, Onions, I wish she hadn't done it; I think it was a great mistake. One ought to stick to what one was brought up to. It's only unsettled her more than before to go floundering about among all these mysteries which the priests can't possibly explain properly. I think that's why they go in for all this incense and fancy dress and *omnia saecula saeculorum*, to cover up the fact that they don't really know who they're chanting and mumbling at. I wish Heather had listened to me. If only I'd been at home. . . .'

'Mm,' Oliver felt drowsy. He let John ramble on, catching desultory remarks here and there. Dimly, half-listening to the wireless, he heard John say something three or four times, before his brain registered it as something worth paying attention to.

'And she thinks I'm criticizing her,' John kept saying. 'Me, of all people. If she only knew, my God, if she only knew!'

'If she only knew what?' asked Oliver, opening his eyes.

'Oh, nothing. I wouldn't bore you with it. It just' – John gave an unamused laugh – 'it just seems so fantastic you telling me she thinks I'm too good for her, when all the time . . .'

'Spill it,' said Oliver, for John obviously wanted to be pressed into the luxury of confession. 'What have you done? Robbed a bank?'

'Wish it were as simple as that. I could tell her that, but this – I could never make her understand. She'd be terribly hurt.'

Oliver turned off the wireless. 'If you want to talk about it,' he said, 'get on with it. If not, shut up.'

'I haven't told a soul,' John said. 'I could never tell Heather, yet I feel such a swine keeping it from her. It's been preying on me ever since I got back.' Oliver could not see his face. His voice came disembodied from the arm-chair in the panelled dimness at the other side of the room. Up and down swung the heel of John's slipper, while the other foot tapped on the floor, a tom-tom accompaniment to his words.

*

'It was when I was in Australia, waiting to come home, after the cruiser had got us away from Burma. I hadn't seen Heather for nearly two years; I'd never even seen Susan at all. There was a bit of a hold up about getting home. I knew I might have to wait an age for transport – well, that was understandable; there were sick and wounded to be thought of first. In any case, the Jap war wasn't over then, and there was a chance I might be drafted to some other regiment out there. There wasn't much left of mine. They gave me indefinite leave and a certain amount of back pay and told me to stick around and get myself fit. I was a bit moth-eaten.

'I was dying to get home. We'd all talked of very little else since we were captured – that and food. And yet I was dreading it too, in a way, because when Heather and I had been together last we hadn't been making much of a go of it. You weren't at home, of course, so you wouldn't know, but we had a holiday up in Scotland, a second honeymoon, it should have been, but I couldn't

239

do a thing right. Heather didn't enjoy herself. I bored her – made an awful ass of myself.

'You ever been to Melbourne? Pretty fine town. There's something invigorating about the air of that country too; you feel you can tackle anything. That's why I want to go back. Heather doesn't want to, and I suppose it is asking rather a lot to make her uproot herself, especially when I bore her. She'd be even more bored with me if she hadn't got her family and friends to fall back on. Of course she'd make new friends; Heather is pretty quick at making friends, I don't know how she does it, but it would all be very strange at first.

'When I first got there I wasn't feeling too good – starvation mostly, I suppose, and I'd had the inevitable dysentery. Of course I made a beast of myself on the food, and got gastric trouble. I went to a doctor and he put me on a diet, gradually increasing – you know the kind of thing – and soon the boy began to feel pretty fit. They've got steaks out there as big as your head, and as much butter as you can eat, real farm butter, and cream with everything, thick, yellow cream. There was a place I often used to go to lunch, Charlie's Buttery, it was called, where you eat up on stools and this chap Charlie would knock you up bacon and eggs and then sling you a great lump of pie with about half a pint of cream on it. He knew where I'd come from, so he always did me extra well.

'It was there it started actually, in Charlie's Buttery, at lunch-time – no, half a sec – or was it dinner? No, it was lunch, because I remember how dazzling the sun was when I went out into the street afterwards. The pavements there are very white, you know, and the sun just bounces up off them and hits you smack in the eye. A hat doesn't help much because the glare comes up underneath.

'Well, this girl – but I haven't told you about her yet, have I? She was on the stool next to me, and I'd noticed she'd done herself pretty well. You know what ridiculous little appetites most women have, always thinking about their figures. This girl had had a hamburger. I watched Charlie frying it on the griddle behind the counter; it always fascinated me to see him flip them over. She had fried potatoes with it and then she had two helpings of raisin pie and ice cream, and then she asked for a second cup

240

of coffee. Then she put on some lipstick, like girls always do automatically after a meal, whether they need it or not, then she climbed down off her stool – she was only a little thing – and went to the door. Of course old Charlie called out to her, quite politely, to remind her she hadn't paid. She turned round and smiled. She had a funny, crooked smile, with a dent in one corner of her top lip where she'd fallen off a bicycle when she was a kid.

'"I'm sorry," she said, "I haven't any money." Just like that. Some nerve, you know. Charlie didn't know what to do; in fact, he was much more embarrassed than she was. He was a soft-hearted chap who hated any trouble. If a drunk ever came in, he used to sweat blood in case they started any funny business and he'd have to call the police. I felt an awful ass, I mean, it was no good pretending I couldn't hear what was going on because I was the only other person in the place. It was late for lunch. So then this girl tells him she'll stay if he likes, while he calls the police. She didn't look much more than a kid, you know, but full of spunk.

'"I thought I might as well have one good meal," she said, "before I was arrested for vagrancy!"

'"Are you sure you haven't any money?" Charlie asked her. She came back to the bar to show him inside her purse, and it was then I noticed how shabby all her things were. She gave the impression of being smart; you know how some women can wear any old clothes and make them look pretty good. She was very thin and pale too, and I saw then that she was older than I'd first thought her.

'Well, what could I do? You'd have done the same, any mug would. Of course I paid for her lunch. She didn't want me to, but, in a queer way, she didn't seem interested enough to protest much, as if things like money weren't important to her any more. It wasn't a lot in all conscience; Charlie's wasn't the Ritz, where you pay for the furniture and the waiters' laundry as well as your food. I was terrified she was going to be horribly grateful and cling to me or something, but she was grand. She just thanked me very prettily and walked out. Wouldn't even let me see her home, though I'd have liked to.

'I didn't go back to Charlie's for a week as it happened, and when I did I got a shock.

'"That girl's been in every day looking for you," Charlie told me. "She'll probably come in today." Lord, I'd have bolted if I hadn't already ordered my food and could see it sizzling under the grill. Sausages, I was having, with tomatoes and spaghetti. Sure enough, I'd hardly got my teeth into it when in she came. People had kept coming in and out, but when she opened the door I could feel it all down my spine. You know how it is when you're expecting someone. She simply came up to me, planked down on the counter the exact amount I'd paid for her lunch and went away without a word. Of course, I couldn't let her get away with that. I mean, if she was so poor that she couldn't pay for her own lunch, I couldn't take any money from her, so I got my hat and dashed out after her. Perhaps it was that time I was thinking of when I said the sun was dazzling. I know it was glaring hot as we stood arguing on the pavement with people bumping into us and prams having to go round.

'No wonder she fainted. At least, I thought at first it was the heat, but it turned out afterwards she hadn't had a thing to eat all day. I managed to get her into a taxi before a crowd collected. After what she'd said about being arrested, I didn't want any policeman coming along. I told the man to drive into the Park where it was cooler, and when she came-to I got her to tell me her story. It was the usual story; at least, one of them. You probably think I was a mug to fall for it, but honestly, Onions, I could tell she was genuine.

'If you could have seen her ... Stella, her name was, and she was so thin that her cheekbones went up into points. I thought I was thin enough when I came out of Burma, but there was nothing of her at all. She had T.B., you see. That's why she couldn't get a job. At least, she kept taking them on and not being able to stand up to it. That's how she got the money to pay me back, by working all day in one of those dressmakers' workrooms. She said it had just about finished her, and she wasn't given to exaggerating – quite the reverse, in fact. She made very light of her story. But I must tell it you in the right order. I'm afraid I'm telling this rather badly, but the whole thing happened in such a short time that the sequence is a bit muddled.

'She'd been in a sanatorium in England for two years and been discharged as cured. Her mother was a widow – did I tell you

242

that? They hadn't much money. She was engaged to a boy who hadn't much money either, and while she was in the sanatorium he'd gone off to Australia to follow up some vague offer of a better job. So what does this ass of a girl do but dash after him as soon as she can. As she wasn't strong, her mother didn't want her to go all that way alone, but if you knew Stella you'd know that no one could ever tell her what to do. She'd put all her savings into paying her fare out, and when she got there she couldn't find her boy. No wonder. She hadn't told him she was coming, simply gone rushing off into the blue in the excitement of not being cooped up any more in the sanatorium, which she'd hated.

'She followed up various addresses and eventually heard he was in New Zealand. She decided to wait until she could earn enough money to follow him, and got some dressmaking jobs; she was very good at sewing. But while she was waiting she got a letter from him, sent out again from England, to say he thought they'd better call the whole thing off – they'd been too young – he didn't want to tie her down while he had no prospects – you know the old excuses. It was pretty obvious he'd found someone else. I'd like to get my hands on that young swine. Still, he'll be feeling pretty bad now if he's got my letter.

'It was then that Stella realized that she wasn't cured at all. She went phut – partly from shock, of course, and had to give up her job. Her landlady found her coughing her heart up one morning and took her to the hospital, and of course, when they'd taken an X-ray, they told her she'd have to go to another sanatorium. Marvellous ones they have out there too, but she wouldn't go. Not Stella. She had hated the other one and couldn't face it again. She was so unhappy, anyway, that she didn't care if she did die. She told the doctor she'd go home and get her things and told the landlady she was going to the sanatorium, but of course she never went back to the hospital. She went and hid in some awful little room in a slum. Oh yes, they have slums all right, even in Melbourne. She'd spent most of what was left of her money paying off her landlady, so she had to get a job; but, as I said, she couldn't do it.

'What would you have done, Onions? Would you have handed her over to the hospital? I know that would have been the sensible

243

and the right thing to do, but I didn't do it. Perhaps the sun had gone to my head. I took her back to my room at the hotel, and then d'you know what I did – me, the respectable married man, the stooge that Heather thinks is too virtuous? I went out and found a flat and rented it.

'I won't bore you with details, old boy. We lived in that flat for two months. I suppose I shouldn't say it, but I was jolly happy. I'd been pretty lonely drifting round Melbourne with food as my only interest. Stella was happy too. She was sweet. You'd never have thought she was so ill; she was always so gay and lively – too lively, of course; it didn't do her any good. We had awful fun. I hadn't a lot of money, but we used to poke around and find the funny little restaurants. Sometimes we'd go dancing. I know Heather always says I can't dance, but I could all right with Stella. She was so pathetically light, you could hardly feel her. It seems like a dream now; I can't imagine myself being the hero of anything so romantic, and honestly, Onions, it was romantic. There was a tune they were playing a lot: "Call Me Back" . . . I suppose it all sounds terribly common or garden to you, just like anyone else's affair, but it didn't to us. Did I feel guilty? No. I was so far away, it was like being in a different world. The ties weren't very strong. And I'd just had Heather's letter about becoming a Catholic. I was very sore about it.

'Stella knew I was married, of course, but we hardly ever talked about it. If ever two people lived in the present, it was us. Good thing we did, because it only lasted two months.

'She'd kept going for so long at a pitch beyond her strength that when she got ill she just went pouff – like a candle. I took her to the same hospital where she'd been before, and the doctor told me off for not making her go to the sanatorium. Of course I should have, but – I wonder. She could never have been really strong again, and at least we had our two months in that silly little basement flat – quite the worst sort of place for her. She didn't live the life of an invalid. We never talked about it, just as we didn't talk about my being married. We shut everything out, like we'd draw the curtains after tea when the weather got colder and shut out the feet going by in the street.

'It was after she died that I wrote that letter to her boy. I wish now I hadn't, but I needed an outlet for my feelings. I drifted about after that, not doing anything very much, and pretty soon I got my passage home.

'You do see, don't you, that I could never tell Heather? It wouldn't be fair. She's been so good all through the war, and it can't have been much of a picnic for her, with all the work she's had to do. People like Stanford – there's nothing in that. Why shouldn't she have some fun? I never seem able to give her any.

'Stella and I had more fun in two months than Heather and I in all the time we've been married.'

*

John got up. 'I say, could I have another drink?' he asked. 'All that talk's just about dried me up. You asleep? I hope you are, because I never meant to tell anyone, but it's been rather a relief, you know, to get it off my chest.'

'D'you know what?' said Oliver, coming out of a reverie. 'I think you should tell Heather.'

'God, no, I couldn't. How could I ever make her understand that it was something entirely separate, that doesn't affect our relationship at all? You know what women are; it would upset her dreadfully. And she's upset enough with me already as it is. It would be fatal. I wouldn't have the guts.'

'That's just it,' said Oliver vehemently. 'She's always complaining you haven't any guts. She even makes a grievance of the fact that you never look at another woman, and says, it's not much of a compliment to her that you're simply faithful from lack of temptation. Go on, be a man. Tell her. At least it would bring you off the saintly pedestal to which she so objects.'

'It's easy for you to talk,' said John, standing before the fireplace with his drink, his head dropped forward between the yoke of his shoulders. 'Shut away here, you've forgotten what life is really like; you're all theory.'

'All I know is, I get more ideas about life than ever I did when I was so busy living it. My advice is pretty good. I advised Vi to marry Fred, and look what a success it was. I believe it's my mission in life now to lie here and hand out sage counsel. John, don't be a mug. Oh Lord, there's Heather coming back now. Why don't you tell her tonight? Stage a terrific scene up in your room while she's mellow with the free drinks of Stanford's friends.'

'I couldn't face her,' John said. 'I'll fly up and pretend to be asleep when she comes up. Call her in and keep her talking a bit there's a good chap. I couldn't face her tonight. I feel too muddled.'

It was Elizabeth, being brought back in the doctor's car. Oliver called her in and she came, looking very tired. She looked as if she had been sleeping in the car; her eyes were as hazy as a waking child's and a strand of corn-coloured hair had escaped from the neat roll. She put up her hand and tucked it in.

She told Oliver that she had seen Lady Sandys safely into a comfortable room. She had been very quiet during the drive, not knowing her, of course, but amenable.

'She thought it was a hotel we had taken her to. She kept wanting to ring down to the restaurant to ask them to send up a nice little dinner for two. Then she was upset because there was a draw-sheet on the bed, kept threatening to send for the manager, and called the nurses chambermaids. I heard two of the nurses who'd helped me put her to bed laughing afterwards in the corridor, so I saw the Sister and told her we didn't want any of that. I think she'll be all right there. How's John? Has he been very worried?'

'Oh, dreadfully,' said Oliver. 'He's talked of nothing else.'

CHAPTER 10

BEFORE she left, Miss Smutts, always the soul of tact, said to Heather: 'Cheer up, misery. Worrying won't make it any better, though there's no doubt it was your fault, and you can't deny I warned you. But I never was one to say: "I told you so." What's done's done, *I* say, and it may all be part of some higher plan we puny mortals aren't meant to understand.'

'Take her away, John,' muttered Heather, whose eyes were still suffused with sleepiness and hangover. 'And for God's sake don't miss the train and bring her back again.' Miss Smutts, whose luggage all seemed to be in brown-paper parcels and knitting-bags, drove away quite perkily with John, taking leave of Oliver with a 'Toodle-oo'. She was looking forward to her holiday at Malden, where there was a good cinema and a café that sometimes had lemon-curd tarts, and where her sister's credit with the tradespeople was good. It would be a nice change.

It was true what John had told Oliver, that Heather would hardly speak to him. Indeed, she would hardly speak to anyone; she wallowed in her imagined position as an outcast. John said that at meals she was silent and picked at her food with a fork, and when Toby came over on Sunday morning to play chess with Oliver and stayed to lunch, Heather went straight to her room when she returned from her second Mass of the day and sent a message by David to say she was not hungry and would not come down. She became ostentatiously wrapped up in the children and mothered them jealously, even advancing their bath time so that John was deprived of his half-hour with them after tea. Never had Susan and David been taken for so many walks. Mrs North said it was a mercy the weather was fine, or she would have wheeled them to death from over-exposure in her anxiety to be out of the house as much as possible. She went out often in the evenings, not saying where she was going, and taking the car without asking whether anyone else wanted it.

If she happened to be in the room when John came in with the daily telephone bulletin from Birmingham, Heather would walk out, or deliberately pick up something to read. John, who would never learn, tried sometimes to draw her into the conversation. 'Sounds better that, doesn't it, Heather Bell?' he would appeal. 'If she's enjoying her food, there can't be much wrong with her.'

'It's no good asking me,' Heather would answer. 'I'm not supposed to know anything about psychology, that's quite evident, isn't it? You'd better ask Elizabeth.'

No one had thought that they would miss Violet so much. There could be no finesse or innuendo when Violet was around. Her noise and downrightness had a harsh, carbolic effect on an unhealthy atmosphere.

Poor Mrs North was always saying: 'I do miss Violet, d'you know it?' Violet had often been trying, but at least she could

247

understand her uncomplicated nature, and when she was difficult it was in a straightforward way that could be dealt with by straightforward talk. Violet had so far sent one postcard with 'X marks our window' and a picture of their farmhouse hotel on which she had forgotten to put the 'X'.

The only person to whom Heather would talk was Oliver, and even with him she still maintained her defiant attitude.

'This house is getting impossible to live in,' she said, roaming round his room in her restless way. 'It beats me how you can lie there so contentedly in this depressing atmosphere, but then, of course, they *like* you; that makes a difference.'

'But, ducky, we all adore you,' said Oliver lightly.

'Like hell. Disapproval simply shrieks at me every time I come into a room, thinly veiled under a patronizing tolerance which is worse. If John thinks I've behaved so badly, why doesn't he say so? I wish Vi were here. If I said something foul to her, she'd say something foul back, instead of turning the other cheek for more, so as to put me in the wrong. And look at the way John never asks me who I'm going out with. He just sits there dumb and hurt, but you can see accusations streaming out of the top of his head. And why shouldn't I go out? *He* never takes me anywhere. He always wants to sit at home and read. Why shouldn't I have a little fun?'

'Oh, quite, quite,' murmured Oliver.

'D'you know what he said to me today? He said' – she mimicked John's slow voice – 'he said: "Heather Bell, why don't you occasionally read something else besides magazines and library novels? You'd get much more relaxation from a good book." So that's to be the latest thing! He's going to educate me. If being educated means you've got to spend all day over one chapter of those dreary books of his where the foot-notes take up half the page – no, thanks. D'you know, Ollie, I wish he'd just once do something really awfully wrong, some-thing that was crazy and impulsive. I wish it had been him who sent Muffet off her rocker, I do honestly. *I* shouldn't bear a grudge against him like they do me. I'd think all the better of him for showing a little human weakness.'

John and Heather's marriage was going to pieces in their hands. Oliver was furious with them, and furious with himself for being a bedridden spectator, condemned to watch helplessly the disintegration of something that could have been built into happiness. Go on, he told himself. Do something; help them, since they're incapable of helping their own silly selves. You always pride yourself on handing out such wise advice. Hand out some now, now, when it really matters.

He got to work again on John. 'John, I wish you'd tell Heather what you told me the night when – on the night of Vi's wedding. I'm sure it would help. It'll give her a shock, maybe, but it might shock her out of this absurd behaviour – give her something else to think about besides herself.'

'It won't,' said John mulishly. 'It'll make her think about being jealous, and I wouldn't blame her; she'd have every right to be.'

'All right, then, but at least that would be a normal, healthy reaction, and you could get your teeth into a good old normal row, instead of this futile, concocted antagonism that has to be fostered because there's no real cause for it.'

'I wouldn't dare,' said John. 'I haven't the nerve. She's fed up enough with me already; this would only make it worse.'

'It wouldn't. It would give her quite a new idea of you. I told you what she said about wishing you'd show a little human weakness, didn't I? Well, if your little interlude with Sylvia isn't human weakness, what is?'

'Stella,' said John absently. 'But Heather didn't mean that. She doesn't mean half she says.'

'I tell you what; if you won't tell her, I will. Yes, I would; I've got interfering enough for anything these days since I've had nothing else to do. And I warn you, I'll probably tell it all wrong.'

'You wouldn't honestly?'

'I'll swear I will if you won't.'

'I don't know. I'll have to think. . . .' Oliver did not wonder that Heather got irritated with John when he put on that baffled, ox-eyed look, behind which you could almost see his mind wavering about like a piece of cobweb. 'Of course,' he said presently, 'I suppose she couldn't really be jealous of someone who's – who isn't alive?'

Couldn't she? thought Oliver, but he said: 'No, no, of course not,' to encourage John.

'And I have felt the most frightful cad keeping it from her all this time. It would certainly take a load off my mind. You really think I should – – ?'

'Oh, Jonathan, I've *said* so. I'm not going to say it again; I haven't the breath to waste. Look, there's my ultimatum. If you don't tell her tonight, I will.'

'She's going out tonight,' said John, seizing hopefully on the excuse.

'Oh, yes, to Stanford's birthday party. I thought he'd asked you both.'

'I won't go to that man's parties,' said John sulkily. 'I said I didn't feel up to it.'

'Well, tell her before she goes. And look here – I'll bet you a quid she doesn't go. She'll forget all about that facetious little Air Force tyke and stay home to argue it out with you.'

John squared his shoulders and looked like Churchill in Britain's darkest hour. 'I'll tell her,' he said grimly.

Oliver spent the rest of the afternoon and evening chuckling inside himself to think how he had managed the affair. He was getting pretty good; first Violet and now Heather and John. What should he turn his master mind to next? He felt despotic, positively matriarchal. He felt he ought to have a lace cap and a parrot that swore like a sailor and an ebony stick to rap on the floor when he wished to give orders to his satellite household.

He woke early the next morning to the immediate knowledge that he was pleased about something. He had been enjoying one of those vaguely romantic dreams where nothing happens on which you can put your finger when you wake. You know that you enjoyed the dream, but you can't remember why. It hovers like a forgotten tune just out of reach, while you clamp your eyes shut and try to go to sleep again to find the wistful sweetness in which you have been basking all night, and in trying too hard wake yourself thoroughly and lose the dream beyond recapture.

But it was not the dream that contented him this morning. He knew why he was pleased: it was about John and Heather. His mother had come in last night to tell him that they had both gone to Stanford's party after all. Heather had gone with Stanford, since he arrived to fetch her, and John had asked permission to use the family car and followed them shortly afterwards.

So it had worked. The matriarch had been right again. Lying watching the early-morning birds, Oliver wished very much that he could have heard what passed between John and Heather. It was none of his business, but he had been such a busybody all along that he was rapidly losing all delicacy. It was an immense satisfaction to know that he had been right. If this were the beginning of a new understanding and they were going gradually to come together again, what a glow he would feel to have had a hand in it! He lay now and glowed already, his brain maundering on ahead into a rose-tinted future, and when Elizabeth came into the room, which was filled with a dusty gold by the sun shining through the drawn curtains of the side window, he turned on her a beaming smile.

'Morning, Liz!' he called. 'Morning's at seven, etc. Look at that sun on the dew. All's very much right with the world this morning.'

She came towards him and put down the cup before she spoke. 'I'm afraid all's very much wrong with the world,' she said seriously.

'Oh, that's only liver. You should take a – –'

'Listen, Oliver,' she said, and something in her face reminded him suddenly of the face of the MO with the pink cheeks and the little black moustache who had told him he had got to lose his leg. It was the bad-news face of someone who wished they did not have to be the one to break it.

'Listen,' Elizabeth repeated. 'Heather hasn't come home. What shall we do? Do you think I ought to tell someone?'

'She and John were probably so late at the party that they decided to stay the night somewhere,' Oliver said, not worrying. Rather a good sign this.

'But John didn't go to the party.'

'He did. Ma told me he'd taken the car out.'

'Not to go there. He told me he was going to the pub. He looked rather queer; I didn't want him to go.'

'My God,' said Oliver slowly. The glow was rapidly chilling into an icy apprehension.

'And when I dressed this morning,' went on Elizabeth, 'I found this note in the pocket of my white overall. Heather had evidently put it there knowing I wouldn't find it till the morning.

It says: "Be a brick and look after the children for me for a bit. Give the enclosed to John."' She showed Oliver a folded square of paper.

'Typical Heather dramatization,' said Oliver, trying to speak lightly. 'Have you read the note?'

'The note for John? Of course not.' Elizabeth looked offended.

'No, I suppose not. I'd love to know what's in it, though.' He squinted at it against the light. 'What a temptation for an honest man. Liz, you don't think – no, she couldn't have. She wants to give John a fright, I suppose. Silly, dramatic little fool, acting like someone in a film, and calmly landing you with the children. You wait till she comes back. I'll sober her up.'

But Heather was not coming back. John came downstairs heavily, with his eyes fixed on space, dropping a foot on to each stair like a very old man. He came straight into Oliver's room, moving like a sleepwalker. 'Onions,' he said, and had to clear his throat because his voice was hoarse, 'Heather has gone off with Stanford Black.'

Oliver expostulated, argued, refused to believe it, long after his brain had accepted it as true. All the time, there hammered at the back of his mind the insistence that it was his fault. It was a terrible thought, and it began to blot out all other thoughts, even his anger with Heather and his pity for John. He knew now how Heather had felt about Muffet. No wonder she had harped on it. He could imagine a thought like this haunting one's waking hours for ever and shadowing one's dreams. It was quite an effort to bring himself back to John.

John stood hunched like a bear in his dressing-gown, staring out past Oliver at the long shadow of the tree clump, pointing diagonally down the sparkling hill. The letter dangled from his finger-tips. 'I don't blame her,' he kept saying. 'How could I expect her to do anything else after what I told her? Selfish idiot that I was, kidding myself it was fairer for her to know, when all the time it was because I wanted to get it off my chest and stop feeling guilty.'

'But what happened? What did she say when you told her?'

'She'll come back, of course,' John reassured himself, nodding. He went on with his soliloquy, while Oliver went on with his question.

'But what did she say?'

John looked down at him in a tired way. 'She was furious,' he said simply. 'She wouldn't listen properly at first, because she was dressing to go out, but when she realized what I was trying to say she swung round on that tapestry stool of hers with her hairbrush in the air and stared at me as if she thought I was mad. Maybe I am. She let me finish – of course I told it all in a muddle, leaving out half the things I meant to say – and then she turned round with her back to me. I could see her face in the glass. You hear about people's faces being livid. Hers was – a sort of greyey-white.'

'But what did she *say*?' Oliver almost screamed.

'She said,' recited John in a flat voice, 'she said to think she'd been faithful to me all these years and led a deadly life, when all the time I'd been gadding about – you know the kind of thing. She said I was a hypocrite, pretending to be so virtuous. She called Stella a tart. I tried to explain about it not making any difference to her and me. I reminded her that Stella was dead. That made it worse.'

'Why?' Oliver tried to probe him out of the musing silence into which he had fallen. 'Why worse?'

'She said it was disgusting of me to try and excuse myself by pitching a sentimental story. She said why couldn't I just say I'd had a mistress in Australia and leave it at that. She said she supposed the next thing I'd tell her would be that I only did it out of kindness. She wouldn't talk any more after that, wouldn't answer me. She finished her hair – I could see her hands were trembling – got her coat and bag and went downstairs, to write the note, I suppose. I went into the kids' room; David's bedclothes were all on the floor. While I was tucking him up I heard her come back into our room and rummage around. I thought she'd come back for something she'd forgotten, but she must have been packing a bag. I didn't dare go in again; I wish I had. Perhaps I could have stopped her. That swine Black – he must have asked her to do this long ago, you know. Then I heard his car come up the drive – that foul car of his with the outside exhaust – and she rushed out to him before he had time to come into the house. You want to see her note?'

'Not much.' Oliver took it. It said: 'Have gone where I'm more appreciated. Will write to you. E. will look after the children until I've calmed down a bit and decided where to take them.'

'She can't do that.' Oliver looked up. 'She can't have the kids.'

'What should I do with them?' John spread his hands helplessly.

Sooner or later they had to tell Mrs North. She took this enormous catastrophe far better than she took minor ones, but later in the day she suddenly felt so tired that Elizabeth put her to bed.

Elizabeth was a rock. She made no comment on Heather. She was so busy looking after the children, Oliver, and Mrs North, helping Mrs Cowlin in the kitchen, putting food before John in the hope that he would eat it, dashing off in the car to do the shopping, answering the telephone, cancelling Mrs North's bridge date with Mrs Ogilvie and fending off Mrs Ogilvie from coming round instead, that she had no time to talk to anyone. John did nothing but talk. Oliver grew so weary of hearing him go over and over the same ground that he had to get Elizabeth to manoeuvre him out of the room. John went upstairs then and talked to Mrs North, hour after hour.

Oliver thought he felt worse than at any time since his illness. He had certainly never felt so unhappy. That night he lay wide awake, cursing himself for a meddling fool, seeing how he had been carried away by his vision of himself as an oracle. Seeing that he had spoken from theory, fitting the thing together mathematically instead of humanly, so pleased with himself for being so wise that he had never paused to consider just how wise he was.

He heard the stable clock strike one and two, and by the time it struck three the gathering cloud of black depression had submerged him completely. But no one was going to pander to his ego if he had a mood now. No one was going to be bothered with his whims and try to coax him with special food and ask him whether he would like a bottle of wine opened. He would not even get the gratifying appreciation of a relieved household when the mood lifted. Probably no one would know he had had one. Serve him right. He wished that he was older, now that he appeared to be doomed for the rest of his life to useless introversion, since what he had thought was useful extroversion had failed so miserably. He would never get better, of course; that always went without saying when he had a *cafard*, and he would grow into a querulous old man who was bandied around the family, a nuisance to everybody, unable to die, and when he did, without even any money to leave to the people who had looked after him.

On top of all her other extra work, Elizabeth had remembered to make his tea. Oliver eyed the thermos sourly. Trust her not to forget a thing. What right had anyone to be so perfect? It seemed almost like an accusation. He was beginning to understand more and more how Heather had felt after her disastrous mismanagement of Lady Sandys. How could he go on living in the same house with John? But he had no Stanford Black to run away to. Perhaps he would run to Mary Brewer's pub – run on one leg and go hopping into her bedroom that would have dark leaning furniture with big knobs, and a rush mat by the washstand. Mary Brewer would sit up in a narrow bed in pleased surprise, wearing green stockinette pyjamas and a hair-net. Her underclothes would be lying over a chair. He could see the suspender belt and the black woollen stockings she wore with her uniform.

All the same, he thought grudgingly, it was a good thing Elizabeth had made the tea. He poured himself a cup, took one sip, and hurled the rest out on to the lawn. The tea was half cold; she had not screwed the cap on properly. So you're not so efficient after all, he thought, illogically quite pleased, in spite of having no tea, to catch someone else out in a fault, however slight.

Mrs Ogilvie could not, of course, be kept away for ever. Two days after Heather's flight, when there was still no word from her to say where she was or what she intended to do, Mrs Ogilvie arrived with a book for Oliver, all about the spiritual adventures, mostly depressing ones, of a mutilated soldier. With her unerring instinct for trouble, she had no sooner stepped into the hall than she scented that something was wrong. She nosed about until she thought she had tracked it down.

'And where is Heather?' she asked, when Elizabeth, with the children hanging on to her skirts, brought the tea-tray into Oliver's room.

'Why,' said Mrs North quickly, a little too quickly, 'she's

255

gone to stay with friends in town, mm-*hm*. Elizabeth's looking after the children.'

'*Really?*' asked Mrs Ogilvie. 'Now, isn't that nice for her? I'm sure she can do with a change from domesticity.' She did not ask why Mrs North's eyes were so red behind the pince-nez and her puffy cheeks unsuccessfully camouflaged with so many layers of white powder. She did not ask why John refused anchovy toast and sat staring into space with his hands hanging, jumping and answering at random when he was addressed, nor why Oliver was in such a bad temper that he did not even look at the title of the book before putting it down on his table, but her busy eyes said it all for her.

When Elizabeth came to fetch David for his bath, although he went readily enough, he had to say: 'When is Mummy coming home?'

'Soon, my lamb,' said his grandmother.

'No, but when? I say *when*?' David dragged against Elizabeth's hand. 'Termorrow? Day after? Day after day after day after that?' John looked like the Spartan boy who had a fox under his shirt.

'She'll come home soon,' said Elizabeth, bending down. 'You'd like her to have a nice long holiday and enjoy herself, wouldn't you?'

'She never said good-bye to me,' protested David in the whine which he had recently developed because he had discovered that it exasperated Heather into giving him what he wanted.

'Come along, dear,' said Elizabeth brightly. 'Listen! I can hear your bath running.' As she took him away, Mrs Ogilvie gave herself a brisk little nod, which plainly said: 'There is something funny going on round here.' Indeed, a less acute perception than hers could have sensed the distressed atmosphere of the house.

She had just time to circulate her suspicions in the neighbourhood when, as if to confound her, Heather came home. She came home very late at night in a hired car, which she stopped at the far end of the drive, and she let herself in quietly and crept into Oliver's dark room with a quick 'Don't be frightened, Ollie, it's me. I don't want to see anyone else yet.' He was inordinately pleased that she had come straight to him. Although she could not know of his responsibility in the affair, it seemed that because

256

she came to him and said: 'I want to talk to you first,' he was forgiven.

'Well,' he said, not knowing what to say. 'Well, have you come back for good, or just to get your toothbrush?'

'For good,' she said in a small voice. 'No, don't turn on the light. Can I sit on your bed; it doesn't hurt you now, does it?' She perched on the end of his high bed and he could see her outline dimly against the night sky. Her head, with its clumpy shape of soft hair, was framed in one open casement of the side window of the bay. She twisted and put her head out, leaning her hands on the sill and breathing deeply.

'Mm,' she said, turning back again, 'it's good to smell the garden. I feel as if I'd been away ages. I've been staying in such a horrid hotel, Ollie, in Kidderminster of all places. It makes the whole thing sound like a music-hall joke, doesn't it? My window had loops of dirty lace curtains and looked out over a yard where cats made love in the dustbins. The cupboard door wouldn't stay shut unless you put a chair against it and there was a spider that came up the waste-pipe of the basin.'

Oliver was so bursting with a question that he thought she must have heard him thinking it.

She gave a little laugh. 'I know what you want to ask. No, he wasn't. In fact we haven't been together at all, except just at the party, and I didn't stay there long. I hadn't wanted to go at all, but of course we had to, as he was the host. No one will believe me, I know, but I've spent these three days all on my own. How are my children?'

'Blooming. Haven't missed you at all.'

'I suppose I ought to say it was the thought of the poor little motherless darlings that brought me back, but it wasn't that specially. I just came because I wanted to. Ollie – –' She paused, looked down and plucked at his eiderdown. 'I've had the most extraordinary experience.'

'What?' he asked, and waited for her to find the words to begin.

'It happened at the party, of all the unlikely places. I was in the bar of that dreadful roadhouse – you know – the Spotted Dog. All little triangular glass tables and chromium chairs and notices saying: "Eat, drink and be merry, for tomorrow we'll have a hangover."' All the time she was talking she was plucking feathers busily out of his eiderdown, as if it were an important task.

*

'How shall I tell you?' she asked, throwing back her head and looking at the ceiling for inspiration. 'Shall I begin at the beginning? I don't know how much John's told you. You know what we rowed about? Oh, yes, I suppose he told you ages ago, long before he screwed himself up to telling me.

'I was livid. You know how it's been with us for ages – ever since he came back really. I did try, honestly I did, though I know you won't believe me, but I just felt so – so *wrong* all the time – nervy and jumpy and seething inside and ready to fly off the handle the moment anyone, particularly John, spoke to me. I did try, Ollie. I used to go to church and pray and pray, and then when it didn't make me feel any better I felt let down. I mean I'd thought that being a Catholic was going to help me, like it did Blanche Arnold, and when I found it didn't, I felt I'd got no one on my side and I didn't see how I was going to go on. I had nothing. Not that I expected to see a vision of the Virgin Mary wreathed in roses or be wafted up to heaven in a kneeling position or anything like that, but I wanted help – guidance, peace, self-control, whatever you like to call it – and I wasn't getting it.

'That business about Muffet put the lid on it, as you know. I felt ghastly about it, and because I was accusing myself all the time, I tried to vent my mortification by accusing everyone else of accusing me, though I dare say they weren't. I went and confessed it all right, but it didn't make me feel any better. It made me feel worse, in fact, to think that what I'd been taught to believe in was just so much meaningless ritual. I was just about at the end of my tether when John sprung his little fairy story on me. Poor darling, he did tell it so badly. I'm sure it was very romantic, but he made it sound anything but.

'It was the last straw. I had been thinking of clearing out before, you know, because I felt I couldn't cope with this house any longer, and Stanford had made the sinful suggestion more than once, and it made me so mad to think that some small dregs of loyalty had kept me here faithful, while all the time John had put one over on me. I just boiled over. I never thought twice about going; I just went. I *couldn't* have stayed here. Could you, Ollie, under the circumstances?

'I didn't plan ahead – separation – divorce – I didn't think as far as that. I just thought I'd clear out with Stanford and then decide what to do. I didn't mean to come back. I know none of you like Stanny, but I've always been fond of him. We get on very well together and he'd always been sweet to me. It was refreshing to get a bit of expressive stimulating admiration instead of just dumb devotion. That makes me a typical magazine heroine, I suppose. Depressing, isn't it, to think that all women have a standard set of reactions? I thought it would all be so easy, just to drop everything and live in the present for a bit. Even John had done it, after all, and he seemed to have a pretty good time.

'Well, Stanford was thrilled, of course, in a rather triumphant, I knew-you'd-come-to-your-senses-sooner-or-later kind of way. We went to this rather grim party. I never have liked his friends particularly. They're all right on a party, and I've got on quite well with them and had fun, but that night I just couldn't stand them, especially that Doris woman with the teeth and the violet lipstick. They seemed so commonplace. Of course, they couldn't know the terrific thing I'd done and what I was feeling like. You know how you feel when you've been in a skid and fetched up half an inch off a telegraph pole – shaken and trembling and sick. I felt like that, and every time I thought about John and Elizabeth finding those letters and what you'd all say, I felt even sicker. I knew I'd never be able to go back. It seemed more and more irrevocable, and that made me feel sad. Then when I'd had a drink or two, some poisonous concoction of that familiar barman with the drooping eyelid, I felt sicker and sadder still.

'Stanford was being awfully sweet to me. He kept coming up and whispering that we'd clear out soon; he knew where we would go. He said he'd got a room all fixed up for us at a quiet hotel on the river and we'd go there over the week-end and discuss what we'd do when he had to go back to Ockney. One thing I must say, he's very efficient in a situation like that. He made it all so easy. Lots of practice, I suppose.

'"Happy?" he kept asking, and I'd say "yes, rather," but I

259

wasn't at all. The thought of him suddenly wasn't giving me any comfort. You may laugh, but it's been a comfort all this time to know there's someone around who thinks you're marvellous and is only too ready to tell you so, and that you're not appreciated by your husband. Just what you want to hear. But now that I'd got him I found I didn't want him, not awfully, and he was all I had got. No wonder I felt sad.

'Everyone had gone through to the restaurant to dance. Stanford and I were alone. He'd gone to the bar to get another drink, and it was then it happened. I always thought that kind of thing only happened in church, and I expect you did, but, d'you know, it doesn't.

'How will I tell you? How can I make you understand? Promise you won't laugh or scoff, or, if you want to, wait till afterwards.

'Well . . . well, you know one jabbers a lot of automatic stuff about the Peace of God which Passeth all Understanding, and parsons with plums in their mouths intone it at you on the wireless and it doesn't mean a thing. I suddenly – there in that sordid bar – I knew what it meant. I felt it, Ollie. I didn't realize at first. I just felt warm and comfortable and not unhappy about the future any more. It was like someone making a fuss of you when you don't feel well; like someone taking your hand – someone friendly, who you're sure knows more than you do about everything – and saying: "it's all right; you don't have to worry. I'll look after everything." That was all. That was my extraordinary experience. I expect you think it was the drink. Well, you can if you like.

'All the struggling and frustration I'd been through in church, going all the wrong way about it, strenuously saying all the prayers without properly knowing what they meant, thinking that I could achieve something by getting up early in the cold and saying ten decades of the rosary very fast and putting rather more than I could afford into the plate – after all that, what I'd been trying for just happened to me in that bar without my doing a thing about it.

'I felt all right then. I told Stanford I wasn't going with him, and I was able to argue quite calmly; it all seemed rather remote and unimportant. I didn't tell him why, of course; he'd have thought I was tight, like I expect you do. I told him I couldn't leave the children and that I hadn't the guts to leave my security and face social ostracism. I didn't want to hurt his feelings by making him think I didn't want him. Of course he was hurt — any man would be — and he kept on asking me why I'd suddenly changed my mind, but in the end he was awfully nice about it, and offered to drive me home. Like a fool, I never thought that if I went home then I'd be in time to tear up the letters; I could have made some excuse to go into Elizabeth's room and sneak them out of her overall. I only knew that I didn't want to come home yet; I wasn't ready. I wanted to go somewhere quite on my own, where no one could get at me till I'd thought things out.

'I didn't tell him that. I said he couldn't possibly leave his own party, and he saw that — he's always such a good host — and he saw, too, that I couldn't possibly stay. Luckily, there's a garage attached to the Spotted Dog, and I managed to get a car, and when the man asked me where I wanted to go I said Kidderminster. You may well ask why, but I'd happened to see it on one of those maps with puns and funny drawings while I was waiting in the hall, and it was the sort of place where I wouldn't be likely to meet anyone I knew.

'When we got there I asked him if he knew where I could stay, and he took me to this hotel. He knew the proprietor, luckily, because I'd never have got in anywhere else at that time of night. It didn't matter it being such a squalid place, a sort of commercial travellers' one-night stand. It was better, because I was sure not to meet anyone. I just wanted to be quite alone. I wanted to hide from you all and Stanford and everybody. Queer place to go into a kind of retreat, wasn't it, the King's Head, Sharpe Street, Kidderminster? The tablecloths had Worcester sauce stains on them and there was one very old, broken-down chambermaid called Ruby. The bell in my room didn't work, anyway, even if I had wanted her. Supper was at half past six — high tea rather, with tea that left brown stains in the cups, and slabs of factory cake, and then you either went into the saloon bar or did what I did which was go to bed. How I slept, Ollie. The first real sleep I've had for weeks and years. Perhaps that's why I feel so well. I felt rather bad thinking of Elizabeth getting out of bed to shut the children up when they wake early, but I have had them all this

261

time, and I know she gets up with the lark, anyway, to do the boiler. There's a lot of good in that girl, Ollie; I don't know whether you've realized it.

'There you are, darling, there's my pathetic little story, my dim little tribute to the Catholic faith. I see now that it all goes back to meeting Blanche Arnold in that nursing home. Although I couldn't make anything of it till now, that was all part of the shape of it, because when I did, when it really mattered that I should, it made it so unmistakable and important.

'Don't be afraid that I'm going to be a changed woman, or get religious melancholia or anything. It's just that I know now what I'm going to do. Instead of always trying to alter John, I'll have to alter myself, just enough so that we can fit in together and get the best out of each other instead of scratching around trying to find the worst. Does that sound awfully righteous? It isn't meant to be; it's meant to be common sense.'

*

'I think I'll go to bed now.' She yawned and leaned her head against the window. He could tell by her silhouette that she was completely relaxed. It was the first time he had seen her so relaxed since the old days when she used to fling herself down to sleep in odd corners.

'Of course,' she said slowly, 'I'm dreading facing the others. I think John will understand, though. D'you think he'll take me back? I should look pretty silly if he wouldn't. Has Ma been very upset? I do hope she'll believe I haven't been with Stanford, because she's so moral she'd never get over it, even though I have come back. She'd think of it every time she looked at me. I think perhaps we'll go out to Australia after all and do what they call making a fresh start. After all, if John could be happy in Melbourne with the consumptive Stella, he can be happy with me – happier perhaps; he always did like plump women better than thin ones.

'If Stanford rings up, I'm out, or dead. Good night, darling. I think I'll sleep in Vi's room. You might tell Elizabeth when she wakes you and she can break the glad news, or you can, and then I shan't feel quite such a fool coming down. I shall feel a pretty good fool, though. Still, I suppose one's got to pay some price for three days' debauchery in Kidderminster. Did you know the air there has got one of the highest soot contents in Worcestershire? One of the commercial travellers told me.'

Oliver slept well and lay so still that in the morning there was still a dent on the end of the bed to tell him that he had not dreamed it, and when he pulled the eiderdown up against the chill of the early morning air a little pile of feathers drifted down on to the floor.

CHAPTER 11

THE house had never known such a quiet summer. John had started work again in London, and Heather and the children had gone to live with him in his mother's new flat in Maida Vale. Lady Sandys, who had done well in Birmingham, had been moved to a rest-home in the outer suburbs, where they could visit her more easily. She was so much better that she was demanding to know why she could not go home. They told her that she had had a nervous breakdown, due to delayed war strain, which she was quite ready to believe. Being one of those people who say 'I have a horror of war,' as if everybody else loved it, she was not surprised that it had affected her more deeply than those people who scampered about in navy blue overalls and berets, really *enjoying* the air raids.

Although she objected to the neighbourhood and to the matron of the home, who called her 'My Lady Lou' and almost gave her woolly bears to play with, Muffet was quite happy playing bridge and writing the memoirs of her life in green ink. She only had occasional lapses now into oddity, and there was talk of her going with John and Heather to Australia if they definitely decided to migrate.

Fred was so short of labour that Violet and Evelyn and even Elizabeth were sometimes out all day helping on the farm, and Oliver was outside now most of the time, wheeling himself round the flatter parts of the garden, or sitting on the lawn, or in the recess of the yew hedge where people used to watch the tennis. Mrs North said she was haunted by the echo of her own footsteps as she dusted and tidied the rooms which there was no one to make dusty or untidy.

She did not like the heat, and she kept the house curtained and cool. When Oliver wheeled himself through the french windows into the rose-scented dusk of the drawing-room, he collided with the furniture, because it seemed pitch dark after the garden. When she sat in the garden, his mother kept to the shade of the cedar tree, while Oliver basked, against orders, in the full sun, with his father's old Panama hat tipped over his eyes and a sawn-off pair of flannel trousers pinned across his stump. Dr Trevor would not let him have his artificial leg yet, as he did not trust him not to do more with it than his heart could stand.

Now that he needed so little nursing, Elizabeth had been given the chance to leave, but after all these months of seeming never to have taken root, she preferred now to stay and help with the house and farm. Her rounded arms were taking on the colour of a brown speckled hen's egg and her corn-coloured hair, bleaching in the sun, looked fairer still in contrast to the tanning skin, which made her eyes look bluer and her teeth whiter. She did not seem to want to go. Oliver gathered that she was thinking seriously about Arnold Clitheroe, and did not consider it worth while starting another job if she were going to be married. It would mean living in Golders Green, with a week-end cottage at Virginia Water, so he supposed she planned to make the most of the real country while she could.

He saw her and Evelyn coming down to tea one day from the hayfield on the other side of the hill opposite the house. They came over the top of the hill, and he watched them all the way down, Elizabeth in a blue dress and Evelyn in boy's shorts and a bright yellow shirt. Half-way down, they broke into a run, and soon their legs were going faster than their bodies, like bicycles without free-wheels. He heard them laughing as they disappeared under the lip of the Ha-Ha wall that divided the garden from the hill field.

Mrs North puttered out of the house with the tea trolley like a shunting goods engine. She wore a striped tussore dress, white buckskin shoes with buckles and a straw hat with a flopping brim, which she pushed up to look down the garden through her dark

264

spectacles. She looked different without her pince-nez; softer and cosier, more English, more like anybody's mother.

'What are those two playing at?' she asked. 'I can see them fooling around trying to climb the Ha-Ha at the highest place. Why don't they come up the steps like sensible people? I do wish they'd hurry; I just can't wait to tell Evie about her father's letter. Oh, Evie!' she called. 'Oh, Elizabeth!' No wonder she found the heat trying. It made even Oliver, who could soak up sun like a lizard, feel hot to see her fussing round the tea table, rearranging plates, going in and out of the house, and calling out at intervals to two people who would come, anyway, sooner or later.

'Oh, my,' she said. 'Violet said she might be stopping by for tea. That'll mean another cup. All this going backwards and forwards makes my legs feel like melting candles.'

'Why not let her get it when she comes?' Oliver asked with the indolence of someone who knew he could not go himself.

'She'd only break it. Do you know, she's broken nearly the whole of that tea set I gave her. I found Fred eating his tea off a tin flan dish when I went over the other day. And it wasn't even tea-time. They have the craziest regime: tea at half past six, and they were aiming to have supper after that at half past seven – macaroni pudding, in this weather! Violet was eating a hunk of cold suet roll for her tea. Imagine, they have hot steamed pudding for lunch every Saturday, whatever the season. Still, I reckon Fred's lucky to get any food at all, though Violet's really becoming quite a good little cook since she's consented to let me give her a few hints. She will use the same pan for everything, though, without scouring it properly in between. That's not very hygienic, you know.' She pronounced it hygi-ennic, and stood for a moment gazing wistfully at a vision of her land where washing-up machines and rubbish pulverizers and cornerless floors could make the most casual woman sanitary.

'Here they are at last. Well, come along, you two! My goodness, anyone would think you didn't want your tea. I've got a surprise for you, Evie.'

'Strawberries?' Her freckled face fell again as Mrs North shook her head. 'Much more exciting. Your Pa's coming over next month to stay awhile and then take you back to the States.'

Evelyn's skinny bare legs waved in the air as she solemnly

265

turned head over heels and then rolled down the bank on to the lower lawn. During the anticlimax of climbing back up the bank, she remembered that it would be polite to say: 'Of course, I don't want to leave here – but oh, Auntie Hattie! Did he say anything about the ranch? Has he got my horse yet?'

When she had gone in to wash, Mrs North said to Oliver: 'I shan't tell her the other news yet. Bob said he was going to write and break it himself. Once she gets used to it, she'll probably like the idea of having someone to take her mother's place. She can't resent it. After all, she never knew Vivien; she was only a baby when she died.'

'She could be jealous of someone taking Bob away from her, though. She seems to adore him.'

'Bob wouldn't let that happen; he's too nice a person. He adores Evie, too. It's just that he's never had the time for her and she's always been parked with nursemaids and convenient sisters. But now that she's older he'll probably take more interest in her, and this Irene, of course, will be able to make a home for the poor kid. I only hope she's the right type. I never have trusted Bob's taste since he got himself so involved with that terrible girl who played the 'cello, remember?'

'Irene,' said Oliver. 'I'm sure it's Ir*e*ne, not *I*reen.' They had this argument about twice a week until Bob's arrival.

But when Bob Linnegar and his new wife arrived it turned out that she was never called either Irene or *I*reen, but Honey. Everyone, even Evelyn, must call her that.

'She can't call her Mother,' said Bob piously, mentally removing his hat to the memory of his first wife. Evelyn had no intention of doing anything of the kind. She did not like Honey, who was tall and *svelte*, with a thirty years' trail of interesting experiences behind her, which now, at forty-seven, showed in her face if not in her figure. Honey did not like Evelyn very much either. She did not like any children, especially unsophisticated ones. She arrived, however, laden with presents to make a good impression: a fabulous doll, dressed by Molyneux, which could take in drinks and get rid of them, a cabinet of paints good enough for an artist, boxes of chocolate and candy, and some precocious little dresses.

Evelyn had taken the doll shyly and politely, holding it as

awkwardly as Violet held a baby, and had left it upside down in a chair for days until Mrs North took it away. She had taken the paints to school to show her friends and she had passed round the chocolates once and then disappeared with them for the rest of the afternoon.

The dresses terrified her. Mrs North, afraid of offending her new sister-in-law, had at last argued Evelyn into trying them on, but she would not come downstairs and show herself, nor could she ever be found afterwards when Mrs North wanted to fit them for altering.

'Beastly, horrible things,' Evelyn told Oliver through the window. 'Weeny short sticky-out skirts like lampshades and blouses with words written all over them and great big soppy bows instead of buttons. I *couldn't* wear them.'

'I suppose they're what children wear in America, so she thought you'd like them, too. It was jolly kind of her to bring you all those things, wasn't it?' he said in a propaganda voice.

'I don't like her,' said Evelyn sombrely. 'She looks like a devil.' This was rather true. Honey's face was long and narrow, with high cheekbones and thin, sarcastic lips, painted to look fuller. She had long greenish eyes and her eyebrows were plucked to go down in the middle and up at the sides. Her nose was not beaky enough to spoil her appearance, but it was bony and sharp, with cutaway nostrils. She wore her hair parted in the middle, with the front locks rolled into a black horn over each temple. She was extremely elegant, with perfect legs and feet and liked all her clothes, even her suits, to cling everywhere. Her nails were talons dipped in venous blood and she liked musky perfume and barbaric, clanking jewellery and huge shiny handbags.

She had brought presents for Oliver, too, books and sweets and cigarettes and a half-mocking sympathy, which said: 'I understand you: you are my type. You and I are grown-up in this rather juvenile world.' Once, when she leaned over him to point at something in his paper, Oliver felt frissons travelling up and down his spine, and put it down, for his own peace of mind, to her nails. For Honey was attractive, in a serpentine, unwholesome way, to men, but not at all to women.

Bob was crazy about her. He was a noisy, good-tempered, middle-aged man with a large fit body and a round grey head too big for its brain. His voice carried everything before it, not only by its volume, but by the sweeping things it said. You could never have an argument with Bob. If he said a thing was so, it was so, and you soon learned to spare yourself the effort of contradicting. He would make the most fantastic statements and stick to them, shouldering aside all disagreement, like a buffalo coming through pampas grass. Mrs North had always adored her brother, and his presence in the house woke her from her long comas of domestic absorption. She seemed to get less tired, and she could sit down and forget what was in the oven if he were talking to her. She could pass a clock ten times without looking at it and next quarter's telephone bill would show that she had been less extravagant on TIM. She worried less and laughed more. She was as gay as a girl and reverted more and more to her mother tongue, which she refurbished with the latest expressions which she picked up avidly from the Linnegars.

Evelyn, who had not seen her father since she was old enough to realize him as anything more than a vast male presence, was a little afraid of him. She had worshipped him in her mind, encouraged by her aunt, and she worshipped him in the flesh, but from a safe distance, prowling round on the edge of the company, watching him, coming quickly to him if he called her, but slipping away as soon as the conversation side-tracked him from the bear's hug he was giving his daughter. She swallowed all his stories and electrified her school with the information that New York was built on a foundation of rock no thicker than a paving stone and that an American train went so fast that its sound followed it through the station and had to have a signal of its own. She believed everything he told her, and he told her what he thought she wanted to hear.

When she asked him about the ranch, he said: 'Oh, sure, sure, we'll have a ranch, with a swimming pool and whole herds of cattle and wild ponies and cow-punchers and hill-billies. You can have Gary Cooper too, if you want.'

'I think I'd rather have Rodeo Ralph, if you don't mind,' said Evelyn, whose knowledge of film stars was confined to the retrogressive, second-feature cinema to which she sometimes went with Violet and Fred. 'He could be head groom, but of course I shall look after my own horse myself. Have you bought him yet?

What's he like? Oh, I do so want a chestnut, with golden lights in mane and tail, but of course' – she looked at him anxiously – 'if it's not, I'm sure I should like another colour just as much.'

'You shall have the finest, high-steppingest chestnut in all California,' said Bob expansively. 'You shall come with me and choose one. We'll go on the Santa Fé Chief, in a state berth with satin sheets and perfume coming out of sprays in the wall. You start lunch in the Grand Central and get half-way across the continent before you've done.'

'I've seen a melon,' said Evelyn cautiously. 'In a shop. Aunt Hattie said she wasn't rich enough to buy it. Are we rich enough, Daddy, to buy a very big ranch?'

'Acres and acres of it.' Bob spread his arms and Oliver saw Honey frown at him and tap her foot. They did not intend to live anywhere but in New York, where an apartment was being fitted out for them by a fashionable interior decorator who looked like being Honey's next experience.

Oliver thought it was about time someone started breaking it gently to Evelyn where she was going to live. It should also be broken to her that Honey was a permanency. She did not seem to realize that she would be going back to the States with her and her father. She thought he would leave her over here now that he had got a daughter for company.

'If she's coming with us, Uncle Ollie, I'm not going,' Evelyn said determinedly, eating her supper in his room in a skimpy woollen dressing-gown with her hair in pigtails.

'But that's the whole idea of their coming over here, to take you back with them,' said Oliver.

'They don't want me. When I go out for walks with them, or in the car, which I don't like because Daddy drives too fast, they talk to each other all the time and it's dreadfully boring. She won't let him talk to me. If he starts and we're just enjoying ourselves, she calls out: "Oh Ba-arb!"' She gave a good imitation of her stepmother's twanging city accent. '"I've gotten a stitch in my side, or a thorn in my finger, or a stone in my shoe" – you know how she's always shamming she's got something wrong with her. Then he fusses over her like Heather used to do with Susan when she cried. She wouldn't be any good on a ranch. She'd always be getting colds or hurting herself or getting her

269

toenail trodden on by one of the horses. She kicked up an awful shindy when Dandy trod on her foot, and it couldn't possibly have hurt because he hasn't any shoes on, and he's so light, anyway. He's stood on my toe loads of times and I haven't minded. Look.' She kicked off her slipper and showed him the crinkled, blackened big toenail of anyone who has much to do with horses.

'Fred doesn't like her either, because she said his bulls ought to wear knickers. He thought that was rude and so do I.' She tore savagely at the crust of bread and butter sprinkled with sugar and her pale-lashed eyes brooded their dislike of her stepmother.

Oliver cleared his throat. 'Perhaps you won't live on the ranch just at *first*,' he said tentatively. 'You might live in New York for a bit; you'll love that. You live in a flat like a palace with beds like clouds, higher up than the top of the Wrekin, and the lift takes you up in one go – swish – without stopping.'

'Daddy said we were going to have a ranch,' said Evelyn doggedly.

Oliver sighed. 'Probably later on you will. You could leave Honey in New York while you and he went to California.'

'He wouldn't go without her. He won't go anywhere without *her*.' Which was true.

Bob followed his new wife about like an infatuated St Bernard. If she got up, he would ask where she was going, and when she was sitting down he would ask her if she was comfortable and did she want anything fetched and wasn't she tired and wouldn't she like a small shot of rye, of which he seemed to have brought an inexhaustible supply in his baggage. When they had been at Hinkley for a week, Honey decided that her hair needed resetting and her nails resharpening.

'I'll make an appointment for you with my man in Shrewsbury,' Mrs North said obligingly, already moving towards the telephone. 'It's only a little place, but Mr Meechayul is a very skilled man. He used to be with Antoine.'

'Thanks a lot, Hattie,' said Honey with a patronizing smile, 'but I couldn't go to anyone but Julian in Dover Street. He always does me when I am over here. Barb is going to take me up to town. Have you wired the Dor*ches*ter yet, dear?'

'Blimey,' said Violet, flabbergasted, 'all the way to London to have your hair washed? You must be potty.' Her status as Mrs Williams with a home of her own and no one to tell her what to do all day had given her more poise with people like this. Instead of being paralytic as she once would have been, the uneasiness which Honey's presence caused her manifested itself in an outspoken bravado of rudeness.

'You ought to hold your head under the pump like I do,' she went on. 'We haven't had any water at the cottage since the drought.' Honey shuddered and leaned well back as Violet reached across her for another piece of cake.

'Say, isn't that terrible?' she said. 'I'd just pass *out* if I didn't have my bath every evening.'

'I should think everyone else passes out if you do that in this house. There's never enough hot water for more than one bath at night.'

'Violet!' Her mother quickly changed the subject. 'You never told me you hadn't any water. That's terrible. Why don't you and Fred come up here for baths?'

'Should think you'd got enough people having baths without us too,' said Violet, glad to have the point handed to her. 'We're O.K. You ought to see us washing in the morning. Fred pumps while I wash, then I pump while he washes.'

'Quite a charming little idyll,' said Honey, lighting a cigarette and blowing smoke down her nostrils, and Bob made everybody jump by going 'Ha-ha-ha!' like the hooter on a calliope.

When Evelyn heard that they were going to London for the week-end, she went dead white and stared at her father unbelievingly. 'But you can't, Daddy, you can't. It's my school sports. I *told* you!'

'So you did. Say, isn't that just too bad? You'll have to tell me all about it, hm?'

'But you promised you'd come. You know I might win the high jump, and I wanted you to see me. All the other girls' parents go.'

'I'll come of course, dear,' said Mrs North, 'and perhaps Violet and Fred will too.'

'Yes, I know – thanks awfully – but I mean – well, you always come, and they know you. Nobody's got a father who's an American, and I did so want him to come. Daddy, do. They have lovely teas,' she said hopefully. 'Miss Mann makes the most super baps, with strawberry jam and cream – –'

'What in heaven's name is a baps?' asked Bob.

'A bap,' said his sister. 'It's a sort of round, doughy thing you make on a griddle.'

'You mean a hot biscuit,' said Honey.

'Not a *biscuit*,' said Evelyn scornfully. 'Biscuits are things like this.' She waved a *petit beurre* furiously under her stepmother's nose.

'A cracker,' murmured Honey.

'Oh, don't let's have that old argument again,' said Oliver wearily. 'You'll have to get used to talking about crackers, Evie, when you go to the States, or no one will know what you mean.'

'I'll say biscuit if I want to,' said Evelyn stubbornly, 'and they'll jolly well have to understand.'

'You'll go hungry,' said her stepmother in a catty little sing-song.

Evelyn was understood to mumble that she'd rather starve than talk that potty language, as she slouched out, aiming a kick at a table leg on the way. They heard her go upstairs, bang, bang, bang, against the back of each step.

'Oh dear, her shoes – –' said Mrs North. 'That's her only good pair. I shall have to talk to you about her clothes, Honey, before you take her back. She'll need a completely new outfit; she hasn't a decent thing to wear. I've been letting her run wild, I'm afraid, and she's nearly always in pants, so it hasn't really been worth buying her anything good. And there's nothing in the shops – –' She was horrified to find herself apologizing to her sister-in-law.

'Oh, sure,' said Honey. 'Archer can take her to Maceys and get her fitted out. She's been a children's maid; she'll know all about it.'

'Don't let her get fussy things,' said Mrs North, who hated the thought of her poor Evelyn in New York. 'Those dresses that you brought were very lovely, but I'm afraid she'll never wear them.' She gave a half-hearted laugh. 'She's quite a madam, I'm afraid, in her likes and dislikes.'

'She'll have to dress like an American child and not like a stable boy when she's over there,' said Honey, looking hard. 'She's too darned independent altogether for my way of thinking.'

272

'Now, Honey,' said Bob uneasily. 'Now, Honey.'

'Look, Bob,' said Mrs North, knowing that it was no use suggesting that Honey postpone her hair appointment, 'why don't you take Evie up to town with you? She wouldn't mind missing the sports for a treat like that, especially if you won't be there. Do take her and show her a good time. She hasn't been to London since she was old enough to enjoy it.'

'Why – –' Bob glanced at his wife, who was looking more than ever as if she had just come up through a trapdoor in a green magnesium flash. 'Why, I don't know – –'

'It's impossible, Bob. We've planned to go all sorts of places she couldn't go. It wouldn't be any fun for her. What would she do?'

'What she really wants to do,' put in Oliver, 'is to take the longest journey there is on the Underground and then come back by as many different buses as possible.'

'If you think,' said Honey, 'that I'm going to spend my weekend exploring London's transport system – –'

'I'll take her another time,' said Bob largely, 'take her up and give her ice-cream and take her to movies and theatres and anything she wants.'

'You'll hardly have time, dear,' said his sister, 'if you really mean to sail at the end of the month.'

'I can make time for anything. How d'you think I made a success of my business? It's a mathematical fact that you can make a day have more than one thousand four hundred and forty minutes if you know the right trick. You go with Evie and see her win the races, Hattie, hm? She loves you.'

Yes, she loved her aunt in a safe, familiar way, but she loved her father with a deluded worship that was heading her straight for a broken heart.

Elizabeth, who had been on holiday since before the Linnegars arrived, came back just before they left. She looked very smart in a new suit and a new pair of shoes and a little straw hat like a boater on the back of her head. Oliver goggled at her and made a rude whistling sound. She twirled round for him. She seemed self-satisfied. 'Like it?'

'Not half. And a new bag too – let's look. Pigskin. Must have cost the earth; you never bought that on the salary we

273

pay you. No, don't tell me; I know. Well, he has good taste in bags, I'll say that for him. Been in London all the time?'

'Mostly. Elspeth and I went to her people for a week.'

'Go to your people at all?'

'Once,' she said, shutting up her face.

'I see. I – er – yes. Er – your father all right?'

'Yes, thank you.'

'Oh, good,' said Oliver over-heartily. He often wondered just what crime Mr Gray had committed that she would never talk of him. She went out to find Mrs North and came back almost at once.

'Why is Evelyn crying?' she asked accusingly.

'*I* don't know. Is she?'

'She's in her room, face downwards on the bed. I couldn't get a word out of her.'

'Poor little devil. She's got something to cry about, as a matter of fact.' He told her about Honey and Bob. He told her everything. He told her about the sports, and about the London trip that never came off; he told her how badly Bob had broken it to her that they were not going to live on a ranch but in a thirtieth floor apartment in New York and that Evelyn would go to High School every morning with Honey's maid Archer. It took quite a long time. It was a relief to have someone on whom to unload it, and Elizabeth was always a good listener. She did not ask irrelevant questions or break in like most women to tell you some parallel experience of her own.

'I do wish she hadn't got to go,' Oliver said when he had finished. 'But Bob wants her, and she is his child, even if she does seem more like ours. It's rotten for the kid not having a mother, and having Honey is worse than having none. Still, I needn't tell you that. You should know.'

'Why do you say that?'

'You not having a mother, I mean.'

'Oh, I see. Yes.'

On Sunday, the day before the Linnegar family were to leave for Liverpool, there was to be a rally of the local children's Pony Club in the meadow opposite the house. The events would take

274

place on the flat ground, the spectators, proud mothers, disapproving Nannies, and possessive grooms, could watch from the hill. Violet and Fred had been working like blacks to arrange it. All the day before, Oliver watched them building jumps, knocking in poles, marking out a judging ring and a paddock with sheep hurdles. He had wheeled his chair to the edge of the lawn and shouted directions at them until the rain sent him indoors.

'Let's pray it doesn't rain tomorrow,' he said to Evelyn, when she was having her last supper but one in his room.

'I don't care if it pours,' she said raptly, 'as long as I win the jumping. Daddy doesn't think I can ride, you know. Did you hear him say riding lessons in an indoor school?' The scorn in her voice was tremendous. 'If he sees me win the jumping, perhaps he'll buy me a horse.'

'You couldn't very well keep it in New York.'

'I'd find somewhere. I'd keep it in the back garden.'

'Skyscrapers don't have back gardens, darling.'

'Oh, Uncle Ollie.' Over a plate of cornflakes, she looked at him like Electra. 'I don't want to go.'

'I know you don't now, but there'll be all sorts of things you'll have there that you can't get here. What about all that ice-cream and chocolate you were always talking about?'

'Oh that. I was only a baby then. And I hadn't thought about leaving Dandy. After all I've taught him, and he's such a wonderful jumper – touch wood for tomorrow. How can I bear it? I cried yesterday. Elizabeth came in, but I didn't tell her why. I didn't want to make her cry too.'

'Elizabeth never cries.'

'She jolly well does. She cried once like billy-o when I was sleeping in her room. Ages ago it was – when that girl was here that smoked cigarettes all the time and said Bloody and David and I weren't allowed to.'

'What was she crying about?'

'She wouldn't tell me. I offered her a bit of chocolate, but she wouldn't have it, so I suppose she had a tummy ache. That's enough to make anyone cry, isn't it, Uncle Ollie?'

'It is indeed. Oh – good evening, Honey. Lord, is it time for drinks already? I haven't mixed them yet.' He wheeled himself

275

across the room to the cocktail table. Evelyn paced sedately after him carrying her mug, plate, and spoon. 'Good night, Uncle Ollie,' she said.

'Get me the ice before you go to bed, there's a good girl.'

'O.K. Wish me luck for tomorrow.'

'You bet.' Evelyn went out without appearing to notice that her stepmother was in the room.

'What's happening tomorrow?' asked Honey chattily, helping herself to one of Oliver's cigarettes.

'You know perfectly well. The Pony Club show. It's the ambition of Evie's life to win the jumping. I think she will too,' he went on eagerly, with his back to her, forgetting to whom he was talking. 'That pony may be only a little fellow, but he jumps amazingly well for an Exmoor. He's got that unusual length from the stifle to the hocks, you know; I believe that's what does it. It was smart of Vi to pick him out at that age. Evie's worked awfully hard on him, and she's done wonders too. She's got far more patience with a horse than most grown-ups. If only she can keep him from running out to the right tomorrow . . . . He gets his head down, you know, and yaws on the bit, and of course she's not strong enough to haul him in. Oh, excuse me,' he said as Honey gave a delicate yawn, 'I was thinking aloud; I didn't mean to bore you.'

'She's too obsessed by horses, that child,' said Honey fretfully. 'It's all she can think or talk about. High time she was taken into civilization, if you ask me. She'll have to take the straw out of her mouth and get herself a few social graces, or my friends will think I've mothered a moron.'

'Poor kid,' said Oliver rudely, 'if you're going to try and turn her into one of those harassed little prodigies one sees on the films.'

'Don't be ridiculous, Ollie.' She called him 'Ar-lie', in a caressing drawl. 'I only mean she must be a bit more sociable. You're not exactly sociable yourself, are you?' Her voice was low, but by the frissons in his spine he felt she was coming near his chair. She was, much too near. 'You don't like me a lot, do you?' she murmured, close enough for him to smell her.

'Not much,' he said briskly, jogging the cocktail shaker in a businesslike way.

'Well, that's just too bad, because I like you such a lot.' She passed his chair, lightly touching his shoulder with her finger-tips and leaned against the table in a mannequin attitude, stomach flat and pelvis tipped forward. 'I think you're a pretty swell guy,' she said, with a college-girl candour that did not go with the crevasses worn into her face between the nose and the corners of the mouth, and the vitiated texture of her skin. 'It's too bad you've fended me off all this time, because I know we'd have so much in common. I understand how it is with you, you see, on account of I had to lie up with my back all that time when I was a very young girl. I got so lonely. People used to visit with me, of course, but I used to long for someone to talk to – intimately. I used to read poetry, just the way you do – Shelley, Keats, Siegfried Sassoon. . . .'

Oliver's brain began to panic, and the reflection that Siegfried Sassoon could hardly have been writing poetry when Honey was a very young girl was its last coherent thought. He began to feel suffocated, on the point of breaking out into a sweat. He wanted to let out a yell, spring out of his chair, and pelt into the fresh air.

He wondered why she suddenly took her eyes off his and tightened her mouth, before he realized that Evelyn had come back into the room.

'There isn't much ice, I'm afraid, because the fridge isn't working properly,' she said, going round Oliver on the opposite side to Honey and putting the bowl carefully on the table. Although she was untidy about her clothes and hair, she was a neat-fingered child. She never spilled or slopped things, and she could be trusted to help Mrs North with the flowers without leaving wet marks on the furniture under all the vases.

'You wait till we get to New York,' said Honey, who had not entirely abandoned the pretence of being sweet to Evelyn. 'My fridge is three times as big as yours and has a rotary mixer for making ice-cream. What do you think of that?'

'I don't like ice-cream,' said Evelyn crushingly. 'At least I did until everybody kept trying to make me like going to America because of the ice-cream.' She went out with dignity and Honey shrugged her bony shoulders and held out a hand for her drink. Oliver watched her predatory fingers curl round the stem of the glass like a claw.

'Funny kid,' she said. 'Say, Ar-lie, do you think she'd care all that much if Barb and I didn't show up at this affair tomorrow? After all, we don't know anything about horses, and I want so much to take him over to see those people at Much Wenlock or whatever you call it. My greatest friend, Ellie Bamburger, gave me their address and she'll think it so odd if we don't go.'

'You're not going,' said Oliver firmly. 'At least, I don't care what *you* do, but Bob must stay here. She's set her heart on it.'

'But I can't go on my own; I can't drive a car with a right-hand drive.'

'Well, hire a car, go on a bicycle, hitch-hike, anything you like, but you're not taking Bob away from here tomorrow. It was bad enough about the sports; if you spoil this for Evie, I'll kill you.'

'My gracious, don't be so intense.' Honey laughed at him. 'Actually, darling, I have rung this Mrs Barnet and told her we'd both be over to tea. She wants so much to meet Bob, and I didn't think it would matter all that much.'

'Listen, Honey,' said Oliver, gripping her wrist in his vehemence and feeling as if he had grasped the handle of an electric shock machine on a pier, 'if you don't let Bob stay and see Evie ride tomorrow, I'll strangle you – like this' – he began to twist her wrist – 'quite quietly and comfortably. The wheel-chair murder, the paper will call it; they'll make quite a thing of it.'

'Ollie!' She tried to pull away her wrist, half frightened, half enjoying it. 'What are you doing? You're hurting me!'

He twisted a little harder. 'Good. I just want to make sure you understand. Now do you promise, or do I break your arm now and your neck tomorrow?' He felt like Buck Ryan.

'Ollie – stop it! Oh! Yes – yes, of course we won't go if you feel that way about it.'

He dropped her wrist and she stood rubbing it carefully, contemplating him with admiration. 'My, aren't you strong? Quite a lad, aren't you – don't care what you do, and all that?' She mocked him. Then she became serious, and dropping her head, gave him a sultry look. 'It certainly is a pity you and I couldn't have got together. I believe we could have had a lot of fun. Oh, don't be afraid,' she purred, 'I'm not making a pass at you. No kidding, Ar-lie, I do like you so much. I admire you. I've wanted to tell you before, but I was afraid you'd snub me. You're kind of a chilling person, you know. I've wanted to tell you that I just couldn't be sorrier for you. You're so brave and so cheerful that a lot of folks might not realize how badly you must feel, but I know how sad it is, when you're so young. . . .'

'I'm not all that young,' Oliver said, 'though I suppose I must seem so to you.' For some time after she had gone he glowed with the satisfaction of having achieved the kind of remark that usually only suggests itself about half an hour too late.

It poured with rain again on Sunday morning, and Evelyn had a fight with her aunt about whether she was to ride in a mackintosh. Her desperate face, plastered with damp red hair, presented itself at Oliver's window while he was eating his lunch. He had been kept in bed for the morning as a precaution against the fatigue of an afternoon's sociability.

'Uncle Ollie,' cried Evelyn, her face streaming with rain or tears. 'I can't, I can't.'

'Don't often hear you say that,' said Oliver with his mouth full. 'Ma's always complaining you think you can do anything. What can't you?'

'Ride in this awful school mac. She says I must, but it's got no slit in the back and it's much too long, and Daddy said once I looked like an orphanage child in it. I *can't* wear it. What's the good of having that new riding jacket? I shan't get wet; you don't when you're moving. Oh, do speak to her, don't let her make me wear it. She says I mustn't catch a cold because of travelling tomorrow, but I don't care if I do. I don't care if I catch a cold and die after today.'

'Calm yourself,' Oliver said. 'I'll see what I can do. Go and have your lunch and don't say any more about it, and I'll talk to Ma.'

'Oh, Uncle Ollie, you are a darling, you are a pet,' she gabbled. 'I do love you. How can I bear to go away and leave you, with your poor leg and everything? There'll be nobody to ride in the hill field for you to look at. Will you write to me? Promise? Not that she'll probably let me read it; I bet she'll open all my letters and take them away.'

'Who's she?'

'You know quite well, so don't be governessy. I say, do you

279

think it's getting any lighter? Do you? I'm sure I did see a teeny bit of blue sky then. How big is a Dutchman?'

'Evie,' called Elizabeth, coming into Oliver's room with his pudding, 'go and have your lunch. We started ages ago.'

'I couldn't eat anything. How d'you think I *could*, when I feel sick whenever I think of this afternoon?' Evelyn was surprised at her obtuseness.

'Have this biscuit and cheese then.' Oliver handed it out of the window.

'All right, if you promise – you know what.'

'O.K., O.K., don't pester me. I've said I would.' She went away, looking tiny in the tent-like mackintosh, nibbling abstractedly at the sodden biscuit.

The grooms and children who had arrived with ponies during the morning had sheltered at the farm, but after lunch, when the rain became a drizzle and then a few gusty drops and then ceased altogether as the wind rose and blew the clouds away, they began to emerge and dot themselves about the hill field. While Elizabeth was helping Oliver to dress, Evelyn burst into the room, unrecognizably spruce in a shirt, and tie, her new tan riding jacket, and stiff jodhpurs that stuck out in a point on the seat and made her legs look like matchsticks.

'You mustn't come in here like that when your uncle's dressing,' said Elizabeth.

Evelyn took no notice of her. 'Uncle Ollie, I believe in God,' she announced. 'After you'd asked Aunt Hattie and she still said yes I must, I thought I'd have to kill myself. Then I thought of something else and I went into Dandy's stall and prayed and prayed, just like the girl in the book who prayed and the bread got cooked, only I prayed for it to stop raining. After today, I think I'll be a saint and pray all the time. I can do anything. I could pray and make it start raining – only I'm not going to; I didn't mean that,' she added hastily, glancing out of the window in case God had misinterpreted her rash statement. 'I'm going to get Dandy out now. He's been sweating like anything; I'm sure he knows. Will you watch me? There's crowds of people there and some of the ponies are awfully big. The Master's come. Oh, Uncle Ollie, he is marvellous. He's come on one of the Hunt horses, a topping big grey, you must see him. He's brought a couple of hound puppies with him too – they're frightfully well trained, much better than the ones Vi's walking.' She dashed away, leaving the door open.

'Isn't it silly,' said Oliver. 'I feel as nervous about her winning that jumping as if she were my own child. I'm sure I shall be awfully wet when I have a family – drool at the mouth and dote. You won't, though. You'll be scientific and sensible, and when they don't win things you'll say it's good for their characters. Poor little things, it would break my heart to be their father, but I don't suppose Arnold Clitheroe will mind. He thinks everything you do is marvellous.'

Elizabeth opened her mouth to say something and then closed it again. 'Why do you always call him Arnold Clitheroe in that tone of voice?' she muttered, bending down to tuck a rug round his legs.

'It's such a funny name,' he said simply. 'I can't help it. Am I ready, Liz? How do I look?' He cocked his head at her. 'Oh, my cigarettes.' He patted the breast pocket of his jacket.

'In the right-hand pocket, and your matches.' She went behind him and started to wheel him out of the room.

'You're a marvel. I couldn't do without you.' He said this several times a day, meaninglessly, because soon he would have to do without her. 'No, don't push me as if I was a pram. Let me go under my own steam. You might leave me that much self-respect.' He put his hands on the outer wheels and, giving them a tremendous shove, went bowling over the floor and nearly ran into his mother in the doorway.

'Careful, darling!' She skipped aside. 'I was just coming to ask you if I look all right. Do I look sporting enough?' She wore a green tweed suit over her best corsets, a green satin blouse with a diamond brooch, a cab-driver's hat with a feather on one side, and shoes that were comparatively low-heeled for her. 'I can't walk in these brogues,' she complained, kicking out the little feet that always looked unequal to her weight, 'but I do want to look right. I never know how these country women manage to look so dowdy and so right at the same time.'

'You look a perfect English gentlewoman,' Oliver assured her, and she believed him.

'It's this medal,' she said, proudly touching her lapel, where a blue and gold badge proclaimed that, although she hardly knew one end of a horse from another and was afraid of both, she was a member of the local Pony Club committee.

'Honey looks just terrible,' she said with satisfaction. 'She's wearing that umbrella-shaped dress she got at Worth's and that hat that makes her look like Carmen Miranda. Bob, of course, looks just right. That man does have the loveliest shoes.'

'No more talk about them not being here this afternoon, I hope?'

'She hardly spoke a word at lunch. Just sat there with her Mona Lisa smile while Bob fussed round her as if he were her slave. I do hate to see him making such a fool of himself over that woman, Ollie. I hope he'll get used to her soon and settle down before she makes a monkey out of him. I reckon it's because he married late. He was just like this over Vivien, though, when they were first married, but she was always such a sweet person.' She sighed. 'Evie would have adored her. She adores Bob, though, doesn't she? Half the reason she's so excited about this afternoon is because she wants to show off to him. He's out there with her now, striding about and being most fearfully English, don't you know.' She put on what she imagined was her ultra-English accent. 'Where are you going, darling, down to the end of the lawns? You'll be able to see it all from there.' She took hold of the back of his chair and he turned round and removed her hand from the rail.

'Let me go on my own,' he said like a testy old gentleman. 'Why does everyone treat me as if I was paralysed?' As he wheeled himself away from them down the corridor, he heard his mother say to Elizabeth: 'It's a good sign, isn't it? He's getting so independent. . . .'

He sat enthroned on top of the Ha-Ha wall above the meadow and several people came up to talk to him from below. The M.F.H., a long, lean, tanned man who was the idol of all the children and many of the local females, rode up on a huge grey horse with scarred legs to tell Oliver he was expecting to see him hunting again next season.

'I don't know,' said Oliver. 'I don't see how I – –' He glanced down at his missing leg.

'Course you will,' said the Master, yanking his horse's head away from the lawn, which he could crop without lowering his neck. 'When I was with the Southdown there was a chap, been turning out for years with a cork leg. They weren't so good in those days, of course. He had to ride with it stuck straight out and it used to catch on gateposts and knock him off as easy as tipping your hat. Funniest thing you ever saw.'

'It must have been,' said Oliver doubtfully.

'Oh, old Saunders didn't mind. He used to lie there in the mud waving his leg and wait for someone to come and put him back on.' He kicked the grey in the ribs and, putting a horn to his lips, cantered round the field like the Pied Piper, with a string of hero-worshipping children kicking and beating their ponies after him.

Mrs Ogilvie came and planted herself on a shooting stick and talked up at Oliver with her hands on her spread knees. 'What a very chic woman your uncle's wife is,' she told him. 'So *American*, if you know what I mean. You're looking peaky, old boy. Been overdoing it?'

'On the contrary,' said Oliver. 'I never felt better.'

'You'd never admit it; that's you all over. I always say you're a stayer, a game one, if ever there was. It's the breeding, you know, like with horses. An ounce of blood is worth an inch of bone.' She always adapted her conversation to suit the occasion. This afternoon all her similes were horsey; when she went to a flower show she called her friends blossom, and children were thrusting shoots. At the cinema she tinged her talk with obsolete Americanisms, and at a dog show she all but barked.

'See my grandson out?' She jerked her head to where a terrified little boy like an uncooked shrimp was doing the splits across the broad back of a Shetland pony no higher than a large dog. 'Game as they make 'em. I've told Richardson a hundred times not to let go of the leading rein, but would you *believe* it, I found my little topper trotting about on his own as pleased as Punch while the man was away over in a corner coffee-housing with his pals. Rank Socialism, you know, but what can one do? Servants

283

have no idea of loyalty these days, and of course this government's gone to their heads. What news of John and Heather? They don't seem to come down much these days.'

'That's because they're so happy up there in their flat,' Oliver said. 'They're getting madly domesticated. Heather makes rugs in the evening.'

'How splendid!' cried Mrs Ogilvie, disappointed to find no hint of a family feud.

The first class was being judged for the best rider under ten years old. Mrs Ogilvie's grandson had refused, with screams, to enter. Oliver saw that Bob had somehow talked himself into being one of the judges and was swanking about in the middle of the ring with the Master and a woman in a mackintosh, who looked like Dorothy Paget and ran the local riding school. Evelyn and Dandy were going round in perfect harmony, the pony's little legs going like oiled clockwork, Evelyn with her hands still and her head high, scarcely rising from the saddle, and beautifully, with a well-timed dip of her body, leading Dandy off on the inside leg when the riding-school woman bellowed: 'Canter!'

But the judges, infuriatingly, were not looking at Evelyn. Bob was, but he did not count. The other two would concentrate on a smug little boy in miniature boots and a jockey cap, who was tittuping round the ring on a professional show pony with a plaited mane. He wore a little hunting stock and his gloves were very bright yellow and even his behind looked conceited. He did not even smile as the woman in the mackintosh handed him the red rosette and caught the pony a slap on the neck that echoed round the field. He had known he would win. So had she; he was one of her pupils.

Fred, who was riding about on his farm cob, a bad-tempered animal with a tail like a worn-out stair brush, looked more of a person than he did on the ground. Violet, in a red polo sweater, grubby breeches and canvas leggings, was galloping about on foot picking up fallen poles, spacing out potatoes for the bucket and potato race, being a turning point or a starter or a winning post or the victim of the needle and thread race, and tightening the girths of children in danger of being swung upside down as their grass-fed ponies' stomachs shrank with the exercise.

Some of her dogs had got out, and the young setter kept rushing about barking hysterically among the ponies' legs and being yelled at for a bloody dog and why the hell couldn't people keep their tykes under control. One or two of the mothers thought that Major Ferney should be more careful of his language at a children's show, but others shrugged their shoulders and said: 'He's always like that nowadays; he's getting absolutely sodden.'

In the intervals of yelling at children who could not control their ponies for ham-handed little bastards who ought to be riding donkeys, Major Ferney ambled over to Oliver and leaned against the wall to blast the government and Russia and the farmers and the weather and his own catarrh.

Evelyn was second in the bending race, and rode up to Oliver wearing a blue rosette, her face holy with joy. 'Did you see us, Uncle Ollie, did you see us? Wasn't he super? He never put a foot wrong. Fancy him beating that black pony, I never thought he would.' She did not say 'Fancy me beating that great girl in pigtails who tried to jostle me out at the start'. The credit was all Dandy's; she wanted all the glory for him. The pony's brown sides were black with sweat, his forelock had got tangled in the browband of his bridle, grass and foam had dirtied the bit on which Evelyn had spent so many hours of burnishing last night and the hair on his neck was rubbed into a curly lather by the reins. His wise little eyes were wild with the unusual excitement and he kept throwing up his head and hurling a challenging neigh into the air as if he were a stallion.

'I should give him a bit of rest before the jumping,' said Oliver. 'Calm him down a bit or he won't know what he's doing. And for God's sake keep your weight on that left rein. And watch that double bar; I saw the Master telling Vi to put it up a notch.'

Evelyn nodded vaguely. She was too excited to pay much attention to what anybody said. 'I'm going to walk him up and down on his own while the others have tea,' she said. 'Aunt Hattie keeps trying to make me go in and have some, but fancy anyone thinking of tea on a day like this.'

The Master came up and said: 'Good show, Evie. That's a nippy little brute of yours. What is he – New Forest?'

'No, he's an Exmoor,' she breathed, adoring him.

'Hm,' said the Master to Oliver. 'Should have said he was a

Forester with that length of leg, and he's not such a slug as most Moor ponies.' Evelyn sat there in heaven, making Dandy stand like a Hackney show pony while the two men discussed him. She was at the peak of her existence. Her mind and body, her thoughts and memories and expectations were crystallized into the glorious present. She had forgotten yesterday and tomorrow and that there was any other world except the hill field or any people except those gods who talked the language she loved. If anyone had said to her: 'You are going to Liverpool tomorrow and the day after that in a ship to America, where you will wear dresses and hats and walk on pavements and smell petrol and scented women instead of summer grass and hot horses,' she would have been as shocked as a sleep-walker too roughly awakened.

At tea-time neglected mothers and nurses came into their own. Picnic baskets were unpacked and children were made to get off ponies and sit on rugs. 'On the *rug*, Miss Sheila, I said, not on the wet grass. Just look at the seat of her breeches, 'm. I shall never get that green off.'

Rich ponies had blankets to wear and grooms to walk them up and down, abjuring them with mock harshness as if they were real horses, when they tried to eat grass. Proletariat ponies were tied to the fence and allowed to eat as much grass as they liked and put their forelegs through their reins. One of them lay down and rolled on its saddle, and mothers screamed and men ran up to buffet it to its feet, where it gave itself a soul-searing shake and laughed at them. It did not mind being cursed; it had had its roll. Violet stood under a tree eating a bun and holding half a dozen ponies and the big grey belonging to the Master, who was having tea in the house with the Norths.

Half-way through tea Oliver suddenly realized something, excused himself and wheeled himself rapidly out across the lawn and down the ramp which had been made for him where the steps used to lead to the lower lawn. He scanned the field without much hope. There were the picnic parties, there were the grooms, there was Violet in a happy coma, letting the grey rub sweat off its face on to her jersey, there was Evelyn, walking Dandy soberly up and down like a professional stable-boy.

Mrs Ogilvie detached herself from one of the nearest parties and stood below him with legs out-thrust like Napoleon on a little mound at Rattigan. 'I forgot to tell you,' she called. 'I met Mrs Linnegar by the garage just now when I was getting our tea out of the car. She asked me to tell you they were just going off to their friends and wouldn't be back late. And, Ollie,' as he started to manoeuvre his chair round, 'don't go away, I want you to meet a great friend of mine; she writes books. Ollie!' But he pretended not to hear, and although out of the corner of his eye he could see the friend to whom Mrs Ogilvie was always offering him as copy, approaching reluctantly, he completed his turn and started back to the house. He could not always get up the ramp if the ground was sticky. He could not get up now. He pushed at the wheels till his arms ached, but he kept rolling ignominiously back on to the lower lawn, nearer to the persistent bleatings of Mrs Ogilvie, who, mercifully, was not agile enough to climb the Ha-Ha.

If only he could kick this blasted chair into a flower-bed and walk up. Elizabeth saw him struggling and came running out of the house. 'Wait!' she called. 'Don't strain yourself. I'll push you up.'

'I can *do* it,' said Oliver crossly. He gave a final thrust just as she put her hands on the back of the chair and got up the slope with her assistance.

'What's the matter?' she asked, walking behind him.

'Nothing. What d'you mean?'

'I ought to know when anything's the matter with you by now. Your face is as easy to read as a child's.' This did not make him feel any better. He told her what was the matter.

'What do you expect? You didn't really think they would stay, did you?'

'He's supposed to love the child. How can he be so inhuman?'

'He's not. He's just obsessed. That's how it will always be for Evie now. He'll break her heart over and over again, until finally she gets so tough she won't have a heart to break any more.'

The children were being collected for the jumping contest, which was the chief event of the afternoon. Evelyn was to jump fifth. The first pony had already been shooed into the ring and was sulking its way over and through the jumps, when Evelyn realized that her father was nowhere to be seen. She kicked Dandy out of the crowd of ponies in the paddock and quested up and down the field, asking anyone she knew. 'Where's Daddy?' she asked Mrs North. 'Where's Daddy? I must wait to jump till he's here. He wants to see me.'

'He should be somewhere around,' said Mrs North cravenly, looking about her so that she did not have to look at Evelyn.

'Where's Daddy?' Evelyn asked Violet, who was standing by one of the jumps. Violet shrugged her shoulders.

'I'll have to change my place, Vi. I can't jump till he comes. Will it matter if I swop with Michael Roberts?'

'Don't *fuss*, Evie, and take Dandy out of the way. Look out!' Evelyn pulled Dandy back as a roan pony thundered up to the jump with its knees going very high, ears pricked, nose thrust out and quarters gathered for a tremendous leap, and at the last minute stopped dead with its neck still stretched towards the jump, while a very small girl in a blue jersey and a beret described a slow parabola and sat neatly in the brush fence, setting up a wail that brought her mother running flat-footed down the hill. Violet picked her up, plumped her back on the roan pony, said: 'You're all right, Amy; take it again and let him see you mean it,' ran back a few yards with the pony, whipped it round and gave it a terrific baroosh which got it over the jump without it or its rider quite knowing how they got to the other side.

'Now what's the matter, Evie?' She looked round, but Evelyn had gone.

'Fred, have you seen Daddy?' Fred scratched his head, tilting his cap to an absurd angle, and looked round, resting one hand on his cob's table-top quarters. 'Isn't that him over there?' He pointed to a man whom Bob might possibly have resembled if he had grown a moustache, lost most of his hair, and changed into a plus-four suit and a pork-pie hat with flies in the band.

'Elizabeth, where's Daddy? I can't jump till he comes! I promised him he should see me.'

'I expect he's somewhere about. You go ahead and jump, and mind you win. Look, you'd better go back to the paddock; they'll be calling your number soon.'

Could anybody find the courage or the right words to tell her? Oliver thought, but when Evelyn came riding towards him and stared up at him with agonized eyes, all he could say was: 'Perhaps he's in the house, watching from a window.'

'Oh, but he must – – Oh, hold my pony a minute, could you, please? I must just – –' Evelyn jumped off and flung Dandy's reins at a nervous little man who was standing near. She scrambled up the protruding stones which made steps up the Ha-Ha, stumbled at the top, picked herself up and tore up to the house, negotiating the grass bank on all fours.

They had called her to jump twice before she reappeared at Oliver's side. 'I've looked in all the rooms; he's not anywhere,' she said desperately. 'Oh, Uncle Ollie, he *must* be here. Where is he? It's not even as if he was so small I couldn't see him.'

Violet was beckoning sweepingly at her to come down. The pony in the ring crashed through the last jump and, exalted with having knocked so much over, bolted away to the edge of the field before its rider could stop it.

'Come on, Evie!' called the Master. 'You can't keep missing your turn.'

Even he could not deflect her. 'Tell them to let me wait till last,' she whispered to Oliver. 'I'll go and see if he's at the farm.' She was gone again before he could stop her. 'Can she jump later?' he called. 'She's gone to get her whip.'

'What's the matter with her?' grumbled the woman in the mackintosh. 'She'll miss her chance altogether if she doesn't look out. Come on in then, Stewart, and remember what I told you about your hands.'

The smug little boy in the boots and jockey cap had finished a clear round and cantered out of the ring with his pony flicking its tail in contempt for the size of the jumps, and two other children had bucketed their way round before Evelyn came back, running under the wall, her eyes still scanning the field.

'Seen him?' She wavered uncertainly below Oliver, looking palely up at him like a little pond creature.

'Here, I wish you'd take your horse,' said the little man plaintively, who had been holding Dandy at arm's length, gyrating as the pony moved so as to keep face to face with him.

'Come on, Evie!' They were yelling at her again from the ring, and the children in the paddock were goggling at her like a herd of sheep at a fox.

'What's the matter, old girl, got stage fright? Come on, you go in there and win! Hup, she goes!' Mrs Ogilvie put her hands under Evelyn's knee and gave her a leg-up that nearly shot her over the other side. Evleyn gathered up her reins, still looking vaguely round. 'I was waiting . . . I couldn't see Daddy . . . I wanted to . . .' She stood in her stirrups and craned over the heads of the crowd.

'Gracious heavens, is that all? He's gone out to tea; no wonder you couldn't find him. Get a move on now!' She gave Dandy a slap on his quarters that made him start forward, nearly jerking Evelyn out of the saddle. The crowd made way for her and she cantered into the ring, flopping about like a sack of potatoes. Dandy liked jumping, and he got himself over the post and rails and the two brush fences, but when he came to the wall, which, in practice, had needed all Evelyn's concentration to make him face, he simply stuck his head sideways and down, thrust out his lower jaw and bore her out to the right through a gap in the hurdles, scattering the spectators, while Evelyn sat on him like a passenger, barely pulling on the reins.

'What's the matter with her? What's the matter with her? Oh, damn!' Violet danced up and down in her disappointment. She turned her back and slouched away as Stewart trotted smartly back into the ring, was given the red rosette, and cantered twice round the ring with it in his mouth, the ripple of applause sounding thin in the open air.

Evelyn and Dandy had disappeared towards the farm. Oliver wheeled himself across the lawn, through a flower-bed and into the kitchen garden, from the far end of which he could see the garages. He had thought he heard a car on the drive, and as he reached the path by the marrow-bed he saw the family car lurch into the yard in the style in which Bob always cornered. He drove into the garage and from within came the destructive crashing which was Bob's way of shutting car doors.

He and Honey emerged and Oliver was just going to call out to them, when he saw Evelyn come walking slowly round the corner of the garage with her toes turned in. 'Well!' Bob hailed her. 'And did you win, young lady? Don't tell me – I know you did. My family always win anything they want.'

'You *said* you'd be there,' Evelyn said incredulously. 'You said you wanted to see me jump. You went out to tea.'

'Sure, sugar.' Honey had her flapjack raised and was twiddling her horns of hair. 'Grown-ups have important dates they can't always put off to please little girls, you know.' Evelyn did not seem to hear her. She was still staring at her father.

'Yeah, sure,' he said, busy with the garage doors. 'It was just too bad, but I'll see you another time, hm? What d'you think Mrs Barnet gave me for you? Why, where's she – –?' By the time he had finished with the stiff old lock and turned round, Evelyn had gone, back round the corner to the stables.

'Sulking,' said Honey, and linking her arm in Bob's, she smiled up at him as they sauntered into the house.

'But she must go,' Mrs North said for the twentieth time. 'She's his child; I can't interfere. He wants to take her. He must be fond of her; he just doesn't understand children very well.'

'He's not fit to have a child,' Oliver said, also for the twentieth time since his mother had come down in her dressing-gown to hash the matter over. 'And it's no good your keeping on telling me that children are better with their own parents, because I shall just keep on saying it depends on the parents.'

'Maybe it will turn out all right,' said Mrs North, trying to make her voice sound hopeful. 'Bob's such a sweet person, you know, even if he is a little thoughtless. He'd never let that woman spoil Evie's life.'

'What's he been letting her do ever since they came here, then?'

'That's just infatuation, dear,' said Mrs North patiently, as if Oliver were too young to understand about sex. 'They'll settle down. You wait, in a few years' time Evie will be coming back to see you and laughing to think how she once didn't want to go to New York.'

'"Didn't want" is putting it mildly. I can't bear to think about tomorrow.'

'There she is, poor little lamb, with her bags all packed; just one left open to put in her golliwog in the morning. She'd never have gone to sleep if I hadn't given her that half aspirin. She never cried, though, but it was that lost kind of staring look that got me. And she hasn't eaten a thing all day. She's not fit to travel. Bob will be lucky if he gets to the States without a sick child on his hands.'

'She can't go,' repeated Oliver, who could think of nothing else to say.

'It's no good to keep saying that,' said his mother quite irritably, 'and you know it. There's nothing we can do about it, so we might as well stop upsetting ourselves and talking each other into imagining all kinds of things. She'll be all right. She's his child; he's got to take her if he wants to, so don't let's talk any more about it.' She emptied an ashtray into the paper basket and reversed a few books that Mrs Cowlin had turned upside down in the bookcase when she cleaned the room. 'Of course, it isn't as if she'd enjoy the life,' she said, reopening the discussion she had just closed. 'You saw what she's been like all day. This is what she loves. It's too bad she couldn't have spent all her childhood in a place like this, but then again, she'll have opportunities a lot of children would give their ears for.'

'She can't go,' said Oliver flatly.

'You're quite right, she can't go,' said Elizabeth in an unusually masterful voice. It was so unlike her to butt into a conversation that they both turned and stared at her standing in the doorway in a blue and white spotted dressing-gown over pale-blue pyjamas.

'Well, don't *you* start,' said Mrs North. 'We've been telling each other for the last hour she can't go, when we know all the time it's got nothing to do with us. I'm going to bed and take a Slumbello. D'you know, Elizabeth, I never touched drugs till September the tenth, 1944 – that was when I got the telegram about you, Ollie – but my nerves have had more shocks in the ten months since then than in the whole of the rest of their life. What a year this has been, Ollie! Everything that had to happen in our family has happened, just about. How's Evie?'

'Sleeping now.' Elizabeth still had that unusually determined look on her calm face. 'She sat up a little while ago when I went in, grabbed hold of me as if she was drowning, and yelled out that she didn't want to go. She was more or less asleep, of course, but it shows what must be going on in her brain. All those awful things she said to her father when he went to say good night, and he got so silly and shouted – excuse me, Mrs North. I suppose I shouldn't talk like that about your brother.'

'Go right ahead.' She spread her hands resignedly. 'Oliver's been slanging him good and plenty for the last hour.'

'He's not fit to have a child,' repeated Oliver, who seemed incapable of making any more than a kind of gramophone accompaniment to the conversation.

'She'll be worse again tomorrow,' said Elizabeth. 'How can you send her out to that life? You can't let her go.'

'Well, really, Elizabeth,' said Mrs North with the coldness arising from an uneasy conscience, 'I think it's hardly your business.'

'It is my business,' said Elizabeth firmly and shut the door. 'That's why I came down. I want to tell you something.'

'I don't want to hear any more about Evelyn going to New York,' said Mrs North wearily. 'It's settled she's going, so there's no need for everyone to get so dramatic about it. Really the way you two go on, one would think no one had ever had a stepmother before.'

'Oh, yes, people have had stepmothers,' said Elizabeth bitterly. 'I'm not going to talk about Evie, I'm going to talk about myself. I wasn't even going to tell you. I wasn't going to tell anyone, not ever; but perhaps if I do now, I can make you see, and you'll have to do something. You can make most people do what you want, Mrs North, so surely you can manage your brother.'

'Don't give me that line of talk,' said Mrs North. 'I'm much too tired to go for flattery. What do you want to tell me? Make it snappy, whatever it is, because I want to get to bed. Believe it or not, but I, even I, have had enough talk for one night.'

'I wasn't ever going to tell anyone,' repeated Elizabeth. She sat down on the footstool, crossed her feet neatly, arranged her dressing-gown over her knees and linked her hands round them, leaning back and staring before her. 'When a thing as shattering as that happens, you don't tell anyone, because it's part of you. It's the things that haven't really gone deep into you that you tell, and pretend they're your innermost feelings.'

Mrs North looked at Oliver and raised her eyebrows. Elizabeth had never talked so introspectively before.

'I hope you don't mind my talking about myself,' went on Elizabeth, with the deference born of habit, because she had every intention of talking about herself, whether anyone minded or not. 'It won't take long. It's quite an ordinary story, I suppose. It must happen to lots of people, though that's no reason why it should happen to one more – Evie, I mean.

*

'You know, I think, that my mother died when I was quite young – twelve and a half, to be exact; two days before I was going to be twelve and a half. We always celebrated half birthdays in our family. We loved anniversaries and celebrations and presents, so we found every excuse to have them. My mother and father celebrated everything: not only their wedding-day, but the day they met, the day he first kissed her, the day he proposed by letter, and the day he got her answer back. They always gave each other something – flowers or sweets – not anything much, you know. We weren't terribly well off, but comfortable enough. We had a little house in Wimbledon, with dahlias in the front and a coco-nut for the birds and a lawn at the back where you could sit and watch people driving off the fourteenth tee of the golf-course. I expect Oliver would say that's typically suburban, because he's rather a snob about things like that, but nobody who hasn't lived there can possibly know how nice it was. I don't know if you think so, but it always seems to me as if the sun used to shine more in those days. Surely we had whole weeks of it in the summer, but now we get excited about two sunny days running.

'My father worked in London and always, if we were not going to be back before him – if I had a dancing class, or we were going out to tea – my mother would leave a present on the hall table for him to find when he got home, or if not a present, a note. Always something. Then when we got home he'd have done something: laid out my night clothes – probably the wrong ones – or cleaned the shoes, or made something for supper. I dare say it all sounds rather ingenuous and silly told like this, and I don't care if you think so, because it wasn't.

294

'I loved my mother. She was like me, and always understood what I was getting at, but I think I loved my father more. He was a sort of hero and God to me, like Evelyn's father used to be to her. He was gay. He wasn't big or boisterous or jolly; he was quite a little man really, with a soft moustache and brown eyes, and he was just quietly gay. He didn't sing about the house; he hummed. He had his own tunes, about two or three of them, so you always knew who was coming. It reminded me so much of him when I read that book about Gerald du Maurier: how his father was always singing *Plaisir d'Amour*, so you could hear him before he turned a corner. My father made his songs his own, just like that. *Greensleeves*, one of them was. For a long time after – but I haven't got to that yet – I couldn't bear to hear it played or sung, but I've got over that long ago. I've got my life very well ordered. Things don't upset me.

'We none of us thought about our life ever changing. We never visualized getting any older or richer or poorer, or living anywhere else, or being turned upside down by a family crisis. Our life was just us, just right. We were never deliriously happy or miserably depressed. We were content, secure, and snug. Smug, you'll say, I suppose.

'My mother died having a still-born baby, which she hadn't wanted, because the three of us had been so happy we didn't need anyone else. They didn't want another child but me. I can say that now without conceit, because it's like talking about another person. What I was then, I'm not now. After she died, I remember being ashamed of a thought I had. I remember thinking that I'd rather it was her than my father. If he had died it would have been the end of everything. As it was, I still had him, and I had a sort of new pride in looking after him all by myself. I must have been quite grown up for my age, to be able to run the house. My mother had taught me how to cook and clean and do accounts, and although we had a morning maid, I used to find plenty to do when I wasn't at school. My father used to let me miss school often, so that we could do things together. That's probably why I'm so badly educated.

'Quite soon, surprisingly soon, he started humming *Greensleeves* again, and we realized we had made a life for ourselves. A different sort of life, of course, and one always had the feeling in the back of one's mind that there was something missing, but we were more intimate, and we enjoyed feeling responsible for each other. We still stuck to the present-giving, though we left out my mother's anniversaries; we weren't quite all that sentimental. Before, it had been my mother who bought the things for him; now it was me, and I loved that. He paid for them really, because if I wanted to give him a present he had to give me more pocket money, but that didn't matter.

'At the week-ends we used to go for long walks with our dog. He was my dog really, but he liked my father better. We were both mad on walking, and my legs got frighteningly well developed. I was rather thick and square in those days, but it all went afterwards in hospital, because of the food. Sometimes we walked over Wimbledon Common, across Robin Hood Corner through Richmond Park to that hotel – fancy forgetting its name – all green tiles, where you used to be able to get stone ginger and pickle sandwiches. Sometimes we'd take a bus or a train into the country and walk all day. Hiking, they call it now.

'Am I making my life sound frightfully dull and goody-goody? I don't think I was really a prig; I was just rather ingenuous and unenterprising. I had no ambition, absolutely none. I never wanted anything but that life in Wimbledon. The other girls at school used to plan how they were going to be famous, but I didn't even want to have a job. I just wanted to stay at home and be the perfect little housekeeper. My father was very interested in food, not greedy, but keen on it in the right way, and he was fun to cook for. I can remember holding my breath sometimes when I put a dish on the table – *Œufs mornay* perhaps – oh, yes, we'd been to France in the holidays – in case when he tried it the eggs would be hard and he'd be so disappointed. I'd rather have it that way than someone like Lady Sandys. Remember how she used to smoke during meals and never notice what she was eating?

'I didn't want to marry either. We talked sometimes about a mythical husband for me, with a kind of patronizing pity for any man who thought he could possibly intrude. I didn't see how I was ever going to like anyone as much as my father. I suppose psychologists would say I had a father-complex. I dare say I had, but it made me jolly happy.

'It was when I was nearly sixteen and going to leave school in a few months' time that he met my stepmother. He'd been out to dinner without me and I was in bed when he got home. On the hall table I'd left him one of those twopenny packets of biscuits you used to be able to get – remember? Four biscuits with a bit of cheese in the middle; he loved those. I heard him humming as he opened the front door. I called out to him to come up and laugh about the people he'd met, but he didn't hear. I heard him go into the sitting-room and make up the fire, and I heard him move his arm-chair in front of it and creak about getting his pipe and things, and I fell asleep before he came up.

'When I went down the next morning to get the paper for him to read in bed, he hadn't touched the biscuits. I know that doesn't sound so important. You could say he hadn't seen them, or he had had a good dinner and wasn't hungry, or he was leaving them there to take to work. I told myself all that, but it didn't help. I left them there and he didn't take them to work, so I threw them away. He'd never snubbed me before. I couldn't say anything to him about it, and that was the first secret we ever had.

'Well, the rest of the story is the usual Wicked Stepmother saga, and full of self-pity on my side, so I won't dwell on it. She was very domineering and completely selfish and he loved her. That was all, but it was enough to change our whole life. You wouldn't think a man could possibly change so much, but he could and did, and the whole of my world changed with him. It all went, everything, even the humming, because she didn't like his tunes. She liked modern music, and she said *Greensleeves* reminded her of singing classes at school. She didn't like walking, because she had varicose veins, and she always wanted to do indoor things at week-ends. We didn't have things like *Œufs mornay* any more, because she was a food crank and wanted salads and nut cutlets and wholemeal bread. She would hardly let me into the kitchen after she saw me once testing the heat of milk for junket with my finger – well, you *have* to, don't you, Mrs North? – because she said I hadn't been scientifically trained in the preparation of food.

'I know I said just now that I was grown-up for my age, but actually I don't think I can have been. I didn't understand the first thing about love or sex. I couldn't understand, I just simply

297

couldn't begin to see why he wanted her. He had always been enough for me, and he still was, but suddenly I wasn't enough for him; that was what shook me. I kept asking myself how I'd failed him, and I used to think of petty little things – that I wasn't a good enough cook, or that I never starched his shirt collars right, and try and put it down to that. Until I remembered that she would never wash anything; she used to send even handkerchiefs to the laundry because of spoiling her hands, and that her ideas of cooking were most certainly not his, although she was rapidly converting him. They used to take in a dreadful little paper called *The Dietician*, and it was agony to me to see him poring over this little pamphlet affair with its cheap type, instead of the daily crossword puzzle which we'd always done together.

'When I tried to get him back to me by leaving things for him in the hall, she'd take them away before he could see them, and say: "I won't have your rubbish lying about." He thought that I was sulking because I never gave him presents. He was getting so changed that he thought that *I* was changing, and she was always having digs at me to him: saying I was a moody adolescent, and how queer it was that I hadn't made any close friends at school. I hadn't needed any before.

'I couldn't even talk to him. Of course he'd asked me whether I was happy about it and told me how nice it would be for me to have a mother, and I thought, if you really think that, it's no good trying to make you understand. I resolved never to get so attached to anything or anybody again, because then I could never be so hurt. I'd die if I was hurt like that again. I never want to get so fond of one person, or even a set of people, or a place, or a way of living, that I should mind losing them so terribly. I know people sometimes think I'm disinterested and detached, but I'm sure it's the best way to live if you want any peace of mind. It's not safe to have all your eggs in one basket; a platitude, I know, but it's surprisingly true, like all platitudes.

'I had to get away. I couldn't bear the house so changed. She moved all the furniture and had the wallpaper stripped off and the walls distempered and the carpets taken up and slippery mats put down and the boards stained with varnish that smelled of fish. She spent twice as much money as I used to when I ran the house, and I wondered how my father was managing, but I couldn't ask him. They used to give a lot of parties and ask people they didn't really care for, just because they were people. My stepmother was crazy about Bridge, and she taught him to play Contract, though he'd always sworn he'd never learn anything but Auction, and they were for ever having parties with refreshments standing about on dumb waiters and cider and lemonade and tea brought in at nine o'clock.

'A friend of mine had left school to be a nurse, and when I was sixteen I left, too, and went to a children's hospital. You can start there before you are old enough to start your general training. When I was old enough I went to a larger hospital which was a training school. At first, I used to go home on my day off each week, but each time there was less and less of me in the house, until in the end it didn't seem like my house at all. I used to think of it as her house. It didn't even seem like my father's. It didn't smell of him and his things any longer. It smelled of her.

'One week when I went home my dog wasn't there, and she told me he was getting so old and decrepit it had been kinder to have him put away. My father backed her up, though he wouldn't meet my eyes. He knew as well as I did that Dumbell had loved his life. It didn't matter him not being able to go upstairs; he didn't have to go upstairs. It was the week after that that I made some excuse not to go home – said I wanted to study or something – and that was the beginning. After that, I often slept at the hospital on my day off, which was horrid, because you didn't get any breakfast, and as we shared rooms the other girl used to wake you up at six when she got up. It was better than going home, though, and feeling as if I'd butted in on something, and as often as not finding my bed not made up and dust-sheets over the furniture in my room.

'I got friendly with Elspeth, the girl I go and stay with in London, you know, and sometimes I used to go home with her. She pestered and pestered me to take her to my home, until at last I had to.

'It was awful. I was so embarrassed. I'd rung up my stepmother and asked her most humbly, hating myself for being so servile, whether we could possibly have tea. She knew we'd only have a short time there, because we had to be back on duty, but she hadn't got a thing ready for us, and when I asked her if we could have tea, she said: "I suppose so, if you get it yourself. I don't see why I should make a skivvy of myself for you and your friends." And can't you hear Honey saying something like that in a few years' time when Evelyn wants to take a friend home? I can.

'My father tried to approach me once or twice to find out why I hardly ever went home, but how could I tell him that when I did I felt like a visitor, and an unwelcome one at that, and felt that when I left I'd got to thank my stepmother for having me? Once, he started to give me a highfalutin, pious sort of talk about jealousy and young people thinking they knew better than anyone else how to lead their own lives. He thought it was me who had changed, when all the time it was him.

'After I'd finished my training I went on taking jobs in hospitals, as my one idea was not to have to live at home. After two years as a staff nurse and a junior Sister, I found I couldn't bear the life in a female institution any longer. I could feel myself getting like the other Sisters – everybody does in the end, you know – and it frightened me to hear the way I'd sometimes catch myself talking to some soft new little probationer who still thought nursing was a noble and charitable profession. I took up private nursing, because there was more money in that, and I had to be independent. My father needed all he earned to satisfy my stepmother, but in any case I wouldn't have taken any money from home, and I never shall. I must always be independent. Now when I gave him presents on his birthday and at Christmas, it was my money, but somehow it made it less of a present than in the days when it had been his.

'I hardly ever go home now. I don't know whether that hurts my father, but he's got used to it. He's quite happy with her, I think. She's got rather ugly since the war, because she was terrified of the raids, and because she couldn't get all her cranky foods and wouldn't eat the ordinary rations, so she's got very thin and her skin's all dry. It flakes off her face under the powder, and her teeth are getting discoloured. Pretty soon, I suppose, she'll have them all out and have a false set and then she'll be beautiful again. Not that I ever thought she was; her nose is too near her chin, but my father did, and so did her friends. They would keep telling her so, which was such a mistake.

'Well, you know the rest. Dr Trevor got my name from another doctor I used to do a lot of work for, and I thought it sounded like a nice job, so along I came. It has been a nice job, too; I don't know whether you realize how happy I've been. I know you've thought me unfriendly and secretive because I wouldn't talk about myself or my home, but I never wanted to tell anybody. I never would have told you now, but it's just that I can't bear to see Evelyn faced with that sort of life, and you being such a happy family, I was afraid you didn't understand what it's going to mean to her to be pushed out.

'Have I made you see, Mrs North? Can you do something? You must do something, find some excuse to keep her here. Never mind if it is going to offend your brother. It's too late to stop him marrying that woman, but it's not too late to stop Evie suffering for it. You must do something – anything, to stop them taking her to New York.'

*

When his mother had gone upstairs, still undecided whether to take her Slumbello and sleep on it, or lie and let things sort themselves out in her head, Oliver said to Elizabeth: 'Turn on the light. I want to look at you.'

'I don't look very nice. I haven't got anything on my face.'

'I can stand that. But I must,' he said, as she switched on the centre light, 'see what a girl looks like before I tell her I love her. It's such ages since I said it, and I've never meant it before.' Elizabeth stood by the door, one hand still on the switch, frowning, not knowing whether he were serious or not.

'Don't look so sceptical,' he said. 'I do love you so much. I have for a long time, as a matter of fact, but there hasn't been a propitious moment to say it till now. It's all right, I can love you. It's you who aren't going to get attached to anybody, remember, not me.'

'You're just talking like that because I pitched you a hard-luck story.'

'Don't be absurd, and couldn't you come a bit nearer? It's a bit of a strain to carry on this sort of conversation at a distance.'

She did not move. She looked rather frightened. 'I don't know what to say,' she said. 'You see, I – –'

301

'You don't have to say anything; I'm not asking you for anything; I'm simply making a statement, and all I ask is that you should come a bit nearer so that I can see how you're taking it.'

'Oliver, I've got to tell you something. I meant to tell you before, but when I got back from my holiday this business with Evie was on, and I thought I'd better wait with my bit of news. I'm going to be married.'

Oliver tried to pretend it was not a shock and a terrible disappointment that made him feel physically sick. 'If you mean you're engaged to Arnold Clitheroe,' he blustered, 'that's no news. It was written all over you when you came back from London. I was wondering when you were going to tell me. Well, you've got the security you were looking for, haven't you? A nice, coldly calculated security, which means that you don't have to work any more, and you don't have to go home, and Arnold has plenty of money and is a bit of a stick, so there won't be any emotional upsets. Poor old Arnold Clitheroe, of course, doesn't count. He loves you, poor fool, with a humble devotion that will make no demands on you.'

'Oliver, stop it.' She came over to him now. 'How can you be so horrid? You twist all my words and make me out to be something despicable. You sound as if you hate me, and yet a minute ago you said you were in love with me.'

'Oh, that's nothing,' he said airily. 'I'd be in love with any reasonable-looking girl under the circumstances. Patient and nurse, you know; it's one of the oldest situations. Don't let that worry you.'

'Oh!' she cried, and her face got red. 'I hate you! Oh, I hate you!'

'Good, good!' he jeered miserably. 'I like to see you let yourself go for a change. Go on, cry, I don't care. Let your back hair down. I wish you would, too. Why do you wear it like that? It looks like some damned awful yellow draught extinguisher.' He shot out a hand and pulled at the ribbon round which her thick hair was rolled. She put up her hands and stepped back, but the ribbon was off and her corn-coloured hair was falling round her cheeks and neck as far as her shoulders, hiding her furious, weeping face.

'God,' he said softly, 'the times I've wanted to do that when you were leaning over me with that damned stuff half an inch from my face, and smelling of hay and apples.' She did not hear. She was half-way to the door, stumbling because she had lost one slipper and was blinded with hair and tears.

CHAPTER 12

AFTER all their talk, Evelyn solved the problem on her own by waking next morning with a temperature of a hundred and one and the blotchy beginnings of a rash all over her chest. Obviously she could not go with measles to Liverpool, much less to New York. Berths were scarce, and Honey, who had had enough of England and rationing, would not forfeit hers, so she and Bob decided to sail alone.

It was as simple as that. Mrs North, who had lain awake all night trying to decide what to do, felt quite cheated to find that it had been settled without her. She had arrived at a beautiful plan about five o'clock in the morning, taken two Slumbellos and slept stertorously through people coming in with tea and break-fast and news of measles until she woke at midday with a splitting head and the knowledge that she had forgotten something it was imperative to remember.

Still half doped, she groped her way downstairs to find out what it was. Elizabeth, hearing her go into Oliver's room, came in with a cup of coffee. 'Well,' she said, 'there must be about a grain of morphia in those pills. You've been sleeping like the dead for twelve hours.'

'I didn't take them till dawn.' Mrs North shook her head to try to clear it. Her hair was still pinned up and cold cream glistened in the corners of her nostrils and the folds of her chins. Without her glasses she looked small-eyed and undressed. 'I was thinking things out. I've decided what to do about Evie, but I – did I tell you what it was? I can't quite remember. I can't seem to think straight at all.'

'You don't have to.' Elizabeth smiled. 'It's decided itself.' Mrs North was amazed to hear of all the things that had hap-pened while she slept. That anyone but she should have discovered the spots on Evelyn's chest, she, who was such a specialist in rashes; that they should have sent for Dr Trevor on their own; that Bob and Honey had already left for Liverpool – it was disappointing to have missed so much.

'You might have woken me when Hugo came,' she said.

'I did look in,' said Elizabeth, 'but you didn't wake, and he wouldn't hear of disturbing you. I think it's only a light attack; he thinks so, too.'

'But Bob!' Mrs North was gradually beginning to take things in. 'I haven't said good-bye to him. How could he go off like that without saying good-bye? Why didn't he come in to me?'

'He did,' said Oliver and Elizabeth together, and, hostilely polite, each offered the other the chance to speak.

'They must be some pills,' Oliver said, 'if you can sleep through that. He said you did stir and mumble at him, but Honey was screeching at him from the car that they would miss their train, so he had to go. He's going to ring up tonight and settle about Evie. But by the time she's over this he'll be safely in New York and so busy interfering with the people who've been running his business much better without him that he won't have time to remember about having her. He won't come over again for ages – Honey will see to that – and Evie obviously can't go alone, so it'll all blow over and she can go on living with us, at least until he's got rid of that woman.'

'What do you mean, darling, got rid of her?'

'You don't expect the marriage to last, do you?'

'I hope not,' she said, and put a hand to her mouth guiltily. 'Maybe I shouldn't say that. I think I'll go up and put some clothes on. Imagine not being dressed at this hour! I haven't slept like this since Heather was born. What about lunch, Elizabeth? Oh, have you? You are a good girl. You look as though you could do with a Slumbello yourself, dear; you look all washed out. Didn't you sleep well?'

'I'm quite all right,' said Elizabeth, turning away.

'Miss Gray,' said Oliver loudly, 'is the happiest girl in the world. She's going to be married.'

Mrs North looked at him quickly and then ran to overtake Elizabeth. 'But isn't that *too* exciting!' She looked back at Oliver once more and he saw that she was still uncertain whether her fears had not at last been realized, so before she could say anything embarrassing he said: 'She's going to marry Arnold Clitheroe, her friend in London, you know.'

As she knew nothing about him, Mrs North enthused as if it were all desperately romantic. She kissed Elizabeth warmly and said a lot of spontaneous, affectionate things. 'But this means you'll be leaving us; that's not so good.'

'Yes, quite soon. Arnold wants to get married soon so that we can have our honeymoon before the winter. I'll stay and see Evie through measles, of course, but Oliver's all right now; he doesn't need a nurse.' She nodded coolly towards him.

'Oh, sure.' His mother looked at him thoughtfully, wondering how he felt about all this, and he foresaw nights and nights of fending her off when she came downstairs to discuss it.

Elizabeth could now take Arnold's sizeable diamond from the ribbon round her neck and wear it on her engagement finger, where it caught Oliver's eye every time she did anything for him. He did not want her to do anything for him. He insisted on getting in and out of bed on his own and dressing himself, although it took him twice as long, but he did not want her near him. He made the excuse of wanting to learn to manage on his own before she left. 'And I don't want you infecting me with measles,' he said. 'I've never had them and I don't intend to now.'

Dr Trevor had at last sent a man down from London to measure him for his artificial leg. It was to be a mechanical miracle, according to the man, and Oliver would be able to do as much with it – nay more – than he had with his real one. 'Oh yes,' said Oliver sceptically. 'I'll play football the day after I get it, I suppose.'

'Oh, come,' the man laughed indulgently, rolling up his tape-measure, 'we mustn't try to run before we can walk, must we?'

But he would be able to get about, and his heart was behaving itself. He and Fred had many talks about their future co-operation on the farm and Oliver drew out some of his savings and bought a stud bull, wheeling himself down to the farm to see it arrive with more interest than he had ever felt before in the cattle. It began to look like quite something of a life. Whatever he had told his mother, he had always known at heart he could not marry, hadn't he? He would never be properly fit; how could he marry? So what difference did it make to him if Elizabeth was going to marry Arnold Clitheroe? None. It got everybody tied off very neatly.

During these last days Elizabeth was almost like a ghost in the house. She nursed Evelyn efficiently and devotedly, but her trunk had gone to London and she herself was so soon to follow it for good and she seemed surprised to find herself still at Hinkley. She drifted about, pale and slightly apologetic, unable to settle to anything and avoiding Oliver as much as possible. Once or twice she seemed as though she wanted to try and be reconciled with him, but he snubbed her almost before she had opened her mouth. Women always wanted it both ways. He was not going to have any of this 'Can't we still be friends?' business.

When Evelyn was better and sitting up in bed with a tray of tin horses on her lap, Elizabeth was given the week-end off to go to a party in London with Arnold. She would be coming back for a few days to complete the month and collect the rest of her things.

It rained on Saturday, and as Oliver could not go out, he did not bother to get out of bed. He did not feel very well. When he told his mother that he had a headache, she, being preoccupied with what she was going to tempt Evelyn with for lunch, told him it was the muggy weather, which did not make him feel any better.

In the evening he asked for Bovril and biscuits instead of dinner, and Mrs North said: 'Oh, darling, don't tell me you're going off your food when I've just got Evie to start eating again. It's such a worry to me. I was going to come and have dinner in here with you, but if you don't want any I shan't bother. I'll just have some soup in the kitchen.'

'You can't talk about people not eating.'

'That's different. I'm starving, but I've begun dieting again. I haven't really been able to get down to it this last year; there's been so much to think of, what with one thing and another, but I'm really going to try and reduce now. You'll be going around with me soon. We might do a trip to London, hm? And you won't want to be seen with a stout mother.' She waited for an appropriate answer, but he did not feel up to making it, so he smiled instead and she went away.

After he had sipped the Bovril and left it until it got too cold to drink, and had nibbled half a biscuit and thrown the rest out of the window, he read and listened to the wireless, but he was bored with his book and the B.B.C. and himself. He began to wonder what Elizabeth was doing, and tried for the hundredth time to picture the man with the impossible name. She had shown him a snapshot, taken in such dim weather that he could hardly tell which was Arnold and which was the background, but he looked slightly better than he had expected. Oldish, of course, too old for Elizabeth, although he still seemed to have all his hair, and his figure, though peg-topped, was passable. He looked prosperous and kind and not very clever; a nice safe husband if ever there was one. In the background was a tall, narrow house with a conservatory; in the middle ground, Arnold and a long glossy car; in the foreground, an inbred-looking poodle.

The party was to be in the private room of one of the smarter London hotels. He had allowed Elizabeth to tell him that much. The hosts were two business men, on a visit from the North with their wives, to retaliate for the party given last week at an equally smart hotel by London business men and their wives. The menu would be practically identical, Oliver reflected, and neither the brandy nor the jokes any better. The only difference would be that Elizabeth would be there and Arnold Clitheroe, who perhaps had not shone much last week, would shine tonight with a reflected glory. Oliver did not mind betting she could knock spots off any business man's wife. But she was practically a business man's wife herself. Would she become befurred and bosomy and go in for elaborate hats? She would never let her hair down now. The wives of middle-aged business men did not go in for shoulder-length bobs and swinging pageboys. She would perhaps cut it short and have it waved close to her head, and she would go to the hairdressers too often from boredom, and it would soon get to look stiff and brassy.

It was one o'clock when he woke up and wondered whether to have some tea. Although he was not technically an invalid any more, his mother still pampered him with his thermos, and his milk last thing at night. She would probably go on pampering him and he would slide from invalidism into old age with no perceptible hiatus. She was right about the muggy weather. He felt hot and sticky and he threw off his blanket and lay with only a sheet over him. He had smoked too much because he had had a restless day, and his mouth felt dry. He still had the headache, and a backache as well from falling asleep sitting up over his book. He did not really want any tea, but it would be something to do. He was just unscrewing the cap of the thermos when he heard the sound of a car in the drive. Who on earth? He always seemed to be hearing cars in the drive when the rest of the house was sleeping. It made him think of Heather, and the times when she had burst into his room.

It was Elizabeth who burst in this time, and she had been crying again. This was too much. She was almost offensively reserved for nine months and never seen to shed a tear, and now she had cried twice in the last three weeks, told her life story, and got herself engaged to a man with ten thousand a year.

She came in, switched on the light, banged the door, and stood with her back against it, looking defiant. She wore a white evening dress and her hair was caught up at the side by a sparkling clip and fell round her neck in just the daffodil bell which he had been thinking she never would have.

'Whose car?' he asked sternly.

'Mr Peploe's, bless him. He never minds turning out for your family,' she said.

'You are not my family,' Oliver said, 'but Clitheroe's.' He was killing time until she chose to tell him what she was doing here when she should be in the ladies' cloakroom talking about servants to the business men's wives while the business men were having one for the road and talking whatever business men talked about when their wives imagined they were telling *risqué* stories.

Elizabeth shook back her hair. It obviously felt unfamiliar against her neck. She did look pretty, though, even if she had been crying. 'I just caught the last train,' she said. 'Heaven knows why. I've been wishing all the way down I'd stayed in London. I mean, if I had to run away, why run all the way to Shropshire?'

'Yes, it's hard on Mr Peploe,' murmured Oliver, 'but harder still on Clitheroe.'

308

'Oh, shut up about Clitheroe,' she said desperately. 'I never want to hear his name again.'

'My dear!' Oliver suddenly felt so light-headed with happiness that he could only be facetious. 'Don't tell me he's turned out to be a snake in the grass. What's the man done? Aren't his intentions honourable after all? I see you haven't given him back his fur coat; that wasn't very ethical of you, Elizabeth. If you want him horsewhipped, he'll have to come here, because I don't feel well enough to go to London. I haven't been well all day,' he said plaintively.

'I'm sorry,' she said absently, and then blurted out: 'I couldn't do it, Ollie! I couldn't do it. All my plans – the life I was going to have – I was so sure – –' she rushed forward, fell on her knees by the bed and spread her lovely hair all over his chest. He moved her head gently off the scar over his heart and began to stroke her hair. She was crying again. That made the third time in three weeks.

'Tell your Uncle Ollie,' he said. He took back what he had thought about not wanting to be friends just the same. He would like to be friends with her.

'It was at the party,' she sobbed. She was a bit hysterical, and with her face buried in his pyjamas she was difficult to follow. 'It was awful – at least, I didn't think so at first, because it was just like lots of things I've been to with Arnold and his friends, but half-way through I suddenly realized how awful it was. I suppose it was after my third glass of champagne. One of the men kept calling me Little Lady. He's Arnold's best friend, and he'd always have been coming to the house.

'It was all so dull, and I didn't fit, though I was the dullest of all. I kept trying to be bright and laugh at the jokes, but all the time I felt I'd like to go away and yawn till my head split in two. I was the youngest by miles, but I was Arnold's fiancée, so that made me the same age as the others. Arnold was asking them all to the wedding and telling them where we were going for our honeymoon. Torquay, you know, and I'd wanted to go to the real seaside, but Arnold loves Torquay. He likes hotels with glass verandas and five courses for dinner and people with napkins over their arm showing him dishes before they serve them, and he will talk knowingly about wine, although I'm sure he knows nothing about it. Oh, Ollie, he is so stuffy. If that's security, I don't want it, it makes me feel so old.

'One of the men said: "I always thought old Clith was the perfect bachelor; shows you never can tell, doesn't it?" and Arnold raised his glass towards me and said: "It's love, gentlemen, love that makes the world go round." I suddenly felt suffocated and I was afraid I was going to cry, so I made some excuse and went to the Ladies. The attendant asked me if I wanted my coat, so I said to myself: Why not? And without thinking twice about it, I hared down the corridor and out into the street and there was a taxi waiting, just as if it was meant.

'Wasn't it awful of me to run out on him? I don't know what he'll say to his friends. All the way down in the train, I kept imagining him searching frantically round the hotel with his eyes getting closer and closer together. He'll be so hurt, but I'll never be able to explain. Having kept up this act with him for so long, I'd never explain what I was really like and what I really wanted.'

'What do you want?'

'I want you!' she wailed like a child.

It was enough to make anyone's heart thump and pound and the blood sing in their ears, particularly someone whose heart and blood were prone to do that even when not kissing the girl one loved.

'D'you know,' he said dizzily, 'I haven't kissed anyone since I was knocked out. I'll have to get into training.'

She sat back on her heels and looked at him. 'Oh, Ollie darling, you look awful!' she cried. 'Not a bit well,' assessing him in a motherly, not a professional way. 'Oh, what have I done? I've upset you!' She put her hand on his heart. 'Ollie!' She was professional now. 'Let's look at your watch.' She counted, her eyes widening. 'Darling, your heart – oh, what have I done?' He wagged his head at her and grinned. He felt very odd, as if his head had come right off and were bowling round the top of the walls.

His heart was going so fast that it was making him sweat. When she had taken his temperature she was in a panic. No nurse should panic like this just because the patient is a little ill. 'Kiss me,' he said foolishly, and reached out his arms, but she was farther away than he thought, and he clutched the air and nearly fell out of bed.

She put him back. 'Do be careful. Oh dear, what shall I do? Your pills . . . yes . . .' He saw her at the corner cupboard, miles away. 'Damn,' she said from the distance, 'there aren't any.'

'Never mind the pills,' he said thickly, but she did not seem to hear, so he wondered whether he had spoken at all.

'I've got some in my room,' she said, nearer now. 'Lie still till I get back. Oh, look at you, all uncovered!' She drew up the blanket, and, as there were no more, pulled off Arnold Clitheroe's fur coat and laid it over his chest.

When she got back he was laughing weakly and rather inanely, with a lolling head. 'What's the matter?' she asked, wondering whether he were delirious.

'It's too funny,' he said, and it was difficult to get the words out clearly. 'It's a good thing you're going to marry me and not be a nurse. What a nurse!'

'Here are your pills,' she said soothingly. 'Take them. I'll hold the glass for you.'

'I don't want pills. I've just had a look at my chest. If you'll take this damned great fur rug off me for a minute you'll see I've got measles.'

Mrs North, pattering down the stairs to see who was making all that hysterical laughter, found it was Oliver, with a temperature of a hundred and three and looking it, and a girl in a long white dress with her hair all over the place, whom she did not at first recognize as Elizabeth.

MORE ABOUT PENGUINS
AND PELICANS

Penguinews, which appears every month, contains details of all the new books issued by Penguins as they are published. From time to time it is supplemented by *Penguins in Print*, which is our complete list of almost 5,000 titles.

A specimen copy of *Penguinews* will be sent to you free on request. Please write to Dept EP, Penguin Books Ltd, Harmondsworth, Middlesex, for your copy.

In the U.S.A.: For a complete list of books available from Penguins in the United States write to Dept CS, Penguin Books, 625 Madison Avenue, New York, New York 10022,

In Canada: For a complete list of books available from Penguins in Canada write to Penguin Books Canada Ltd, 41 Steelcase Road West, Markham, Ontario.

ONE PAIR OF HANDS

Monica Dickens

Tired of the life of a debutante Monica Dickens decided to be a cook-general. This uproarious backstairs view of the English upper classes in moments of comedy, drama, selfishness, and childish pique holds the reader's attention from first page to last with that 'exuberant vitality' which Compton Mackenzie finds in the work both of Charles Dickens and his great-granddaughter. Here is fun, wit, malice and – in the face of the tartars who rule on both sides of the green baize door – courage. You can also discover how to cook a *crème brulée*.

'There must have been some dull patches in Miss Dickens' kitchen career, but there are none in her book. The high spirits which first made her think of getting a cap and apron infect its pages, and she has an appreciation of character which may well be inherited. Nearly everyone will want to read this irreverent chronicle from below stairs' – *Time and Tide*

'Glorious entertainment' – *Daily Mail*

'Riotously amusing as the book is in parts, Miss Dickens also manages to make it a social document' – *The Times*

ONE PAIR OF FEET

Monica Dickens

'A brilliantly funny account of the first and only year of her training to be a nurse. . . . Her funniness on the subject she chooses is far from being facile or irresponsible. She is shrewd, and she shows not only a quick eye, but an excellent heart. . . . Her character sketches of sisters, nurses, public-ward patients, the grandees of the private wards, and the grandees of the town are little masterpieces' – Elizabeth Bowen in the *Tatler*

'Is this as good a book as *One Pair of Hands*? The answer is that it is much better. The cheerful impudence is still there. The power of observation and the family eye for a comic character are in better form than in her early work. And there are occasional touches of genuine and unforced pathos' – J. B. Priestley

'The most striking thing about the book is, that for all the emphasis on trivial irritations, monotony, hardship, mental stultification and lack of appreciation, Miss Dickens succeeds, almost in spite of herself, in conveying the essential nobility of the profession and the supreme satisfaction of a life saved' – *Listener*

MY TURN TO MAKE THE TEA

Monica Dickens

As a cook-general Monica Dickens irreverently recounted how other people's crockery came to pieces in *One Pair of Hands*, and as a nurse how the hospital wards thundered under *One Pair of Feet*. In *My Turn to Make the Tea* she rounds off the record with an account of those glorious months when she helped, as a cub reporter, to put the *Downingham Post* to bed each week.

'Anyone who has been a junior reporter will recognize the truthfulness of the picture the author paints ... I take off my hat to Miss Dickens as the most entertaining junior reporter ever to enter a newspaper office' – Howard Spring in *Country Life*

'Vivacious ... wherever her eye falls, it finds the exact, significant detail, and her ear for dialogue is unerring ... All in all, Miss Dickens is bringing the word Dickensian up to date' – *Observer*

'It is a book which will be read, as it has been written, with enthusiasm and with pleasure' – *The Times Literary Supplement*

FLOWERS ON THE GRASS

Monica Dickens

After the sudden death of his young wife, Daniel Brett turns his back on security and sets off in search of the free life he knew as a child.

In this account of his adventures, Monica Dickens uncovers a wealth of reputable and disreputable characters to delight the reader.

LOVE IN A COLD CLIMATE

Nancy Mitford

The story of coldly beautiful Polly Hampton, her aristocratic parents and the denizens of Alconleigh, reintroduces many of the characters made familiar in *The Pursuit of Love*.

Sharpening her charm, wit and 'engaging heartlessness', as well as a good deal of perceptive observation, on this privileged circle, Nancy Mitford creates her own world of froth and fun and, at the same time, gives a shrewd appraisal of the upper classes in twentieth-century England.

DON'T TELL ALFRED

Nancy Mitford

Many of the characters in this novel need no introduction to the thousands of admirers of *The Pursuit of Love* and *Love in a Cold Climate*, as, once again, Nancy Mitford gleefully charts the cracks in society's upper crust.

The scene is Paris, where Alfred (husband of Fanny, the narrator) has been posted as Ambassador. What with the exigencies of Parisienne *haute société*, the demands on the personal toilette, exquisite Northey (the social secretary) and her love life, plus the vagaries of her own children, Fanny has *no* chance, whatsoever, of sinking back into comfortable middle age.

'Delicious imbroglio' – *Daily Telegraph*